The Summer *of* No Attachments

LORI FOSTER

The Summer of No Attachments

ISBN-13: 978-1-335-50318-3

The Summer of No Attachments

HQN
22 Adelaide St. West, 40th Floor
Toronto, Ontario M5H 4E3, Canada
www.Harlequin.com

Printed in U.S.A.

The Summer of No Attachments

Chapter One

Ivey Anders shoved back a wayward curl and gently secured the dog against her body so it couldn't move while her tech, Hope Mage, carefully clipped away the twisted wire. The poor thing, a stray by the looks of it, had gotten itself tangled pretty tightly and one hind leg was in bad shape. Ivey wanted to get it to the clinic where she could properly assess the damage.

Mud caked the fur, making it difficult to find any other injuries just yet, but there was one astounding fact Ivey couldn't ignore.

Behind her, the homeowner groused that the dog had likely been stealing eggs from his chicken coop.

Voice calm, temper mostly in check, Ivey said, "You didn't hesitate to call me, did you, Marty?" It was well-known that Marty was not a fan of dogs, or cats for that matter, and mostly considered them a nuisance. However, they'd come to an agreement some time ago. Marty, who owned a fair amount of wooded acreage, was supposed to call her if a stray showed up, and she, as the local vet, would take care of the "problem" for him.

Laura, his wife, was quick to say, "I called." Defiant to Marty, she added, "Soon as I heard the poor thing, in fact."

Which didn't mean much. The animal might have been there for hours. Possibly more than a day, though Ivey couldn't bear the thought of that.

"She's pregnant, you know." Refusing to take her eyes off the dog and unwilling to raise her voice since it might frighten the animal more, Ivey said, "If she took an egg, it would have been from starvation—and you already know I would have compensated you for it."

Affronted, Marty grumbled, "I wasn't worried about one egg, just don't want to lose my chickens." He cleared his throat. "If it helps any, I was out here this morning and she wasn't caught then. Afternoon I watered my garden, and that's why there's so much mud. So I doubt she was hung up there more than a few hours."

The fist around Ivey's heart loosened just a little. "That helps tremendously, Marty. Thank you."

More times than she could count, Ivey had taken on problems with stray animals who needed special love and care. It didn't matter that she'd been working as a veterinarian for years now, seeing all manner of hurt, neglected or just plain ill animals. She still loved them all, and when one hurt, she hurt with it.

"No thanks necessary," Marty complained, his tone gruff with insult. "Not like I'd let an animal suffer."

Ivey had a feeling their definitions of *suffer* varied a bit, but she realized this mattered to him, and she was too grateful to quibble so she just nodded.

"Almost got it," Hope murmured, and with one last clip, the wire loosened. "There." Fingers gentle, she disentangled the dog's leg, exposing a painful wound.

Ivey murmured to the small animal all the while, cooing

softly, petting and holding her secure. The second she was able to sit back on the muddy ground, she pulled the dog into her lap. With her face close to the top of the dog's head, she whispered, "There now, that's better, isn't it? We'll get you all fixed up, I promise."

"Here." Slipping off her zip-up hoodie, Hope offered it to Ivey to wrap around the dog. "Do you want me to get the carrier?"

Busy swaddling the dog, careful not to jar her, Ivey shook her head. "She doesn't weigh more than ten or eleven pounds. I'll carry her to the truck and we'll see how it goes." Feeling mud seep into the seat of her pants, she realized she couldn't get up without letting go of the dog. Lifting a brow at Hope, she said, "A little help?"

"Oh sure." Hope caught her under one elbow, and Laura hurried forward to take the other, giving her the leverage she needed.

Marty stepped back to avoid getting muddy.

Carefully, the two women got Ivey on her feet. The thick mud was heavy on the seat of her pants, dragging on her stretch jeans that had loosened throughout the day. At least her rubber boots wouldn't be ruined. Since they treated all sorts of animals, including those on farms, she and Hope each kept a pair at the clinic.

"Let's go." Plodding forward, Ivey led the way to the truck. Halfway there, the dog started panting. Concerned, she hastened her step, not at all worried about getting mud on the truck seats. "No need for the crate. Just get us back to the clinic."

Picking up on her angst, Hope ran around to the driver's side and got the truck on the road in record time. "Everything okay?"

"Not really, no. Something's wrong."

"What should I do?"

Poor Hope. A sick cat had kept them an hour past closing, and then Marty had called… "I'm sorry." Ivey barely took her gaze off the stressed dog. "Do you think you could assist me at the clinic?"

"Of course I will! You don't even have to ask." Frowning, Hope muttered, "Did you think I'd drop you off with a dog in distress? Tell you good luck?" She snorted. "Have I ever done that?"

She and Hope were close enough that Ivey knew she'd inadvertently insulted her. "No, you haven't. But it's Friday night after a very long day."

"It's Friday night for you, too, you know."

"What a sad situation for us both." Despite her worries, Ivey chuckled. "Most women would have plans, and yet we never do."

"You have Geoff."

Ivey made a face. "Lot of good that does me." Likely Geoff was settled on the couch already, watching sports or playing a video game. The excitement had left their relationship a long time ago, so she doubted he'd even notice her absence.

For her part, Hope never dated. That bothered Ivey a lot, but she loved Hope enough that she would never pry.

Smiling at her friend, Ivey said, "I'm glad I won't have to do this alone."

"Not ever," Hope vowed. "Even if by some miracle I ever do have something worthwhile lined up for the weekend, I'd still be here for you, okay?"

Her friendship with Hope meant so much more than any other relationship Ivey had, including her lackluster romance with Geoff. "Smartest thing I ever did was hire you."

"I'm so glad you did," Hope whispered. "Otherwise we might not have become friends, then where would I be?"

"Let's just agree that we're better off together." Though Ivey was ten years older than Hope, they'd still hit it off from the start, meshing together as if they'd been lifelong friends. Where

Ivey was take-charge and sometimes a little too outspoken, Hope was an intent listener with an enormous heart.

Ivey often wanted to challenge the world, and Hope, sadly, wanted to hide from it.

Or more accurate, she wanted to hide from any interested men.

Hope had an affinity with animals, plus a gentle but sure touch. She was never squeamish, but she exuded sympathy. Ivey valued her. The clients loved her. And the animals trusted her.

Unfortunately, they were still five minutes away from the clinic when the dog went into labor. "This is definitely happening," Ivey said, doing what she could to make the animal comfortable.

Leaning closer to the steering wheel, Hope drove a little faster. "Be there soon."

They'd barely gotten in the door when her water broke. Hope ran ahead to prepare an area, moving with practiced ease as she opened an already cleaned kennel and set up a whelping box, then filled it with bedding material. The box had three tall sides to contain the coming puppies, and one low side for the mother to step out for food and water.

Knowing Hope had it in hand, Ivey began cleaning the dog as quickly and efficiently as possible. She managed a cursory job, removing the worst of the mud, when Hope rejoined her. "We're all set."

"With luck we'll have enough time to clean and wrap her leg before she gives birth." Usually that happened within two hours after the animal's water breaking, so they didn't have a minute to spare.

A day that had already been long just turned entirely endless.

One month later, bright and early on a sunny Monday morning, Ivey came into the clinic through the employee door around back. May in Sunset, Kentucky, was a time for short sleeves, sunglasses and summer fun.

Ivey had the first two and was working on the third in her own sweet time.

Honestly, she felt good. Better than she had in a while. Like she'd recently cleaned out her closets to get rid of outdated styles, or as if she'd shed ten unwanted pounds.

With a grin, she thought it was more like two hundred unwanted pounds. Named Geoff.

Things had been going downhill for a while, and finally, Friday night, she'd mustered her backbone and broken things off with him. What an awful confrontation that had been!

Later that night she'd second-guessed everything she'd said to him.

Saturday, with Geoff gone and her day open, she'd been at loose ends, wondering what to do next.

By Sunday she'd realized the freedom.

And now, Monday, she chose to see the world in a whole new light.

Geoff did not. He'd called twice on Saturday and twice on Sunday. Each time he'd started out cajoling and ended up making nasty accusations.

Because she, awesome woman that she was, couldn't be swayed. Not by a man who had taken her for granted.

Regrets? Nope, she had none.

For two years she and Geoff had been a thing. A loose thing. A thing with no real goals. A dead-end relationship type of thing that was more about convenience for him and uncertainty for her. It had left her unsatisfied—in more ways than one. It had left her uncertain about her own appeal. It had left her feeling needy, but no more.

She didn't need marriage.

She didn't need a partner.

Sex... Well, okay, she liked that every so often, but that didn't

require a committed relationship. This was going to be her summer of no attachments. If she needed physical comfort, well, by
God, she could "hook up" like so many people did. Find an attractive guy, one who could hold her interest for a few hours,
and then move on.

It was her new MO. Freedom. Putting her desires first. It
didn't matter that she'd been born an old soul with no interest in partying or bars or clubs. In college, when everyone else
had reveled on the weekends, she's volunteered at a local shelter.

Now, being a beloved—by the animals she treated, at least—
local veterinarian, her days were fairly mundane. And once she
left work, her evenings were mostly dedicated to Maurice, her
aging cat. Geoff hadn't liked Maurice much. Maurice had felt
the same about Geoff.

She should have trusted her cat. At fifteen, Maurice had very
good instincts.

As she made her way through the clinic, Ivey heard barking and smiled. Daisy, the little Jack-a-bee dog she'd rescued
from Marty's farm, still lived at the clinic with her three adorable puppies.

Making a beeline to the private kennel where Daisy slept each
night, Ivey called out, "It's me, love."

Anticipation silenced the barking.

The second she opened the door, Daisy's tail started swinging, but her big beautiful eyes were filled with wary adoration.
The plump little puppies tumbled over one another in play, paying no attention as Ivey came in to sit close to the little dog. She
scratched under Daisy's chin and petted along her back.

"You're such a sweet girl. Still so shy though." Her leg had
healed nicely, though she now had a scar. She'd been through
so much, but from the birth of the first pup she'd been such
an excellent mama. "What did you go through, baby, to make
you so timid?"

Ducking her face, Daisy snuggled closer.

"It's all right, love. You can be timid if you want. I don't mind."

During the day, Daisy had free run of much of the clinic, as long as it didn't involve the areas where other animals might run into her. The puppies were kept contained with a low temporary barrier across the bottom of the kennel door. Daisy could step over it, but the puppies could not.

Sighing, Ivey figured Daisy would loosen up in her own time and not before. Hope would be in soon, but until then, she opened the door that let Daisy and her puppies into a small enclosed yard with grass and sunshine, then she went about rinsing the water bowl and refilling it with fresh water, and putting out dry food.

Daisy immediately found her favorite spot to enjoy the sunshine. The puppies followed, one happy to nurse, one chasing a fly, the other plopping down to nap near her mama's neck.

There were plenty of enrichment items in the outdoor pen, like toys, chews and flexible tunnels, ensuring Daisy got exercise and the pups could play and learn.

Oh, how she'd miss them if...*when*, she found them homes.

Hope stepped up beside her. "You're not fooling anyone, you know."

"I have no idea what you mean." She knew *exactly* what Hope meant.

Hope followed Ivey as she headed inside to check the schedule. "You say the right words, but anyone seeing your eyes knows you aren't going to part with Daisy, maybe not with her babies, either."

Was she really that transparent? "It just bothers me." Without waiting for Hope to ask, Ivey explained. "People see the puppies and automatically want one." In a high false voice, she said, *"They're so little and cute."* Then with an eye roll, "They look right past Daisy, but she's what the puppies will look like in a few more months. Puppies don't stay puppies. If they don't love the dog—"

Hope raised a hand. "You're preachin' to the choir, sister. If I was allowed to have pets in my rinky-dink apartment, I'd be all about Daisy." She made a face. "And okay, the pups, too. Heck, I'd start my own menagerie."

Ivey grinned as she watched Hope flip back her dark, baby-fine hair. It was a gesture Hope used when making a point. A sort of "Hmph" expression.

"You'll find a new place soon." Not that Sunset had a lot of rental properties. Most people tended to buy their homes, but at only twenty-one, Hope wasn't quite there yet.

"Well, speaking of that...could I ask a favor?"

Since Hope never asked for anything, of course Ivey said, "Anything."

"A lakefront home out by Marty's farm was recently sold. A big house with a lot of land. I don't know if you remember it."

"It's surrounded by woods, right?"

"Yup, that's the one. The people who lived there had a guest-house that the wife's mother lived in. Now that the mother has passed, they decided it was all too much for them, so they sold it, and the new owner wants to rent out that space."

Finally catching on, Ivey put down the report she'd been skimming and turned to Hope with a grin. "You're thinking of renting it?"

Excitement made Hope's dark blue eyes brighter. "It's so beautiful, Ivey. Near the lake and still close enough to the clinic that I wouldn't have a long drive to work. And it's private. I mean, I can see the main house, but I'd have my own driveway and my own little deck." She drew a breath. "I already talked to the owner—a single father who's new to the area—and he's holding it for me until I go there tonight to check it out. After that, he'll have to show it to other people."

Immediately, Ivey knew the issue. "You want company when you go?"

Now that it was out in the open, Hope seemed to wilt with relief. "Would you? I know it's dumb, but I just can't—"

"Hey." Ivey leaned against the counter and smiled. "I'd die of curiosity if I didn't see it, too. And, Hope? You don't have to explain to me, okay? I get it."

"Thank you." Hope blew out a breath. "It's right after work, but I only found out this morning or I'd have said something last night."

"Maurice won't mind waiting a little longer for his dinner. Odds are he'll be sleeping until I get home anyway." If she thought too much about how Maurice had slowed down, she'd turn melancholy.

Searching her face, Hope asked, "What about Geoff?"

"He's history. Both gone and forgotten."

Surprise took Hope back a step. "That was fast."

"Happened Friday night, actually."

"Why the heck didn't you tell me?"

It was true, they usually shared everything, yet this time Ivey had hesitated. She picked up the report again, turned it in her hands, then admitted, "At first, I wasn't sure how I felt about it."

"So you didn't want to discuss it?"

She gave it some thought. "I think I just needed to come to terms with it first."

Just then the receptionist, Karen, breezed in with her usual cheerful greeting as she quickly set up for the day's appointments.

Ivey spoke to her a moment, going over the upcoming schedule.

When she finished, she took Hope's arm and steered her to an exam room. They both liked Karen a lot, but she was known to gossip.

Voice low, Ivey explained, "Geoff was a mistake going nowhere fast. I decided I was better off without him."

"Okay."

Ivey noticed that Hope didn't disagree with her on the mistake part.

"So…" They both heard customers arriving. Closing the door quietly behind her, Hope asked, "What does Geoff think about it being over?"

With a roll of one shoulder, Ivey said, "Who cares?" And she did her best to make it sound convincing.

Folding her arms, Hope leaned against the door. "Was he in agreement?"

"Not exactly."

One dark brow elevated. "Did he ask what he could do to fix things?"

Deadpan, Ivey repeated, "Not exactly."

"So he's been an asshole?"

Ivey fought the grin but lost. "That word sounds so funny coming from a sweet girl like you." Very rarely did Hope curse, and she was almost never unkind—except to jerks who deserved it.

Leaning in, Hope enunciated carefully, "Asshole," with exaggerated effect.

Ah, that was just the injection of humor Ivey needed. The snickers started, grew into hilarious laughter, and finally, a minute later, faded into chuckles. Falling against each other, the two women fought for breath.

Once they'd mostly recovered, Hope wiped her eyes. "Full disclosure. I never liked him."

"You don't like any men."

"Not so! I like them just fine as long as they aren't…"

"Don't say it."

"Assholes."

Slapping a hand over her mouth, Ivey fought in vain to get it together.

Hope helped by stepping away and straightening her shoulders, smoothing her hair, tugging at the hem of her shirt—all in an effort to quell the humor.

Knowing she had to do her part, Ivey tucked flyaway spirals

of her too-curly hair back into her band. "So." She had to clear her throat twice to suppress the twitching of her mouth. "Did you want to ride together or separate?"

"We might as well arrive separately since we'll be closer to where you live. It'll save you from backtracking."

"Then I'll follow you there." That way, they'd arrive together, saving Hope from any awkward moments. "Until then, it sounds like the waiting room is filling up, so we should get to it."

They stayed busy for the rest of the workday, and with two emergencies they had very little time for lunch. A few hours before closing, a storm drifted in with clashes of thunder that shook the ground and bright flashes of lightning that split across the darkening sky. It made the animals more fractious, and the humans less agreeable. Poor Karen had to constantly mop the waiting room floor because Ivey, Hope and the two other techs stayed nonstop busy.

Ivey made a point of thanking her repeatedly, but luckily Karen was an upbeat sort who tackled every job with a smile. It took a lot to dent her buoyant attitude.

One day, she might have to expand her business, Ivey thought. Maybe take on another vet so she could have more time off. But for now, she enjoyed keeping things small. She knew everyone in Sunset, knew their pets and how they fared.

The only upside to being so swamped was that she had zero time to dwell on her failed relationship...

No. She hadn't failed.

She'd reevaluated.

Knowing Hope waited for her, Ivey went to her office, grabbed her purse—and found she had a dozen missed calls and text messages.

All from Geoff.

With a small wince, she scrolled through the texts. They seemed to come an hour apart, lodged in and around phone calls.

Hey babe just wondering how you are

I called but you didn't pick up. Busy?

Seriously, did he have no idea what hours she worked?

No reason to ignore me. That's a bitch move.

Ivey's eyes narrowed.

I might stop by your place after work.

I won't be there, you jerk. And don't you dare disturb my cat!

I think we should talk about this. Call me.

That one was from ten minutes ago.

She didn't want to talk to him—they'd said it all Friday night and even if she'd been inclined toward second thoughts, he'd helped cement her decision with the ugly way he'd tried to blame her for everything.

So instead of calling, she texted back, Busy tonight. Then, so he wouldn't accuse her of having a date, she added, I'm with Hope.

As soon as she sent it, she wanted to kick her own butt. She didn't owe him explanations. So she added, Besides it's over. Then she fought the urge to type Sorry.

God, being a nice person was a handicap when it came to ending things. Ivey shoved the phone into her purse and met Hope at the back door. Everyone else had already left.

"Are we running late?"

"By only a few minutes," Hope said. "I called and he said it's fine. He and his son just finished dinner."

Together, keeping an eye on the stormy sky, they headed to their respective cars in the empty lot.

"So he has a son?"

"I guess." Hope stepped around a puddle. "I don't really know much about him, but if the guesthouse looks as good on the inside as it does the outside, it's worth every penny of what he's asking for it."

"Then let's hope it is."

Corbin Meyer looked at his son—still a shocker, that one—and wished he could figure him out. Justin was tall for his age, long and lanky with chronically messy brown hair that resisted any sort of style, blue eyes full of resentment and distrust, and enough excess energy to power a locomotive.

Determining how to expend that energy in a constructive way would be a trick. A move had been in order, but Justin made no bones about his disgruntlement.

He probably wanted his mother back. In his heart, Corbin knew it was better that she'd bailed on the kid.

Justin wanted to keep his friends, too, but they were in his old neighborhood near southern Ohio. Not an area Corbin would settle in.

Justin definitely wanted his familiar life back, but Corbin hoped, with time, he would grow to love his new life more. Kids were adaptable, right?

Like he had a freaking clue.

Hands in his pockets, Corbin leaned in the doorway to his son's room and cleared his throat. "Knock, knock."

Justin didn't look up.

"The rain's stopped. I have someone coming by to look at the rental property in a few minutes. You need to go with me when I show it to her."

"Why?" Still without eye contact.

The words *because I said so* tried to break free, but Corbin remembered how he disliked that answer as a kid, so he swallowed it and tried for something more reasonable. "Because you're ten, and I'll feel better having you with me."

He got the eye contact finally, and it seared him. "Why?"

Sighing, Corbin came in to stand closer. "You don't like that we moved. I get that. Change is tough."

Justin snorted.

"Does that mean you agree or disagree?"

He shrugged.

"So you think I'm too stupid to understand?"

Wariness flattened Justin's mouth. "Didn't say that."

"Good. Because I'm far from dumb. And you're far from dumb, too, so I know you understand. Neither of us had much choice with the move, but we're here now and I for one am looking forward to our future."

Justin mumbled something he couldn't catch. And maybe he didn't want to know anyway. "I figured there were a few things we could do to try to make this adjustment easier. First, before I get back to work, I figured we'd buy some bikes."

Glancing up, Justin asked, "Bikes?"

"One for me, one for you. Here in Sunset, there are plenty of winding roads for us to ride on. I like staying fit and you're obviously a strong kid. We could ride around and explore things. What do you think?"

"I don't know how to ride a bike."

Corbin's heart broke just a little, but hopefully he hid it. "So we'll practice here on the property first, where no one will see us. Hell... I mean, heck." Cursing was a problem now, and Corbin struggled with it daily. "I haven't ridden in years, so we can both get the hang of it again, then we'll tackle the town."

Banking his enthusiasm, Justin asked, "Okay?"

"We'll buy some floats, too, and get you a life preserver so we can do some swimming. I'm told the lake water is still a little cold, but we can take it, don't you think?"

Interest sparked in his eyes. "Yeah."

"I need a promise from you first though. No going near the lake unless I'm with you."

That got his chin up. "Why?"

The kid did love that word. "Because I just got you and I damn well don't want to lose you, that's why." The urge to reach out and ruffle his hair was strong, but Corbin had already learned not to. Justin pulled away every single time. "In fact, any time you're in the lake, you'll wear a life vest."

"Whose rule is that?"

Taking the question as interest instead of resistance, Corbin went to the end of the bed and sat. It was a new twin bed, for a small new addition to his family.

"My brother and I were raised near a lake. My mother was crazy strict about us never swimming alone or without a life preserver. She swore there was a nasty undertow, and if we got hit in the head we'd be pulled under, and it would be tough to ever find us again." Now that he considered it, Corbin decided that he, too, would wear a life belt. What if he was swimming with Justin and he got hurt? No, he'd never put the kid through that, so they'd both be extra cautious.

Justin's eyes rounded and it dawned on Corbin that he might be needlessly scaring him, dredging up nightmare images better left to Jason Vorhees in Camp Crystal Lake, from the Friday the 13th horror series. He'd already learned that his son had a fascination with all things horror-related. He didn't need Corbin encouraging that grisly interest.

But then again, this might be one of those lessons where a healthy respect for danger would be a good thing. "It can happen," Corbin insisted, "So no going to the lake without letting me know. But hey, we'll pick up some fishing gear, too, all right? In fact, after we show the guesthouse, we can walk down to the lake and check out the dock." They'd only moved in three days ago, and the time had been filled with setting up furniture and unpacking. "We'll grab a flashlight and look for frogs. What do you think?"

One narrow shoulder shifted with grudging curiosity. "If you want."

"I do." Standing again, Corbin gave in to the need to gently squeeze that proud shoulder, pretending he didn't notice how the kid froze. "Grab your shoes, okay? We need to go meet her now."

After he left the room, Corbin freed his smile.

Little by little, he'd win over Justin. It had only been a few weeks, so no doubt he was still adjusting to the shock, especially since he'd been dumped on Corbin like he didn't matter, with no looking back. He pitied Darcie, though. She'd gifted him with a son, and in the process she'd also given up something pretty phenomenal.

Or at least it would be phenomenal once Corbin got the whole parenting thing figured out.

Chapter Two

Ivey stood with Hope in the driveway, taking in the outside of the one-bedroom house. She loved the setup for Hope, and judging by her friend's expression of awe, Hope loved it, too.

Though it no longer rained, steady drips fell from everywhere, leaving both women damp. The difference was that Hope's glossy, baby-fine hair only went a little limp, while Ivey's turned to dandelion fluff.

"There are no outside stairs, which makes it a little more secure," came a deep male voice from around the house.

Ivey took in the congenial smile of an *extremely* handsome man, then transferred her gaze to the boy following behind him.

"You enter from inside the garage," he said, gesturing toward it. "Either by using your garage door opener, or there's a keyed lock on the door around the side. I can show you how to manually open the garage door, too, in case the power goes out, but that's only likely to happen in bad weather...like today's storm."

Going mute, Hope stepped a little closer to Ivey, leaving her to do the introductions.

Ivey held out a hand. "Hello. I'm Ivey Anders. I work with Hope and came along to see the place."

Six-plus feet of striking masculinity stepped forward. The humid breeze had mussed his brown hair, and his golden-brown eyes smiled. "Corbin Meyer. Nice to meet you." His much-larger hand held hers only briefly before he reached back and gently brought the boy forward. "This is my son, Justin."

Wearing a ball cap backward, hands shoved into the pockets of his loose cargo shorts, tennis shoes a little ratty, Justin muttered, "Hi."

In the normal course of things, Ivey didn't pay that much attention to men, but she *was* shopping around again—right? Not that a single father seemed like a great idea...unless he looked like Corbin.

Hope nudged her.

"Oh yes. Sorry. It was a long day." She worked up a smile to cover the awkwardness. "This is Hope Mage. You spoke with her. She's actually the one interested in the place."

"I hope you like it." Flexing some nice muscles, Corbin easily lifted the double garage door. "Room for two cars, or whatever. I believe the previous owner had a car and a golf cart. They were elderly and used the golf cart to get to and from the lake for fishing. By the way, if you do take it, you're welcome to do that. Fish, I mean." He waved toward a spiral staircase in the far left corner. "That leads up to the main living area."

Ivey glanced at the boy who, instead of following, stepped over to the side of the driveway and lifted a wiggling earthworm that had washed up with the rain. Fascinated, she watched him carry it to the base of a tree where an exposed root broke through the grass.

When he released it, Ivey put a hand to her heart. "What a heroic thing to do."

The boy glanced at her in surprise. So did Corbin and Hope.

"What you just did was so kind. Thank you for that, Justin. I always do the same when I see the poor things out of the ground."

"You pick up worms?" Justin asked.

"Absolutely. For the same reason you just did."

"Because they dry out otherwise."

"Indeed they do. Birds like to find them, so sometimes it's okay. Circle of life and all that. But I can never resist saving them when I can."

Swiping his hand on his shorts, Justin sidled closer. "Do you save bugs, too?"

"Of course." She nodded at Hope and said in a conspiratorial whisper, "Neither of us are squeamish about bugs."

"Even cicadas?" Justin looked at Hope with glee. "Do they make you scream?"

Hope laughed. "I don't mind most bugs, but yes, those little devils are creepy. I don't scream, but I do dodge them when I can."

A huge smile broke over Justin's sweet face. "My mom used to scream real loud." He straightened his shoulders. "I always had to get the bugs before she squashed them."

His mom used to? Ivey wondered about his mother, but of course she didn't ask. "I imagine here by the lake, you'll find a lot of insects. Snakes, too. Are you familiar with snakes?"

"We didn't see none in the city." He turned to scrutinize Corbin. "You afraid of snakes?"

Without missing a beat, Corbin said, "Remember I told you my brother and I grew up near a lake? We saw a lot of snakes. Snapping turtles, too. It'd probably be a good idea for you to know the safe ones from the ones you should avoid."

"Avoid them all," Hope suggested. Then to Ivey, "I'm so glad we don't deal with reptiles."

"I'm a veterinarian," Ivey explained to Justin. "Meaning a doctor for animals. Mostly dogs and cats, but also farm animals. As Hope said, we don't treat reptiles."

Blue eyes widening, Justin asked, "You get to work with dogs and cats?"

"What a perfect way to put it. Yes, I get to. Isn't that wonderful?"

"Yeah." He shot another sly glance at Corbin. "I've never had a pet."

Again, Corbin seemed to skate right through the awkwardness of that disclosure. "How about you and I discuss it, maybe after we've shown the house?"

Justin's mouth fell open, his expression turning to exhilaration. "You mean it?"

Now with a smile to rival his son's, Corbin nodded. "I won't ever say anything I don't mean, okay?"

Such an odd exchange. To Ivey, it almost seemed like father and son were strangers. She and Hope shared a brief look.

Corbin ignored it. "Right up these stairs."

Ivey took the lead, followed by Hope, Justin and then Corbin.

"I had it cleaned, but not much else," Corbin said. "The paint still looked okay to me, but if you take it, feel free to brighten it up."

The stairs opened with a three-piece bathroom to the left, the only bedroom straight ahead, and a living room/kitchen combo to the right.

The space was small but had definite charm. Ivey watched Hope and saw the way she glanced into the bathroom, then moved more quickly into the bedroom as her excitement built. A mirrored closet ran the length of the wall opposite from where the bed would probably go.

Ivey followed Hope as she entered the corner kitchen that was certainly big enough for one petite woman, but would make entertaining difficult.

Not that Hope ever entertained, not even to date. She kept to herself and other than occasionally grabbing a meal or seeing a movie with Ivey, she spent her evenings at home. Alone.

In the living room, sliding doors opened to a deck over the garage. All the windows made the rooms feel bigger, and with the woods off the back and one side, the lake on the other, the small house offered plenty of privacy.

Hope turned to where Corbin stood back, arms folded, just outside the kitchen, giving her a chance to look around. "I *love* it."

"Glad to hear it." He moved closer but still gave Hope plenty of space. "Justin and I only recently moved in ourselves, and we still have a lot to do to the main house, but I figured this place was ready to go."

"It is, and if you don't mind, I'll take it."

"Well, that was easy." He glanced down at Justin. "We don't mind at all, do we?"

Taken aback by the question, Justin lifted his narrow shoulders in uncertainty. "Guess not."

Casually but also with caution, Corbin put his hand on the boy's shoulder. "We were going down to the lake to check it out, and we already have plans over the weekend. Monday and Tuesday I have errands to run and I don't know how late I'll be. We could finalize paperwork next Wednesday, if that works for you."

"I understand. You'll want to do a background check." Hope dug into her purse. "I brought my proof of income and a letter from my employer."

"Me," Ivey said, lifting one hand.

As Corbin accepted the paperwork, he fought a grin and lost. "So Wednesday works?"

"Yes…as long as you promise to hold it for me?"

"Consider it yours."

Blowing out a deep breath, Hope laughed. *"Thank you."*

Ivey grinned, too. Obviously Hope loved the place. She knew it was as much the private location as it was the nearness to work. Hope liked people, dealt well with pet owners, but she didn't socialize and preferred not to run into locals after work.

Just as they were heading out, Ivey's phone started ringing.

She saw it was Geoff and rejected the call. Before she could get it back in her purse, it rang again. Locking her jaw, she silenced the phone.

When she looked up, she found Corbin watching her. The man had the most compelling brown eyes. His irises were caramel, circled by a darker brown. Thick black lashes, too. Kind eyes, she thought. But also…bedroom eyes.

When his mouth quirked, she realized she'd just been standing there staring at him. Heat flooded her face. "Sorry about that. I was just…taking in the view."

"The view?"

She gestured lamely at him, up and down his body, then she realized what she was doing and dropped her hand. "I'm sure you're used to it."

Clearly holding back a grin, he nodded at her purse where she'd stuffed the phone. "Everything okay?"

"Just dandy."

Her tone sent one of his thick eyebrows up but he looked more amused than offended.

"Sorry." It wasn't Corbin's fault that Geoff was a pain in her backside. "Just a pesky ex." *Oh my God, just shut up, Ivey.*

"Not taking no for an answer?"

Appalled at herself, she pressed her lips together. This was why she needed to go it alone for a while. It seemed when it came to men, she had no filter. Geoff claimed that was one of the things that had annoyed him most. The ass had rattled off a list once she told him she was done. As if by naming all her faults, she'd suddenly…what? Realize she was to blame for their failed relationship and be thrilled to have him after all?

Corbin was still watching her, so she said, "Conversation is only important if he's talking. Otherwise, he doesn't listen."

"Then I imagine he misses a lot."

Why the hell was she detailing her breakup to a perfect stranger? "Ignore me. Sometimes I speak without thinking."

"Or with sarcasm." He grinned.

Ivey did a double take. "I wasn't being sarcastic when I said you're hot."

He actually laughed. "Somehow I missed you saying that."

"But you knew what I meant. Why else would I stare?" Her phone buzzed with an incoming text. Growling, she turned it completely off.

"I meant," Corbin said carefully, "you were a little sarcastic about your caller. But I'd say you're allowed, especially when provoked."

Doing her utmost to rally, Ivey hitched her purse strap over her shoulder. "I promise, I'm better with animals."

"And rescuing bugs. Two admirable traits."

Admirable? She realized Hope was heading back down the stairs, Justin following her, so she felt safe whispering, "If you do decide you'd like a pet, let me know. I can point you in the right direction."

His gaze warmed even more. "Thank you, Ivey."

The way he said her name, all deep and husky while looking into her eyes, started a slow burn. *My, oh my.*

Was he flirting? Or was she just desperate for an ego boost?

And seriously, did she want a single dad flirting? At the moment, she didn't understand his and Justin's dynamic at all. He seemed like a terrific, very attentive father, and then suddenly he and his son were like visitors instead of family. Very odd.

Before she got ahead of herself, she should find out more about him, and with that decision in mind, she headed down the stairs.

Aware of Corbin right behind her, she carefully descended then stepped out of the garage. An early evening sun broke through, turning the wet surfaces into a sauna and making her hair frizz even more. If she were flirting with Corbin, that would bother her.

But she wasn't. No, definitely not. Her rioting hair didn't matter and was an inescapable fact, anyway.

Oblivious to the weather, Justin hunkered down on the lawn to look for more bugs. He was a cute kid, with his innocent blue eyes and loads of curiosity.

"If you find any that are dead," Ivey suggested, "put them aside and you can feed them to the fish later."

"Found one," he said immediately, and to everyone's consternation, he stuffed it into his pocket.

Corbin winced. "Guess I better go find him a container. Thank you both for coming out. I'll see you Wednesday, Hope." His gaze shifted to Ivey, lingering a moment. "And maybe we'll see you around town."

Despite everything she'd just told herself, she sort of hoped he did.

Corbin was a little disappointed that Hope came alone on Wednesday. Did that mean she trusted him? He doubted it.

He had a feeling something had happened with her that made her noticeably reserved with men, so trust would be slow in coming. He was careful to keep his distance in the open garage and to ensure Justin was within range. A kid, Corbin was fast discovering, changed the undercurrents of everything. Mostly in a really great way.

Hope's background check was fine, not that he'd expected anything different. And Ivey made a nice reference. It hadn't taken more than a single trip into town for groceries to hear about her animal clinic and all the amazing work she did. On the way to get fishing equipment, he and Justin had driven by the clinic. Her small gravel parking lot had been packed.

He heard a crack and leaned out of the garage to see Justin using a stick to hit rocks toward the lake. It struck him that his son had a good swing, plenty of speed and strength. He also had accuracy, so the rocks didn't come anywhere near the guesthouse and the main house was to the left and behind him.

"Have you played ball?" Corbin asked him.

"Just in the street with friends." Justin tossed a green walnut into the air, swung his makeshift bat and sent it soaring.

With a whistle, Corbin watched it disappear past the trees. So some baseball equipment would be next on his list. He wondered if the town had a team...

"This is so wonderful," Hope said, drawing his attention back to her. "Am I able to move in right away?"

"Whenever you want." He handed over two sets of keys and a garage door opener. "Also, these are my numbers. One for the landline at the house, the other my cell. As I said, we haven't been here that long, so I don't know of any problems. But if something should come up, feel free to call. I'll be working mostly from home, so you shouldn't have any trouble reaching me."

Corbin kept the offer as impersonal as he could, and still her gaze avoided his.

Forging on, he said, "This is a refrigerator magnet with all the local emergency numbers. I imagine you already know them, but the realtor gave me two, so I'm sharing."

"Thank you."

"Justin and I picked up kayaks, fishing equipment and floats a few days ago. We'll probably use the lake often, but if you want some privacy there, either for a party or just a few friends—"

"I won't."

The quick, firm denial stymied him for a moment before he continued. "Or if you and Ivey want to swim uninterrupted, just let me know in advance. There's plenty of property between us, but both our paths converge to the lake and there's only the one dock."

"I'm not much of a swimmer, but thank you."

At a loss, he finally said, "Well, Justin is. I think the boy is part fish."

Hope hesitated, then cautiously said, "You and your son... He hasn't always been with you?"

Nice that she would come right out and ask. He'd prefer that over curious assumptions any day. Corbin looked to ensure Justin wasn't within hearing range. He found him swinging from a tree limb, luckily not more than a few feet off the ground.

So many things about his son made him smile.

"It's a relatively new situation. Actually…" He hesitated, but Hope would be living close, so she'd be seeing Justin again. He didn't intend to spill his guts, but the words just came out. "I wasn't aware I had a son until his mother brought him to me. She wanted time to herself."

What an understatement. Darcie had claimed she had a right to her own life and he could do the parenting gig from now on. Justin had stood there, his head down, hearing it all.

Corbin felt anger surging inside him again, but he had only to look at Justin—*his son*—and gratitude overwhelmed him instead. True, he hadn't wanted a child, and to that end he'd done his best to prevent it. Not once, not even as a teen, had he indulged in unprotected sex. Clearly, condoms weren't foolproof, because Justin was here now, and he was his. Corbin knew he'd spend the rest of his life being the best father he knew how to be.

As Hope looked at Justin, empathy darkened her eyes. "Wow, I'm so sorry. This must all be really hard for him."

"He keeps it to himself, but I think, I hope, we can work through it together." He looked down at Hope, at the way she avoided his gaze. She'd parted her baby-fine hair neatly in the middle, and silky bangs fell over her forehead. She had a slight figure, was incredibly shy, at least around him, and her blue eyes were shades darker than his son's.

She commiserated with his son, and Corbin commiserated with her. Maybe because, in some indefinable way, she reminded him of Justin. Every bit as wounded, wary and guarded. Already he felt protective of her, but then, that was part of his nature. His mother, bless her, hadn't tolerated apathy of any kind. The adage "boys will be boys" was pure nonsense, she said, and there was no excuse for boys to be less compassionate, less aware, than girls.

From what he'd gleaned so far, Justin's mother had pretty much left him to raise himself. She'd explained that he was a handful, headstrong and determined to run wild. Corbin saw no evidence of that. Yes, Justin was a healthy, active ten-year-old boy with plenty of energy. But Corbin had once been the same, so he didn't see that as unusual.

Hope shifted beside him. He realized he'd been quiet too long, lost in thought. "Sorry."

Her gaze shot to his in surprise, but didn't stay there long. "For?"

"My mind wandered." Looking up at the mature trees of every kind, at the bluer-than-blue sky, Corbin breathed deeply and smelled the lake and the wild honeysuckle that grew along the perimeter of the woods. "It's been a lot to take in, but I'm hoping this place will be good for us." *Maybe it would be good for Hope, too.*

She gave him a tentative smile. "It is very peaceful here."

"There's plenty to do, a lot of ways to keep an active boy busy." And they were far from the city and Darcie. He believed Justin's adjustment would be easier without his mother's insults, not that she'd mentioned any plans of visiting him anyway.

She'd been clear that she was handing him over—for good.

When he saw Justin bring his legs up to climb the tree, he knew he needed to wrap it up. Stepping away, he said, "I won't hold you up any longer. Remember, if there's anything you need, just let me know. It'll be terrific having you as a neighbor."

"Thank you," she said. "For everything."

After a nod, he joined Justin, smiling at how easily he scaled the tree. Standing near enough to catch him but unwilling to inhibit him, Corbin said, "When I was your age, I had a tree house."

Now hanging upside down, Justin eyed him. "For real?"

"My brother and I built it with my mother's help."

"Your dad didn't help?"

It amused Corbin to have this conversation with Justin up-side down. "Dad had already passed away, but Mom took up the slack." He'd given Justin a condensed version of his family already, but he didn't want to overwhelm him with details yet. "What about us building one?"

Eyes lighting up, Justin swung around and dropped to his feet. Then he scowled. "I don't know how to."

"I do, and I'd enjoy showing you."

Skepticism showed through the excitement. "You mean it?"

Every damn thing he offered, big and small, Justin treated like an unexpected gift he couldn't quite trust. Of course a dad would build a tree house with his son. Sooner or later, Justin would come to expect some things as his due.

"Why not?" Hoping to break through his son's invisible wall, Corbin put his arm around him. He tried to make the gesture casual, but it wasn't. He literally ached to touch his son, to roughhouse, to hug him, to feel the little-boy-softness of his skin and to breathe in the sunshine in his hair.

For now, he'd call it progress that Justin didn't shy away from the nonchalant touch. "Let's go explore and see if we can find a tree closer to the main house that will work."

Bolting ahead, Justin yelled back, "I know a good one."

Laughing, Corbin broke into a run, too.

Friday afternoon, using her only break to drink tea and devour an egg salad sandwich, Ivey considered what Hope had shared a few days ago. It made sense, given the relationship she'd wit-nessed between Corbin and Justin.

All things considered, Corbin seemed a very attentive par-ent, and Justin didn't seem any more temperamental than many kids his age.

Corbin hadn't yet contacted her about a pet, but the man had certainly been busy.

By now, everyone in town knew that they'd moved in, and the rumors were that Corbin was made of money. He spent enough to give that impression, buying things that most people collected over time. Kayak, paddleboard, floats, lawn furniture, a wrought iron patio set, fishing gear, sports equipment... It was as if he'd moved in empty-handed and then filled every space for entertainment.

According to Hope, they were now building a tree house, too. From one of her windows, she had been able to see them in the tree, putting up a platform, both of them shirtless.

She'd been very complimentary in her description of Corbin's chest. Ivey had been imagining that ever since.

When did the man work? And what type of work did he do?

Because Sunset was a small town, she knew that he'd hired landscapers for the lawn and a few locals to expand the dock. And...

Honestly, she spent far too much time thinking about him. So much time, in fact, she hadn't given any other guys the time of day. Just as Corbin's presence had gone through the gossip mills, so had her newly acquired status of *single*. A few locals had tried to engage her in conversation, and one had even offered to buy her coffee.

She'd been carefully polite in turning them down, claiming a busy schedule. After all, she'd die if anyone thought she was still pining for Geoff. The truth was that she only thought of Geoff when he contacted her, and with him, she wasn't quite so gracious.

When would she see Corbin again? Maybe she could—

Hope stuck her head into the office. "Sorry, but you have company."

Ivey's heart leaped and for a single second she thought that Corbin had stopped by to see her. Maybe she'd conjured him with her daydreaming. Quickly tamping down her expectations—and needlessly smoothing her hair—she decided he probably wanted to find out about a pet. She was already smiling when Geoff stepped in and closed the door behind him.

Well, hell. All her expectant joy evaporated.

No way could she block the scowl from her face. "What are you doing here?"

His charming smile never slipped. "You won't take my calls, so what choice did I have?"

"You *could* get the message that we're over."

"Right." Moseying in like a man without a care, he propped a hip on the edge of her desk. "And I have. I get it. We're over." With false humility, he added, "I screwed up."

Cleaning her hands on a napkin, then gulping down the last of her herbal tea, Ivey shrugged. "Wonderful. So why are you here?"

The charming smile warmed another watt. "Since our old relationship is over, I thought we might try a new relationship."

That had to be a joke. She wasn't known for her diplomacy, so surely she'd gotten her point across. But just in case, she looked him in the eyes and stated, "No," without a single blink.

"Don't be so hasty, babe. We've known each other a long time, we're friends, right?"

Hearing the endearment made her mouth flatten.

"Come on, Ivey. You were attracted to me once."

Once…past tense. Yes, Geoff was a good-looking man. Fit, tall enough so that she didn't feel gangly beside him, his brown hair neatly trimmed and his blue eyes sparkling.

She didn't care anymore. Never again would she be romantically involved with him, but something more casual? If he truly meant mere friendship, she could probably handle that.

To make sure, she asked, "Friendship? Certainly. Not yet, but sometime in the future, that would be fine." She pushed back her chair. "Unfortunately, we'll have to discuss the finer points another day. I have patients waiting."

When she started around him, he caught her arm. "Ivey,

wait." His thumb rubbed above her elbow in a not-so benign way. He stepped up close behind her. Too close. "If I have to start as friends, hey, I can work with that." His voice dropped and his warm breath teased her temple. "But we could be friends with benefits, don't you think?"

Oh good Lord. His attention now was so ironic, she could laugh. Seriously, she'd given him every opportunity to show interest, to find even a spark of chemistry, and he'd chosen to play games on his phone instead.

Now that she'd ditched him, he wanted convenient sex? Less than a month ago, she'd repeatedly offered convenient sex, and he'd turned it down.

She said with exaggerated humor, "No, I don't think so. Thanks anyway."

"We were good together, babe."

She'd thought so, until he'd lost interest. Whenever she tried to initiate things, it had always been a toss-up whether he'd be agreeable or not. Lately, the scale had tipped to the negative and she had no desire to put herself through that type of rejection again.

"We might have been once." Back in the beginning. "But not for a while."

"Ouch. I'll take that one on the old ego." He put a smiling kiss to her temple.

Which prompted her to shove away from him. She was just turning to face him, ready to hit him with some hard truths, when another knock sounded on the door and it opened, bumping her in the back.

She moved forward, which brought her closer to Geoff, before she turned...and found Corbin and Justin standing there.

Corbin lifted both brows, and oddly enough, he appeared cheerfully determined. "Hope said it was fine to come on in. Maybe she didn't know you were busy."

Belatedly, Ivey realized that Geoff had both hands on her

shoulders. She quickly shrugged him off and took a step for-ward again. Closer to Corbin.

Heart quickening in pleasure, she said, "Geoff was just leav-ing." Had Hope sent Corbin in specifically to interrupt? Such a true friend. Pretending Geoff wasn't there, she smiled. "It's so good to see you both again. Come on in. I'm sorry I don't have more room—Geoff, if you wouldn't mind?" She nudged him away from the only extra chair.

Justin, being a sweet kid, jumped in with buzzing energy. "We're here about a pet!"

It was nice to see him so animated. "Is that so?"

"You said you could give us some guidance?" Corbin casu-ally stepped in front of Geoff beside Justin's seat.

Really, there was no place for Geoff to go but out. He reached past Corbin and cupped Ivey's cheek. "We'll talk more about this later."

Rearing back from his touch, Ivey said, "I'll be busy all week." The way she bared her teeth felt more like a snarl than a smile. "Thanks, though."

Geoff's face fell dramatically.

Yeah, she could have been a little smoother, but as she'd al-ready admitted, that wasn't her forte. Talking to animals? That she managed quite well. Dealing with worried pet parents? Piece of cake. Pushy exes? Not so much—especially in situations like this one where they were all crowded together in her office while her schedule backed up.

Geoff shot a look at Corbin, then an equally suspicious look at Justin before turning and dragging away. He acted like a de-feated man, but she wasn't buying it. He likely missed her comfy couch and the free food she provided more than he missed her.

The second he cleared the room, Ivey closed the door and fell back against it. "Whew. That was tense."

"Was it?" Corbin asked, as if he hadn't thought so. He glanced down at Justin. "What do you think?"

Justin shrugged. "I want a dog."

Both adults laughed. The kid had a one-track mind that didn't include adult problems.

"Tell you what. Give me fifteen minutes to catch up, then we can discuss it."

"Or," Corbin said, "we can come back when you're finished here."

"When I finish, I need to get home to Maurice." So that Corbin didn't misunderstand, she quickly added, "He's my aging cat. Fifteen minutes?"

"Sure."

"Perfect." She opened the door enough to slip out. "I'll be back as quickly as possible."

As she worked her way through two routine office appointments, Ivey wondered why she was so giddy. Absurd. The man was here to discuss a pet for his son, not to see her personally. None of that stopped her from smiling her way through a dog's vaccinations and a follow-up with a cat who'd been stung by a bee. Both animals were doing well and the pet owners were lovely people.

On the return to her office, Ivey realized that she should have sent Corbin to the break room where he and Justin could have gotten a drink or a snack. She hastened her step, opened the door and found them studying the graphs on the wall, some showing the skeletal makeup of cats and dogs, another showing the devastation of heartworms, and another listing types of dogs and their temperaments.

"That was quick," Corbin said. "I hope that means the vet appointments weren't for anything serious?"

"So far today, it's been busy but ordinary. Hope can handle things for a while, so let's talk about dogs." She smiled down at Justin. "Big or small?"

He shrugged. "I don't know."

Inspiration hit, and she said, "I have some puppies here. Would you like to see them?"

He nodded fast.

"This way." As they walked to Daisy's room, Ivey explained how she'd gotten her. "Her leg is okay now, but she'll always have a scar because the fur won't grow there. The puppies, however, are perfectly fine. They won't be ready for adoption for at least another three weeks, but this way you'd have first pick." She opened the door to the outside pen.

Daisy immediately perked up, then saw the unfamiliar people and shyly hunkered down. The puppies, however, charged forward, making Justin laugh.

Ivey and Corbin stepped back and watched in companionable silence. In the middle of the yard, Justin plopped down and allowed the puppies to crawl all over him.

Corbin stood close beside her. She could feel the heat of him, even smelled some masculine scent, like maybe soap or aftershave. It made her breathe more deeply. The way he watched his son, a small smile on his mouth, made her heart turn over. In so many ways, he was incredibly appealing, physically and emotionally.

"Thank you," he said.

Good Lord. Had she given those compliments out loud? Ivey stared up at him in question.

"For this." He nodded at Justin. "I'm hoping the dog will keep him company when I have to work."

"Oh?" Seeing that as the perfect segue, she asked, "What is it you do?"

"I'm an IT program and project manager. I'm able to work from home, but there's a lot of virtual meetings with technicians, teleconferencing and phone calls. When Justin joined me..." He shook his head, discontent with that phrasing. "When I realized I had a son, I took an extended leave of absence, but I have to get back to work eventually. I'm hoping a dog will keep him company when I'm unavailable." He hurried to add, "I'll be home with him, so of course I'll be accessible if he needs me, but I'd rather he play outside—where I can see him—than just watch TV or play video games."

He'd covered a lot of ground, as if assuring her that he understood his many responsibilities as a parent. "It can all be overwhelming, I'm sure."

"Maybe. It's been fun though. Challenging." He rubbed his hands together. "He's adapted so much better than I could have hoped."

"Children are resilient. And you're good with him, so I'm sure that helps."

He glanced at her. "Hope told you the situation?"

"She did, yes. Is that okay?"

"Of course. I assumed she would." He had his gaze on Justin, then his smile widened. "Such an amazing kid."

Ivey managed to tear her attention away from Corbin's profile to glance at Justin, then couldn't look away. On his belly, inching forward, Justin held out a hand...to Daisy.

Ears flattened in worry, but with her tail swinging, Daisy sniffed his hand. She didn't move away.

Stunned, Ivey whispered, "Daisy is afraid of everyone." Her eyes went glassy with emotion, especially when the dog allowed Justin to gently pet her with only one finger. "Oh, he is an amazing little boy. Oh my." She swallowed heavily. "This is incredible."

Corbin kept his voice as low as hers. "He has a lot of love to give." His gaze never left his son.

"Justin?" Ivey called softly.

The boy looked over his shoulder, his expression somber. "Are you keeping her?"

"I wish I could." Ivey wished that so very much. "But Maurice is afraid of dogs. He's old and—"

"I want her."

Her heart positively melted. She had to draw deep breaths to keep from tearing up.

Looking every bit as fragile as Daisy, Justin asked, "Is that okay, Dad?"

Given the poignant expression on his face, Justin hadn't called him that often. There was so much emotion evident. So much pride.

To bridge the moment, Ivey said, "She's a Jack-a-bee. A mix of a Jack Russell terrier and a beagle. I'm guessing she's around four years old. Twelve pounds, which is smaller than many." Daisy hadn't had an easy go at life so far, but finding a forever home would help her to blossom. "Once she warms up to you, she likes jumping and running, and she loves to howl."

Justin stared at Corbin, waiting with mixed hopefulness and defiance.

"I think that would be terrific," he finally said, his voice gruff. "Clearly she likes you."

"Yeah." Justin urged her into his lap, then put his cheek to the top of her head.

Ivey couldn't help it. She leaned into Corbin, letting their arms touch. "We can't separate her from her puppies just yet. They're barely five weeks old."

"I don't mind waiting," Justin said, and he laughed as one of the puppies tried to climb him and tumbled over.

"God," Ivey murmured. "I really love your kid."

"Yeah." Corbin put his hand to the small of her back. "I'm pretty nuts about him, too."

Chapter Three

Hearing Justin call him *Dad* was like a powerful punch to the heart, leaving Corbin raw. The tree house hadn't done it, nor the bike or even the thought of a boat.

But that little dog had done the trick.

He watched the careful way Justin explored the scar on the dog's leg, tracing it with his fingertips. Emotion damn near took out his knees. One day, he'd be able to show his son how much he loved him, but his plan was to go slow, to give Justin time to adjust, to let things happen in their own way. Too many decisions had been taken from Justin already: a new parent he didn't know, a new place to live. A new way of life.

He deserved to make some decisions for himself, like what dog he wanted to adopt...and what to call Corbin.

Today felt like they'd made incredible strides.

"Why don't we leave him to get better acquainted while you and I talk?" Ivey asked.

Corbin realized they stood very close together, his arm around her, his hand open on her narrow back…and she didn't seem to mind. He'd been so absorbed watching Justin, he'd reacted without thinking. Touching her had seemed right, natural, even necessary, so he had.

Since discovering he had a son, women hadn't factored much into his thoughts or plans. He'd been too intent on figuring out the future and all the ways he wanted to make life better and more secure for his son.

But now? With this particular woman?

He liked Ivey a lot.

Her smile made him want to get even closer. So many things about her drew him. The fact that she liked Justin obviously helped, but it was more than that. Though she seemed to consider it a fault, her refreshing bluntness amused him. It was appealing how she openly cared for Hope. He appreciated her focus on animals, her contributions to the community. So many people had already sung her praises.

And she was currently unattached.

Added to all that was her unique but appealing looks. He liked the vibrant way she smiled, how she often fussed with her wildly curling hair and how her slender hands moved when she talked.

Turning to face her, Corbin dropped his hand. "Lead the way."

"We're going just inside," Ivey explained to Justin. "You'll be all right for a few minutes?"

In a mumble, he protested, "I'm not a baby."

"Of course not. I wouldn't even consider allowing a baby to take Daisy."

Good answer, Corbin thought, impressed with how quickly Ivey had replied.

Nose wrinkling, Justin looked up to ask, "Is her name really *Daisy*?"

His disgust made Corbin grin. "You don't like it?"

Flashing a guilty look at Ivey, he said, "Not really."

"What would you name her?" Ivey asked.

"Something cool." His mouth twisted to the side while he considered options. "If she was a guy dog, I'd name her Freddy, like Freddy Krueger."

Corbin stalled.

Ivey, bless her, merely laughed as she walked back toward Justin. "You know that movie?"

"I've seen every horror movie there is."

"You have, huh?" Sitting down on the grass with him, she asked, *"Alien?"*

"All the Alien movies. I liked *Alien vs. Predator* best, though."

"Oh, that's my fave as well. I love that they combined two awesome franchises."

More engaged than Corbin had ever seen him, Justin sat up a little straighter. "Since she's a girl, I couldn't name her Freddy, but I could have named her Ripley."

"Ripley is amazing, right?" Now Ivey wrinkled her nose. "I wish they hadn't killed her off. I was really bummed about that."

"Yeah, me, too. They could bring her back though…or is she too old now?"

"Sigourney Weaver? Pfft. She could still pull it off."

Corbin felt like an outsider. He didn't mind, since Justin was so engaged. But seriously, Ivey liked horror movies? He was more an action flick–type guy. He knew Justin was into them, it was one of the things his mother had explained right off.

Stick him in front of the TV with a horror channel and he won't bother you.

So far, Corbin and Justin had kept busy with other activities. Never, ever, would he let Justin think he was a bother.

His brother, Lang, got into the whole horror genre, but for some reason, it surprised him that Ivey did, too.

Justin screwed up his face in deep thought. "There aren't as many girls in horror."

"What about Alice from *Resident Evil?"*

Justin shook his head. "I know a girl named Alice and she's not nice."

"Hmm. I can see how that wouldn't work then."

He considered things. "Hey, I know! What about Laurie Strode from *Halloween*?"

Ivey's chin tucked in. "You've seen the Halloween movies?"

"'Course. And all the Friday the 13th movies. *Jason X* was the best cuz it was funny, too."

"Oh, um…" She cast a helpless look at Corbin. "You approved that?"

Now that he'd been included, Corbin stepped closer. "I knew he was a fan, yeah." He ruffled Justin's hair. "Your Uncle Lang will be thrilled."

"He likes scary movies?"

"The scarier, the better."

"Me, too!" Leaning closer to Ivey, Justin confided, "The Texas Chainsaw movies creeped me out. They were kind of gross."

Her brows went even higher. "Yes, they were."

"But I liked *Army of Darkness*. Ash is awesome."

In a deepened voice, Ivey said, "This is my *boom*stick!"

"Ha!" Laughing, Justin rocked the little dog. Her tail waved and she settled against him. Mimicking Ivey's tone, Justin said, "Come get some."

"Good one!" Ivey grinned.

On the outside again, Corbin smiled at their antics, but didn't understand any of it.

"Tell you what." Ivey reached a hand up to Corbin, and he obligingly helped her stand. Dusting off her backside, she said to Justin, "You can rename Daisy anything you want. She'll be your dog, and she's smart enough to adapt."

He put his cheek to the dog's head. "You don't think she'll mind?" The dog licked his face.

Wearing a soft expression, Ivey shook her head. "I think she'll love that you love her, period. Now, I do need to have that talk with your dad, so sit tight and we'll be right back."

Grabbing his hand again, Ivey towed him into the clinic, closed the door and collapsed back against the wall with dramatic effect. "He's seen all the Friday the 13th and Halloween movies!"

Corbin discovered that he liked her theatrics, too. She nearly wailed those movies in accusation, but why? With a shrug, he said, "Sounds like he's seen every horror movie there is." So that she wouldn't blame him for that, he added, "I wouldn't have thought explicit horror was okay for a kid his age, but apparently his mom disagreed." Overall, he assumed Darcie had done everything she could to keep Justin out of her way. Corbin knew he would be very, very different.

Ivey leveled a frown at him. "My guess is his mother didn't care."

"Yeah, unfortunately that seems true." The muscles in his neck tightened. "From what I saw, Darcie had an issue with drugs. She seemed high when I got him from her, and she made it clear she resented him."

Ivey touched her mouth. "In front of him?"

"Yes, and that kills me. I should have been there all along, but I didn't even know about him."

"How exactly did that happen?"

"I dated Darcie a few times when I was seventeen, nothing even close to serious, then suddenly she moved away. I barely noticed. At seventeen, I was busy setting up college, helping my mom around the house, gaining my independence and all that." The excuses didn't sit well now, especially when he thought of Justin as a baby. "Out of the blue, Darcie contacted my mother and said it was critical that she get hold of me. Mom was traveling, but arrangements were made, we met at a park...and she had Justin with her."

"That must have been a shock."

"Not at first. I just assumed she was married and had a family. But right there in front of him, she said I was his dad and it was time for me to step up." His muscles coiled, his stomach cramping. "God, that poor kid just stood there, stiff-necked and fighting tears." He turned away again, knowing he'd see that awful scene, that he'd feel Justin's pain for the rest of his life.

"Did you question it?"

"In front of him? Hell no. He was already being put through enough." He pressed a fist to the wall. "She had all his stuff with him. While I stood there trying to figure out what to say, she tossed his things into my SUV. Justin wouldn't look at me, but I could see he was terrified, and that made up my mind."

"You took him."

"Of course I did." Knowing his expression was grim, he turned back to her. "She gave Justin a hug, told him she loved him but that she needed a change, and she said he'd have a good life with me."

Ivey watched him. "I can't imagine how you must have felt."

"I was more concerned with how Justin felt. I asked him to give me just a moment with her, then I went with her to her car to finish discussing things."

"She sounds like a very disturbed woman."

"To say the least. She'd met a guy, she said, and he didn't want kids."

"Never mind that she already had one?"

Any time Corbin thought of that day, he found it difficult to breathe. "I asked her if it was forever, or if she'd be back soon, just disrupting his life more. She laughed, Ivey. I was so afraid Justin would hear her that I let it go."

"I think my heart is breaking."

Exactly how he had felt. How he *still* felt several times a day. "That first week was awkward as hell. I realized I needed documents, but I waited until Justin had gone to bed one night before I called her. She said she'd mail everything to me."

"Did she?"

"Yes. Birth certificate, his last report card, a few things like that." He worked his jaw. "I got worried, contacted a lawyer and now I have sole legal and physical custody, too."

Surprise flashed over Ivey's face. "She signed off on that?"

"It all happened in a whirlwind, so I doubt Justin knows. It doesn't seem fair to put that on him, too. The thing is, if Darcie wanted to see him, I wouldn't cut her out. But never, not under any circumstances, will I let her take him away from me. Not now."

When her small, soft hand rested on his chest, Corbin went still. She stared up at him with understanding, and intent. Eyes that had looked bright green in the sunshine now appeared hazel in the dimmer indoor light.

He covered her hand with his.

"I'm sorry for all of that," she said, "I really am. You know he's a terrific kid."

"Yes, though I don't know how that happened."

"Does he talk about his life before you?"

"Little tidbits here and there. Like random things will pop up out of nowhere. We got fast food one day, and he told me that one of his mom's boyfriends liked the same place and would usually bring him a burger from there. Or when he accidentally closed his fingers in the door, and he refused to cry or even say much. I told him I'd be shouting and he said big boys didn't do that." Frustration flexed his jaw. "I asked him about friends, but he just shrugged and said most of the kids in his building were older. He said his mom liked to sleep late, so he watched a lot of TV."

Her hand patted his left pec. "But *Halloween*? *Friday the 13th*?"

A little lost, Corbin shook his head. "Halloween mask and hockey mask, right? Full disclosure, I've never watched them, but of course I know about them." When she winced, he asked, "They're extra bad or something?"

"Oh, Corbin. You should really watch one." Her voice dropped to a whisper. "They're equal parts sex with horror."

"Sex?" *Ah, hell.*

"A lot of, ahem, female nudity. Well…" She gestured at her breasts. "Mostly T&A, as they say in the movies."

For the moment, the ramifications eluded him. "T&A, huh?" Tits and ass. It amused him how Ivey said it.

Tilting closer still, she breathed, "Graphic sex."

Good God. Moving past her, he opened the door enough to peek out at Justin. On his back, with Daisy on his chest and the puppies climbing over him, he looked like the average, carefree, fun-loving kid.

Closing the door again and leaning against it, he groaned. "How do I start censoring something he loves? Something he's been allowed to watch?"

"You're his father. You can make those decisions that are best for him."

She made it sound so easy, when he knew it wasn't.

Sympathy eased her frown. "Listen, I grew up on horror movies. Like Justin, they're my favorites. I have an attic full of old toys, comic books, posters, you name it. My mother was very lenient, but she drew the line at all things sexual."

"No T&A?"

She gave an airy wave of her hand. "I sneaked around it, as all kids do. But if she'd known, I'd have been grounded for a week. If it helps, I can make recommendations on horror that doesn't include nudity. Predator and Alien are both terrific franchises. *Army of Darkness* is more campy fun than anything else, but it sounds like Justin's already watched it. *Goonies* or *Silver Bullet* would be more age appropriate for him. Do the whole Jaws series. Sharks are always good for a startle. Oh, and *Gremlins*! Total kid movie."

While Corbin listened in awe, Ivey concentrated. "I know! The Godzilla movies. Those would be good, too." She heaved a sigh. "When you get home, do an Internet search for horror movies for kids, or something like that. This weekend, I'll go through my attic and see if there's anything I can bear to part with."

Seeing an opening, and smart enough to take it, Corbin said, "I bet Justin would love to see it all."

Her eyes flared a bit as if with inspiration. "That's a wonderful idea. Would you like to come over? I work a partial day every other Saturday, but I'm off Sunday. Well, unless there's an emergency. Then I'd have to—"

Corbin laid a finger against her lips. Really soft lips, he noticed. "Sunday would be perfect, and if something comes up, just let me know. I'll give you my number."

Her lips puckered slightly, and she drew a deep breath through her nose.

"Okay?"

When she nodded, her lips teased his finger.

Get it together, Corbin. It amazed him how being with Ivey like this helped to blunt the pain of what he knew of Justin's past. The reality still tortured him, but with Ivey, it wasn't quite as bad.

Fighting his own instincts, he dropped his hand to his side. She immediately licked her lips and damn, that was provocative. Time to refocus, and fast. He got out his phone and, casual as you please, asked, "What's your number? I'll send you a text so you'll have mine, too."

Not quite so casual, she recited hers. Corbin got the impression she didn't pass out her number often, but then, neither did he. It was different here, in Sunset. Instead of hooking up at night with a woman in a club, he'd met a veterinarian on a rainy afternoon while leasing out a guesthouse with his son nearby.

If someone had asked him a year ago, he'd have denied such a thing was possible. Now? In so many ways, it felt incredibly right.

When her phone pinged with the text, Ivey smiled.

"Why don't you tell Justin?" Corbin suggested. "He'll be excited." Realizing he'd imposed on her busy day, he asked, "Or do you need to get back to work?"

Gazing up at him, Ivey nodded, then shook her head.

His mouth twitched. "Yes? No?"

She noticeably gathered herself. "Sorry, I got distracted. It's not often a gorgeous man gives me his number."

Damn, he enjoyed her praise. He knew he wasn't an ogre, but he'd never had a woman be quite so open with her compliments. "Gorgeous, huh?"

"No reason to be modest."

"I'm not." Though he wouldn't have described himself that way. How did she constantly get him off track? "Do you expect me to believe guys—gorgeous or otherwise—aren't interested in you?"

"I don't know. I was with Geoff for so long that…" She cut herself off to assure him, "But I'm ready to get back out there."

"Good to know." Not kissing her took great concentration. It helped that Justin was nearby, waiting for him.

"That was my plan, you know. I was going for variety."

"Variety?" He wasn't sure he liked the sound of that.

"Geoff was such a grind toward the end that I sort of swore off commitments. My new plan was to focus on me and what I want."

Fascinating. "Solid plan. So…what is it you want?"

She shrugged. "Convenience? I know I don't want another slug taking up space on my couch, especially when he's not…"

She stopped abruptly, and damned if heat didn't tinge her cheeks. "When he's not what?" Corbin prompted.

Her chin lifted. "Let's just say if I make time for a guy, he better be worthwhile."

Was she talking sex? Tantalized by that thought, Corbin propped a shoulder on the wall and regarded her. "How's that going for you?"

The question caught her off guard. "What?"

"Getting back out there."

"Oh." She cleared her throat. "Well, I've been busy, so…" She rushed on with, "If you're interested, though, I'll find time."

"Count me interested."

She opened her mouth, then closed it. "Okay." She nodded. "I'll shut up now."

No way could he contain his laugh. He trailed two fingers over a fluffy curl, ending with a stroke against her cheek. "Don't ever censor yourself on my account."

"I tend to go on."

"You speak your mind and I like it."

Her smile came slowly before she checked the time. "I dragged you in here to discuss the dog and got totally sidetracked. All the T&A talk threw me off."

He opened his arms. "Lay it on me."

Without hesitation, she launched into her concerns. "I'm thrilled that he wants Daisy, please understand that. I love her so much and I badly wanted her to find a good home. I knew it'd be crazy difficult for me to accept someone as her owner, but I think Justin will do a great job with her, especially after seeing them together."

She'd rattled that off so quickly, Corbin had a difficult time keeping up. "But?"

"Daisy—or whatever he decides to call her—is a very energetic dog. She's smaller than many, but makes up for it with sweetness. Because she's still skittish, she's going to need a lot of attention. Adapting from her life here to your home will take patience."

Such an amazing, big-hearted woman. "We'll be very good to her, Ivey. I promise."

"I can't guarantee she won't chew on stuff or piddle on the floor or—"

"Hey." Cupping her cheek again, he let his thumb tease near the corner of her mouth. Her skin was incredibly soft and warm.

"You have my word. I'll supervise Justin and together we'll make sure she's well loved. Okay?"

She deflated with a sigh. "Yes, I believe that, or I never would have agreed." Hesitantly, she asked, "While the puppies mature, I don't suppose you'd bring Justin by every so often so Daisy can get to know him better?"

Glad that she'd suggested it, Corbin smiled. "That's a terrific idea. Justin would love it."

Her gaze searched his. "And you?"

Ah, the straightforward approach. He had no problem with that. "I'll enjoy seeing you again."

Making no bones about her relief, she blew out a breath. "Great. Now I really do have to hurry." Without waiting for him, she opened the door and rushed back out to the small yard. "Hey, monster fan, sorry that took so long."

"It did?"

Clearly his son was so involved with Daisy and the puppies, he hadn't even noticed.

Ivey laughed. "Have you decided on a name for her?"

"I was going to go with Ripley, but I might just leave it Daisy." The dog sat in his lap, face tilted up while Justin stroked her back. "She probably wouldn't like someone changin' her name."

"I'm sure you'll make the right decision." Ivey reclaimed her seat beside him. "I have a couple of ideas and you can let me know what you think. Your dad already agreed, so it's up to you."

Justin cast Corbin a wary look. "Okay."

Corbin was getting used to that expression. Sometimes it seemed that Justin feared him. After all, a man who could give so much could also take it away. In time, he hoped Justin would learn to trust him, to rely on him. Until then, maybe he needed to pull back a little. Not with the dog; that was a great idea, he believed that. But he could slow down the pace with everything else he bought. He might be overwhelming Justin with all the gifts.

Ivey spoke as if she were imparting great secrets. "When I was your age, and all through college actually, I amassed a *huge* collection of horror stuff."

Justin's eyes widened. "Do you still have it?"

"It's all packed up in my attic, gathering dust and maybe cobwebs."

"Like a horror scene," he breathed in awe.

She nodded. "Exactly. But I thought, if you're brave enough, you and I could go up there and check it out."

Clutching Daisy to his chest, he shot to his knees. "For real?"

Delighted, Ivey said, "For real. There are toys you could look at, most still in the packaging, though, because to collectors, those are worth more. I also have magazines, comics, books, posters. Let's see, some lunch boxes, holiday props, masks, clothes…" Running out of steam, she wrapped it up with, "All kinds of things. So Sunday? Are we on?"

"Heck, yeah!" He looked back at Corbin, cautious again. "It's okay?"

Corbin repeated, "Heck, yeah." He knelt down beside them. "The other thing is that Ivey would like us to visit the dog here whenever we can, so she can get used to you before we take her home. I told her we could fit that into our busy schedules."

Justin smiled. "We're not that busy."

God, how he loved that kid's smiles. "So we're all set." He stood, then took turns hauling each of them to their feet. "We should let Ivey get back to work now."

As if on cue, Hope stuck her head out the door. "Sorry to interrupt, but the Mathersons are here."

"I'll be right there." To Justin and Corbin, Ivey explained, "Their dog had a pretty serious surgery and this is his first follow-up. I need to run, but it's been a lot of fun and I'm already looking forward to Sunday."

As she quickly strode into the clinic, Justin gave his attention back to Daisy, taking the time to cuddle her, to whisper to her, all in all, breaking Corbin's heart just a little.

He put his hand on Justin's narrow shoulder. "She has a nice setup here. She'll be fine."

"Yeah. She's got her babies to keep her company, huh?"

"I'm sure she's a very busy mama."

Justin looked at the pups as they played. "Think she'll miss them?"

"Ivey will find good homes for them."

Nose scrunched, Justin squinted up to Corbin. "Yeah, but will Daisy miss them?"

Without an answer for that, Corbin chose to deflect. "Why don't we ask Ivey on Sunday?"

"Okay." After kissing Daisy on the head, he set her down carefully with her puppies. As they left the fenced-in yard, Justin asked, "What are we going to do now?"

"I don't know. What would you like to do?" Corbin considered the ice cream parlor, maybe a bike ride or a trip to the lake.

Sly, a little hopeful, Justin suggested, "We could look at boats again."

Damn, hadn't he just ruled out more purchases? Who was he kidding? If it made Justin happy... "Is that what you want to do?"

"It was fun, right?"

"Sure." He rested his hand on Justin's back...and was thrilled when he didn't pull away. Currently, Justin was all hard angles, bony knees and elbows and shoulder blades, wrapped up in little boy sweetness. Touching him touched Corbin's heart. "I suppose we have time for that."

They were just reaching his car when Justin said, "I like her."

"Daisy?"

"I meant Ivey. She's pretty cool, huh?"

"Very cool." He'd moved them to Sunset so Justin could find a new focus. Now it looked like Corbin had found one as well.

★ ★ ★

As soon as Ivey and Hope wrapped up with the last patient, Ivey locked the front door, fell back against it and burst out with, "I have a date."

Equally excited, Hope squealed. "That's why you were out there talking so long?"

"Yes. Well, I should explain it's not a date-date."

One hand on her hip, Hope asked, "So what kind of date is it?"

"The kind where Corbin and his son come to my house to go through the attic with me." She laughed. "You know what? Maybe it isn't even a date. But he did say he looked forward to seeing me again, and they plan to stop in every so often so Justin can visit with Daisy before he takes her home."

Jaw loosening, Hope breathed in shock, "You're letting him have Daisy?"

Not an unexpected reaction. "Trust me, I'm as surprised as you are. Oh but, Hope, that little boy looked at the puppies, looked at Daisy and chose *her*."

"Okay, that's incredibly sweet." Still looking unconvinced, Hope said carefully, "It's just that I always assumed you'd somehow keep her."

"You know I'd love to, but Maurice wouldn't like it. He's always hated dogs. And since I'd have to leave them there alone when I worked, I'd spend all my time worrying."

"I guess." Hope pursed her mouth. "What about the puppies? Have you found homes for them yet?"

"No one that I'll actually let have one." And that was a problem. "I still have a few weeks to figure it out."

"If nothing comes up, we could just keep them here. Like little mascots."

Not a bad idea. "What about you? Are you allowed to have pets in your new place?"

Struck by that thought, Hope opened her mouth only to close it. Finally she said, "I don't know. I could ask, though, right?"

"Absolutely. Corbin is a super nice guy. If he doesn't want you to get a puppy or two, he'd definitely tell you so."

"Two?"

Trying not to laugh, Ivey headed back to the office to get her purse. "If you took two, they could keep each other company."

"There is that."

Delighted that Hope didn't sound against the idea, Ivey asked, "I could bring it up with Corbin, if you want."

"Thanks, but I have to be able to deal with him. Might as well start with something easy like this. So far he's not hard to be around."

Karen stuck her head in the doorway. "Unless either of you need anything else, I'm heading home."

"We're on our way out now, too." Ivey hitched her purse strap over her shoulder and turned out the light. As they all stepped out together, she said, "As always, Karen, we couldn't get by without you."

"Just don't forget it," Karen teased, and hurried along her way.

Once she'd secured the back door, Ivey stopped Hope from going to her car. "How are you doing?"

"I'm good, why?"

Hope was never truly *good*. The trauma she'd suffered in her past still influenced her in so many ways. Few knew about it, but Ivey and Hope had grown close quickly and they shared just about everything.

Ivey took in Hope's puzzled expression and wasn't sure if she should even bring it up. "Never mind."

"Oh." Realizing what Ivey was actually asking, Hope shook her head. "You mean me with guys and the fact I'll be living so close to Corbin and on my own and everything."

That pretty much summed it up. "When are you moving in?"

"Starting tonight, actually." With new anticipation, she

hooked her arm through Ivey's. "I have my essentials boxed up, a bunch of my clothes, plus a sleeping bag. I paid some boys to help move my bed and dresser over the weekend, but I splurged and bought a new love seat and a few tables. They'll be delivered early next week."

"Wow." So many questions, but Ivey started with, "What boys?"

"High school guys who work at the grocery. Three of them. They seemed nice and they're always polite."

If Ivey had to guess, they were probably extra nice to Hope. Not only was Hope pretty, she was also incredibly sweet. "And you aren't nervous about it?" Usually Hope got tense around any male who was close to her age of twenty-one. High school boys could be anywhere from fifteen to eighteen.

Pausing, Hope stared out over the rear parking lot, empty now except for their two cars. "It was four years ago. I figured it was time to push myself a little. Sixteen-year-old boys seemed like a safe bet. Plus it'll be daytime and I'll have all the windows open, so…" She shook her head. "I have to start somewhere, right?"

Ivey wanted to hug her close, but many times that resulted in each of them getting weepy. So instead she made a decision. "I'll go with you Saturday after we get off work, and I'll cancel my plans with Corbin for Sunday so I can be there with you—"

"No." Laughing a little, Hope gave in to the hug that Ivey had resisted, but she kept it brief, a quick squeeze of affection that said what words couldn't. "You're excited about seeing Corbin and I'm excited to hear how it goes. Plus…this is on me, Ivey. I want to start putting the past behind me."

"You don't have to do that alone."

Her smile trembled, and she leaned in for a longer, softer hug. "How is it you're so much more understanding than my own mother and sister were?"

"I don't know. I guess they were too close to it, too close to you, so they had a different perspective."

Hope shook her head. "No, they just blamed me. They were so excited about my sister marrying him, all because he had money, and they seemed to think I deliberately messed it up."

Fury surged, but Ivey held it back. She knew the story, and it still made her want to vent on people she'd never even met. "Money should never come before family. More importantly, you were only seventeen, for God's sake. Should you have let him rape you?"

It was odd, but Hope always reacted positively to anger on her behalf—maybe because, as she'd said, she didn't get that reaction from her own family.

A ghost of a smile chased off her gloom. "Overall, I think they really just wished I'd kept quiet so no one else knew. Then my sister could have gone ahead with the marriage and gotten her hands on the family's wealth."

"Ridiculous. Money is not that important." Yes, Ivey did well enough, always had. Her parents had raised her in an upper middle-class neighborhood, and though she hadn't gotten everything she'd wanted, she'd had everything she needed.

"No, it's not." Hope unlocked her car and opened the door to let out the day's heat. "I haven't seen either of them since then, and other than a card for holidays, they haven't contacted me."

"They should be ashamed."

This time Hope smiled without reserve. "I tend to agree. I miss them, but I'm not sure I could ever go back to that town anyway. Too many ugly memories."

Once everyone had found out about the attempted rape, Hope had been under scrutiny, especially since her sister didn't immediately break things off with the bastard who'd tried to force himself on her. One day, Ivey thought, she'd go there herself and give them all hell.

For now, she figured Hope needed a change of subject. "So you're camping out in the new place tonight, huh?"

"I'm really looking forward to it, so please don't worry."

"I'll try not to, if you'll send me a few texts just to let me know how you're doing."

"Deal. Now get home to that grumpy old cat. And, Ivey?"

"Yes?"

"Love you."

Oh, if Hope had been her sister, a whole lot of people would have been demolished. "Love you, too." They parted with smiles.

With luck, Ivey thought as she made her way to her car, the move would be good for Hope. Just the fact that she planned to live so close to Corbin was a good sign.

Had Corbin noticed Hope's apprehension? Ivey would bet yes. He wasn't an obtuse man. Still, maybe she'd have a little talk with him, just to ensure he understood the way of things. Perhaps he'd keep a close eye on Hope? She'd give that idea some thought, maybe discuss it with Hope tomorrow.

And then on Sunday, she'd see Corbin again. Crazy how much she already looked forward to it.

Chapter Four

Hope smiled as she pulled into the long drive to the guest-house—now *her* house. After work she'd done a little shopping for necessities, like coffee, cereal, milk, lunch meat, condiments and bread. She was incredibly excited to settle into the new space.

Even the driveway was beautiful. Tall trees of every variety offered welcome shade. Honeysuckle left a sweet scent in the air. And the birds, so many birds, sang their little hearts out. The privacy, the beautiful setting… God, it made her heart happy.

For so long it seemed she'd struggled to make ends meet, to gain her true independence. Leaving home at seventeen, especially in the emotionally devastated shape she'd been in, had thrown her priorities out of whack. Anger had vied with fear, but luckily that kept her determined to keep going.

With Ivey's help, she'd gotten her two-year degree while working at the clinic, too. Soon she'd be able to continue her education so she could eventually be a veterinarian. Ivey's clinic could really use the help.

Who needed the social scene when she had her work, a friend like Ivey and wonderful goals? She didn't. She didn't need her family, either. Could she forgive them? Yes. But four years had passed and not once had they said they were sorry. Why would they when they'd never acknowledged that she was a victim?

The stroll down memory lane lasted right up until she turned the curve in the drive and saw the man looking around her house. She hit the brakes so hard, dust and gravel spewed up around her, drawing his attention.

Shading his eyes, he looked toward her.

Her heart jumped into her throat and lodged there, making it difficult to draw a breath. Backing out in a quick escape seemed like a good idea, but he smiled and waved to her. When she didn't drive forward, he started to approach.

He was as tall as Corbin, a little bulkier with strength, and from what she could see of his face, very handsome.

She didn't care.

Holding a white ball cap and wearing reflective sunglasses, he could be anyone. His clothes looked like the typical summer T-shirt and cargo shorts with sneakers, except that the body beneath was different. More honed with muscle.

Locking the doors, Hope put the car in Reverse in case she needed to speed away. Didn't matter how idiotic she might look, not when fear ran rampant inside her, urging her to flee, making her fight hard to remain in control.

"Hello," he called out, pulling off the glasses, showing friendly light brown eyes and dark lashes. Yep, very handsome.

And it *still* didn't matter.

When he reached the side of the car, he leaned down to look in. For a second, he just stared, then his smile warmed even more. "I'd about given up hope of finding anyone home."

Hand shaking, Hope opened the window a tiny bit. Knowing she frowned, that she didn't look the least bit welcoming, she asked, "Who are you?"

"Lang Meyer, Corbin's brother." He waited for her to introduce herself, to maybe open the window more, and when she didn't, his smile slipped. "I wanted to surprise him with a visit, but he's not home and not answering his cell. Any ideas?"

Yes, she had ideas. Like maybe he should go wait at Corbin's house instead of hers. "He lives in the bigger house over the path in the woods."

Bracing a hand on the roof of her car, he nodded. "Right. I have his address and I tried there first. When I didn't find him, I went down to the lake in case he was swimming. Saw this house through the trees and figured—"

"He's not here."

Straightening again, he slowly replaced his sunglasses, put the cap back on his head and shoved his hands into his pockets. He wasn't smiling now, but his tone still sounded congenial. "Got it. Sorry I bothered you."

Hope watched him turn and stride away, and in that moment she hated herself for being such a coward. Her fears had made her unkind, bordering on outright mean.

Lowering the window more, she called out, "Wait."

He paused, but three seconds passed before he faced her again. She could see his dark eyebrows raised over the top rim of his sunglasses.

Clearing her throat didn't remove the vise of uncertainty trying to steal her voice, but she forced the words out anyway. "Corbin was with my friend earlier. She might have an idea where he's gone. If you'd like to wait, I'll call her."

After a long hesitation, he nodded. "Thank you. If I hadn't been so long on the road, I'd head into town and kill some time until he returns, but—"

"It's not a problem. Just let me get parked first." Hope reached for the garage door opener, but then withdrew her hand. Being inside the building with him would feel too confining, so instead she stopped the car right outside the garage. Taking her phone from her purse, she put in a call to Ivey.

Her friend answered on the third ring. "Hey, chickie, what's up?"

"Well, Corbin's brother is here?" Yeah, that didn't explain anything, especially since she posed it with so much uncertainty.

"Here, where?"

"My new place."

Sharpened awareness came through in the way Ivey asked, "You're okay?"

Lowering her voice, Hope whispered, "In my car, doors locked. He's just standing there." Looking gorgeous and waiting. "He does resemble Corbin, so I believe him."

"You want me to shoot over there real quick?"

God bless her, she could always count on Ivey, even when it was horribly inconvenient. "No, I'm…" Fine? Was she fine? Hope shook her head. It didn't matter. "He said he's been calling Corbin but no answer. Any ideas where he might be?"

"I'm sorry, no. But if they're on the beach, Corbin's signal might have dropped. You know how it is there. For every phone service that works, another doesn't." Then with decision, "I'm coming over. Stay in your car. I'll be there in ten minutes."

"You don't need to—" Hope realized that Ivey had disconnected and wondered what to do with Lang.

As if he sensed her unease, he kept his distance this time when he asked, "Any luck?"

That in itself was a surprise. Most men either ignored her nervousness or tried to tease through it. Mind made up, Hope lowered the window enough to poke her head out. "She's…um, coming over. She'll be here any second."

"You say my brother was visiting with her?" As if relishing that idea, he nodded. "I'd love to meet her."

"Yes, well…" She couldn't continue to cower in the car. Anyone with eyes could see this man and Corbin were related. And he certainly didn't act threatening. In fact, he was considerate, keeping his distance while not making a big deal of it. "I'll try calling Corbin, too." Going for stealth and likely failing, she asked, "What's his number?"

Taking two measured steps closer, Lang rattled off the number while Hope put it into her phone. It rang three times before Corbin answered.

It startled Hope to hear his voice, since she'd believed Lang that Corbin wasn't picking up. But he had known Corbin's number by memory, so that counted as something. "Hey."

"Hope?" Corbin murmured something, probably to Justin, then asked, "Everything okay?"

"I think so." Keeping a wary eye on the guy, she said, "Your, er, brother is here?"

"Lang?" He laughed. "No kidding?"

Watching Lang smile again, she explained, "He called but you didn't answer, so he…came to my place. That is, the guesthouse."

"We were out on a boat for a test drive. Guess we lost the signal. Good thing you were around. I'll be there in just a few minutes. Tell him not to budge." Then he, too, disconnected the call.

Hope released a tight breath. Forcing herself, she opened her door and stepped out but stayed close to the car. "He'll be here any minute. He said he was out on a boat, so his cell service didn't work."

Face falling, Lang asked, "Did he buy a boat?"

The ridiculous expression shouldn't have been so engaging, yet it was. "I have no idea."

"I hope not, or part of my surprise will be ruined." He looked around again. "This is a great place. Really quiet."

"I agree, especially since it's close to town, and to where I work."

"Yeah? Where's that?"

"The animal clinic." *Why in the world would I tell him that?*

"Really?" With his sunglasses in place, she couldn't see his eyes, but she had the sensation of being looked over. "Seems right."

Had he just checked her out? Her stomach jumped at the possibility, but not in an altogether unpleasant way. "It's actually your brother's property."

He eyed the small house again, then vaguely gestured toward the woods. "I thought he lived over there."

"He does, but he's renting me the guesthouse." Her lips clamped shut. She *never* volunteered information and didn't know why she'd gone so talkative now.

"That's a nice score." His grin went lopsided. "Hope he's giving you a good deal?"

"I couldn't afford it otherwise." The words left her mouth uncensored, shocking her. Unlike Ivey, she didn't chatter. Or at least, she hadn't until now.

"While we wait, will you tell me about my nephew?" Without crowding her, Lang moved slightly closer. "That is, if you've met him?"

"I have." Despite herself, she softened. This was one subject she didn't mind. "Justin is very cute. Tall, too. And a little shy."

"He probably got the height from our side of the family, but shy? No, definitely not a Meyer trait." He rested against one of the garage posts supporting the deck. "Does he look like my brother and me?"

"You've never seen him?"

"Small phone photos, that's all. Soon as I heard about him, I put my business up for sale. Luckily, it went fast so I packed up and drove here." He held out his arms. "You can probably tell how anxious I am."

"A little," she admitted, charmed despite her caution. "Well, Justin does have brown hair, but I think it's lighter than yours. I don't remember his eye color, sorry." She wanted to ask him about his business, but if she did, would he feel free to ask her more questions?

Just then, Lang perked up. "You hear that?"

Tires on the gravel drive made a distinct and recognizable sound. "It's probably my friend. I assume Corbin would go to his own house."

But no, that was Corbin's SUV coming around the bend in the drive. He stopped behind Hope's car, hurriedly got out and greeted his brother with open-armed enthusiasm.

"Lang! I didn't know you'd be here or Justin and I would've been home to greet you."

"Surprise." Wearing a wide grin, Lang strode to his brother and the two men engaged a bruising bear hug with a lot of back thumping and laughter.

Hope caught herself grinning, especially when she saw Justin's wide-eyed amazement. Clearly he was as overwhelmed by his uncle as Hope had been.

Immediately Lang freed himself to face the boy. "Holy smokes, you *are* tall! You sure you're only ten?" He approached Justin with consideration. "Here I had visions of a little squirt, but you're nearly as tall as me."

Scoffing, and fighting a smile, Justin said, "No I'm not."

"Close enough." To Corbin he said, "The kid looks sixteen, not ten."

The expression Corbin wore could only be called pride. "He definitely looks older."

That made Justin puff up, too.

It fascinated Hope, seeing the easy way Lang dealt with him, how comfortable he was meeting his nephew for the very first time.

"We were both tall, right? Mom's mentioned that often enough." Corbin put his arm over Justin's shoulders. "I should warn you that your Uncle Lang is the wild one. Don't believe anything he tells you."

"Ha! It's your dad who got into all the mischief. Me being three years older—"

"Which makes him an old man at thirty."

"—it was my job to get him out of scrapes. Kept me busy around the clock."

No one had noticed Ivey parking behind them, but as she stepped out, she said, "If he's old at thirty, then I'm ancient at thirty-one, so my guess is that you want to take back that insult right now."

Oops, Hope thought. Not because of Corbin's comment; clearly Ivey was teasing about that. But her friend was more dressed down than usual. She wore loose shorts, ancient flip-flops, an oversize T-shirt, and she'd stuck her fluffy hair into a haphazard knot on top of her head that looked like it might explode free at any moment.

Corbin laughed. "Ivey, you're here, too? This is like a party."

Ivey raised her brows while fighting a smile. "And that crack on age?"

"Consider it retracted, although dressed like that, you look closer to twenty, so you've got a leg up on this old man."

Lang feinted with a lunge, Corbin jumped back and Justin laughed out loud.

Hope's gaze met Ivey's. Males, they silently agreed, had a very different way about them.

Corbin did hasty introductions all around, then ended with, "So what do you think, Lang?"

"That you have great taste in women."

Ivey choked.

Corbin said, "True, but I meant about your nephew."

"My nephew. Damn, I love the sound of that. I'm getting all choked up now." Belying that statement with another grin, Lang closed in on Justin. "You'll have to forgive your uncle his excesses, but what the hell? I come from a family of huggers, okay?" Without waiting for Justin to agree, he swung him up and into a wide circle, making Ivey dart away and causing Justin to laugh hard.

Patting Corbin's arm, Ivey said, "I'll let you boys get to it," and she walked over to Hope.

"Stay for dinner," Corbin offered. "Both of you. If I know my brother, he's starving. And I'm finding that Justin is an empty well. I could order up some pizzas. They deliver out here, right?"

"They do," Ivey said, but deferred to Hope on the invitation.

Hope hated to be the party pooper, but it couldn't be helped. "Thank you, but I've got a lot of stuff to unload."

"She's staying the night," Ivey volunteered, while missing Hope's subtle gesture that she should go along. "The rest of her things will be delivered over the weekend, but until then, I'll help her set up what she has with her."

Lang had surely noticed already that her passenger seat and the entire rear of her small hatchback was packed full. Rather than comment on it, he lifted Justin's arm, lightly squeezed his biceps, and said, "Yup, plenty strong enough." He held out his arms. "That means you have three strappin' menfolk here willing to help, so just tell us where to put what."

"And once we're done," Corbin added, "we'll all go over to my house for pizza. Deal?"

Hope could see that Ivey wanted to but was holding back so she didn't put Hope in an uncomfortable position. The funny thing was that here, with the brothers' laughter and open affection, she didn't feel as on edge as usual. "I could eat," she finally said, surprising Ivey, though the guys didn't seem to realize how rare it was for her to socialize, even in a small group. "Thank you."

"And since Maurice is already fed and napping again," Ivey said, jumping on board, "you can count me in, too."

Hiking up his loose shorts in a take-charge manner, Justin strode forward. "Ready when you are."

It was the first time Ivey could recall seeing Hope relax around men. But then, Corbin and Lang continually heckled each other with good-natured insults while paying a lot of attention to Justin, praising him on everything from his strength, his speed, his intelligence and his good looks, which they both made clear had been inherited from them.

They were so relaxed together, it appeared to relax Justin, too.

Each time Hope laughed, Ivey wanted to grab her up for a tight celebratory hug. She'd give a lot to see Hope live a carefree, happy life. Her peace of mind had been stolen from her at the sensitive age of seventeen, and until today, it seemed a permanent mark had been made on her psyche.

Now she was flourishing right before her eyes. Ivey couldn't have been more thrilled.

"Everything okay?" Corbin asked, nudging his way into the tiny kitchen to help empty a few more boxes.

She gave him an easy smile. "Yes, actually."

His gaze lingered, grew warm. "You look pleased about something."

"I am." Peeking around him, she saw that Lang, Hope and Justin were getting the last few boxes from the car. "I've never see her like this."

"Comfortable with men?"

Very perceptive. "You and your brother are so casual about everything, I think it's difficult to be stressed."

He tugged on one long crimped curl that had fallen loose from her topknot. "One of these days, you'll tell me about her."

"Yes, I think I might." It was strange, but in such a short time, she trusted him.

His attention dropped to her mouth. "What would you think if I kissed you before the evening ended?"

Oh wow. "Seriously?" Awareness flooded her system, setting her nerve endings alight. "I'd think that was pretty awesome."

They heard footsteps coming up from the garage, so Corbin brushed his fingers over her cheek and stepped back. "Soon, then. Maybe when I walk you to your car tonight?"

The fast way she nodded earned a soft laugh from him. Ivey

didn't mind amusing him. She'd be anticipating that kiss every minute until then.

The guys didn't tease Hope when she shook out her brand-new sleeping bag in the bedroom. Instead, Lang knelt down to check it out, smoothing his hand over the material. "Cushy. Lots of padding." He twisted to look at Corbin. "You remember those old sleeping bags we used in the backyard? Man, it was like sleeping on a beach towel. No stuffing at all."

"How could I forget?" Corbin asked. "We used them in our tree house, where all the mosquitoes felt free to feast."

"We have a tree house, too," Justin boasted. "Well, almost. We're still working on it."

"He's a workhorse," Corbin said, again with his arm over Justin's shoulders.

"I noticed." Lang came back to his feet. "I think you hauled more than your dad and me combined. Maybe you'll be strong enough to get us up the tree in our old age."

"The way your brother tells it," Ivey said, "we're already in the old-age category."

Clutching his heart as if she'd just pierced it, Corbin pretended to stagger, leaving Justin to laughingly prop him up. "I'll never live that down."

Ivey gave him a playful shove. "So, that's it?" She turned to Hope. "Anything else you need done?"

Satisfaction glowed in Hope's expression. "Nope. I'm all set, at least until my furniture arrives."

All set and clearly excited by the prospect. Ivey would remind her again to check in, just so Hope would know she wasn't alone.

Again proving himself to be a great guy, Corbin said, "There are floodlights off the balcony and behind the house. They're bright enough that you can see all the way to the lake."

"The electric bill—" Hope began.

"Isn't a problem. You pay a flat rate, so don't worry about that. It's added into your monthly payment and the bills come to me."

For that alone, Ivey could kiss him. And kiss him again.

Maybe a little more than kissing. But then, she was sort of looking for any excuse to get nearer to him. When she'd started this new campaign of being footloose and fancy-free, not once had she counted on a guy like Corbin.

Funny that him being a great dad only made him more interesting. She wasn't sure how hooking up would work with him having a ten-year-old son, but for now, she enjoyed getting to know him better.

And yes, she realized that was the exact opposite of her plan, but who cared? He was nearby, incredibly good-looking, interested and… There she went, making excuses again.

"Speaking of the lake…" Lang smacked himself in the head. "I left a surprise for you and Justin over at your house, but now I'm concerned it might be a duplicate."

"You hear that Justin?" Corbin led him toward the stairs. "Let's go see what Uncle Lang has brought you."

"Uncle Lang," his brother said with a big, satisfied grin. "I'll never get tired of hearing it."

"Will you be the best uncle ever?" Ivey teased.

"Naturally." Assuming a lofty expression, Lang stated, "I excel at all I do." With that, he shot a quick, suggestive look at Hope, making Ivey stiffen.

Her friend never liked male attention, and in fact, it set her on edge. Outright flirting or innuendo tended to leave Hope floundering.

But Lang moved right along, adding, "I have no doubt I'll win the uncle gig, too. Just watch."

When Hope only chuckled without a single sign of unease, Ivey felt her heart turn over. She couldn't wait to get Hope alone to ask her about her reaction to Lang, but for now she enjoyed seeing her relax and have fun.

Together, they all tromped over the path in the woods to Corbin's house. Branches spread out overhead, and exposed roots tried to trip her up. Corbin stayed close, occasionally holding back a weed, once removing a spiderweb with a stick.

When Justin ran ahead, Corbin called, "Wait for us," but Justin didn't slow and Corbin didn't seem to mind. "That boy has one speed, and it's fast."

Ivey smiled with him. "Typical of kids his age, I guess."

Lang said, "I remember always being in a hurry."

"And I remember always beating you."

"A challenge!" Lang broke into a flat-out run, and Corbin immediately gave chase.

She and Hope shared another look. "Should we?"

"Heck, yeah." And just like that, Hope took off, too.

Wow. She'd had no idea Hope was so fast! Laughing while struggling to catch up, Ivey ran as fast as she could in flip-flops... and skidded to a halt when she found the others all staring at Corbin's driveway, where a very nice inboard boat sat in shining splendor.

Holy smokes.

Pleased with himself, Lang stood with arms crossed while Justin and Corbin circled the boat.

Finally Corbin looked up. "You didn't."

"You already know I did." Smug, he took a bow and said, "Surprise."

Astounded, Corbin rubbed the back of his neck. "It's big."

"Not too big for the lake. I checked before getting it. If you take the cover off and climb inside, you'll find a tube, skis, rope, jackets...everything you need."

Corbin's mouth hitched on one side, giving him a lopsided grin. "Wow." To the women, he said, "My brother is sometimes overly extravagant."

"Pfft," Ivey teased, totally deadpan. "It's just a boat," and that had both men chuckling.

Justin couldn't seem to take it in. "You bought it for us?"

"Yup. What do you think? Am I the best uncle ever or what?"

Taking everyone by surprise, Justin launched himself at Lang and got swung up into a big hug. "You are!" Ninety miles a minute, he explained, "Me and Dad were looking at boats, but he said it was a big decision and we had to take our time and now we have one and it's bigger than the one we rode in today."

As Justin drew a breath, Lang said, "I'll teach you to water-ski, okay? Or your dad can. He was better at it than me."

"Truth," Corbin said, turning to the women. "Either of you ski?"

Hope shook her head. Far as Ivey knew, she hadn't even been in the lake, or worn a swimsuit, since the assault.

"I've gone tubing, but only when the driver swears not to deliberately dump me." Making a face, Ivey said, "Geoff drove a friend's boat once, and there was nothing fun about it."

Corbin sent her a shrewd look. "Yeah? Why's that?"

"He *did* dump me, the jerk. And back in the cove where I just knew there'd be big turtles and catfish and all kinds of snakes." The memory irked her all over again. "I made him take me home and the whole thing was a fiasco."

Lang said, "Geoff sounds like a—"

"Bad driver," Corbin inserted, giving his brother a frown and sending a quick nod Justin's way. To Ivey, he said, "Our mother would ride in a tube and we knew if we dumped her, there'd be hell to pay. I promise you, you can trust both of us."

Lang crossed his heart, but added, "For the record, I like getting dumped." He stuck his hat on Justin's head. "What do you think?"

"I don't know." Justin lifted his shoulders. "I guess I will." He moved away to circle the boat again.

"So." Hands on his hips, Lang surveyed his brother. "You hadn't yet bought a boat, right?"

"I was trying not to overindulge," Corbin said.

Ivey couldn't take it a second more. "Not to be nosy, but you're saying you could have bought a boat like that, too?" Pretty sure it had to cost eighty thousand or more, not that she knew boat values since she'd never considered one herself, much less one so fancy. Then to Lang, "And you can just grab a boat like that as a gift? To give away?"

Corbin hedged, but Lang shrugged it off as nothing. "Yeah? Corbin didn't tell you?"

"No," Corbin said. "I haven't yet shared my financial records with her."

Ivey laughed. "The two of you should take this act on the road. Together, you're hilarious. And hey, it's not like being financially secure is a bad thing."

"It's not old money," Corbin said with a shrug. "Early in Mom and Dad's marriage, he turned a rundown sporting company into a thriving business. They reinvested everything for years, expanding across the country. After Dad died, Mom took over, though she's no longer involved in the day-to-day running of things. Lang and I have stock, of course, and investments of our own."

"So you don't need to work?"

"Don't *need* to," Lang said. "But we both do."

"It's an ethical thing," Corbin explained. "And we'd be bored in no time if we didn't stay busy."

Proving none of that meant anything to him, Justin asked, "Can I look inside?"

"You bet." Lang started unsnapping the cover of the boat. "Why don't you and I explore it while your dad gets that pizza ordered? I'm starved."

"Me, too," Justin said, already climbing up the trailer's wheel well with the nimbleness of a monkey.

Smiling fondly, Corbin put a hand to Ivey's back and urged her toward the house. "Hope? You want to come in with us or check out the boat?"

Fingers laced together, bottom lip caught in her teeth, Hope looked longingly at the boat.

Catching her expression, Lang said, "We could use your help. Grab that side of the cover."

For a few seconds more she hesitated, then sent a smile at Ivey. "I'll help out here."

Oh my, oh my. Gently, Ivey said, "I'll be right inside if you need me."

Hope nodded and headed over to the boat, dutifully grabbing the cover and helping Lang roll it back.

Bending to Ivey's ear, Corbin said, "You look stunned. Is it really so unusual for her to join in like this?"

She glanced back, but just then, Hope seemed exactly like what she was: a young woman interacting with a handsome man who'd been flirting with her. "I'm more thrilled than anything else," she whispered, "but it is surprising. Normally she'd do everything she could to dodge a man who seems a little interested."

"Will she be okay out there?" Concern plain in his expression, Corbin glanced back, too. "Justin is a good chaperone. That kid misses nothing. The thing is, my brother can be outrageous."

"No way. Really?" Because that had been insanely obvious from the start, Ivey chuckled. "I hadn't noticed."

In reaction, Corbin gave her a brief hug.

She liked that far too much, but holy cow, the man was solid and warm. He even smelled good, causing her to draw a slow but deep breath.

"Understand," Corbin said, "Lang wouldn't cross a line. Not ever. Flirting, though? Can't rule that out."

"I get the feeling he probably flirts with every woman."

"True, but he's being a little more attentive than usual." They reached the front door and Corbin released her to unlock it, then waited for her to enter.

Curiosity had her doing a quick perusal of everything she could see. The house was immense with an open floor plan, including a loft over the great room. Casually decorated with plenty of plush seating, it wasn't at all ostentatious. "This is nice."

"Thanks. I like all the windows that face the lake, and the deck out back, too. My biggest issue is the master suite is there." He pointed to a door between the foyer and the great room. "The other bedrooms are either upstairs or down. I was worried Justin would be nervous sleeping on a different level in a new house, so I took one of the rooms upstairs nearer to him. We're across from each other with the open loft between us, so still plenty private, but it means I have to come downstairs to use the master bath so he can have the bathroom upstairs."

Taking that all in, Ivey blinked. "I grew up in an older home with one bathroom and we all shared, so I'm sure you'll survive."

The playful mockery had him laughing out loud. "Maybe I'll look at the stairs as daily exercise."

"There you go."

Evidently more amused than insulted, he pointed to another set of stairs to the left of the foyer, leading down to a lower level. "I'll put Lang downstairs, and don't judge me, but he'll have his own bathroom, too."

Impressed, Ivey asked, "How many bedrooms altogether?"

"The master, which isn't being used, two upstairs and two down. Three and a half baths. But hey, property around here is way less expensive than I'd expected."

"And you're loaded." She poked him with her elbow to let him know she was teasing.

"Don't let Lang fool you. We're comfortable, but you won't see either of us living in a mansion or buying a private jet or anything."

She made a face of bogus disappointment. "So you're not filthy rich? Bummer."

"Ah, so that's why you're interested?" he teased right back. "You're after my money?"

Boldly looking him over, she sighed. "What other reason could there be? I mean, you're hot and all, tall and fit. Undeniably sexy." She fanned her face. "You're also funny and friendly, with all the makings of a great dad and loving brother, but—"

Grinning, he said, "Stop right there before I blush."

Ivey snorted. "Money doesn't impress me anyway because I'm comfortable, too. Why, just last summer I totally bought my own kayak."

"No kidding," he said, playing along.

"It was a spur-of-the-moment decision." She peeked up at him, caught his grin and struggled to look sincere. "I didn't have to save for it or anything. Just drew the cash from the bank."

"Wow. So if *I'm* a money-grubber, you're my ticket?"

The humor broke free, and she chuckled. "Yeah, we small town vets are all about the paycheck." She rubbed her fingertips together as if holding money. Leaning into him, she admitted, "I sometimes get paid with the barter system, like a deal on a new roof or landscaping. One time this kid kept my grass cut for a month in exchange for his dog's surgery."

Corbin's grin softened to a tender smile. "You did that for him?"

"His family already struggled, and he kept busy with high school and a part-time job. But he loved that aging dog so much. He'd always kept up with vaccines, flea treatments and stuff like that. When the dog needed a tumor removed, the family wasn't sure what to do. An expense like that wasn't in their budget and might have meant skipping a payment on other bills." She lifted her shoulders. "What else could I do?"

"Some people would refuse services." His hands framed her face. "But you? You found a way to work it out."

They'd moved from friendly to intimate in a heartbeat—and she didn't have a single complaint. "I love animals, and I love people who take good care of them."

His thumbs brushed over her cheeks. "Damn, but you're amazing."

Her heart started tripping, especially with the way he looked down at her, as if memorizing each of her features. Very ordinary features, she knew. Put all together, she wasn't a hag, but she'd never had a guy like him look at her quite like *that*.

"What?" His thumbs went below her chin, tilting her face up more. "You don't know how amazing you are?"

"I'm just me." A small town vet who'd so far led a fairly mundane life. "No man's ever said I was amazing before. Only Hope. She compliments me all the time."

"Men can be stupid—and Hope is right."

Resting a hand on his chest, she countered, "Obviously, not all men."

"No." His gaze moved over her face, settled on her mouth, and he drew her closer. "I promise I won't be stupid."

Making promises to her? *Be still my heart.*

Trying to play it off, to be more lighthearted than she felt, Ivey mused, "Not rich but not stupid. That really balances things." Then to give herself a moment, she got serious again. "Hope has gotten really good at avoiding situations that make her uncomfortable, so she must be enjoying your brother's antics."

He accepted the topic switch, releasing her from the intensity of his gaze, dropping his hands and taking a casual step back as if the heart-throbbing moment hadn't happened. "So is Justin. It's damned rewarding to see how easily he's accepted Lang. It'll be a good thing to have him here, though I'll admit, the boat is a little overboard."

How nice that he acknowledged what she wanted without her having to spell it out. He'd effortlessly picked up on her cue without making it awkward. Every moment with him made her want more, but how much more? And what about the unrestricted, unattached attitude she'd planned to adopt?

She'd met Corbin and all her newly declared objectives had flown right out the window.

"So," she said as he led her toward the kitchen. "You don't want a boat?"

"Sure I do. We live on a lake." His hand went to the back of his neck, his expression pained. "I'd been debating the pros and cons of getting one."

"Now you won't have to." The eat-in kitchen opened to a spacious formal dining room. Beyond that was a covered deck with a screened-in porch. All around her, the greens of the trees were visible, but the real kicker was the sight of the setting sun.

"This is absolutely beautiful."

"I think so." Pulling his gaze away from her again, Corbin leaned back on a counter. "So far, life here has been good. Justin is settling in, getting used to things." He rubbed his mouth. "I want him to know he's loved, not because of what I give him, but because he's mine. Because I'll take care of him and protect him. It's hard to know if he's struggling when I keep getting carried away and surprising him with new stuff."

"You don't want him to think you're buying him." Ivey touched his arm. "But he's a smart little boy, and kids—like animals—have a sixth sense when it comes to BS. They know when people are genuine and when they're not."

"I hope you're right." He tugged her a tiny bit closer. "I feel like I have ten years to catch up on. I'd like to show him everything, tell him everything, *give* him everything as soon as possible. I've had so many luxuries through my life, but more than that, I had parents who loved me. Until Dad passed away when I was twelve, they were always there, always supportive, and after he died, Mom filled all the empty places the best she could."

"Does your mother live nearby?"

He shook his head. "About four hours away, but she's indulging a hot romance right now." His mouth quirked. "Some dude she met at bingo. Nice guy, no kids of his own. He's *crazy* about my mother."

"You like him?"

"I like seeing her happy." Reaching up, Corbin smoothed her hair again, then teased a springy curl between his fingers.

"Normally she'd have been here by now to meet her grandson, but they're doing this big drive across the country in his RV. Lots of touristy stops along the way."

"Sounds fun." Very aware of the gentle way he played with her hair, Ivey smiled.

"Justin is excited about the gifts," Corbin went on, "but not nearly as excited as I am giving them."

"Everything is still very new for both of you. I'm sure you'll get it in check." It felt incredibly natural, sharing this moment with him. Ivey put her hand to his jaw. "In the short time I've known you, he's already warmed up and relaxed more."

Turning his head, Corbin kissed her palm. "Sunset is a good place. It seems to have that effect."

"I think it's your love that's doing it."

"God, I do love him. It was only minutes after Darcie dropped that bombshell on me that I started feeling it. By the end of the day, I was consumed with the need to protect him. I wanted to make him feel secure."

"Does he miss his mom?"

"He never says, but he must, right? I tried talking to him about it once, but he shut down and since then, I don't want to pressure him."

"He just needs time. Keep being so attentive and understanding, and you'll get there."

His gaze flicked from her eyes to her mouth and back again. "I hope you're right."

Giving in to the impulse, Ivey went on tiptoe and put her mouth to his. A gentle kiss of reassurance. At least that's how she'd intended it. But once her lips touched his...

Chapter Five

He hadn't been prepared, but once her body went flush against his, he got with the program real fast.

What was it about Ivey that struck him so hard, got him talking about very private matters and thinking very intimate things? He'd known her only days but it felt like years.

She brought fun with her whenever they visited, and he never knew what she might say, where she might verbally go. She laughed with him, and sometimes at herself, which told him she was a good sport who didn't take herself too seriously.

God knew he found her attractive, too. Her light brown hair was a mass of tiny, wild curls as unpredictable as Ivey herself. Her big green eyes could be bold or filled with concern, bright with teasing or soft with concern.

She looked great in her business wear, but dressed down like this? Shorts and a tank shouldn't have been so sexy, but on Ivey, with her smiles and her protective nature and the love she had

for animals in need, it came together in the sweetest, most irresistible package, hitting him like an emotional punch.

Getting involved should have been the very last thing on his
mind. He had a full plate arranging a new life with a son he
hadn't known about, relocating to a new area, setting up house,
getting to know the people.

Hectic as that might be, Ivey just seemed to *fit*. Effortlessly.
Where he felt like he was working on everything else, with Ivey
he was just…comfortable.

And against his body? Yeah, she fit there, too. Only the fact
that Justin, Lang and Hope were nearby kept him from getting
carried away.

Well, and Ivey herself. He'd felt it when she pulled back earlier, so he'd tried to chill. Pressuring her in any way was the
very last thing he wanted to do. Regardless of how he felt, he
could and would tamp down any urges that went too far, too fast.

But Ivey had been the one to up the ante again—and he was
incredibly glad. The way she kissed him, or more like attacked
his mouth, made him think she hadn't been properly appreciated in far too long.

Her ex had to be the biggest tool alive.

As she adjusted and readjusted, she continually took the kiss a
little deeper. She tasted sweet and hot, felt soft in his arms, and
he loved the hungry little sounds she made…

The laughter reached them, along with the sound of the front
door opening. Corbin eased her away, but couldn't resist one
more, soft kiss on her now damp mouth. "I think we were supposed to be ordering pizza."

She touched her lips, her eyes heavy, her expression dazed.
She let out a shuddering breath—then stalled his heart by whispering, "When I decided to add some fun to my life, I wasn't
thinking of a guy with a kid and a comedian brother."

Was she already having regrets? "Meaning what?" She'd kissed
him and now she wanted to rethink things?

"Meaning you're so much more than I ever imagined. Not to say the pickings around here are precisely slim, but…yeah. I know all these guys and none of them ever curled my toes."

There she went again, making him laugh. "Curled toes, huh? Sounds kinky."

Around the corner by the entry, they could hear Lang calling for Justin to hurry up.

Ivey lowered her voice. "I was a teenager the last time I ran through the woods! And all the fun banter? I love listening to you and your brother, and I especially enjoy taking part. Even this, pizza at a guy's house… I haven't done anything like that in forever."

Such simple things, and she appreciated them, same as he did. "I'm glad you're enjoying yourself."

"I am, so very much." She glanced around his kitchen, seeming to take it all in with interest. "Thank you for including me. Far as first dates go, this one is a winner."

"So that's what this is? A first date?" Amused by the way she blushed, he picked up the kitchen phone. He'd found that his cell reception here near the lake wasn't always reliable. Given his business interests, it made sense to have a landline.

"I consider it a date." She wrinkled her nose. "But then, I'm woefully out of practice with this stuff. Geoff and I were together for two years—is it bad form for me to mention him? Probably, but hey, it's true. In those whole two years, I don't remember having this much fun."

Why had she stayed with the putz for so long? A smart, caring woman like her should have demanded more.

He smoothed down one of her curls and watched it spring right back. It made him smile. "I'm having a great time, too, so I don't care what we call it. Just saying, if this was a date, I got off easy."

"Well, I imagine dating with a son is different."

Lang stepped in. "It might have been, but now with Uncle Lang here…" He waggled his eyebrows. "You kids feel free to use me as a sitter whenever you want."

"Where's Hope?" Ivey asked, not at all bothered by Lang's intrusion.

"She and Justin found some creepy-ass caterpillar that I wanted no part of." He shuddered. "Said they'll be right in."

"Wuss." Corbin turned to Ivey. "What kind of pizza do you and Hope like?"

"Anything is fine. Pepperoni and sausage, or load it up. Oh, but no anchovies." She made a face of disgust. "Those things are foul."

"I've always thought so," Corbin agreed, then turned back to the phone.

A minute later, Justin and Hope walked in discussing the bug. Hope said to Ivey, "Justin found the biggest tobacco hornworm I've ever seen. It was huge!"

"Really big," Justin said, bounding forward in excitement. "And fat and green." His taunting gaze slanted toward Lang. "He was afraid of it."

"You disparage me, boy?"

Unsure how to take his uncle, Justin paused, his teasing expression arrested.

Corbin laughed and mussed Justin's hair. "We both disparage you, Lang. You should have outgrown your phobias." Damn Lang for making the boy uneasy.

Catching on, Lang gave Justin a nudge. "Hey, your dad and I disparage each other all the time. It's all in how you do it."

"With love," Hope interjected, and then blushed.

"Exactly. I give Corbin a hard time but I do it with affection." More seriously, Lang put a hand on Justin's shoulders. "As a joke, in fun, it's perfectly fine and I promise I was only teasing back. It takes a lot to insult me."

"Very true," Corbin said. "I've tried but he always laughs it off." Since Justin was back to grinning, he figured they'd gotten past the awkward moment.

"Even though your uncle runs screaming from bugs—"

Lang snorted. "I do not. I just avoid them."

"—he loves horror movies almost as much as you and Ivey do."

That lead-in got everyone talking about favorite monsters and movies. First chance he got, Corbin planned to check out the movies Ivey had warned against, though Lang didn't appear to think anything of it when Justin waxed on about Jason Voorhees and Michael Myers.

Finally the pizza arrived. Lang got out plates and napkins while Corbin offered colas, then they all took seats around the table. Corbin sat with Ivey on his left side and Justin at his right, which naturally put Hope and Lang together. He'd seen his brother in many modes, but this one was new. Lang was all about being the uncle, but he was also acutely aware of Hope.

Corbin gave her a quick, more detailed scrutiny. Sure, Hope was cute, in an understated way. She looked younger than she was and dressed in the plainest clothes imaginable. Dark brown, nearly black hair framed a pale oval face dominated by deep blue eyes. She watched Lang like a sheep fascinated with a wolf, understandably wary but interested anyway. Her reticence was almost painful to see.

Lang must have felt it, too, given the way his expression gentled every time he glanced at her. At thirty, his brother had been around enough to pick up on Hope's shyness and insecurity.

But for the next two hours, everyone lingered over the food, talking, laughing, teasing and altogether having a great time. Being here with his brother, his son and Ivey was as cozy as a family gathering, Corbin thought.

Hope said little, even when Ivey tried to draw her into conversation, but she smiled a lot, taking it in with interest. Justin was just the opposite. He flourished in the group of people, talking nonstop first about the boat, then telling Lang all about Daisy.

Lang, ever a good uncle, asked all the right questions. When the puppies were mentioned, everyone looked at Ivey, but she blew them off, refusing to engage on the subject. It didn't take a genius to know she had divided feelings. With the way she loved animals, she'd probably have a difficult time parting with them.

It gave Corbin a few things to think about.

With a yawn, Ivey stretched. "I have work tomorrow, so I suppose I should get going."

Hope quickly said, "Me, too."

"Awww," Justin complained. It was clear that he hated for the fun to end.

Corbin hated for it to end, too, especially since Justin had enjoyed it so much.

Ivey smiled at him. "Daisy is used to seeing me in the mornings. Even on the days I don't work, I go by to visit with her. And if I stay here much longer, I'm liable to sleep past my alarm, and then I won't have as much time to play with her. Plus I need to get home to my kitty, Maurice."

"Will I get to meet Maurice when we visit?"

"Of course, but remember, he's old and grumpy so we have to be really calm and quiet when we're around him."

"I'll pet him real easy, okay?"

Ivey gave him a smile full of affection. "You were so good with Daisy, I'm sure you'll do great."

Justin beamed.

Lang started putting away the empty pizza boxes. "I have *The Monster Squad* saved to my iTunes account. Since the ladies have to leave, you want to watch it with me?"

"Heck, yeah." Justin glanced at Corbin with open yearning and heartbreaking uncertainty. "You wanna watch with us, Dad?"

He'd never tire of being called Dad.

Wondering if that was another one he shouldn't let Justin see, Corbin shot a look to Ivey, but her easy grin told him it would be fine. "You'll love it. Super fun for all ages."

"I can't imagine a better way to round out a perfect day." The happiness on Justin's face made Corbin feel like he could take on anything. "If you two can wait until I walk Ivey and

Hope over, then yeah, I'd love to watch it with you." Already
he imagined Justin snuggled in close to his side, maybe sharing
a big bowl of popcorn.

"Not a problem." Lang stood there holding empty boxes and
a trash bag. "Justin can show me where to find the garbage can
and maybe whatever room you want me to use?"

Just like Lang to immediately pitch in. Their mother hadn't
raised any slugs. "Justin, why don't you show him the room
downstairs, okay?"

"It's cool," Justin promised. "There's a bed, but the rest is
empty. Dad says we'll put a gym down there." He took the bag
from Lang. "Come on, I'll show you." Then the imp added, "I
found a spider down there the other day."

"Don't taunt me, boy, or I'll be camping out in your room."

Grinning, Corbin watched them go—and realized both Hope
and Ivey were doing the same. Hope actually looked confused,
as if she wasn't sure what to make of Lang, but Ivey looked
merely amused.

"A domesticated man." Ivey nudged Hope. "It's a pleasure to
see, don't you think?"

Hope went pink in her cheeks.

"We were taught well," Corbin explained. Being tidy had become a habit, learned under his mother's watchful eye. Because
he'd been looking at Hope, he saw her flush and turn away—
with a small smile. Interesting.

Putting a hand to Ivey's back, and with Hope preceding them,
they headed out. "Lang is terrific," Corbin said. "I'm glad he's
here, but it's sooner than I expected."

"I guess he didn't let you know he was on his way because
he wanted to surprise you?"

"With a *boat*."

Still smiling, Hope headed for the path that led to the guesthouse. "He said he sold his business?"

"That sounds crazy, right? But we're family, so..." Corbin

stepped ahead of Ivey and moved aside the branches of a prickly bush. It'd make sense to clear the path a little more. He'd see to that soon. "I knew Lang was selling his sports complex, but he got it done quicker than I expected."

"A sports complex?" the women said almost in unison.

Dusk had fallen, yet streaks of red and orange clung to the horizon. Without the baking sunshine, it wasn't quite as muggy. The throaty trill of frogs on the lake mixed with the constant chirping of crickets. It was a peaceful night. He wouldn't mind spending more like it.

"Yeah, you know. Batting cages, indoor soccer, outdoor baseball and softball diamonds—"

"Wow," Ivey said. "It was his, or part of the family business?"

"All his, and it was the perfect job for Lang."

"Because he's athletic?" Hope asked, as she moved around a spiderweb.

It amused Corbin that she was skittish with men but thought nothing of insects. Like Lang, he'd just as soon not tangle with some types of bugs. He wasn't quite as squeamish, and put to the test he'd definitely man up. But given a choice? Yeah, he'd avoid spiders.

"Lang is one of those natural athletes that did well at every sport he played," Corbin said. "He never took any of them too seriously, though."

Ivey snorted. "Does he take anything seriously?"

"Family." Lang would do just about anything for him, their mom and now Justin. "It was hard enough on him when I moved closer to where Justin lived. At first, I didn't want to change too many things in his life, but it didn't take me long to rethink that."

"You wanted a clean break?" Ivey asked.

"Since his mother walked away, and he didn't have any close ties there, it seemed like a good idea. Make everything different but better."

Ivey nodded. "Give him a new focus and a fresh start."

"Lang would have been there right away, but I wanted it to just be us, you know? I figured we should get acquainted before the rest of my family closed in. It's mostly Mom, Lang and me, but we have other relatives we see on holidays. How about you two?"

Hope was suddenly giving all her attention to where she stepped.

Corbin knew he'd said something wrong, but he had no idea what.

Catching his hand, Ivey squeezed. When he glanced down, she gave a small shake of her head so he'd know to let it drop with Hope, but then she followed up with, "I'm an only child. My parents were one and done."

"Because you were a handful?" he teased.

"Probably, though the way Mom tells it, I wasn't bad, just determined to do things my own way. She said I never minded hard work. Honestly, though, I am self-absorbed."

Hope snorted in disagreement.

"When I set my mind on something, I rarely notice anything else going on around me. It was that way in school, in college and when I took over the clinic here."

"Don't buy into that," Hope said with firm insistence. "Ivey is wonderful."

"I agree." Corbin rubbed his thumb over her knuckles. "But the same goes for you, Hope. I mean, anyone who can take over bug duty with my son is okay in my book."

Tension easing, she laughed. "Anytime."

When they reached the driveway of the guesthouse, Ivey stepped away from him, saying to Hope, "I'll walk up with you."

"You don't need to." Hope shot a guilty look at Corbin.

The house was dark, none of the outside lights on, and the night seemed to envelope them. To Corbin, it felt like great ambience, but to Hope? He doubted she felt the same way. She had a very fragile air about her.

"I don't mind," Corbin said, encouraging them. "Justin is with Lang, so I'll wait. Take your time."

Gratitude sparkled in Ivey's pretty green eyes. "Thank you." Once Hope unlocked and opened the side door for the garage, Ivey took the lead.

He had the feeling she'd been doing that with Hope from the start, protecting her when necessary, supporting her where she could and caring for her with her whole heart.

To him, that made Ivey a truly remarkable woman.

Hope and Ivey both kept mum as they went up the stairs, but Ivey felt her excitement crackling until it popped the second they had privacy.

Grabbing Hope's hands, she gushed, "Oh my God, isn't Corbin incredible?"

Hope laughed. "Yes, he is."

"And his brother?" Ivey searched Hope's face, saw her try to look away, but she didn't let go. "Hope? C'mon, don't be coy. Admit it. You actually liked him, didn't you?"

The smile came slowly, then bloomed into a beautiful grin. "It was the oddest thing, but… I felt different with him."

"Oh, honey." Feeling like a proud mama, she drew Hope in for a warm embrace, happier with her news than she was with her own feelings for Corbin. "That is so wonderful."

Hope laughed it off with obvious embarrassment. "It doesn't mean he's interested, too. No, don't say he is because then I might be disappointed if he isn't."

Pressing her lips together, Ivey accepted that Hope had a point. "So," she said carefully, "it's true that some guys flirt and it only means that he finds you attractive."

Automatically, Hope's hand lifted to smooth her hair.

Her friend was not used to worrying about her appearance at all. She was neat, but far from styled. That suited Ivey, because she wasn't all that styled, either. But where Ivey had crazy hair, Hope's dark hair was sleek and shiny, a beautiful contrast to her blue eyes. Add in flawless skin, a gentle smile, and any man would be lucky to catch her attention.

Ivey held her at arm's length. "You have to trust me on this, okay? You are so damn cute, of course Lang flirted. Other men would, too, if you gave them half a chance."

"I never wanted to give them a chance," Hope fretted. "You know how I panic. It's awful and embarrassing, and sometimes I hate myself for it."

Ivey's heart turned over. "Please don't. You have every right to your feelings, whatever they might be." She tipped her head. "And I think with how handsome and humorous Lang is, you have a right to react to him."

Impatient, Hope shook her head. "I shouldn't even be considering it, because. I'm not sure I could do anything about it anyway. If I give him the wrong impression, it could be so awkward." Wrapping her arms around herself, she turned away, her voice dropping to an agonized whisper. "Can you imagine how Lang would react? He probably thinks I'm a normal girl…and I'm not."

Ivey saw her shudder at just the thought of causing herself that much embarrassment. She stepped closer and kept her voice low as well. "If he doesn't understand what you've been through, it could be awkward, but probably not in the way you're thinking." From what she knew of Corbin so far, he was a conscientious man, so she had to assume his brother was the same. They might be worried and unsure of the situation—but in no way would either of them consider Hope abnormal.

Hope swallowed heavily. "Maybe…if a man knew what to expect up front, he wouldn't be disappointed."

"If he knew the situation, I'm sure it would help," Ivey agreed.

Hope spun around. "You would tell him?"

"If you want me to but, Hope, real men, *good* men, would understand."

As if afraid to believe, Hope said softly, "And they're good men?"

"I think so." Ivey considered the repercussions, but she felt she had to press Hope just a tiny bit. Her unheard-of interest in Lang could be an opening, a careful start for so much more. Hope had a well of affection and caring to give, but she needed the right man, and if that wasn't Lang, Ivey would warn him off right now. "So. What do you think?"

"You probably should. If you don't, Lang might just think I'm a weirdo."

Ivey tried a reassuring smile. "Not the impression I got."

"No, I know. But he...well, he got too close outside and... well, you know me. I bolted away like a scared rabbit. He gave me this long, curious look that kept me frozen to the spot, and then he just acted like nothing had happened, but he kept his distance." She covered her face. "He might think I don't like him."

Imagining how that had played out, Ivey nearly winced. She was fairly certain it had taken Lang off guard. As much as she loved Hope, she wanted to be fair to him, too. Catching Hope's wrists, Ivey gently lowered her hands. "But you do *like* him?"

"I barely know him."

"Doesn't matter. Go with your instincts. I knew I was into Corbin right off. And from what I could see, you seemed to like Lang?"

"I really do. Don't you? Don't you think he's funny? And he's already so determined to be a great uncle, and..."

Ivey laughed. "I'm convinced, yes, and I'm thrilled that you're seeing things as they are."

Hope bit her lip. "Because I see him as a nice man who probably wouldn't hurt a woman?"

Oh now, see, that shattered her heart. "Only disgusting creeps would. I can almost guarantee that if Corbin would have been around, he'd have taken your side." He might have even shown the bastard the error of his ways. A girl could hope. "And since Lang is his brother, I'm betting he's the same."

Hope laced her fingers together. "What do you think he'll make of it?"

There was no way for her to know for sure. She had a guess, based on what she knew of Lang so far, but you couldn't always trust assumptions. Plus, as was evident from Hope's family, siblings were sometimes very different. Where one might be honest and caring, another could be selfish and mean.

Ivey pasted on an encouraging smile. "I'll talk to Corbin and we'll go from there. Okay?"

Looking both excited and concerned, Hope agreed. "Please make it clear that I'm not expecting anything, not even interest."

"Of course."

"And if he laughs it off, that's that. Promise you won't press."

"I wouldn't." It was so refreshing to see Hope's anticipation. "Look at it this way. If he isn't interested, then he'll stop flirting, and you'll be able to be around him without worrying."

Hope let out a big breath. "Thank you, Ivey. You're the absolute best."

Such a shame that kindness from a friend earned so much gratitude. In so many ways, Hope still judged others by a four-year distant incident. "I'll secure the garage door when I leave, then text you so you can rest easy. Enjoy your first night here, and remember, if you need anything at all, don't hesitate to contact me."

As promised, Ivey locked the garage's side door, tugged on it twice to be sure and then texted Hope. Already her friend had turned on the outside lights so that the entire area glowed like midday. The only sign of nightfall was the deep shadows beyond the reach of the floodlights and the stars twinkling to life overhead on a deep indigo sky.

Once she got confirmation from Hope, Ivey rounded the garage and found Corbin leaning against a post, long legs crossed at the ankles, his expression thoughtful. Very quietly, she stood there gazing at him. He hadn't yet noticed her as he stared off in the distance, likely pondering the million and one things he had on his mind now that he was a father.

She'd never thought too much about children, other than how they acted with their pets. Some kids disturbed her, those who were allowed to use their cats and dogs like dolls, stuffing them into baby clothes whether the animal liked it or not. Kids who ignored their pets, or worse, took enjoyment in annoying them. It was times like that where she didn't care if she talked too much or if she overstepped. Kids needed to respect animals, period.

Then there were the children like Justin, who instinctively empathized with animals. Some kids were that way. Others had parents who supervised them and taught them how to properly care for pets. She was sure Corbin was that type of parent.

Was there anything at all *not* to like about him? If so, she hadn't found it yet.

Before meeting him, she would have said her preferences leaned more toward messy blond hair, bleached by time in the lake, tanned muscles and blue eyes. Yup, she'd seen a few guys like that playing volleyball on the beach, using their paddleboards or kayaks, some of them fishing off docks—tourists, she had assumed, since she didn't recognize them. She'd even considered them when deciding she was done with relationships. What better way to indulge an easy, meaningless fling than with a hunky guy who wouldn't be around long? Ideal situation, right?

Yet none of them had instantly excited her the way Corbin had.

Now she much preferred light brown eyes and warm brown hair. And those shoulders, those long muscular arms, that—

"Hey."

Busted, Ivey realized he'd caught her cataloguing all the intriguing aspects of his awesome bod. Mentally, she shrugged. He shouldn't look so good if he didn't want her to notice. "Sorry," she said with a grin, starting toward him. "You look good standing there framed in the light like that."

His mouth curled in a very masculine smile. "One of these days, you're going to make me blush."

"But not today?"

"No," he said, his voice gentle. "Not today."

Whoa. When was the last time a man had looked at her with so much heat?

That'd be a great big *never*.

He nodded up at Hope's windows. "Is she okay?"

Yup, Corbin definitely appeared to be the whole package, irresistible inside and out. "She is, for now." Ivey tamped down the urge to jump his bones. "Do you think we could talk about that?"

"About Hope?"

She nodded. "If you have time?"

"If I know Lang, he packed enough for a lengthy visit. He'll keep Justin busy helping him move in."

"For good?"

He shook his head. "No, but I wouldn't be surprised if he stayed with me for the summer."

"You won't mind that?" She couldn't imagine anyone moving in on her, but then, she and Maurice were pretty set in their ways.

"He's my brother," Corbin said.

It must be nice to have close family like that. The thought led her right back to Hope.

"So let's talk first, and then if you still have a few minutes, maybe we can do a little kissing, too?" Thinking that might need explanation, she added, "That kiss in your kitchen sort of rocked my world. I need to try it again to see if it was an anomaly or if you're really that good."

The promise was as much in his eyes as from his mouth when he murmured, "I have time."

Oh goodie. Glancing around, Ivey wondered how far voices might carry. She took Corbin's hand. "Let's get in my car. If we stand out here, we'll get chigger bites."

"Wouldn't want that."

When she reached for the driver's door, he opened the back door instead. "We'll have more room here."

In her little car, they'd still be crowded, but at least the console wouldn't be in the way. "Good idea." She climbed in first, but quickly scooted over so he wouldn't have to walk around to the other side.

Once he closed the door, they were cocooned in deep shadows. He gazed at her. "Now, about Hope?"

Shame on her for nearly forgetting, but with him sitting there taking up so much space, his eyes glimmering in the darkness, the scent of him surrounding her... Well, forgetting to breathe would be understandable.

Ivey cleared her throat. "Lang was flirting with Hope."

"Yes. I think she has him confused. He's used to women actively reciprocating, but Hope seemed very skittish about his interest."

"She's not!" The last thing she wanted to do was discourage Lang, except... "That is, she *is* skittish, pretty much with everyone. But it doesn't mean she's not interested in him."

"In some ways, she reminds me of Justin. Anxious to take part, but afraid of disappointment."

Ivey let out a strained breath. That summed it up pretty well. "When Hope was seventeen, her sister's fiancé tried to rape her."

Corbin went very still. "I wish I was surprised, but I figured it had to be something that awful." He reached for Ivey's hand. "Please tell me the bastard is locked away."

"Oh, how I wish I could." His hand was big and strong, holding hers securely. "The assault was bad enough, but her family...they blamed Hope. Her sister didn't want to break off the engagement, so they ordered Hope to keep quiet about it."

"Jesus."

That he didn't question whether or not it actually happened meant the world to Ivey. To her, it seemed anyone could look at Hope and know she'd gone through a terrible ordeal. But on top of that, Hope had a great many facts to back her up.

"The man's family has wealth and influence, and without her own family's backing, Hope knew she didn't stand a chance in court. If she'd told her family about it first, they might have talked her out of saying anything at all. But it happened at a swanky party. She went upstairs to use the restroom while most of the guests were outside."

Repeating it hurt, so how much harder must it have been for Hope to live through it?

"He'd followed her, and the second she stepped out of the restroom, he was on her. At first, she didn't know what to think, so she didn't scream or fight as she might have with a total stranger. She'd known him for months, and she didn't like him at all, but she hadn't guessed that he could do such a thing."

"Her sister's fiancé? No, of course she didn't." Corbin lifted her hand to his mouth and pressed an encouraging kiss to her knuckles.

Best to just get it over with. "He dragged her into an empty bedroom." Her voice lowered to a raw whisper. "He left bruises on her, Corbin. In terrible places." Her throat felt thick. "But my girl fought him hard. She raked her nails over his eye and that hurt him enough that she was able to get away. As soon as she was out of the room, she started screaming for help. Several people reached her before her family got there and took her to a secluded room."

"And despite all that, her family didn't back her up?" He sounded as angry as she often felt.

"They wanted his money. Hope's sister thought she'd misunderstood. Her mother thought she'd overreacted." Ivey's fingers tightened on his. "Before anyone knew who had attacked her, the police were called. I've seen the photos from that day, and believe me, there was no misunderstanding. She left, of course, and she hasn't heard from her family since."

"God, that's harsh." He freed her hand to put his arms around her, holding her close. "I'm glad she has you, Ivey."

"We have each other."

For a minute, he just held her, his hands moving up and down her back, occasionally giving her a squeeze, then he kissed her temple. "You want me to talk to Lang, tell him to back off?"

"Actually...no. This is the very first time I've known her to show any interest at all. Usually if a guy looks at her, she gets as far from him as she can. Your brother didn't pressure her, and that's good, but he probably needs to know that Hope moves at a different pace. Unlike me, who by the way, is totally hoping we can work something out sooner rather than later, Hope hasn't even been kissed in four years. If Lang isn't the patient type, or if he's going to consider her dysfunctional or something, then yeah, he better back off or I'll demolish him."

Corbin gave a soft laugh. "If my brother was that way, I'd help you." He tipped up her face. "But, honey, he's not. He's a good man. I'm proud of him."

"I assumed." Sadly, Hope couldn't.

"I can't speak for him, so I don't know his intent, but I can make sure he understands the situation."

"That's what I figured." Ivey licked her lips. "Darn it, we should have done the necking first." Hard to follow up such a sad, depressing topic with kisses.

"Look at it this way." Corbin pecked the tip of her nose. "We'll have something to look forward to." And with that disappointing conclusion, he opened the door and helped her out.

Chapter Six

On Sunday morning, the skies stayed dark and the air was static. By midmorning, the storms had started and the electricity went off and on before dying completely. It was Ivey's day off, but she worried about Daisy and the puppies, so much so that a few hours before Corbin and Justin were due to visit, she decided she had to collect the animals.

Luckily, there were no other animals at the clinic just then. Knowing she'd be back home in plenty of time, she bundled up in a rain poncho, stepped into her knee-high rubber boots, grabbed her purse and headed to the garage. The second she backed out of the driveway, the windows were awash with rain. It came down so hard and fast, the wipers could barely keep up.

Worried about Hope as well, Ivey called her, put the phone on speaker and set it on the console while she drove.

"Everything okay?" Hope said at once.

"The power is out here. What about you?"

"Yes. Of course I didn't think about candles or anything, so

I might be running out to the store if this lasts. Good thing I got my bedroom stuff set up yesterday because we sure couldn't have moved it today."

"So the boys came through?"

"They were super nice, even though they had to navigate those narrow stairs with my mattress and box spring. I gave them all generous tips."

"Because you're a generous person." Sheets of rain washed over the street, causing Ivey to drive very slowly. "I wish I could have helped you more with your move." Not that she could have gotten a box spring and mattress up those stairs.

"You were working, and besides, I enjoyed it." Hope hesitated, then confided in a whisper, "Lang offered to lend a hand."

And Hope hadn't shared? "You big sneak! Why didn't you tell me?"

With a laugh, Hope said, "I turned him down, but, Ivey, it was so nice of him. He asked, I thanked him and said I could handle it, and he said if I changed my mind to let him know. He didn't press so I'm guessing you talked to him?"

"To Corbin, who I'm sure shared."

There was a long pause. "How did he take it?"

"Corbin? He was rightfully angry on your behalf." Just as she'd known he would be. "He couldn't speak for Lang, of course, but he agreed it would be best to let him know, just so he didn't come on too strong." Tentatively, Ivey asked, "It worked?"

"I think so." With an agonized groan, Hope said, "This is all so uncomfortable, but still, I'm glad it's out in the open. I mean, just among us. I wouldn't want all of Sunset to know."

"Of course not. I'm sure it won't be repeated."

"Lang gave me his number."

Ivey could hear the tempered wonder in her friend's voice and it made her smile. "Do you think you'll call him?"

"No. At least, not anytime soon. But it's nice having it. I, um, gave him my number, too."

Wow, talk about progress. "Good for you."

"I still can't imagine me doing anything with a guy."

"You don't have to imagine it," Ivey said quickly. "Just let things progress naturally. Conversation first, okay? That's a big first step." The phone began to fade in and out, and she knew she was losing Hope. "I have to go, okay? Sketchy connection. If you need anything, please let me know. Love ya a bunch."

"Love you, too. Drive carefully."

A near-continuous flash of lightning gave a strobe effect against the darkened sky as Ivey parked close to the back door of the clinic. A slight overhang helped shield her from the downpour, but she was still drenched in the time it took her to unlock the door. Icy trickles snaked down the side of her face and into the neck of her rain slicker. Her rubber boots slipped on the linoleum floor when she stepped inside.

Concerned for Daisy, she hurried through the dim interior until she reached the right kennel. All was silent, but then Daisy probably didn't hear her with the fury of the storm all around them.

When she opened the door, Daisy launched into startled, maniacal barking until she realized it was Ivey. Then she hunkered down in a low rush, her puppies following. Obviously Daisy was relieved to have company.

"I know, baby, I'm so sorry." Plopping down to sit on the floor, Ivey cuddled them all. For fifteen minutes, she soothed the frazzled animals. Once they were calmer, she loaded them into a carrier with soft blankets. The second there was a slight break in the storm, she dashed out to her car and secured them in the back seat.

Her phone, which she'd left on the console, showed she'd missed a call from Corbin.

Assuming he'd have to cancel, disappointment swamped her. Yes, she understood. After all, being out in the mess wasn't pleasant. But she'd been looking forward to the visit all morning.

She returned the call right before she pulled out onto the road. Thanks to the faulty connection, they could barely hear each other, but she caught enough to hear Corbin's surprise that she was out in the storm.

She had an equal surprise in knowing he and Justin were on their way. Something about them being out and about when the storm started, so if she didn't mind, they were going to be early.

It didn't require a glance in the rearview mirror to know she was a complete and utter mess. The rain always amplified her hair to impossible heights, and her frizzy curls had already sprung free from the hood of the slicker. Pretty sure the chill in the air had pinkened her nose, too.

But hey, Corbin wanted to visit, she wanted to see him, so they'd both just have to suffer her appearance. "Come by whenever," she said loudly so he could hear her over the storm. "I'll be home in ten more minutes."

Because traffic was nonexistent with the storm, she made it in eight—and Corbin's SUV was already in her driveway. When he saw her, he got out to manually open her garage door for her, since the power was out, and she slowly drove in past him. Before she even left the car, he was inside, with Justin dashing in behind him.

The boy wore a brand-new bright green raincoat, rubber boots and a smile of anticipation. Corbin had on a windbreaker, which hadn't done a thing to protect his head. With both hands, he pushed back his sodden hair.

Ivey stepped out to greet them. "I know why I was out on the road, and I'm guessing Justin will be pleased. But why were you guys out?"

"It was only drizzling when we left," Corbin explained. "I thought we'd get something to eat before coming over, but the weather changed our plans."

"We bought me a raincoat instead," Justin said, admiring his neon boots with icky black spiders on them.

"You look very sharp." Without thinking about it, Ivey lifted her own boot, bright yellow with chickens…and realized she'd worn shorts. And her knees were soaked. And she had goose-flesh. "My, uh, boots are cute, too, don't you think?"

"I like mine better," Justin admitted.

She choked on a laugh.

Corbin cocked a brow at her knees. "I think they're very cute."

Time for a subject change! "Guess what?" She tipped her head toward the car. "I have a surprise in the back seat."

"What is it?" Justin tried to peer in the window around her.

"I couldn't bear the thought of leaving Daisy and her babies alone at the clinic in this weather, so I brought her home."

Instead of appearing happy, Justin's face fell. He quickly looked down, hiding his gaze from her.

"Justin?" Gently, Ivey moved closer to him. "You don't want to see Daisy?"

"Are you keepin' her now?"

"What? Oh, honey, no. She's your dog, I promise." At that, he perked up. Ivey couldn't resist brushing back his damp hair. "I just didn't want her to be alone, that's all."

"But you said your cat wouldn't like her."

"True. I suspect Maurice will get all grumpy, give me dirty looks and then hide under the couch. Or maybe the bed." She cupped his cheek. "But you're here now, so you can help me introduce them. What do you say?"

Suspicion narrowed his eyes. "She's still my dog?"

Ivey crossed her heart. "I promise."

The concern disappeared from his face, replaced with glow-ing happiness. "I'll help for sure. Daisy likes me, right?"

"Daisy adores you." Ivey opened the back door, and there was the little dog, her nose pressed to the side of the carrier, her tail going crazy.

Poking a finger between the wire bars of the carrier's door

to touch Daisy's nose, Justin bent to speak to her. "Hey, Daisy. Are you scared, girl? I'm here now."

Corbin caught Ivey's hand. "Thank you."

"For?"

He nodded at Justin. "I'll take the carrier in."

"All right." She gathered her phone and purse from the front seat, then hurried ahead to the door. It opened into her mudroom, which housed Maurice's litter box.

And... Maurice had been busy, so it wasn't the most pleasant welcome for Corbin or Justin.

"Sorry." She grabbed the air freshener and liberally sprayed the air.

"You have a cat," Corbin said, "so a box is a reality. We don't mind, do we, Justin?"

Face scrunched up in distaste, Justin mumbled, "Guess not."

There in the doorway to the hall sat Maurice, blocking their way with his imperious posture, his incredulous expression taking in the humans and the carrier with accusation. When he sniffed the air, Ivey could almost hear him demand, *A dog? You dared bring home a dog?* Fluffy gray fur bristled on end and his tail poofed out to twice its normal size. Arching his back, Maurice glared.

"Let me get him," Ivey said, but when she reached for him, the cat gave her a grumble of betrayal and shot away.

"Maurice," she called. "Don't be like that."

A very rusty meow came back at her as the cat scurried down the hall and disappeared.

"Well, damn. He's going to sulk for hours now."

Corbin and Justin glanced at each other, then grinned.

"You talk to your cat like he's a person," Justin said.

"Well, yeah. He's been my buddy for fifteen years." She rubbed her forehead. "Like me, Maurice is set in his ways." Giving up on that for the moment, she turned with a smile. "First things first. We can leave our wet boots in here and hang our slickers on those pegs. Let me get out of my stuff first, Corbin, then I'll take the carrier from you." She quickly toed off her boots and set them beneath a bench, then shrugged out of her dripping poncho.

Watching her, Corbin's brows went up again.

Glancing down, Ivey saw why. Her oversize white T-shirt was more damp than not, and it clung to her braless breasts.

Thank goodness Justin had all his attention directed to removing his new boots.

Jerking around, presenting Corbin with her back, Ivey said, "Oops, I better change. I'll only be a moment. Make yourself at home." Face hot, she exited as quickly as Maurice had. Flying down the short hall, past the kitchen and into her bedroom, she very quietly closed the door and dropped back against it.

Good Lord, she'd given Corbin a peek with his ten-year-old son right there. Her face flamed with mortification. The only saving grace was that Justin hadn't even noticed her faux pas.

For a few seconds she fanned her hot cheeks, then finally stepped away from the door and into her small bathroom.

Ack! Worse and worse. Her hair had spiraled completely out of control. In a rush, she tried to smooth it down, but it didn't help. She curled her lip and growled at her own image.

Some women wore the super-curly look with panache. She wasn't one of them.

Knowing she couldn't take the time to primp, not with Corbin in her house for the first time, two animals bound to conflict and the storm still raging, Ivey went back into her room and stripped off her clothes.

What to wear, what to wear?

She heard a bark and, in agony over the circumstances, grabbed another T-shirt, this one dark gray with the word NOPE printed in bold white across the front. She found black-and-gray pajama pants and had just finished pulling them on when a tap came on her door.

"Ivey?" Justin said in a whisper.

In two big strides, she reached the door and pulled it open. "What's up, kiddo?"

Beaming at her, he took her hand and urged quietly, "Come see."

Curious now, very aware of the trust in his gesture, she followed along—and found Corbin sitting on the floor, his long legs stretched out, Daisy and one puppy on his lap...and Maurice close to his side.

Oh, my heart. She pressed a hand to her chest to contain all the emotion trying desperately to explode.

With one hand, Corbin gently rubbed Maurice's neck, smoothing down his unruly fur. With the other, he kept the puppies contained. Every so often, he bent and nuzzled against Daisy's little round head.

The sight of it completely did her in.

"Neat, huh?" Justin squeezed her fingers. "Come on. We gotta go real slow cuz Dad says your cat is nervous."

"Your dad is a very smart guy." Never in a million years did she think Maurice would get that close to a dog. Usually he didn't even like people. For certain he'd always avoided Geoff.

She couldn't have been in her room more than ten minutes. How had he pulled it off?

Releasing her, Justin got down on his hands and knees and crept forward. Maurice eyed him, then stepped into Corbin's side and started to purr.

That did it. Pretty sure she fell in love at that moment. Not that she'd known Corbin long enough, but hey, her cat trusted him.

It wasn't an earth-shattering thing. More like a feeling that sank into her bones.

She, too, lowered herself to keep from startling the cat, then scooted up to sit beside Maurice. The cat's long graying whiskers curled around his face, as did the longer fur above his eyes, giving him a forever-disgruntled air, only contradicted by the rumbling purr.

"He's a sweet old guy, aren't you, Maurice?" Corbin stroked along his back. "You don't mind one scared little dog visiting, do you?"

As if in answer, Maurice stretched out to sniff Daisy. The dog froze, only her tail moving as she waited to see what would happen. When one of the puppies tried to join in, Maurice gave it a swat. The pup sat down and stared.

Justin snickered. "It's okay, buddy." He lifted the pup into his lap.

Ivey sniffled. "Oh, you two sweethearts." They were both utterly wonderful. "I'm not emotionally equipped for all this today."

"They'll get along," Corbin said.

"But Daisy is still my dog," Justin cautioned.

That got her snickering, which got Corbin grinning, and pretty soon they were all laughing softly.

And none of the animals minded.

Hope raised a fist to the storm, but it raged on all around her. So stupid.

"How could you get stuck?" she asked herself for the twentieth time. After a big, resounding boom, the power had gone out for good. At only two in the afternoon, it looked like early evening, the black clouds and gloomy skies blocking most light. Knowing she'd have to get at least a flashlight, she'd bundled up, gotten in her car, backed out...and off the driveway into the swampy yard where she remained.

Damn it, she was a good driver! How could that have happened?

She wasn't sure what to do, but she'd need her car before Monday morning because she had to go to work. Ivey was visiting with Corbin, and no way would Hope interrupt.

Biting her lip, she considered things. Was Lang alone in the bigger house? Or had he gone out, too?

When her phone rang, she jumped so hard it felt like her heart had bounced against her rib cage. Without seeing who it was, she swiped her thumb over the screen and yelled, "Hello?"

There was a second of charged silence, followed by a laugh. "Catch you at a bad time, Hope?"

Her jaw dropped. *Lang.* "I'm sorry! It's the storm... I can barely hear with the rain so loud against the roof of my car."

"You went out in this mess?"

"Um..." She looked through the window where it appeared a pond was forming around her car. "Sort of?"

"Sort of, meaning what?"

"I was going to the store for a flashlight and candles and stuff. Maybe something to eat that didn't need to be cooked. But... I'm stuck."

Calm and patience personified, he asked, "Stuck where?"

"In my driveway?"

"You don't know?"

She narrowed her eyes. "In my driveway."

"How'd that happen?"

Was he *laughing* at her? From somewhere usually hidden, her temper popped out. "I'm hanging up now."

"No, wait." She could still hear the grin in his voice. "That's why I called. I was going out to the store, too, and was going to ask if you needed anything, but hey, why don't I just pick you up and we can go together?"

Several things happened at once. Her heart jumped into overdrive. Heat rushed over her skin. Dread threatened, but it ran neck and neck with eagerness. "I, um..."

"Hope." His tone sounded incredibly gentle. "We could hit up the store, then grab food and after that I can take a look at your car."

"It's stuck in the mud," she explained, because she wasn't yet ready to address anything else. "I'm afraid if I keep trying to get it free, I'm only going to tear up the yard."

"True enough. So what do you say?" He waited. Almost as enticement, he added, "I could be over there in three minutes."

Before she overthought it, Hope closed her eyes and blurted, "Okay." Then she clenched all over.

"Awesome." Still, she didn't hear any great inflection in his tone. No pressure, but no real excitement, either. "Stay put. I'll bring a towel."

As soon as he disconnected, she thought she might hyperventilate. The air inside the car seemed to thicken and grow hot. Deliberately, she slowed her breathing. It helped the tiniest bit. She sat there, frozen, a morass of tingling nerves, until his headlights came up the driveway. *He's safe*, she told herself. *He understands. It'll be fine.*

Ivey wouldn't steer me wrong.

That last reassurance did the most to calm her panic. Out of every person she'd ever known, she trusted Ivey the most. Sometimes, Ivey was the *only* person she trusted.

Pulling up beside her passenger door, Lang put his truck in Park. When he pulled on a hat, she realized he was about to get out, which guaranteed they'd both end up soaked. That got her in gear.

Waving for him to wait, she turned off her car, grabbed her purse and climbed over the console so she could dash straight into his passenger door. With one last withering glare at the angry skies, she pulled up the hood of her coat, opened the door and dashed toward his truck.

The door opened before she reached it, but the truck was high and it took her a second to clamber in.

Sodden, dripping everywhere, she looked up—and caught Lang's indulgent smile. The roomy cab of his truck seemed to shrink around her until she was too close to him, could see only him, smell him, *feel* him—

"A little wet out there, huh?"

The ironic words interrupted her building tension, allowing her to work up a smile. "A bit."

In a very matter-of-fact way, he handed her a big beach towel. "I don't think it'll be too difficult to get your car out once this rain lets up. It looks like you went into an existing rut, meaning plenty of other people have ended up in that same spot, too."

With the edge of the towel held to her dripping face, she peeked over at her car. If others had gone off the driveway in that same spot, she wouldn't have to feel like such a dolt. "I see."

"It wouldn't hurt for Corbin and me to put more gravel there. I'll ask him about it when I see him again."

"Thank you."

"No problem. Warm enough?"

God, he was so nice and so casual about everything that it just naturally helped her relax. "Yes, thank you." While drying herself, she tried to think of something to say. Very little came to mind. "I really do appreciate this. I wasn't sure what to do."

"Hey." He started to reach toward her, but pulled back again right away. "Call me anytime, okay?"

She nodded, but that led to another thought. "How long will you be here?"

"With Corbin?" He shrugged. "A while. Long enough to really get to know Justin and to make sure my brother is okay."

"Why wouldn't he be?"

"You can't know, Hope." He stared out at the storm, then fixed his gaze on her. "A guy finding out he's a dad, and not of an infant but a kid who's been around for ten years? That's a tough one. Like this tsunami of emotion, compounded with guilt and anger. Corbin's working it out. He's a great dad already but I can tell he's still struggling with his thoughts and feelings, like trying to find some footing in the whole single-parent routine."

As dry as she could get, she folded the towel and put it on her lap. "You two are close."

"Corbin and me? Yeah, we are." Some distant memory put a grin on his face. "We always got along, even when he was a pain in the ass, but after Dad died..." The humor faded. "I think we teamed up to make Mom feel better. And since Mom was working to make us feel better, it was like this dysfunctional love fest for a while there, with each of us trying to put a happy face on our situation."

"I'm sure that had to be difficult."

"Losing Dad was the pits." His voice lowered, grew a little rough. "He and my mom... They epitomized the perfect couple in so many ways. Losing him was really hard on her. At fifteen, I felt like I had to be the man of the family."

"That's awfully young."

He snorted. "Especially with my mom. It took her no time at all to realize what I was thinking, and she set me straight real fast."

Forgetting that she was alone with a man for the first time in four years, Hope refastened her seat belt and asked, "How'd she do that?"

"She sat Corbin and me both down and we talked it out. She made it clear she was still the boss—and the woman does like to be bossy, let me tell ya. She said she appreciated our help, and she loved us for being so considerate, but that she wanted us to go on being our usual selves, meaning into mischief and some-times messy and nowhere perfect, and she'd go on correcting us, and we'd all just have to make do with our grief because that's what would've made my dad happy."

What a wonderful way to tackle sorrow. "I can almost pic-ture that, your mother talking to her sons and the love you all feel for each other."

He put the truck in gear and rolled forward down the drive. "Don't think it was all roses, okay? As boys, Corbin and I were loud, rambunctious, argumentative little knuckleheads who got into too many scuffles. But that's most kids, I think."

"Sounds like you two know what to expect with Justin." This was nice. More than nice. Other than Ivey, she hadn't had such a long, detailed conversation in a very long time, at least, not about anything other than a client's pet.

"Maybe, but so far Justin has been different. Not really sullen, but often more subdued than I'd like. I think he's buried some pretty big worries down deep inside him."

Surprised by that observation, she said, "You think?" To her, Justin appeared to be a very sweet boy who smiled often.

As he pulled onto the main road, Lang rolled a shoulder. "The thing is, you're subdued, too, so you might not have noticed."

Why that insulted her, she couldn't say, except that for the first time in forever, what someone else thought mattered to her. "Not everyone is outgoing and enthusiastic."

He briefly glanced at her, but the dark skies and continued rainfall kept his attention on the road. "No, they're not. Some people are shy, some very sweet. Some just naturally quiet."

And some were cowards. Smoothing her hand over the damp towel, she avoided looking at him and said, "I'm all of the above." He held silent, and that felt like encouragement. "I'm also very uncertain."

"With me?"

The windshield wipers worked furiously against the downpour, adding a shush-shush-shush sound to the hiss of tires on wet pavement and the resounding roar of rain against the roof. Honestly, she confessed, "A little less with you maybe."

"I'm glad."

Thankful that her admission hadn't scared him off, she peeked at him. Such a nice profile. Like Corbin, he had a strong jaw and masculine nose, but his hair always seemed to be a little more unruly than his brother's. "I'm not sure why you're different," she whispered.

"Chemistry," he said without hesitation. "It's there between us."

Hope blinked—and watched the firm line of his mouth tip in a half smile. "Chemistry?"

"You know, I don't think you're as delicate as everyone, yourself included, seems to think. So I'm going to lay it out there."

Alarm sparked. "It?"

"Yeah. My thoughts. The truth." He flashed her another quick glance. "Okay?"

Not like she could do anything about it being alone in his truck with him.

He didn't wait for her approval anyway, instead forging on... as if he spoke to a normal woman.

"I think you're pretty hot, Hope. Like that dark, slinky hair of yours and your inquisitive blue eyes." His brows pinched together. "That's what first drew my attention, right? I mean, I'm sure you're used to guys noticing you."

Ha! Fat chance. She wasn't used to that all. Not since... *No.* She didn't want to think of him.

Again, Lang continued without her having to contribute to the conversation. "I'm not a dumb guy, though, so I noticed right off that you were worried. I kept my distance, right?"

"You did." And she'd appreciated it.

"But I was still drawn to you. That small way you smile, as if you're not sure if you should. And the watchful way you kept an eye on me. It was a funny mix of reactions. Not ha-ha funny, but it sort of threw me, thinking you were sexy but getting the message that I should back off, and seeing you look so cute in your indecision."

Ivey had also told her she was cute. Was it true? Sadly, more often than not she couldn't look at herself long enough to notice. She swallowed heavily. "That's not what I see."

"In yourself, you mean?"

She nodded, realized he was watching the road and cleared

her throat. "I've been…" She couldn't say afraid. "Worried for a really long time."

"Four years, I know. Ever since some asshole mistreated you." He blew out a breath. "You know I'm different, right?"

In her head she knew it. Sometimes that didn't matter, though, when her reactions took over. "I do, it's just that I still get jumpy."

Pulling into the grocery parking lot and finding an empty spot very near the front of the store, he put the truck in Park but didn't turn it off. He didn't look at her, either. Staring out at the flooding rain, his jaw clenched and his voice dropped to a whisper. "I can't pretend to know what you went through or how it must have felt." His hands gripped the steering wheel. Abruptly he shifted to face her. "I have a hell of an imagination, though. I spent the entire night thinking about you. I wanted to come see you right away but I figured that'd be over the top."

Caught in his direct gaze, Hope couldn't look away. In the shadowy interior of the truck, his light brown eyes mesmerized her. He hadn't moved closer, but the space between them seemed to disappear, making her breath quicken.

"When I called and found out you were stuck, I was glad." His gaze flickered over her face, across her cheeks, her chin, her mouth, before locking on her eyes again. "Gave me the perfect excuse to come see you."

Hope shook her head. "I can't believe you wanted to."

"That's because you're not a man looking at an attractive woman. You don't see what I see." His hands relaxed, as did his intent expression. "You don't feel what I feel."

Her heart tripped and she whispered, "What?"

"I hope this won't insult you, but protectiveness is top of the list." He considered that, then gave a firm nod. "I want to protect you. I want you to feel safe with me."

Indignation was there, but it was overtaken by curiosity. "I think I do."

He acknowledged that with a quick smile. "I want to get to know you better, too. Do you think we could do that?"

God, she wanted to, but… "I don't know."

"How about we try, and if at any point you feel pressured, just tell me. I'm not perfect, I know that. You need to know it, too."

The grin took her by surprise. "I wasn't under the impression you were."

"Good," he said, all too serious even with her teasing. "Let's face it. There's a good chance I'll trip up every so often and I want you to know up front that you can call me on it."

"So…we'll be spending time together?"

"I hope so. Like this, just being out and about. Or on a date if you want. You're close by so you could join Corbin, Justin and me for a movie in the evening, or a swim in the afternoon."

"I don't own a swimsuit."

"So buy one. Or swim in a T-shirt and shorts."

Warmth enveloped her. She wanted to. Suddenly everything he mentioned sounded exciting, fun and actually *possible*. Feeling a little giddy, she nodded.

"Awesome." He leaned forward to look out the windshield. "I think the rain is lightening up a little. Want to make a run for the store?"

The soft laugh escaped in a rush. He was so casual about everything that it helped her to be casual, too. "Yes, I think I do."

His smile matched hers. "Afterward, you want to grab a bite to eat somewhere? That is, if any place is open in this outage."

She nodded too fast, then couldn't help laughing again. "A lot of places have generators, so…yes. Okay."

Being a seriously funny goof, Lang rubbed his hands together. "Well, this is all progressing more nicely than I could have hoped. Come on, I'll race you."

And before she even thought about it, Hope jumped out and took off through the rain, laughing freely, feeling absurdly happy.

Behind her, she heard the truck door slam and then the slapping of Lang's sneakers right before he drew up alongside her. He even turned to run backward, goading her with, "Come on, slowpoke. Is that the best you've got?"

She ramped up the speed and shot past him, nearly colliding with the automatic doors. They opened and Lang was there, putting on a serious face for the gawking shoppers while she continued to snicker.

Fun. She was having honest-to-God fun, and with a *man*.

In that moment, she knew a whole new world had just opened up to her. She couldn't wait to tell Ivey all about it.

Chapter Seven

Over the next month, Corbin and Ivey fell into a wonderful, comfortable pattern. Instead of Corbin and Justin visiting the clinic, they came by Ivey's house at least three times a week. Justin got to play with Daisy, and Ivey got to enjoy them both. Most nights Corbin brought dinner with him so all she had to do was shower and change. Twice she had insisted on cooking dinner, and Justin made his food preferences clear. Meatloaf was his favorite, but he also loved her fried chicken, declaring it far better than what his dad got from the fast-food restaurant.

Maurice actually *loved* Daisy. When Ivey wasn't home, the pups were kept in the mudroom, but they weren't often alone. When the cat went over the barrier in the mudroom to use his box, he usually stayed to visit. Ivey had found them all together more often than not. It astounded Ivey, since the cat had never before met a dog he didn't hate. Then again, Daisy was a very small, timid dog who treated Maurice like a friend.

Going up to the attic had become Ivey and Justin's "thing."

That first time, my goodness, how Justin loved it all. She could still remember the awe in his voice as he looked around.

"Wow." And then a few seconds later, "*Wow.* This is really all yours?"

"Collected over many years." She put her hand on his shoulder. "You see? I love all things horror as much as you do."

"Maybe more," he enthused, before oh-so-carefully lifting an original *Alien* action figure.

Feeling the excitement of her finds all over again, she made a quick decision. "Let's gather up all the *Alien* stuff and take it downstairs. What do you think? That way you can really check it out without all this dust and clutter."

"For real?" Justin whooped loudly, and the figures had entertained him for a good long while before their visit ended. Rather than put it all away, they moved the stuff into her guestroom.

The next time he was over, they brought down all the classic monster movie posters, as well as a few unique Frankenstein items, like a ceramic coin bank, a few models that she'd put together and painted and a windup doll. Pretty soon her guestroom was filled with her collection. Shortly after that, she began gifting Justin with various pieces.

True, it was a valuable collection, but what did it matter when it only gathered dust in the attic? She knew she wouldn't ever sell any of it. Justin was over the moon for each and every piece she gave him, and that was far more rewarding than hanging on to the stuff.

Lang built a shelf in Justin's room where he proudly displayed each item, but his favorites were the poseable classic monsters. Corbin said he played with those most often.

They were at her house tonight, lingering over pie at the kitchen table while Justin, with all the animals, flipped through old comic books in the living room. Through the open doorway, Ivey could see him sprawled on his back, Daisy curled up on his right, Maurice right beside her and the puppies playing on and around him.

Corbin took his last bite, then sat back, his hands over his flat stomach. "I think I've put on five pounds since you started cooking."

Ivey grinned. "You have not. You and Justin run too often to gain weight." Corbin still hadn't returned to work. Instead, he jogged with Justin. Or took out the kayak. Or swam. They were forever busy.

"When I started running with him, I never guessed he'd enjoy it so much. The kid has mad stamina. More often than not, I'm ready to quit when he's still going strong." Glancing toward Justin, Corbin's voice lowered. "We've got a nice pattern going. Jogging in the morning, errands and chores during the day, dinner with you, then swimming or taking out the kayak before a movie in the evening. I hate to switch it up, but I need to get back to work."

It'd make sense, Ivey knew, if Corbin's time with her had to be cut short. She understood him well enough now to know he would continually build on his relationship with Justin. Anyone could see that he valued every moment with his son, which meant something else had to give. That would likely be some of the time he spent with her.

She got it, but that didn't make it easier. "You said you work from home?"

He nodded. "I gave myself all of May and June off, but July is right around the corner so it's time to get back to it. I'll start with thirty hours or so, but eventually that turns into forty plus."

Ivey reached out and took his hand. Their alone time was extremely limited already, but he usually found a way to kiss her at the end of each visit. He had a lot on his plate and the last thing she wanted to do was add to that.

Hoping to make it easier on him, forcing herself to be stoic, she asked, "Are you trying to tell me we won't see as much of each other?"

"What? No." He quickly glanced toward Justin, then lowered his voice again. "Hell no. I was going to offer a different solution."

Relieved, Ivey smiled. "I'm all ears."

"What would you think of us taking Daisy and the puppies?"

Not what she'd expected. Take the dogs? But…she'd miss them horribly. "I don't understand how that would help."

"Ivey," he said gently. "You don't want to give the puppies away, and neither does Justin. Lang has said he'd help with them all. He's also lending a hand with Justin, but I hate to infringe on him too much since he and Hope are now a thing."

Yes, they were. Nothing too intimate, and they'd yet to share even a simple kiss. But Hope glowed with daily excitement. Lang made a point of seeing her every single night, usually for a walk around the property, or quiet time on the dock watching the sunset. Hope worried that he'd eventually want more and she wasn't sure if she could give it.

But for now, her friend was in a fog of happiness. Even pet owners made note of Hope's lighter mood at the clinic.

"I've gotten very attached to the puppies, that's true."

"And you trust very few people to treat them the same way you would."

She considered that and admitted that she trusted Corbin and Justin both. "Wouldn't that just give you more to deal with?"

He tugged on her hand until she stood, then he drew her around by his chair and urged her onto his thighs. Holding her on his lap, his arms around her waist, he smiled at her. "I was thinking, hoping, that you'd like to join us each night for dinner and maybe a swim." Leaning forward, he kissed her, but with his son nearby he kept it light. "That would make a nice addition to our routine."

Overcome with emotion, Ivey sank against him, her face

turned into his neck, her arms around him. "I would love that so much."

His hand went up and down her spine. "But?"

"I can't leave Maurice each night."

"Does he travel okay? You could bring him. He likes seeing Daisy anyway."

Wow, it truly sounded as if they were combining their lives. She hugged him tighter. "Maurice does fine in his carrier for short trips." Everything seemed to be changing suddenly, but she didn't mind. She already knew how she felt, how she'd felt almost from the first day she'd met him.

"So what do you think? Yes?"

He smelled so good, and she couldn't resist opening her mouth against his throat for just a moment. She felt him stir, and that stirred her, too. Sitting back a little, she nodded. "Yes. On one condition." Not giving him a chance to ask, she said, "Any time it might not be convenient, you only need to let me know."

"Same from you, okay?" He took her mouth in another brief kiss. "I want to spend time with you, but I don't want you pressured to fit it in."

When Justin laughed, they both looked toward him. He held the comic book high while one of the puppies tried to get it. Careful not to disturb Daisy or Maurice, he put the comic on the coffee table and snuggled the pup up close.

Awww. "I love your kid, Corbin. Just absolutely love him."

"I'm glad."

The way he said that and the weight in his words surprised her. She immediately got lost in his golden-brown gaze.

Oh, what she wouldn't give to spend an entire night with him. How that would work, she had no idea, so she didn't say it out loud. But she wanted it. So very, very much.

Carrying the pup, Justin came into the kitchen. "Is this one a boy or a girl?"

Ivey started to scramble off Corbin's lap, but he held onto

her and Justin didn't appear to see anything amiss. Taking the puppy from him, Ivey lifted it high to take a peek, then declared, "Boy." They all had the same coloring without any distinguishing differences yet, other than personality. "There are two boys and one girl."

Tilting toward her, Justin whispered, "How can you tell?"

Wicked amusement lit Corbin's eyes. "Yeah, Ivey. How can you?"

But hey, she'd been a veterinarian for a long time, so she whispered right back, "The boys have penises and the girl does not." Gently, she cradled the pup on her thighs so that his little round belly was up. "You see?"

Very seriously, Justin scrunched up his face and peered at the dog. "Yeah." Typical of a child, he moved right on from that, his curiosity appeased. "Could I name him Freddy, like Freddy Krueger?"

"You still want that name, huh?" She pretended to consider it. "You know, I think he'd like that."

Slyly, he asked, "Could I name the other boy dog Jason?"

Ivey barely swallowed her laugh. "Sure." With a sigh, she added, "And now we're back to the girl pup and the difficulty of a name for her."

"How about Lily? In the comic book, Frankenstein's monster married Lily."

"Oh, that's genius! I think Lily sounds perfect."

Justin edged in closer, hesitated a second, and then his skinny arms went around Ivey's neck and he gave her a fierce hug. Equally stunned and moved by the unexpected gesture, she drew him closer with one arm and breathed in his little-boy smell of sun-warmed hair and skin.

Since she was still on Corbin's lap, Corbin easily enclosed them both in his long muscular arms, then kissed each of them on the head.

As Justin wriggled free, he asked, "Got any more pie?"

Ivey wanted to crush him close again, but apparently his tolerance for affection had its limits and the hug he'd just given was generous. "Yes." Following Corbin's example, she gave Justin a quick kiss on the forehead and handed him the puppy, then kissed Corbin, too, just for good measure, before standing.

Here she'd started out with the intent of having casual fun, and instead she'd fallen madly in love with the family life.

Go figure.

Hands in his pockets, head down in thought, Lang walked through the woods connecting the two properties. With plenty of direction from Justin, he and Corbin had improved the way. A few path lights wouldn't hurt, too, but the moon was bright overhead tonight so he didn't walk into any spiderwebs.

Having just left Hope, he felt…primed.

He wanted her. So damn much.

Yet odd as it seemed, he relished every small sign of her lessening fear. Initially, she'd watched him with wariness, as well as interest. He'd recognized that even if she hadn't.

He'd also recognized the alarm. No woman had ever feared him before. It was an incredibly uncomfortable sensation—so how much worse was it for her?

When Corbin had first explained the situation to him, a variety of emotions had bombarded him. Sure, protectiveness. Lang was a big man with sizeable fists and plenty of brawn. He wanted Hope to see that as shelter, not as a threat. God no, never that.

When he'd chased down his brother to offer support and get to know his nephew, not once had he considered the complication of a relationship for himself. And definitely not with a woman like Hope.

But here he was, mired in need.

The need to touch her. The need to kiss her.

The need to have her trust.

Their relationship was a fragile thing, her skittishness still in evidence on occasion, forcing him to tiptoe on eggshells. Progress was made, though, each and every time they were together. Just tonight, she'd stared at his mouth with singular focus. She wanted him, too. Eventually he'd have her.

And then what?

The house was quiet when he let himself him in through the front door. Corbin and Justin might have already gone to bed, so he took off his sneakers and, without turning on any lights, made his way through the house. He was just about to head downstairs to his room when he heard muted voices upstairs.

Thinking he'd tell them both good night, he went upstairs instead of down.

A low light came from Justin's room. He heard Corbin ask, "What's wrong, son?"

"Nothin'."

Not wanting to intrude, Lang stopped out of sight.

After a brief hesitation, Corbin said, "The thing is, you're my son and I love you. I feel like we're getting settled in, right?"

Silence.

"I can tell when something's bothering you now, just like you'd be able to tell with me." The bed squeaked, and Lang assumed his brother had just sat down. "We're in this together, you and me."

"And Uncle Lang?"

"Yes."

"And Ivey?"

Wow, Lang thought. The kid was bringing out the big questions. He felt for Corbin, knowing the stretch of silence meant he wasn't sure how to answer.

Finally Corbin said, "I care about Ivey. You do, too, don't you?"

"Yeah."

"Is that what's bothering you? Something to do with Ivey?"

It was Justin's turn to be quiet, then in a voice so low Lang could barely hear him, he asked, "Will I ever see my mom again?"

Oh Christ.

Lang put a hand over his eyes, his throat going tight. Hearing the uncertainty in Justin's voice broke his heart as nothing else could. And his poor brother, caught trying to find a way to answer that wouldn't cause the kid more hurt. Damn Darcie for dumping him as she had. He locked his teeth so tight that his jaw ached.

"Do you want to see her?" Corbin finally asked.

"I don't know." Seconds ticked by, each one painful. "She's my mom, so I guess I should."

"Let's not worry about what you should do, okay? Do you *want* to? And listen, bud, there is no wrong answer, okay? No matter what you say, I'll keep on loving you, and I would never—"

"No."

Lang tangled a hand in his hair and gave a small tug. Damn it, his eyes were getting damp.

"So…" Corbin floundered for a moment. "You were asking because you want to know what to expect?"

"Yeah." More rustling in the bed.

Lang peeked in and saw Justin sitting up, his legs crossed yoga style, his bony shoulders hunched. "If I see her, I guess that'd be okay, but I don't want to leave here."

"Never," Corbin vowed softly. "If your mom visits you, it won't change anything. You'll still live with me."

"You sure?" Justin edged closer to him.

"You're mine and I will never, ever let you go." Corbin drew him into his lap and held him close. "I *love* you, Justin. So damn much." He put his jaw to the crown of Justin's head. "Your mom has some things to work out, but I know she loves you, too."

Justin chewed that over. "She sent me away."

"She sent you to *me* because she knows no one will ever love and protect you like I will. She was in a tough spot and she made the best decision she could. Okay?"

Rubbing his eyes and then his nose, Justin nodded. "Okay."

"Good. So…that helps?"

"Yeah." He twisted away and got back under the covers. "Thanks, Dad."

Lang dropped his head silently back against the wall, tortured by his nephew's pain. How could Corbin bear it? He was so proud of his brother for seeming to know the right thing to say and the right way to say it. To give credit to Darcie? No, Lang didn't think he could have, but of course it wouldn't help Justin to know that his mother had completely abandoned him. Corbin had understood that.

His brother was one hell of a man.

Lang stood there in the hall, eyes closed, his thoughts and emotions rioting, until Justin called out, "Good night, Uncle Lang."

His eyes popped open. Oh hell. Busted. Leaning around the door frame, Lang peered in and saw Corbin giving him a sardonic smile.

"Did you want to tell Justin good night?" Corbin asked. "Or were you angling for a hug?"

"I was hoping to be asked." Trying not to look maudlin, Lang grinned and sauntered in.

"I figured." Corbin kissed Justin on the forehead—something Justin no longer shied away from. "Good night, son. If you need anything, or if you want to talk some more, just come to my room, okay? Anytime." When Justin nodded, Corbin stood to give Lang room.

Sitting by his nephew, Lang asked, "You brushed your teeth?"

"Yup." Justin gave a toothy grin to prove it.

"Did your dad read you a bedtime story?"

Curling his lip, Justin said, "I'm not a baby."

"Definitely not, but how about you indulge me?" Lang picked

up the comic book on his bedside table. "This looks like a good one." Werewolf. With some really incredible artwork.

"I already read it," Justin said.

"No kidding? You can read all this?"

Again, Justin said, "I'm not a baby," but this time he laughed.

"Well, *I'll* read it with effect." He gave an eerie, very monster-inspired laugh. "What do you say?"

With new excitement, Justin nodded, then even scooted over to make room for Lang in the bed.

Corbin smiled. "Not more than a half hour, okay? It's getting late."

"You got it." Once Corbin left the room, Lang got comfortable. Justin did as well, snuggling in against his side as if it were a nightly ritual. And by God, starting tonight, it would be. Having Justin there, so close, was something he knew he wanted to get used to.

With exaggerated flair, Lang started to read. Justin was suitably enthralled. At one point, enjoying himself as he did, Lang decided he felt sorry for Darcie. Whatever misguided notions she'd had, whatever hardships life had dealt her, she'd deliberately given up this remarkable little boy.

Someday he'd like to understand her, to know why she'd never told Corbin he was a father, to comprehend what mindset led her to believe she'd be better off without her son. If she'd only told Corbin early on, the entire family would have helped her.

She'd made other choices and tonight, in this moment, he was glad that Justin was with them now.

By the time he finished reading, exactly thirty minutes later, Justin's eyes were heavy and he kept yawning.

Carefully, Lang maneuvered him flat to the pillow and tucked him in. His hair was now smooshed on one side, so Lang smoothed it. "Love you, Justin."

His eyes already closed, he mumbled sleepily, "You, too, Uncle Lang."

Wow. Those profound words burrowed right into his heart, and he knew he'd never be the same. Funny how a man could go from never thinking of kids to loving one with all his heart in such a short span of time.

He set the comic aside, quietly clicked off the bedside lamp and, leaving the door slightly ajar, went to find his brother.

Corbin stood on the covered deck, drinking in the moist night air, listening to the soothing sounds from the lake and trees and wondering if he'd done the right thing, said the right words.

Give Justin up? Never, not under any circumstances.

"Hey." Lang slipped through the sliding doors and joined him at the rail. After a second or two, he asked, "You okay?"

"I am," Corbin said, though he wasn't. Not really. Finally he admitted, "Justin's worries are my own. What if Darcie changes her mind?"

"She signed over her rights to you."

Yes, thank God. Legally, she didn't have a leg to stand on. But morally, did it matter? She *was* his mother. Darcie and Justin had a ten-year history that Corbin couldn't just ignore. "I wouldn't let Justin go, so don't misunderstand. If I had to, I'd fight her in court."

"And we'd win," Lang said, letting Corbin know he wouldn't be fighting alone.

"He's mine and I'm keeping him."

Quietly, Lang said, "I know."

"But that doesn't mean Darcie won't want time with him… or that he might eventually want time with her." Growing tension knotted the muscles of his neck. His hands fisted on the railing. "I'd understand if she did, if he did, but Jesus, it scares me. Knowing what I know now, how could I ever trust her?" Darcie had kept his son from him, and when Justin became too inconvenient, she'd dropped him off like an unwanted pet. She'd seemed high that day, a little unstable, definitely uncaring. Now he kept wondering…what else might she do? If it suited her, would she try to take off with Justin?

Lang put an understanding hand on Corbin's shoulder.

"She has the ability to hurt him so much." Corbin closed his eyes. "It's taken a little while, but now he's happy more often than not. He no longer watches me like he's expecting the worst. He's acting like a little kid again."

"And she could disrupt all that."

Corbin's mouth tightened. "Yes."

Lang turned so that his back was to the railing and he faced Corbin. "I want to ask you something, and I don't want you to hold back."

"Have I ever?"

"No, but you've also never been a dad."

"True enough." Somewhere on the lake, a splash sounded. Bugs darted in and out of the floodlight beams. Clouds rolled over the moon, then cleared again. "Let's hear it."

Lang drew a breath. "I'd like to hang around a while."

That was supposed to be news? "I already figured you would." Justin was a huge lure for *Uncle* Lang, but Corbin knew it was more than that, too. His brother worried for him and wanted to be supportive. Plus he was growing closer to Hope every day.

Lang held up a hand. "Yeah, but I mean, I'd like to stay *here*. Not necessarily in your house, though I've enjoyed it so far."

Finally catching on, Corbin asked, "You'd relocate to Sunset permanently?" That shouldn't have surprised him. Their mom was currently traveling with Hagan in the RV, but he knew as soon as she could, she'd show up, too. It was a nice thing to know that even if something happened to him, Justin would always be protected and cared for. His family would see to it.

Never again would his son be dependent on one troubled

woman who, for whatever reasons, hadn't been able to priori-
tize him.

"That kid's already stolen my heart." Lang looked out at the
night. "But I worry about you, too. Yeah, I know, you can
handle it."

Corbin snorted. "Trust me, sometimes I'm completely lost."

"Maybe. You wouldn't be human otherwise. But damn,
you've already impressed me so much."

"I wish I could be as confident as you." Lately it felt like he
second-guessed his every decision.

"So would it be easier or harder to have me around?" Lang
met his gaze. "I *want* to be here, for you and Justin both, but
only if it'll help and not hinder."

"It helps," Corbin assured him. "Like tonight…" He shook
his head. "I was floundering, man. I wanted to just hug him,
but I didn't want to be dismissive of his concerns."

"He's only ten, Corbin."

"Ten and with the weight of the world on his shoulders. That
was the other problem. How to respect his question without
over-answering it. I didn't want to bring up court or responsibilities or any of the adult things he shouldn't have to worry
about it." He gave Lang a grateful look. "Showing up when
you did helped drag me out of the emotional quicksand, if you
know what I mean."

"I was drowning in it myself, so I get it."

"Good. Then feel free to hang around as long as you like.
The house is plenty big enough for you."

"Awesome." Lang nodded in satisfaction. "Then that's decided."

Together, they stared out at the bright moonlight reflecting
off of the rippling surface of the lake.

It eased some of Corbin's tension, knowing his brother
planned to stay in Sunset. But then what? "I know you, Lang.
You won't be content just hanging out. So what's the plan?"

"I was thinking about that." He folded his arms and leaned on the rail. "Sunset could use a sports complex, don't you think?"

Nope, that didn't surprise him, either. Lang was the highly motivated type who liked a challenge. "People would love it," Corbin agreed. "It's a small town, though, so I'm not sure how lucrative it'd be."

"Meaning I won't get richer?" Grinning, Lang shrugged. "Like you said, I'm thirty now. Not ancient, but I'm ready to settle down a little."

"Ah." Corbin fought his own grin. "Does Hope figure into those plans?"

Lang shook his head. "Who the hell knows? Right now, she's satisfied with just being friends."

Corbin winced for his brother. "Got you caught in the friend zone, huh?"

"It's not a terrible place to be," Lang admitted quietly.

"With Hope?"

"She's different. How I feel about her is different." Lang gave a gruff laugh. "And isn't that screwed up considering I've never even kissed her?"

Awed by his brother's patience, Corbin said, "So kiss her."

He shook his head. "You know what she's been through."

Glad for the diversion from his own turmoil, Corbin pulled up a patio chair and sprawled into it. "There are all kinds of kisses. Start easy and build on it."

"I don't want to rush her."

A simple kiss would be too much? Poor Lang...and honestly, poor Hope. "Has she discussed it with you at all?"

"No. I know only what you told me." Lang worked his jaw. "But I sense things, if you know what I mean. It doesn't take a genius to put the pieces together."

"Bring it up," Corbin suggested. "From what I understand, she's only ever talked about it with Ivey. Talking to you would be completely different."

Lang grabbed a chair, too. "That's the problem."

Feeling philosophical, as if Lang's troubles were a hell of lot more solvable than his own, Corbin shrugged. "You won't know until you try. If she balks, back off, but otherwise…" He let that hang, then added, "She might appreciate your perspective."

Lang considered it but didn't look convinced. "How about you and Ivey? She's a doll, by the way. I love how she deals with people."

"You included?"

Grinning, Lang said, "Hey, she likes me." He tipped his head at Corbin. "But she looks at you like you're Thanksgiving dinner."

Funny how his brother could lighten his mood. "I know and it's killing me." Ivey held nothing back, including her sexual interest. "Eventually we'll get together, but for now, I'm prioritizing."

"Justin first?"

"First and foremost." Where Darcie had failed, Corbin would succeed, in large part because he'd had advantages Darcie hadn't. He knew love, knew what it was and what it wasn't because his parents had shown him. God willing, he'd pass that along to Justin, too. "Luckily, Ivey's been understanding."

"I'm not surprised. She really is terrific." Lang held out his arms. "But, hey, Justin and I could use a few hours of alone time. You know I wouldn't mind. We could take in a movie, or go fishing, or—"

Corbin grinned. "There are probably a dozen ways for you two to amuse yourselves."

"So let me," Lang said. Sobering, he added, "Actually, I could invite Hope along. Justin would be a buffer for her, a way to make her more comfortable. It'd be a win-win for me, and it'd give you some free time, too."

"Maybe," Corbin mused, wondering if it was selfish of him to want time alone with Ivey. Even just a few hours. Long enough to kiss her the way he really wanted.

And more.

Lang sat forward. "I'm here anyway, right? This is one way I can make things a little easier."

"Ivey is coming over each night this week. She's even bringing Maurice." At Lang's questioning look, Corbin said, "Her cat. Trust me, that's a huge concession on her part. The plan is for her to leave the dog and puppies here so Justin has company when I get back to work."

"I'd be great company."

"You can help supervise the dog and puppies."

"Yeah, I can handle that. But what about a date? I can't believe I've offered you a perfect solution and you're dragging your feet."

Was he? At the moment, his relationship with Ivey seemed so perfect, he didn't want to risk changing the dynamics and possibly ruining it. At the same time, they were both adults and the chemistry between them was through the roof. "Next weekend?" Corbin asked.

"Sure. Whatever works for you. As it happens, my schedule is wide open."

Corbin smiled. "I'll have to ask Ivey."

"Like you don't already know she'll be a solid yes." Lang scoffed. "Thanksgiving dinner, remember? She'll be all about it."

Corbin gave in to a satisfied grin. Ivey was rather plainspoken about wanting him. He said only, "I'll keep you posted."

Lang was quiet a moment. "This is nice, right?"

"The setting?" There was something very relaxing about being near the water. It was like your problems got sucked away. "Yeah."

With a twist of his mouth, Lang said, "I meant this." He gestured between them. "Brothers talking. Sharing concerns and shit."

Corbin laughed. "Yeah, that's nice, too."

"Hope never had that." Showing his frustration, Lang rubbed

the back of his neck. "She went through everything and her sister wasn't there for her. What the hell kind of family is that?"

"Not our kind, that's for sure."

"If Hope ever really opens up, she'll like us. As a family, I mean. I get the feeling she could use that foundation, you know? Not that Ivey isn't great because she is. Hope thinks of her as a sister. That's obvious. But her own sister should have backed her up, too, even if her parents didn't."

"No argument from me." There'd been many times in his life when Corbin had relied heavily on his mother and brother, and vice versa. He couldn't really imagine life without them. "Maybe someday they'll come around, but until then, she's got Ivey." Taking in Lang's determined expression, he added softly, "And now us."

"Yeah." Tiredly, Lang got to his feet, then clapped a hand to Corbin's shoulder. "The squirt will be up early. You should get some sleep."

"I'll head in soon." Corbin waited until Lang had closed the sliding doors behind him, then he sat forward, his hands held loosely between his knees. His head dropped wearily. It was a disturbing realization that for the first time in his life, he was actually terrified of things out of his control.

He loved his son. He would do everything in his power to make a good life for him. But he couldn't predict if Darcie would come back, or if she did, that she'd have Justin's best interests at heart.

Chapter Eight

The busy day had prevented their usual chitchat, but Ivey could tell by Hope's breezy attitude that all was still well between her and Lang. She couldn't wait to get details, and to share a few of her own.

She'd spent Monday and Tuesday with Corbin at his house, and to her surprise, Maurice enjoyed the trips. Initially, he'd been a little suspicious of the new location, but he was a smart kitty and recognized Justin right away, and he was beside himself with joy at seeing Daisy again.

Maurice loved to snuggle with the dog. Around her, he seemed younger, friskier and all around happier. Maybe Ivey had been the old grump and just projected that on her poor cat. What a dismal thought.

Things were better now, though. Corbin had even set up a litter box for Maurice. So far he'd turned his nose up at it, but thankfully hadn't had any accidents. Or actually, with Maurice, it would have been an "on purpose," because he did tend to go outside the box whenever something irked him. The cat used ingenious methods to make his discontent known to her.

Tonight Ivey had some of her monster collectibles ready to gift to Justin, so she was doubly anxious to wrap up her day. More and more, she wanted to hand the entire assortment over to him, knowing he'd get a lot more enjoyment from it all than she would just by keeping everything stored. Of course, she'd have to discuss that with Corbin first. It would be a rather extravagant gift.

"Whew." Stepping through the door, Hope slumped back against the wall and used a file folder to fan her face. "What a day. I don't think we slowed down once."

Ivey looked her over. Hope's inky bangs were stuck to one side and heat flushed her cheeks. Perspiration dotted her temples and her shirt clung to her in select places. On top of their busy schedule they'd had two emergency surgeries—which had thankfully gone well—and the air-conditioning had gone on the fritz. It was a very lucky thing that she worked with even-tempered women who persevered.

Smiling, Ivey stripped off her soiled lab coat, dropped it into the bin and then washed her hands in the sink. "You look frazzled. Why don't you head on home and relax?" When Hope bit her lip, Ivey's smile widened. "Or maybe you have something else to do?"

Hope's gaze darted around, making sure Karen and the other tech weren't near, then whispered, "Lang and I are going out on the boat in an hour."

That sounded wonderful. An easy ride as the evening cooled down. "That'll be fun." It thrilled her that Hope had agreed to be alone with Lang. They'd be on the lake, so not really anywhere private, but still, it was another step forward.

"Yes, but..." Hope crowded close and her voice dropped even more. "I bought a bathing suit."

Ivey's jaw loosened before she caught herself and grinned

hugely. "Good for you!" Talk about a big step, this one was a leap. Hope didn't even wear low-cut tops. In fact, she used clothes like a suit of armor, hiding everything she could. "I'm sure you'll look terrific."

"I had thought about shopping around here, but I just couldn't do it, so I ordered it online. It's cute. A black one-piece with a little skirt."

The "little skirt" part tickled Ivey. It sounded just like Hope. "Now you know I want to see it."

Hope quickly dug out her phone and opened her photo app. *"Thank you,"* she said with relief. "I took a picture of myself in the mirror and I'm dying to know if it looks okay." She held the phone to her chest. "But first, you have to swear to me that you'll tell me the truth."

"Oh, honey, I will never, ever lie to you."

"Right, I know that. But some lies are meant to be kind, and the thing is, I want your one hundred percent honest opinion so that I don't make a fool of myself in front of Lang."

Unable to believe she was having this conversation with Hope, that her friend was actually that interested in a man, Ivey crossed her heart. "I swear. Now stop teasing and lemme see!"

With her bottom lip back in her teeth, Hope turned the phone.

Slowly, Ivey took it from her. Holy smokes, even with the suit having a high, round neck and the little skirt that skimmed the tops of her thighs, Hope looked amazing. She had more curves than Ivey had ever realized. Delicate, yes, but so very sexy. "Girl, you're going to rock that man's world."

The second the words left her mouth, she regretted it. What if Hope didn't *want* to rock Lang's world? What if that notion frightened her?

Ivey looked up…and caught Hope's blinding smile.

Glowing in pleasure, Hope asked, "You really think so?"

So pleased she could barely contain it, Ivey gave her a big grin. "I think you're ready to advance things a smidge. Am I right?"

"Actually...yes." Hope hugged herself. "I want to kiss him, Ivey. I think about it all the time." With a soft laugh, she said, "I can't *stop* thinking about it."

Perfect. "I'm sure he's thinking about it, too." Ivey looked at the image again. Hope had slim, shapely legs, gently rounded hips and a tiny waist. The neckline of the suit barely displayed her modest cleavage. "You are such an enticing little package. Lang is going to drool."

"I wish I had bigger boobs."

That got a surprised laugh out of Ivey. "Don't be silly. Big boobs would look absurd on your petite frame." With confidence, Ivey said, "You're perfect as is."

Fretting again, Hope whispered, "What if he misunderstands and thinks I want more than a kiss?"

In many ways, Hope was like a schoolgirl going through her first crush, cautiously seeking new experiences. "Wearing a bathing suit is not an invitation, honey." Ivey handed the phone back to her. "Everyone wears them and it only means you're comfortable enough with him to relax. Lang isn't a dummy, so I trust he'll get it. But you know I'm all about being up front. Why not just tell him you want a kiss, *only* a kiss? That way, there are no misunderstandings."

Karen stuck her head in. "I'm heading out, ladies. I'm in desperate need of a dip in the pool and a margarita."

Laughing, Ivey shooed her away. "You've earned it, Karen. Thank you so much for being with us through thick and thin."

"Thank *you*. If you weren't such an incredible vet, we probably would have lost that dog today and my entire week would have been ruined."

The dog had been hit by a car and for an hour or more it had been touch and go. A grueling experience for all of them.

"He'll still need time to mend, but he's from a good family and they'll baby him."

"Thank God," Karen said, already slipping away. "Everything is locked up except the back door. I'll see you both tomorrow."

As usual, Ivey and Hope gathered their purses together. So often, they were in perfect sync. They each slipped on sunglasses as they stepped outside, and Hope waited as Ivey locked the door. They turned, and together, tripped to a halt.

Geoff was outside his car, leaning against a fender and smiling in welcome.

"Ah, hell," Ivey muttered low. Other than a few texts, she hadn't heard from him in weeks. There had been that one moment at the grocery store where they'd run into each other, but Ivey had greeted him like a mere acquaintance and hurried on her way.

It was totally different to step out of the clinic and find him waiting in the lot.

"Should I stay?" Hope asked in a whisper.

"Absolutely not. Go wow Lang in that bathing suit so you can give me all the juicy details later. And, hon, as always, if you need me for anything, don't hesitate."

Hope cast a quick glance at Geoff. "Same to you, okay?"

"Thanks." With a lagging step, Ivey walked over to Geoff and tried to work up a smile. "Hey."

Geoff reached out to touch a damp curl clinging to her temple. "Rough day?"

Damn it, Geoff had never before been concerned about her days, rough or otherwise. Most evenings he'd made a beeline to the fridge for a beer, then sprawled on her couch to watch television or play on his phone.

She managed a thin smile. "Air wouldn't stay on. The maintenance guy finally got it fixed a bit ago, but it was the end of the day, so...still hot when we left. Should be cooled down by the morning." She'd been looking forward to seeing Corbin, and a delay was just annoying. "What are you doing here, Geoff?"

"I need to talk to you." He straightened away from the car.

Automatically, Ivey backed up a step to put a measured distance between them. Geoff looked stressed, and now that she bothered to notice, he appeared leaner, especially around his face.

Staring up at him, she felt a twinge of concern. "Are you okay?"

"Without you?" His smile was sad. "Not really."

"Geoff," she cautioned gently. "Whatever was between us was long gone before I ended things. You need to move on."

He nodded without much conviction. "I screwed up. I know that now. I got too comfortable, turned into a slug." He blew out a breath. "I didn't take care of you like I should have."

"I don't need anyone to take care of me, but interest would have been nice."

Mouth firming, Geoff looked away. "I was a selfish bastard. I took you and your love for granted."

Sympathy welled up, especially since Ivey was no longer convinced that she'd loved him. "It wasn't all your fault. It takes two to let a relationship sink." Far too often, she'd let things slide, because it hadn't mattered enough.

Totally different story with Corbin.

Very different situation, too, because Corbin had some serious priorities above and beyond a romantic relationship. He put Justin first, rightfully so. To her, that only made him more loveable.

And yet, he was always very aware of her, too.

"You were great, Ivey. Too nice, maybe. But I wanted you to know, I'm going back to the gym now, getting off my butt." Geoff's earnest gaze held hers, and he whispered, "I'll do better."

Oh Lord. An obnoxious Geoff she could deal with. But a contrite Geoff? A humble and sincere Geoff? She scrambled for the right way to respond. Finally, with him waiting expectantly, she managed a tender smile. "That's all wonderful, Geoff, and I'm sure whoever you're with next will appreciate it."

"Ivey—"

"But that woman won't be me." For both their sakes, she had to be firm. "Please understand. Even if you haven't moved on, I have. I'm happy." On impulse, she took his right hand in both of hers. "I want you to be happy, too, but you weren't happy with me."

"I was happier than I've ever been."

"You know that's not true." She squeezed his hand, but when she started to release him, he held on. "We were convenient at first, then just in a rut. Don't you see that?"

"I love you, Ivey. I think I always will."

Inside, she grimaced.

Lifting her hand, Geoff pressed a kiss to her knuckles. "But I meant what I said, if we can only be friends, then I'll accept that."

Tugging her hand free, she said, "Of course we are." She did care about Geoff, and she meant it when she said she wanted him to be happy. He just couldn't be happy with her.

"Then maybe we could get together some time?"

She wanted to deny him, but she didn't have the heart to do that. "Maybe." To keep from giving him false hope, she added, "But you know my hours, and I'm seeing someone else now. I don't have a lot of free time."

"The guy with the kid?"

"Yes."

"Does he love you?"

The question gave her pause. "I don't really know." She hoped Corbin was as emotionally invested as her, but she wasn't about to press him. "We haven't been together that long."

Long enough, though, that she'd miss Justin horribly if she and Corbin weren't seeing each other. Huh. Funny that she hadn't considered that before now. She didn't just love Corbin. She also loved Justin.

And she especially loved being together with them—the animals included.

"Ivey?" Geoff tipped up her face. "Honey, is something wrong?"

Yes, damn it. All kinds of things were wrong. She really needed to find out if Corbin was headed in the same direction as her, otherwise she was setting herself up for devastating disappointment.

None of that was Geoff's business, so she lifted her chin away from his touch and forced a smile. "Sorry. It's been a long, hot, frustrating day and I really do need to get going."

"To see *him*?"

Her smile tightened. "Yes, as a matter of fact." Geoff really needed to face the facts.

"All right, I won't keep you. But, honey, please know that if things don't work out with him, I'm here. In whatever way you want me." He bent to press a lingering kiss to her cheek, gave her a thankfully brief hug and turned to get into his car.

With alacrity, Ivey hustled to her own car, glad that she didn't have to come up with a reply. She used to *sleep* with Geoff, but now, even a peck made her want to smack him.

It took her another hour to get home to Maurice, shower and change and get on her way to Corbin's. Deep down, she was troubled. Despite her resolve, she felt incredibly bad for Geoff. Had she misjudged him? It seemed so.

She didn't regret breaking things off. If she hadn't, she wouldn't be with Corbin now. But could she have been nicer about it? Yup.

By the time she knocked on Corbin's door, she wasn't feeling very good about herself. It was Justin who let her in, and his bright smile buoyed her. Already talking a mile a minute about things the pups had done, ways that Daisy had warmed up and about a cat toy they'd picked up for Maurice, he took her hand and tugged her inside.

Ears up, Daisy came trotting around the corner. When she saw Ivey, she yapped in glee and turned a few circles. Hearing her, Maurice gave a demanding, impatient meow from his carrier.

"They want to visit, huh?" Justin said.

"It seems so." Ivey knelt down and opened the small metal door. Like a regal prince, Maurice sauntered out to the adulation of Daisy. "So aloof," she teased. "You know you're anxious to play."

As the animals turned the corner, Justin followed.

Alone again, Ivey closed the carrier and set it aside. With guilt nagging her, she stood to go to the kitchen where she assumed she'd find Corbin. She'd taken only two steps when he appeared, a cold drink in his hand.

He looked at her, his brows gathering in concern. "Hi."

"Sorry I'm running late."

"You're here now." He bent down and took her mouth in a warm, possessive kiss that did a lot to obliterate her dark thoughts.

She didn't mean to get carried away, but he felt so good she just naturally moved closer. Fingers spread, she slid her hands up his chest to his neck. Around the house, Corbin always wore soft T-shirts that felt so good against her palms and were a treat for her eyes with the way they hugged his muscles.

She, on the other hand, felt rather dumpy in her oversize T-shirt and jean shorts with flip-flops...but she didn't care. Never, not once, had Corbin given her a negative look or comment about her casual duds.

"Mmm," he said in approval of her touch, tipping his head a little and deepening the kiss. His free hand flattened on the small of her back, bringing her into closer contact.

Oh, how she'd love to lose herself in him, Ivey thought. To

have an entire day and night to touch and taste him in all the ways she wanted.

In the other room, they heard Justin laugh, and it effectively pulled them apart.

Corbin stayed close, his gaze searching. "What's wrong, Ivey?"

She let her head drop to his chest. "It was an awful day."

"I'm sorry." He pressed another kiss to her temple, nuzzling gently. "You smell good."

That made her smile. "It's my new shampoo."

"No, it's you." He stepped back and handed her the icy drink, then put his arm around her and steered her toward the kitchen. "Dinner is almost done. I had a late start myself with a meeting that went over. Lang headed off with Hope just a few minutes ago."

That reminded her and she asked, "Did you see her in her bathing suit?"

He shook his head and pulled out a chair for her. "No. Lang went to her place and from there, out on the boat."

Dropping into the seat, Ivey whispered, "Oh, Corbin, she looked *so* good. I can't tell you how thrilled I am that she's coming out of her shell. It does my heart good."

Wearing a crooked smile, he stroked two fingers along her cheek. "I'm glad you're here, Ivey."

She didn't understand his mood. "I'm glad to be here." Blinking up at him, she asked, "Is everything okay?"

"Yeah." He kissed her once more, then turned away to the stove. "Breaded pork chops with cheese noodles and salad, coming up in ten."

"Justin's request?"

"He's a bottomless pit." He deftly turned the chops. "You look exhausted. Tell me about your day."

So nice that he always asked, and that he seemed to pick up on her moods. Sipping her drink, she detailed the surgeries, the failure of the air-conditioning and then, finally, Geoff's surprise visit.

Up to that point, Corbin had given appropriate replies and shown real interest, but now he slowly turned, a fork in hand and a piercing expression in his eyes. "Geoff? Your ex?"

"Yes. He's called and texted a few times, but I rarely acknowledge him." She wrinkled her nose. "He knows my schedule, though, so he was in the parking lot waiting when I came out."

For a second or two, Corbin's jaw worked before he made a visible effort to shutter his frustration. "What did you do?"

"Oh, that was well done. You went from looking pissed to merely curious." When his eyes narrowed, she laughed and joined him at the stove, taking the fork from him and poking at the chops. "I made it clear that we were over. You don't ever have to worry about that. Even if things ended between us tomorrow, I wouldn't go back to Geoff."

"Things aren't ending between us."

"God, I hope not! I was just saying, Geoff is no longer an option, regardless. But..."

He reclaimed the fork, then put it on the stove. "But what?"

It really was funny to see a guy like Corbin acting territorial. Funny and oh-so-flattering. Ivey turned down the burner, then wrapped her arms around him. "How long before Justin joins us?"

Reluctantly, he returned her embrace. "Justin?" he called out.

From the other room, they heard, "Yeah, Dad?"

"Get your hands washed, okay? Dinner is almost ready."

"'Kay."

Corbin squeezed her closer. "Minutes, so tell me quick what's going on."

"Nothing between Geoff and me, I promise." She looked up at him, and decided why not? "I'm falling hard for you, so you see, you have nothing to worry about. I'm the one who should be worried—"

His kiss stole the rest of her statement, but this time it was firm and fast. "No, Ivey. You have nothing to worry about, not where I'm concerned."

Okay...awesome. Glad that she'd brought it up, Ivey grinned at him. "Go, me!"

A reluctant smile led to a short laugh. "Sometimes you're nuts, you know that, right?" He turned her away with a swat on her butt. "But you're also really good for my ego."

"Ditto." Leaning against the counter, Ivey asked, "What can I do to help with dinner?"

"You can quit stalling and tell me what happened with your ex."

True, he already had the table set and he clearly had the meal in hand. "I suppose I should."

"Ivey."

"Geoff is actually misunderstood." There, having said it out loud, she could finally address it. "I feel badly now for think-ing he was such a jerk." The incredulous look Corbin shot her made her sigh in frustration. "Well, I do. You should have seen him today."

"No, thank you."

"Corbin." She watched as he dumped the cheese noodles from the pan into a bowl and set it on the table. "Feeling sorry for someone is not the same as being attracted to them."

"But I'm betting that was his plan. He knows how you are—"

"How am I?"

"Big-hearted," he said with a frown. "Kind and considerate." Such sweet compliments. "Most people are."

"No, many people are not. He's trying to soften you up, Ivey, and I don't like the idea of him waiting around to catch you alone. It's stalkerish."

"I wasn't alone. I was with Hope."

"What if the next time you aren't?"

That...did give her something to think about. "Geoff isn't a threat," she assured him. But it would be horribly uncomfortable to be alone with him.

"Let me guess." Corbin folded his arms. "He wants to be *friends*."

Wow, nailed it. "He, um, did mention that."

Rolling his eyes, Corbin called out again, "Justin?"

"Be right there."

"I'll go check on him," Ivey said. She needed a minute to think without a guy confusing her.

On her way past him, Corbin caught her arm, drawing her to a halt. He looked frustrated and determined as he stared into her eyes. His gaze dipped to her mouth, and then he was kissing her again. This, she decided, was much easier than debating what to do about Geoff.

"Blech," Justin said as he headed for the table.

They immediately broke apart. Corbin looked nonplussed, as if he'd forgotten himself.

Flustered, Ivey patted his chest and turned to Justin. "You think kissing me is gross?" She hauled him close and loudly smooched his cheek, enjoying the way he snickered and wiggled.

When she let him go, Justin surprised her by hugging her hard again. That was the second freely given hug she'd gotten from him, and it meant just as much as the first.

Over Justin's head, she shared a very contented smile with Corbin. "I'm starved and this smells delicious. Let's eat."

Chapter Nine

L ang went perfectly still when Hope, trying to be casual and failing, removed her cover-up and dropped it on the boat seat behind her. It had been enough of a surprise that she'd joined him in the cover-up with her slim legs showing. *Beautiful* legs.

Trying not to stare, unwilling to embarrass her or to upset her with too much interest, he'd given thanks for the reflective sunglasses he wore.

She'd hastily slipped on her own wide sunglasses and asked with a smile, "Ready?"

Wasn't easy, but he'd found his tongue. "Yup. Here, let me carry that." He took her oversize tote bag from her and, going for a nonthreatening move, put his hand lightly to her back.

She hadn't moved away, and his thoughts had been spiraling ever since.

Now, alone on the boat out in the middle of the lake, seeing her in a swimsuit—an insanely modest suit that covered as much as it could—he felt like a high school boy headed behind the bleachers with his first serious girlfriend.

She appeared to be holding her breath, so he slowed the boat until they merely idled over the main body of the lake, then gave her his attention. He even pushed his sunglasses to the top of his head, which made her cheeks bloom with color.

"You look amazing, Hope."

Her tongue slipped out over her lips. "You like it? It's new."

Tenderness nearly overtook sexual interest. Hope looked soft, but she had strength. The innocent expectation in her eyes nearly leveled him. He knew in that moment that he would do everything in his power to see that she was never hurt again.

He'd start with helping her discover her own empowerment. She had it; it was there in her intelligence and her generous nature, and with her desire to move on with her life, to step out of the past and explore the future without fear.

For too long, she'd convinced herself otherwise.

"Yeah, I like it." Seeing her relief, he added softly, "You have killer legs, lady. You should show them more often."

She licked her lips again. "You know why I don't."

"Yeah," he answered softly. "I know." Making sure they were far enough away from other boaters, he half turned toward her. "But it's just you and me out here, and you can trust me."

"I do," she said in a breathless rush. She, too, glanced around, but the few other boaters on the lake paid them no attention. "I was thinking..."

Though his muscles clenched, Lang waited quietly.

"Would you want to kiss me?" Before he could answer, she rushed on. "*Just* a kiss. I want to, and I think I can, but I'm not sure—"

"Just a kiss," he repeated, already standing from the driver's seat, taking a step toward her. He drew a slow breath. *Don't mess this up*, he warned himself. He didn't want to give her too much time to think about it, concerned that she'd become anxious,

or even start to dread it, so he touched her chin to lift her face
and lightly brushed his mouth over hers.

The simple kiss packed a hell of a wallop, at least on his end.
He wasn't at all sure how Hope felt about it.

When he straightened away, she still had her eyes closed.
Smiling, he stroked his fingers over her hair. It was every bit as
silky as he'd imagined. "Hope?"

She swallowed. "That was...fine." Her eyes fluttered open.
"Nice, actually."

"I'm glad." *Don't push it. Don't push it.* Retaking his seat, he
asked, "Fast ride or slow?"

With a suddenly blank expression, she asked, "What?"

The grin almost got away from him. "Want me to drive fast
or slow? The lake's not crowded, so we can either cruise like
we've been doing, or you can settle into the seat, get a hold of
something, and I can show you how much power she has."

Her smile flitted into place. "Fast," she decided. Dropping
into the passenger seat beside him, she braced her feet and said,
"Ready when you are."

That did interesting things for legs, showing the slight muscles
and emphasizing her trim ankles. She was such a small woman...
and she was having such an incredible impact on his life.

Grinning with her, he said, "Hold on," then slowly accelerated
until the wind whipped back her hair and she laughed out loud.
They cut through waves with only a few bounces. Overhead,
hawks soared. Atop fallen logs, flat turtles sunned themselves.

For twenty minutes, he drove them around, keenly aware
of Hope's upturned face, the way the sunshine glinted on her
glossy hair and the utterly serene smile on her lips.

He'd had a few serious girlfriends in his lifetime where love
seemed possible, but he'd never felt anything like this. With
Hope, all the emotions were richer, warmer, sharper.

As he neared the cove at the far end, he slowed considerably. A crane, standing with wings spread, watched them warily. Along the rocky shoreline, a large carp glided just beneath the surface.

Hope stood to look over the windshield. "I've lived here for four years now, and I've never seen this part of the lake."

"Parts of it are shallow." Elm tree branches spread out overhead, shading the area. "I can only go so far into the cove without risking damage to the prop."

"It's so pretty, isn't it?"

In profile, she looked even more delicate. He visually traced her face, from her smooth brow to her inky lashes to the slightly upturned nose and parted lips. He didn't mean to, but he cared for her, he wanted her, so it seemed natural to look at her body, too.

Glancing at him, her smile started to fade. "Lang?"

Damn. Trying to cover his interest, he asked, "Did you put on sunscreen? I don't want you to burn."

Not fooled but apparently not worried, either, she nodded. "I did. I wasn't sure how long we'd be out, so I brought more, just in case."

"Want me to drop anchor here? We could swim."

Her eyes flared. "Here?" Looking around at the irregular shoreline, the towering trees and the dark water, she frowned. "I don't think I'm quite that adventurous."

"Is there anywhere else on the lake you'd be more comfortable?"

"Is there anywhere without fish?" she teased. "No, I'll just observe this time. Is that okay?"

"Hey, whatever you want."

"You should still swim, though. I don't mind."

"Then how about you sit on the swim deck and I'll just take a quick dip?" Hopefully the cold water would have a head-clearing effect.

"The swim deck?" Curiously, she looked around again.

"There in the back. It's made low to skim the water so it's

THE SUMMER OF NO ATTACHMENTS   155

easier to get in and out of the boat." Nonchalant, he turned off
the motor, stood and stripped off his shirt.

He was very aware of Hope's gawking. The sun on his shoulders felt good, but Hope's interest felt better.

Removing the heavy anchor from a locker beneath a seat, he
stepped up to the bow and attached the rope to a cleat.

"You're good at that," Hope said, moving closer to watch as
he secured it. "Is that a special knot?"

He grinned. "The loop in the rope fits in and around the
cleat." Enjoying her attentiveness, he took a moment to explain
the various parts of the boat and how to anchor it. "We'll drift
a little, but not enough to take us too close to the shore."

She eyed his chest. "Are you, um, going to put on a life jacket
or anything?"

"I can swim, but if it'll make you feel better—"

"Yes, please." She lifted her chin. "If you drown, what would
I do?"

"Drive the boat for help?"

Already shaking her head, she said, "I couldn't. I've never
driven a boat."

"After my swim, I'll teach you." They could go slow until
she got comfortable. With any luck, she'd enjoy boating enough
that they could go out more often.

Her lashes lifted and her dark blue gaze locked on his. "Okay,
but before you jump in…" She inched nearer. "Would you mind
giving me another kiss?"

Lang groaned, but again, he didn't want her to change her
mind so he lightly took her shoulders in his hands and drew
her closer. "I will do anything you want, okay? You only need
to tell me."

"Thank you. I want—"

He put his mouth to hers, a little more firmly this time, a little
more leisurely. Her shoulders felt small, her skin satiny, warm
from the sun. She held herself still but breathed faster.

Just as he was lifting his head, her small hand flattened against his chest. Keeping a tight rein on his expanding lust, he teased his mouth against hers.

Still she didn't move away. Ever so lightly, he touched his tongue to her bottom lip.

Drawing a deep breath, Hope whispered with wonder, "I like kissing you."

"Probably not as much as I like kissing you." Which meant he needed to get a grip before he pushed too fast. "I think I should take that dip now, okay?"

She nodded. "Okay."

Snagging up a swim belt and buckling it around his waist, Lang stepped to the swim platform and jumped in. Cold water closed over his head, but thanks to the belt, he popped right back up. Refreshed but still turned on, he folded his arms over the platform and smiled up at her. "Come on. Sit and talk to me."

Gingerly, she stepped onto the platform and lowered herself to sit, but kept her feet tucked to the side. "You're sure there aren't any snakes or big turtles or anything?"

"If there were, I scared them away with my splash."

She smiled, peeked over the side and finally, with a load of caution, dipped her feet into the water. "It's cold."

His elbow touched her knee. At thirty years old, he shouldn't even have noticed that, but he noticed everything about Hope, down to the smallest detail. "It's not too bad. By mid-July it'll be like bath water."

"You're used to lakes, aren't you?"

"We were always around water. Corbin and I learned to swim when we learned to walk. We could spend all day in the water, but Mom wouldn't let us be there by ourselves." He grinned. "She likes to hover."

Hope looked up at the sun. "Did she swim, too?"

"Occasionally." He shrugged. "More often than not, she'd

bring a book to read in the shade, only looking up to yell at us for something."

"Who got in trouble more?"

"In the water? That'd be me, but only because I was always hot-dogging. You know, doing backflips off the dock, or climbing too high in a tree."

Hope laughed. "It's a wonder you survived."

"Being around Justin now, I see it all differently. I'm surprised my mom didn't go nuts."

"He's a great kid."

"Yeah, he is." Lang saw how the heat had flushed her face. "You sure you don't want to get in?"

"Not this time. I'll have to work up to it."

"Then I should probably climb back in." He didn't bother with the little drop-down ladder, and instead hoisted himself up with his arms and plopped down heavily beside her. Lake water sprayed over her legs and arms, and a puddle beneath him snaked over to soak her bottom.

She laughed.

And he *had* to kiss her again. This time, he had her full participation. As if she'd been anticipating that reaction from him, her arms came up around his neck.

Scorched. That's how he felt. And a little lost.

Why hadn't he known a kiss could be like this?

Things had advanced quicker than he'd dared to hope, and he was pondering the best way to enjoy her interest without taking advantage of her lack of experience, when suddenly she jerked away with a screech.

His heart sank as she jerked her feet up and out of the water.

"Something bit me!"

Wait...*what?* That was so far from what he'd expected, Lang didn't quite understand. And he was still breathing too fast.

Hope gave him a shove. "Something's in the water."

"There are all kinds of things in the water."

"Yes, I know that." Exasperated, she stared down at the water again. "It's just that I've never got *in* there."

"You're not afraid of bugs," he pointed out.

"I can *see* bugs. But in that dark water…"

He shook his head, as much to clear it as to deny any danger. He started to question her, but the outraged expression on her face as she peered down into the lake did him in. His choked laugh brought her pointed attention shooting back to him. The signs of humor made her eyes narrow.

That only made it funnier.

She pushed him again, without much heat, then her lips twitched. "I'm serious. Something nibbled my toe."

"Are you okay?" he asked around a smile.

"Yes." She looked at her foot. "All my toes are still where they belong." With suppressed humor, she admitted, "It just startled me."

He curled his hand around her small foot. "No damage done." He glanced into the lake. "There." He pointed at the silvery reflection of a fish. "It's just a little blue gill."

"Aw. It's kind of cute, isn't it?" Keeping her feet on the platform, her arms around her knees, she studied the fish, then glanced at him again. "It could have been something else."

Damn, but she delighted him. "You taste so good," he teased, "I can't blame the fish."

Her expression changed, turned heated. "I think you taste good, too. I liked kissing you, Lang."

"I'm glad. If you want, we can do a lot more kissing."

"With no other expectations?"

"You're in charge. If you ever want more, you'll let me know. Otherwise, kissing is it."

This smile was different. It was a smile of relief and anticipation. A smile of trust.

A smile of power. "Thank you."

Lang knew he'd just lost a big chunk of his heart.

★ ★ ★

Ivey saw the hands of the wall clock tick past 9:00 p.m. She really needed to head home, but she also hated to go. Seated on the floor behind the coffee table, she and Justin competed in a video game. So far, he was skunking her. Badly. Of course, he'd played before and she hadn't, but still…he was only ten. Why couldn't she grasp the movements? Her driver kept wiping out, while Justin's gathered points right and left.

Sitting behind her on the couch, Corbin said, "He's really good at this."

"Hush, you'll distract me." And at that moment, she wiped out for the final time. "Argh!" Dropping the controller, she collapsed back against Corbin's legs and groaned dramatically.

Triumphant, Justin crowed, "I won!"

"Yes, you did." Ivey mussed his hair. "Done in by a child!"

"I'm ten, not a child."

"I'm more than three times your age," she pointed out. "That makes you a kid."

"Huh-uh." Coming up to his knees, his hands on the cushion beside Corbin, Justin said, "My mom said I could take care of myself now."

Silence landed like a thunderclap. Ivey stared at him, horrified, then she reassessed. Surely his mother had said that in some logical context, maybe in encouragement. "She did, huh?"

"Yeah, she said only babies wanted their moms to take care of them."

The horrid disclosure made Corbin stiffen even more. Justin said it in such a nonchalant way, there was no doubting the truth.

"Let's see," Ivey mused, hoping to free Corbin from his tension-induced disbelief. "I'd say you're old enough to take responsibility for some things. Like brushing your teeth without being told? And making sure Daisy has food and water?"

Justin shrugged. "Mom said I could watch myself, too."

Corbin practically jumped on that. "Your mom left you alone?"

"Sometimes." Full of energy, Justin bounced on his knees. "When she had to work or if she had a date. But it's okay cuz I'm ten, now."

Tension vibrated off Corbin. "Where did Darcie work?"

"I don't know." Justin turned as Maurice and Daisy trotted over to him, trailed by the puppies. "She worked at night, though."

Gently, Ivey asked, "When it was dark?"

"Yeah." He no longer looked at them, choosing instead to focus on the animals. The jubilant victory of moments before seemed forgotten.

Ivey didn't want to press, not with him looking so withdrawn, as if he realized he'd blundered into a sensitive topic.

Corbin must have realized it, too. "Ten is getting up there, but as your dad, I enjoy taking care of you."

Justin shot him a quick look. "You and Mom are different, huh?"

"Yes," he agreed. "Very different." Then he went one step further and said, "I won't ever leave you alone at night."

"Why not?"

"For one thing, it's dangerous."

"Yeah, Mom said the same thing. She told me I should come in and lock the door before it got too dark, cuz if I didn't someone might steal me. But sometimes I'd forget." Hugging Daisy close, he whispered, "The lights in our hall didn't work so it was a little creepy at night."

Gathering himself, Corbin sat forward and asked with admirable calm, "Did you leave your apartment unlocked?"

"No. We kept the key under the mat." A puppy chewed on Justin's shorts, making him smile. "But one time, my mom forgot and took it with her."

Ivey welcomed Maurice into her lap. The old cat always

seemed to know when she was upset and needed affection. "What did you do?"

"I slept in the hall." His brows scrunched as he rubbed the puppy's ear, then he said accusingly, "Mom was mad at *me*, but *she* took the key. She made me stay in after that."

Leaning against Corbin, Ivey looked back and caught his gaze. She hoped to convey her support, her understanding, and she wanted to encourage him to remain cool. He looked…ravaged. And no wonder. Little by little, Justin's tone and expression had changed, the upsetting memory coming out of nowhere, which to her, meant it was an important event.

Corbin being Corbin, he pulled together his control. Neither his tone nor his expression showed how wretched this had to be for him. "How mad was she, son?"

Justin rubbed at his nose, his gaze evasive. "Our neighbor, Doris, saw me and she yelled at Mom real bad. I think that's why she was mad at me."

Justin was only ten, so how could he understand an adult's behavior? How would he know that the problem had been with his mother, not with him?

His mouth trembled. "I didn't mean to make her mad or get her in trouble. I swear! I just didn't know what to do."

Ivey put a hand on his shoulder. She felt so much emotion from Justin, and even more from Corbin. She nearly choked on it, it was so strong and turbulent. "Honey, how come Doris didn't invite you in?"

"She did," he said in a rush. "Doris was always real nice to me, but Mom didn't like her so I wasn't supposed to talk to her. Mom said Doris would call the police on her and they'd take me away." He shot a fearful glance at Corbin. "I didn't want to go away. I didn't know about Dad, though." He concentrated on stroking the dog. "Doris told me not to worry, and she gave me a pillow and blanket and sat out there to talk to me until morning."

"Doris sounds like a very nice neighbor," Corbin said.

"Mom said she was a nasty—" he slid a cagey glance at the adults "—B-word."

Clearing her throat, Ivey tried to think of something to say. Justin beat her to it.

"Mom wouldn't let me have pets, neither. And she didn't play video games or race me or *nothing*." His bottom lip quivered as he picked up steam. "She got mad at me a lot, too, and sometimes...sometimes I didn't know when she'd come home!"

Throat closing, Ivey fought to keep her expression impassive. She didn't want to upset Justin more by reacting too strongly.

Leaning past her, Corbin caught Justin under the arms and hauled him up and onto his lap. He clutched his son close, rocking him a little. "You will always know where I am, and you will never be left alone. Okay?"

"I want to say here forever," Justin said, hugging Corbin just as fiercely.

Knowing she was going to cry, Ivey got quietly to her feet and, holding Maurice, headed for the kitchen to give father and son some privacy. Confused by the sadness, Daisy hastily followed her, which meant all three puppies did, too.

Around the corner, Ivey slid down the wall until her bottom hit the floor. Maurice butted her chin and Daisy snuggled up to her side. For years upon years, she'd relied on animals in happy times and sad. Now was no different. People thought she gave so much to animals. In truth, they gave so much to her. She hugged and kissed each animal in turn, taking the comfort they gave, hoping to give some back in return.

Every time she thought of a little boy left alone, sleeping in a hallway, without his mother's care, her heart crumbled a little more.

She was fighting off the tears when she heard Corbin say, "We talked about this, right? I promised you that I wouldn't let anything happen to you. But you're still worrying?"

There were a few seconds of silence where she imagined Corbin smoothing Justin's hair, reassuring him, then Justin mumbled, "It's just that I like it here a lot more. It's fun."

"For me, too."

"And you're really nice."

"I hope so, but I'm also human, which means I might make mistakes here and there." Corbin's tone gentled, and he added, "If I do, it'll be just that—a mistake. It won't mean I don't love you, or that I don't want you here with me."

"Kay."

"Justin…" Corbin hesitated, then forged on. "You can always talk to me. I want you to know that. If you're worried about something, we can work it out."

"But what if you have to go somewhere?"

"I don't have to travel often, and if I did, your Uncle Lang would stay with you until I got back. You'd like that, wouldn't you?"

"Yeah." Justin hesitated, then asked with heartbreaking uncertainty, "You'd always come back, huh?"

"Nothing and no one could keep me away. I promise." There was another small stretch of silence, then Corbin added, "I think you and I need to talk a lot more. There's so much about you I don't know."

"I'm not a baby, I promise."

"No, you're not," Corbin said with affection. "But you are a ten-year-old boy and I don't want you to grow up too soon, okay?"

"I guess."

"Will you promise me that whenever you have something on your mind, you'll let me know?"

"Mom didn't want me bothering her."

"I think your mother had her own issues to work out. I'm very different. I'm already settled, and now we've got this house together."

"And the boat Uncle Lang bought us."

"Yes, and a boat."

"And we've got Daisy."

Ivey heard the smile in Corbin's voice when he agreed. "Daisy is now a part of our family."

"Are Uncle Lang and Ivey family, too?"

"Uncle Lang is my brother, so yes, he's family. Ivey is a very good friend."

"Could she be family?"

Ivey covered her face, her shoulders trembling. Clearly, she shouldn't have been listening in. If she had known they would discuss her, maybe she'd have moved farther away than just the kitchen. Yet here she sat, her heart aching for Justin, feeling sorry for Corbin being put on the spot.

And on pins and needles for his answer.

"Sometimes family isn't related," Corbin explained. "So I think we can call Ivey family."

"Good. Cuz I was worryin' 'bout that."

Bless his little heart. Ivey sniffled.

"Just so you know," Corbin said softly, "I worry sometimes, too. It's the same with Uncle Lang and Ivey. Everyone worries, but it's easier when you share those worries."

"I guess."

That often seemed to be Justin's answer. *I guess.* As if he didn't quite believe what he was being told. What type of life had taught him to be so skeptical at his age?

Understanding that Justin had wound down and wasn't as engaged anymore, Corbin said, "I like it when we have these heart-to-heart conversations."

"What does that mean?"

"It means when we discuss the really important stuff."

"Like how much you love me?"

Ivey stuffed her fist against her mouth to keep from sobbing.

Oh God, Corbin had to be the strongest man alive to be able to bear that without bawling. She definitely wasn't that strong.

"Yes," Corbin said, and there was a note of gruff tenderness in his voice. "I love you very, very much."

Using that same conspiratorial whisper, Justin asked, "Did I make Ivey sad?"

"I think," Corbin said, "that she loves you, too, so she was worried about you being alone."

"She might be cryin'," Justin said. "Babies cry."

"Ivey is definitely not a baby, so you probably shouldn't say that."

"I guess she's cryin' cuz she's a *girl*, huh? That's why."

Corbin laughed. "Now I *know* you shouldn't say that. Ivey is a very strong woman."

"She's still cryin'," Justin pointed out.

"Different people show their emotions in different ways. I hugged you tight because it made me feel better." With a shrug in his tone, Corbin said, "Ivey got a little teary-eyed. It's okay for either of you to cry."

"Do you ever cry?"

"I haven't for a long time. Not since my father passed away." Corbin was silent a moment. "Usually when I feel like crying, I talk to my family. My mother or Lang. Maybe whenever you feel like crying, you could talk to one of us."

"Maybe," Justin promised. "But I won't cry around Ivey, okay?"

"Well, if you ever feel like it, I'm sure Ivey wouldn't mind."

Taking that as her cue, Ivey wiped her eyes and scrambled back to her feet. She peeked around the wall, found father and son watching for her, and so she plastered on a smile. "I wouldn't mind at all, but I do have to admit, if you cry, I'll cry. Heck, if someone on a commercial cries, I usually cry." She lifted a shoulder. "Hope is the same, but our receptionist, Karen? I think you've met her, right? Well, she's a rock. I've never seen her cry."

She realized she was babbling when they both blinked at her. Justin frowned at her critically. "Your nose is real red."

"Yes, I'm what people call an ugly crier."

"I don't think you're ugly," he rushed to tell her. "I think you're real pretty."

Piece by piece, he stole her heart. "You little charmer. Thank you." Her smile actually hurt, because she honestly had more sobbing to do. "I think it's probably time for me to head home."

Just then, Lang opened the door. He wore a huge smile—until he saw Justin on Corbin's lap and the tear tracks on Ivey's face. "Uh-oh." His gaze searched Ivey's face, then worriedly switched to Justin, who hastily rubbed his nose and scrambled off Corbin's lap. Lastly, he looked at his brother.

Quietly he closed the door. "Did I, um, miss something?"

For some reason, maybe because the strain of so much emotion had reached the breaking point, his stricken expression started Ivey snickering. Within seconds, Corbin and Justin had joined her.

They laughed and laughed, which stole the concern out of Lang's eyes and removed her need for more crying. Now she wiped her eyes for a whole different reason.

She suddenly felt wonderful. She loved these people, all three of them, and she didn't think that would ever change.

Wishing she could stay but knowing she needed to get some sleep, she had to call it a night. Bummer, because Corbin's house was starting to feel more like home than her own ever had.

Chapter Ten

The second they stepped outside, Ivey touched Corbin's chest and asked softly, "Are you okay?"

Beneath the porch light, her eyes and nose were still red, her cheeks tracked with tears, and he wanted to hug her as tightly as he had Justin. "Yeah, I am." With one hand he held Maurice's carrier and with the other he kept her close as they started for her car.

She leaned into him, her head on his shoulder. "You amaze me. I'm wrecked, and he's not my son."

"He's with me now, and I won't ever let anything happen to him." Sensing she was about to tear up again, he said, "Actually, I'm encouraged by what happened."

"You are?"

It wasn't easy to explain, but he wanted to share with Ivey. Talking with her seemed as natural as everything else they did. "Justin is starting to open up to me. For the longest time he was too quiet and withdrawn. I got it, I mean, his world had been upended. He was taken away from everything familiar, given over to a man claiming to be his dad. He didn't trust me or anything I said, but he was afraid to tell me so. We were like two strangers living together."

"One of them young and hurt and wary of what was going on?"

"Yes." Justin had been so damned wary. And afraid. "I was set in my ways, blown over to be called Dad and anxious to make up for lost time." He glanced at her. "I found that none of that could be rushed."

"And now?" she asked.

"Now, he's telling me his worries. He's sharing some of what he went through. It eats me up, thinking of the time we should have had together, time I can't get back. But if we talk, if he opens up about the past, we can bridge some of that distance, work through the things that worry him and hopefully make our relationship stronger."

Ivey stopped to stare up at him. Moonlight put a halo around her fluffy hair. "You are absolutely incredible. I've never known anyone like you."

Slowly, he set down Maurice's carrier next to her car in his driveway. "I feel the same about you, Ivey. You've already become a part of our lives." He smoothed her hair, amused when it sprang right back up again, some of the curls tangling in his fingers. "I've got a lot going on right now."

"I know," she rushed to say. "I promise I won't rush you."

Funny, outspoken Ivey. "You can rush me all you want." Bending to her mouth, he whispered, "I like it."

The kiss that followed told him many things. That they'd be incendiary together. That they were inevitable. And that she wanted him as much as he wanted her.

Against her lips, he murmured, "Lang wants to spend Sunday with Justin, which would be the perfect time for us to get together."

"For sex?"

Putting his forehead to hers, he silently laughed, then hugged her close. "Count me on board for that. One hundred percent, okay? But I wouldn't mind taking you out somewhere, too. Dinner or a movie or something."

She kissed his chin, his mouth, then smiled up at him. "I'll cook at my house. If you want to watch a movie, we can stream something." Her open palm moved over his chest, up to his shoulder. "But I really, really want to be with you. I think I'm obsessed lately, because it's all I can think about."

Damn, it was a heady thing to be wanted so much. "Me, too, actually."

Maurice gave an impatient meow. Now wasn't the time to get carried away, not when they'd soon have private time together.

It was getting late, Ivey looked wrung out and she had to work tomorrow, but there was one more thing he needed to discuss with her.

"About Geoff."

Lost, she shook her head. "What about him?"

"I know you said you're not getting back with him—"

"Definitely not."

"But it feels like we have an understanding now, right?"

Her chin angled up. "An understanding?"

Okay, so maybe he jumped the gun on that. Doing a quick mental rewind, he restated, "I want us to have an understanding."

"Meaning what, exactly?"

She didn't sound too keen on it. She might have even sounded a little testy. Screw it. "I think I know what Geoff is up to, even if you may not see it. I don't like the idea of him using friendship as a way to edge back in."

Taking a step back, Ivey folded her arms. "Is it Geoff you don't trust, or me?"

Sensing a trap, he snorted. "Of course I trust you. But Geoff?

No. Not even a little." He drew her closer again. "I could tell you were feeling sorry for him."

"So?" She dropped her arms and leaned into him. "Don't tell me you'd rather I feel sorry for you."

"What? No." The last thing he wanted was anyone's pity. "There's no reason."

"None at all," she agreed. "You strike me as a guy who pushes through problems."

Yeah, not much choice lately. "I do my best. I appreciate having Lang here, and I especially appreciate you." Little by little, her disgruntled expression eased. "You've made everything easier, Ivey. In so many ways."

"I'm glad. I was worried that I might complicate things."

"Never." He tipped up her chin. "So, that understanding? You and me, and no one else." Especially not Geoff.

"No problem." She flagged a hand toward him. "Compared to you, Geoff is still boring."

Why that offended him, he couldn't say, except that it had been a long day filled with emotional upheaval. "So I'm just the better of two choices?"

"Well…yes."

He heard a distinct *duh* in the way she said that. "And if you hadn't met me?"

She leaned in, an impish curve to her mouth, her eyes glittering. "Then I'd have been out seeking a few fleeting moments of excitement." She patted his chest. "But this is better. No risk, and it's all the excitement I can handle."

No risk? Damn it, he didn't like the sound of that, either. "Explain that."

Her shoulders lifted. "Every minute with you is electrifying. It absolutely makes my heart race."

Frustration gathered. "No, I mean that bit about no risk."

"Oh." She edged closer, smiling up at him. "I trust you. I trusted you almost from the moment we met. Somehow I just knew you were a good man. I think it was how you dealt with Justin. How you are with Daisy. And how you looked at me, like you really saw me."

"Of course I see you." He cupped a hand to the back of her head, keeping her mouth close. "Most men are aware of beautiful women." The way she scoffed at that bothered him. "You don't think you're beautiful?"

Her mouth twisted to the side. "Let's be real, okay?"

"Yeah, let's do."

"I know what I look like. I have mirrors, and I have a hairbrush."

That wild, unique, adorable hair… Corbin threaded his fingers into the coiling mass. "Your hair is incredibly sexy."

For that observation he got a rude laugh. "My hair is chaotic. When it rains? Oh my God, it's impossible. Even when I tie it up, pieces shoot out everywhere like it's trying to escape my head."

Damn, she kept him grinning. "Well, I love your hair. I like how it looks and how natural it feels." Saying that, he lightly fisted his hand, crushing a few curls, and then, when he opened his fingers, he watched them tumble free again. "It's silky soft, and I appreciate that you don't load it up with products."

"Products never did any good anyway."

Putting his nose near her temple, he murmured, "It smells good, too."

A little more breathless, she said, "Maybe it's my lotion."

Getting her to accept a compliment was nearly impossible, and yet he found that endearing, too. "It's *you*, Ivey." He touched his tongue to her earlobe, felt her shiver and gently bit. "You always smell so good."

Her hands gripped his shoulders and she tilted her head, making it easier for him to tease her.

"You also have incredible eyes."

Sounding a little dreamy, she asked, "I do?"

"In the sunlight, I can see how green they are, but the gold flecks are there, just waiting, adding a sparkle to your eyes. When the light is dim, like now, the gold expands and takes over."

"Hmm." She breathed more quickly. "I never realized."

"Don't spend a lot of time staring into your own eyes?"

She laughed softly. "No, why would I?"

Instead of answering that, he tilted her back to see her face. "You have an elegant nose."

Her mouth twitched.

"And these lips…" He leaned forward to take a quick taste, coasting his tongue over her bottom lip, and when she opened her mouth, he dipped in for a slower, deeper taste. Voice rougher, he growled, "Your mouth makes me a little nuts."

"Works for me." She put a hand to his jaw, and her amazing eyes searched his. "So you like me a lot?"

Silly, sweet Ivey. "It's safe to say I more than like you."

That truth earned him a radiant smile. "And when I babble? That doesn't put you off?"

A sign of insecurity? He'd put the blame for that on Geoff. "I love how you speak your mind. Anyone who doesn't must be an insecure ass."

"You know, I sometimes wondered. I mean, I do go on, I know that. But I'm not mean about it or anything."

"You're one of the most caring people I've ever met."

Her fingertips touched his mouth. "I'm really glad you think so, because even though that was one of the things I'd planned to work on, now I don't really want to."

"Trust me, Ivey. You don't need to change a damned thing."

"At first, when I was considering how to start over, I'd thought about making changes, but I like me, you know? I like who I am and how I am. I'm overall pretty darned content with who I am."

With good reason. Ivey had it together. Nice house, nice business, respect in her community, a very close friend… "Tell me you have room in that life for a guy with a struggling kid and a wacky brother?"

Sliding her arms around his neck, she gave him a hug. "I love having you guys in my life."

Love. Yeah, he knew he was sinking fast, but how could he not? He hadn't known he needed her until he met her.

And now he couldn't quite imagine facing the future without her.

Soaking in her narrow tub, a scented candle glowing on the edge of the sink and Maurice close by with his catnip mouse, Ivey thought about the day to come. She'd been doing that for more than an hour.

Relaxing. Pampering herself. And anticipating Corbin's visit.

Moisturizing foam drifted around her mostly submerged body. It smelled like lilacs and felt silky to her skin. She'd already buffed her nails and used a deep conditioner on her hair. On her bed, she'd laid out her prettiest matching bra and panties.

Oh, this is nice.

She'd gotten used to speedy showers because Geoff was waiting, yet somehow she knew Corbin would encourage her to take some time for herself.

Because he liked her. As is. A *lot.*

She hugged that knowledge to her, then jumped when her phone rang. Turning to stare at where she'd left it on the closed toilet lid, Ivey frowned.

But it could be Corbin, so she roused herself from her relaxed position, stretched out one arm and snagged the phone.

Not Corbin, but Hope. Ivey answered with a smile. "Hey. What's up?"

"I know you're getting ready for a big date," Hope said. "So I won't keep you. But guess what?"

These days, it could literally be anything. Hope's world was fresh and new, and Ivey had never seen her so happy. "Let's see.

I already know you kissed Lang." Hope had shared that first thing, and it gave Ivey hope that she'd keep pushing forward, and in the process, she'd be able to bury the past. "And Lang kissed you back."

"Don't forget that it was *wonderful*."

Ivey laughed. "How could I forget? That's the best part." Lang had earned a place in her heart forever, regardless of how things eventually rolled out between him and Hope. "So what else has happened?"

"You know he's watching Justin today while Corbin visits you. Well, Lang asked me along! We're going to a movie, then dinner and then to the beach."

The beach was basically a sandy shoreline at the other end of the lake, but a lot of people in the area gathered there at all hours of the day. Sounded like Lang planned to give Corbin plenty of free time. Ivey silently cheered, but because this call was about Hope, she veered quickly back to it. "How fun." The beach would be especially crowded on a Sunday afternoon, so it was a huge step for Hope to go there. "Give me all the details. Movie title, which restaurant and whether or not you're taking that cute bathing suit along…"

"Not just the bathing suit, but I also bought a few floats for us. One is a flamingo—that seems perfect for you."

Ivey laughed. "Oh, I love it! Thank you."

"Mine is this cute tangerine-colored float. I'll use it at the beach, but we'll store them at Corbin's."

"You're really getting into lake life, aren't you?"

"Crazy that I've lived here so long and never realized how fun it could be."

Ivey smiled. It was fun now because of Lang. For that alone, he would always be very special to Ivey.

For fifteen more minutes, she and Hope chatted. Ivey continued to soak, occasionally rubbing the scented bubbles along her arms.

Giving up on his mouse, Maurice circled once, tucked his nose close to his tail and dozed off. Eyeing his fur, Ivey saw that the humidity affected him just as much as it did her. He had little curls everywhere.

Thinking about that made her realize she'd need plenty of time to get her hair in order. So after insisting that Hope catch her up first thing Monday morning, she hung up and reluctantly climbed out of the bath.

She had only an hour before Corbin would show up and she really wanted to look her best.

Corbin arrived five minutes early, not that he was anxious or anything. Ha! He'd thought about Ivey nonstop, about the impression she'd made on his life, and on his son's life.

Unfortunately, another car pulled up to the curb right ahead of him...and he realized it was Geoff.

Recalling Ivey's reaction to his request that she not see Geoff, he forced himself not to overreact. Ivey, with her big heart, didn't see Geoff for the opportunist that Corbin knew him to be. He got out of the car, quietly closed his door and headed for the walkway. Seconds later, Geoff called out to him.

"Hey, you're a friend of Ivey's, right?"

Stopping, Corbin gave himself a second to find a smile and turned. "That's right. And you are?"

"Her boyfriend."

"Ah. Not how she tells it."

Geoff ran a hand through his hair. "Yeah, I meant ex." He eyed Corbin. "I don't recall your name."

"Corbin Meyer." That was as friendly as he could be.

Striding forward, Geoff held out a hand. "Nice to meet you. You're new to town?"

Damn it, he didn't want to engage with the man—but again, Ivey had been prickly over the idea that she and Geoff were friends. "I moved here with my son a few months back." And he'd hooked up with Ivey almost from the start. "My brother is here now, also."

"So you're putting down roots, then."

Wanting rid of me? This smile was more genuine. "That's right."

Pushing his hands into his pockets, Geoff looked toward Ivey's door. "I was just dropping in to see her."

"Bad timing." Lying through his teeth, he said, "We're going out." He would if Ivey preferred it, but he had a feeling neither of them wanted to waste a single minute of their privacy.

Not giving up, Geoff asked, "Yeah? Where to?"

It's called none-of-your-business. Giving him a direct stare, Corbin said, "Usual for a date." Then he stepped away. "I should go, but I'll let her know you stopped by."

"I'll just say hi." Geoff fell into step beside him.

Unbelievable. Irritation growing, Corbin thought about telling him to get lost—and suddenly Ivey's door opened.

Her gaze went from Corbin to Geoff and back again. Smiling, she said, "I was watching for you."

Deliberately, Corbin leaned in and brushed his mouth over hers. As placidly as he could manage, he flagged a hand at Geoff. "He dropped in to see you, but I told him I had dibs on your time." She flushed, and that made him smile. "You look beautiful, by the way—as always." He realized that she'd put on makeup and that her hair was smoother than usual.

"Thank you." She touched her hair. "I tried."

Corbin laughed. Trust Ivey to say the most unexpected things.

With an exaggerated look of apology, she glanced at Geoff. "Sorry you made the trip for nothing, but we really do have plans." She touched her hair again. "And damn it, the humidity is already working against me."

Geoff and Corbin both rushed to reassure her. That Geoff was louder really irked Corbin, but again, remembering how she'd reacted when he'd tried to warn her about Geoff's motives, he stepped back and let her handle things.

"Thank you, both, but you're terrible liars. I can feel my hair getting bigger. Not that it matters now." With a sound that was part sigh, part huff, she turned to Geoff. "Next time you want to visit, please call first, okay?"

"Whenever I do, you say you're busy," Geoff complained.

Corbin barely banked his smile. Ivey was busy nearly every day after work...with him.

She shot Corbin a long look, then moved two steps closer to Geoff. It was ludicrous the way she lowered her voice, because Corbin still heard every word.

"Geoff, we talked about this. I told you I'm involved now, so yes, my free time is extremely limited."

"Sorry." After sending an accusatory glance at Corbin, Geoff rolled a shoulder. "I just wanted to talk."

Ivey appeared equal parts annoyed and sympathetic. She touched Geoff's arm. "I'll call you tomorrow during my break, okay?"

Geoff slowly smiled. "That'd be great, honey, thanks."

"Just to talk, Geoff."

"All right."

"Okay, then. Well..." She stepped back to Corbin. "I'll let you go."

Corbin almost laughed when she latched onto his arm and hauled him into her house. She closed the front door with a click, slid the lock into place and gave him a blinding smile.

Wary of that quick mood switch, Corbin asked, "You're grinning...why?"

"Because you were so nice. You trusted me to handle it and I appreciate that. As you just saw, Geoff can be an ass, but for some reason, he's currently being a very sad ass and I'm glad you didn't pile on."

"If he's sad," Corbin said, still not convinced that anything the other guy did was genuine, "it's because he's only now realizing what he lost."

"Me?" Ivey asked.

"Yeah, you." With his hands on her shoulders, he stepped up against her. "Makes me *almost* feel sorry him." Or not. He knew Geoff wouldn't give up, and in fact, it was kind of creepy the way he'd just shown up.

If Corbin hadn't been there, would Ivey have let him in? He hoped not. "So...you're calling him tomorrow?"

She put her small cool palm to his jaw. "Yes, because apparently I need to make things clear one last time."

"Like?"

"Like I'm no longer interested, I'll never again be interested, and while I'll be polite when we run into each other, I have no intention of hanging out with him."

That did a lot to put Corbin at ease. "Good." He leaned in to kiss her, but suddenly Maurice twined around his ankles. He paused to acknowledge the cat. "Hey, bud, did you miss me?"

"Wow." Ivey smiled down at her pet. "He never greets guests."

Maurice was smart enough that he probably hid when Geoff was around. Kneeling down, Corbin scratched under his chin. "Yeah, we're pals, aren't we, Maurice? Sorry, my man, but I didn't bring Daisy."

Maurice gave him an accusing stare, then sauntered off.

"Oh man, now he's going to pout."

Corbin grinned at her. "I love the relationship you have with your cat."

"Me, too." She gave him an apologetic smile. "Let me grab him a toy to keep him occupied, okay? I'll be right back."

He watched as Ivey opened a cabinet and took out a soft cloth fish, a ball and a squeaky mouse. Maurice looked away when she put them by his front paws.

Propping a shoulder to the wall, Corbin grinned at her efforts as she tried to entice the cat with the squeaky mouse. Finally it worked. Almost reluctantly, Maurice batted the thing, then glared at it as it bounced away, squeaking several times. He stared, twitched his heavy backside, then lunged after it.

Hurrying back to Corbin, Ivey grabbed his hand. "Come on." All but hauling him down the hall, she drew him into her bedroom and closed the door.

Trying not to grin, Corbin asked, "In a hurry?"

"Of course I am." She stared at him with a frown. "Aren't you?"

There couldn't be another woman like Ivey Anders. "Yes." He closed the space between them. "I've wanted you from the first minute we met."

"Same." She slid her hands under the hem of his shirt, then up and over his chest. "I knew you would feel like this."

The touch of her small, capable hands ignited him. "Like what?"

"Perfect." Going on tiptoe, she pressed the shirt up until she bared much of his chest.

She brushed her lips over his heated skin and Corbin burned even more. To make it easier for her, he jerked the shirt over his head and tossed it aside.

"Mmm," she responded. "You are absolutely delicious."

Choking on a laugh, Corbin fingered the hem of her shirt. "How about we have some equity here?"

She flicked her gaze up to his. "I probably should since I went to the trouble of digging out my prettiest underthings."

"Tease." He kissed her thoroughly, his hands in the bouncing mass of her hair, and when she melted a little, he stroked a hand over her waist, under her shirt and around to the small of her back. "You have the softest skin."

Eyes closed, head tipped back, she asked, "Compared to what?"

With another soft laugh, Corbin kissed her throat and eased the shirt up. He could just imagine what she'd say if he told her again how good she smelled, or how her deeper breathing affected him. Wanting her naked, needing to touch her all over, he pulled her shirt up and off.

The bra she'd bragged about was pale pink lace, sheer enough to expose her already tightened nipples. He levered back to look at her. Her shorts rode low on her hips—and what gorgeous hips they were. Generously rounded, they provided a nice contrast to her smaller waistline.

Without him asking, she pushed down the shorts and stepped free. Striking a pose, she said, "See? All matchy-match."

He wanted to joke with her, but he couldn't. He was too turned on.

"Your turn," she prompted. "Equity and all that."

"Yeah, no problem." With haste, he toed off his sneakers, unsnapped and unzipped his jeans, then pushed them carefully past his erection. No sooner had he tossed them to the end of the bed—where the condom in his pocket would be handy—than Ivey was against him, kissing him hungrily, her hands on his rear.

Okay, then.

Taking her boldness as an invitation, he paid her back in kind, opening his broad hands over her lush backside, pulling her in close against him. They both groaned softly at the contact.

He was kissing her, losing himself a little, when suddenly her bra loosened. Looking at her, he realized she'd been busy, reaching back with one hand to open the closure so that the bra cups slipped.

She licked her lips and, watching his face, shrugged the straps over her shoulders and let it drop between them.

Overwhelmed with her honest need, he brought a hand around to her left breast, caressing her, weighing her in his palm. "You are so beautiful."

"My boobs?"

No, she wouldn't get a laugh from him this time. "All of you, Ivey. Every single inch." He moved his thumb over her nipple. "I've never wanted another woman as much as I want you."

She drew in a shuddering breath…and skimmed out of her panties.

He should slow her down, but he couldn't. Not this time. Later, he'd show her how satisfying it would be to savor their time together, but now he wanted her too much.

He removed his boxers, then moved with her to the bed. With every touch and kiss, in the back of his mind he knew this was stolen time. Their moments together would be limited, and he didn't know how he could survive that. Not when everything about her was so perfect.

As he bent to her nipple, first to lick and then to suck, she made a low, rough sound. Hours. He wanted hours to do just this. Enough time to show her…what?

That they were meant to be?

It sure felt that way to him. Yes, he was rushing things, but so what? Already he felt like Ivey was an integral part of his life. The easy part, when everything else felt so damned complicated.

She arched up against him in silent demand—which was surely a huge concession for Ivey, given how she usually spoke her mind. Knowing what she wanted, he lightly moved his hand over her body, discovering all her curves, the texture of her skin, the dip of her stomach and the rise of her hips, until he pressed his palm between her thighs.

Going still for a heartbeat, Ivey groaned.

She was wet and hot, and as he explored her, he discovered she was ready, too.

He had two fingers in her, his mouth at her breast, when she clenched hard and demanded, "*Now*, Corbin."

No argument from him. He reached for his jeans, located the condom in a back pocket and tossed them away. With quickened breath, Ivey watched as he rolled it on, then she opened her arms to him.

He settled over her, took her mouth in a deep, tongue-thrusting kiss and slowly eased into her.

God, so perfect.

Again, Ivey rushed him, her legs coming up and around him, holding him to her as she began to move. Caught up in her urgency, he forgot about control and matched her frenzied pace. Her hands were all over him, her mouth hungry, the sounds she made as sexy as everything else about her, and well before he expected it, she put her head back and groaned out a long, strong climax.

Corbin watched her, soaking in every second of her pleasure, and the moment she eased, he gave into his own release.

Chapter Eleven

"You were even better than I'd hoped for."

Gradually getting his eyes open, Corbin grinned. Leave it to Ivey to say something so unexpected. He came up to his elbows and caught her dreamy smile. "Glad to hear it."

She peeked open one eye, sighed, then closed it again. "Now would be a good time for you to reciprocate."

"Is that so?" He smoothed her wildly tumbled hair, thinking that he could easily be with her forever like this. "Should I tell you how incredible you are?" Getting into that theme, he shifted to the side of her, relieving her of his weight but drawing her close. "Or how you shot my control?"

"Did I?" She seemed very pleased by that. "Was it the matching bra and panties? I always heard guys like that sort of thing."

Now that he wasn't strung so tight with lust, he gave her the laugh she deserved. "It wouldn't have mattered what you wore, Ivey, though I have to admit, they're pretty." He brushed his mouth over hers. "It was you, lady. Everything you do makes me want you more."

"Since I only have two matching sets of undies, I'm relieved. I'd hate to have to spend time shopping."

"I'd rather you spend that time with me."

She stared up at him, her green eyes sparkling. "Me, too."

Suddenly, Corbin had a thought. He gave brief consideration to the ramifications and decided to go for it. "Wouldn't it be nice if we had more private time?"

"Well...yes." She stared at his chest and trailed her fingertips over his shoulder. "But I understand that you have a lot of obligations, and naturally Justin needs to be a top priority."

Yeah, that was one of the things he appreciated most about Ivey, how she truly got his situation and all it entailed. "Wouldn't it also be nice if Daisy and Maurice didn't have to be separated?"

Her expression turned defensive. "I'm not giving up my cat."

"Of course not. I wouldn't ask you to." He squeezed her for being so silly and figured he better get to the point. "What if both you and Maurice came to my house?" The way her eyes widened, he rushed to explain. "You work nearly every day, so it'd mostly be for dinner and sleeping anyway."

Her eyes flared even more. "You want me to move in with you?" Shoving up to an elbow, she squeaked, "You want me to *sleep* with you? At your house?"

Her breasts were a huge distraction as he tried to figure out how to word things in a way most likely to gain her agreement. "You wouldn't have to give up your place or anything, but you could come directly to my house after work. I'm closer to the clinic, anyway. If you're worried about privacy, you can use the master on the main floor."

Her mouth opened and then closed. She blinked fast.

"Look at it this way, Maurice will have company when you're working, and he'll get to hang out with Daisy."

Ivey looked around at her bedroom. "I'd have to bring some of my clothes—wouldn't that bother you?"

"How could it, when you make me feel so good?" Gently cupping her shoulder, he pressed her back in the bed, leaned over and lightly kissed her mouth. "You make things better, Ivey. I'm thrilled to have Justin with me, but I look at the chaos my life has become and it's overwhelming. I'm not just responsible for me anymore, but for someone far more important."

Her smile showed understanding and more. "Your son."

"He's the world to me, but damn, it's enough to keep me up at night." Using only his fingertips, he tucked back her hair. "Then you come around, and somehow it all seems to click into place. I see tomorrow and next week and next month, and I see it all working out."

"You'll make it so. You're such an amazing guy."

Grinning, he touched his forehead to hers. "See? That's part of where I get that optimism. Other than my own mother and brother, I don't think anyone has had that much faith in me."

"I like your mother already."

"Good, because she's going to love you."

Uncharacteristically reserved, especially for a woman who'd hastily stripped and demanded sex, Ivey asked, "Will I meet your mother?"

"She'll show up soon, I'm sure. She's already shown more restraint than I thought she had." In fact, Corbin decided a warning might be in order. "Just so you know, my mother is a louder, more domineering version of my brother. She expects a lot from Lang and me, but usually gives more of herself. She sometimes speaks without thinking—"

"Oh good. We'll have that in common."

"—and she's a hugger. If she doesn't hug you, it means something."

"Like what?"

"Don't worry about it." Within minutes of meeting Ivey, he

imagined his mother would be squeezing her tight. "I promise, you'll be hugged so much, it'll start to annoy you."

That sexy mouth of hers quirked. "I'll persevere." She traced his collarbone. "You're not worried about Justin seeing us together?"

"No. Don't ever think that." Corbin cupped her cheek in his hand. "You're a good influence. With you, he sees how a healthy, independent, motivated woman should be."

Her eyes going incredibly soft, Ivey whispered, "Thank you."

"He needs to sort things out in his own mind, in his own way, but I want to help him however I can. Saying to him that his mother fell short wouldn't be right, especially since I have no idea of why she's done the things she's done." In his heart, it didn't matter. She'd slighted his son, kept Corbin from him, and for that he'd never forgive her. But in his head, he knew he shouldn't judge Darcie too harshly, because he'd grown up with incredible advantages. Not just security, but the solid love and understanding of his family.

"I've wondered that, too," Ivey said. "I'm guessing she didn't have an easy life?"

"Honestly, I don't know. We only dated casually a few times. When Darcie's family moved away, I barely noticed." His mouth twisted. "Now I realize she must have been pregnant."

"And you were only seventeen?"

"Yeah… I believe that happened on the first date." But there was no point to rehashing the past. "I see no problem with Justin knowing you and I are in a relationship." More and more, he realized the truth. "You're the whole package, Ivey. Strong in the most important ways, accomplished and respected and settled in your independence, with a house of your own. But you're also compassionate, energetic and funny. There's absolutely nothing about you that could negatively influence my son."

"You see the best in me." Her smile wobbled, but she lifted her chin. "Thank you."

He saw what was there, what anyone with eyes and even the smallest amount of perception noticed within minutes of meeting Ivey. "Will you stay with me?"

"I'd like that, yes. As you said, I'll have my own house available if either of us needs a break." She peeked up at him. "Promise you'll tell me if, after a few days, you need some space?"

"All right." But he knew he wouldn't.

"Good." She laced her arms around his neck. "And I'll tell you if I do."

His good mood slipped. "You think we'll get on your nerves?" Other than the sleeping arrangement, things wouldn't be that different from what they'd done the past week.

"No, but I don't want to tie you down, so I'm trying to be fair. Let's tackle it one commitment at a time, okay?"

He'd have her with him, and that was the most important part, so he nodded. "Got it." Not to push his luck, but he asked, "Do you think we could start tonight?"

"Um...no." She laughed and gave him a hug. "I'll have to get some things together. But as soon as I can manage it, okay?"

"I'll help however I can."

By the time July rolled around, Ivey had all but moved in for good. Two days after Corbin had asked her to stay with him, she'd managed to get her necessities to his house. Once or twice a week, she brought over a few more things.

And now, it truly felt as if she was part of their family.

A fun perk was that she and Hope saw more of each other, because they all got together often for dinners, boat rides and even quiet conversation around a bonfire. Whenever the guys were busy, she and Hope would relax on their floats in the lake. Her life felt better, more relaxed and easy, than it ever had before.

It was a hot summer evening and Ivey had just showered and changed using the master bedroom, which was where she kept her ever-growing wardrobe from home. Maurice generally slept on the bed in that room, but he didn't seem to mind that Ivey wasn't there.

Though Justin tried taking Daisy to bed with him, she always ended up back in the laundry room with her puppies. They seemed to have gotten comfortable there, as if they considered it their own private room.

All during the day, though, the dogs kept close to Justin, following him as if he were the Pied Piper. Justin loved it, and it did make it easier for Corbin to get back to work.

The pups were now big enough for homes of their own, but no one mentioned that, so neither did Ivey. The thought of parting with them didn't feel right. She was pretty sure Justin felt the same way.

The kitchen was empty when she walked in, but she heard everyone out on the deck. She went through the dining room and out to the covered area. The scent of barbecued ribs on the grill filled the air. Lang stood cooking with Hope sitting nearby. Her friend wore her swimsuit with a beach towel around her waist. Her hair, still damp, was slicked back from her face. She now had a light tan and a perpetual smile on her face.

Corbin reached out a hand to Ivey. Feeling lazy and relaxed, she went to him, and he tugged her into his lap. Maurice stretched out in the sun near the railing so he could keep an eye on Justin and the dogs playing in the yard below.

It was a picture-perfect evening and Ivey knew she was more content than she'd ever been before.

She glanced at Lang and Hope, saw that they were busy chatting quietly and whispered to Corbin, "Geoff called me again today."

Though his expression darkened, his tone was still easy and relaxed when he said, "That's getting to be a habit of his."

"He hasn't called that many times." In the past month, he'd only pestered her three or four times. Since she wasn't at her house very often, she had no idea if he'd tried stopping by there again. She hoped not, but because she always kept their exchanges brief, she hadn't asked him.

Ivey got comfortable with her head on Corbin's shoulder. "I think he's finally grasping reality."

Fingers teasing up and down her spine, Corbin asked, "What makes you think so?"

"I told him that he's a great guy—and, Corbin, overall, he is. I also told him that I'm a pretty terrific person." She kissed his throat. "I know that because you tell me so often."

"Because it's true."

Ivey smiled. She was getting used to Corbin's nonstop praise. Used to it and enjoying it. "Then I explained that he and I just weren't terrific together. My faults irked him. His faults irked me. And the things we liked about each other weren't good enough to make up for that."

"Not like it is between us?"

Teasing him, she asked, "Are you telling me I have faults, now?"

He laughed. "I meant my faults."

She poked him in his firm stomach. God, she loved his body. But it was his attitude, his drive, his love for his family and his determination to bring it all together that really got to her. "I know I have my own, too. But that's it, you know? I *can* tease about it, because we complement each other so much." She'd realized that after the first week had gone so well. Then the second week had been even better. Now every day with him only reinforced the idea that a good relationship was based on compatibility.

Corbin started to reply, when suddenly Justin called out, "Dad, there are ducks on the dock!"

"Hey," Corbin called after him, seeing him running down the slight incline toward the water. "Justin, don't go on the dock without me."

With Daisy and the puppies yapping after him, Justin didn't reply.

Quickly, Corbin stood Ivey on her feet and moved to the stairs leading down to the yard. "Justin, wait for me!"

Maurice sat up, ears twitching.

Pausing on the grill, Lang asked, "What's happening?"

Ivey followed Corbin, but explained, "I guess Justin isn't supposed to go near the water."

Standing at the railing, Hope said, "Too late!" and they all heard a splash.

"Justin." Corbin was flat out running now, his long legs eating up the distance to reach his son. Ducks squawked, Daisy cowered near a tree and the puppies bounded around in excitement.

Corbin reached the dock, his head jerking around as he searched, and then he, too, went into the water.

Ivey waited, her hand to her racing heart, wondering how she could help, what she should do.

A second later, Corbin called out, "I have him! He's fine."

Releasing a tense breath, Ivey gathered the animals as quickly as she could. Luckily, Lang and Hope had followed. She deposited them into their arms so she could continue on to the dock.

T-shirt sticking to his body, his sodden shorts almost falling off and his head hanging, Justin climbed the ladder and stood on the dock.

Corbin hauled himself out beside him. His mouth was set in a hard line and his expression was grim. For a few seconds he just stood there, hands on his hips, his chest rising and falling with each deep breath. Deep breaths that Ivey assumed were a bid for control of his temper and fear.

"You know the rules, Justin," Corbin finally said, his tone moderate. And yet, as he lifted both hands to push back his hair, Justin flinched away.

"I didn't mean to!"

Dear God. Justin reacted as someone who'd been…struck.

Horrified, Ivey resisted the urge to hug Justin close, to promise him it would be all right. She knew it, but Justin needed to know it, too, and she trusted Corbin to handle it.

Corbin's eyes flared, then he hauled Justin close and held him. Ivey saw him swallow twice before he could speak. "Okay, first. I will *never* strike you, son. Not ever."

Justin didn't so much as move. His hands were down at his sides, his narrow back heaving.

"Second." Corbin levered him back to see his face, and his voice grew gruff. "You scared me to death. The rules are there for a reason. Can you tell me what they are?"

Justin didn't meet his gaze, but he nodded. "I can't go in the water alone." Speaking faster, he said, "But it was an accident! The ducks started flapping their wings and I tripped and just… fell in."

"Which is a good reason never to go near the dock without a life preserver. Not for any reason."

"I wanted to see the ducks," he mumbled.

"I don't care if you see a mermaid. A pot of gold. Even if Frankenstein is swimming by. No matter what, you wait for me or another adult, and you always wear a life preserver. Understood?"

Nodding, Justin let his head drop even more. Ivey thought his chin probably touched his chest.

Unable to bear it but hesitant to interfere, she said gently, "Daisy was startled by all the commotion, and the puppies were running everywhere. I doubt they know how to swim yet."

Popping his head up, Justin stared at her. "She's okay?"

"They're all okay, honey. I gathered them up and now your Uncle Lang and Hope are watching them."

"But you were supposed to watch them, Justin. When you asked to bring them all into the yard, you said you would." Corbin put a hand on his shoulder. "Do you remember that?"

Justin nodded in misery. "I was. But I just forgot."

"I know. You're good with them. But this is one of the dangers of being near a lake. I need you to really understand, okay?"

Water dripped all around the boy. He sniffled, but Ivey didn't think he cried. He peeked up at Corbin. "Are you mad?"

"No." Kneeling down, Corbin used the edge of his hand to lift Justin's chin. "We're all human, remember? We all make mistakes. This was a mistake, and it scared me. Bad."

"Cuz I fell in?"

"Yes."

Justin looked over at the water. "I hit my elbow." With a shaky breath, he added, "It scared me, too, when I sank."

"You're used to swimming with a life preserver, but it's entirely different when you aren't wearing one. One day soon we'll go to the beach and I'll make sure you know how to swim, okay? Not that you can skip the preserver, but it'd be good for you to know, just in case we have any more accidents." Corbin drew his own deep breath. "Though I expect you to remember the rules. Got it?"

Justin nodded.

"You scared me, too," Lang said, joining them on the dock. "Corbin sounded panicked, and that doesn't happen often."

"He did?"

"Damn straight." Lang put a hand on Justin's shoulder. "Dads are like that."

Ivey looked back to see Hope sitting in the grass with the puppies climbing on her.

Obviously giving his brother a chance to collect himself, Lang went on, "Your dad told you how our mom was about us swimming, right? Even when we were older than you are now, she had to know when we were in the water so she could keep tabs on us. What if you'd hit your head instead of your elbow? What if you hadn't been able to hold on to the ladder?"

"There's an undercurrent in the water," Corbin explained. "Where you fall in isn't always where you stay. If you'd gotten knocked out…" He briefly closed his eyes in another bid for calm. "If I hadn't found you right away, I don't know what I'd do."

"Cuz you were scared, huh?"

Little by little, Justin seemed less worried and more fascinated. Ivey wondered at that reaction. Had no one ever shown him so much concern?

"I was terrified." Corbin dropped back to sit on his butt. Muscled arms draped over his knees, he regarded Justin. "I need your word of honor that you won't go near the lake alone. Not for any reason."

Quickly nodding, Justin said, "Not even if Frankenstein is swimming."

Corbin's mouth quirked, then he pulled Justin in for another hug.

"Ah, hell." Lang lifted his nose into the air. "My ribs!" He took off running for the deck stairs.

Wearing a grim expression, Justin watched him go. "Did I ruin dinner?"

"No. It'll be fine." Corbin stood. "Let me see your elbow."

"It's okay."

Corbin lifted his arm anyway, then whistled. "I bet that stings."

Ivey peeked to see, then winced in sympathy. Justin had scraped off the skin and it was already bruising. "You can bend it okay?"

"Yeah." He flexed his arm to prove it.

"Let's you and I go get some dry clothes." Corbin glanced at Ivey. "You'll bring in the animals?"

"Of course." She was so proud of how Corbin had handled things, she felt a little weepy. She could use a minute or two to recoup. "Go on. We'll see you on the deck."

"Thanks." One hand to the back of Justin's neck, Corbin walked off with his son.

Ivey dropped down to sit with Hope on the grass. "That was intense."

Hope continued to corral the puppies as they kept trying to scatter. "Ivey, did your parents ever smack you?"

She put Daisy between them, then gathered a puppy into her lap so Hope would have less to contend with. "Once, when I was young, maybe half Justin's age, I remember wandering off at a campsite. Like Justin chasing the ducks, I went after a butterfly. By the time it flew away for good, I realized I was lost in the woods. Nothing looked familiar."

Hope half turned toward her. "What happened?"

"I sat down and cried. Finally Dad heard me, and a few minutes later he came crashing through the woods like a grizzly bear." Ivey hadn't thought about that long-ago day in forever. "He was shaking, his eyes a little wild." She smiled, remembering how relieved she was to see him. "He shook me, gave me a smack on the butt, then he squeezed me tight for the longest time."

"Somewhat like how Corbin reacted."

"Minus the butt smack." She glanced back at the house and saw Lang industriously transferring ribs to a platter. "Later Dad told me that I'd scared a decade off his life. He lectured me for three days on things that could have happened, and how devastated he and my mom would have been without me."

"Come and get it," Lang called out.

"Your dad's reaction actually sounds kind of nice." Standing, Hope brushed off the grass and then lifted two of the puppies into her arms. "I can't remember my parents ever being that angry with me, not even when they knew I'd done something against the rules."

"Like what?" Ivey gathered up Daisy and the other pup. She really needed to figure out homes for them. Eventually. But... not yet.

"I don't know. Like...sneaking out at night with my sister. There was a party at a neighbor's house, and my father had said she couldn't go. I woke when she was climbing out the window, so I went with her."

As they walked up the incline, Ivey grinned. "Somehow I can't imagine you sneaking away for a party."

"I didn't care about that. Not really. But I worried for Charity."

"Charity is your sister?" Surprised, Ivey said, "You realize you've never shared her name before."

Coming to a dead stop, Hope stared at her. "I haven't?"

"No. You've only ever referred to her as your sister."

Bemused, Hope shook her head. "I guess to me, that was the most important part. She was my sister and she'd…stopped loving me." Her eyes widened as she looked at Ivey again. "Over something that wasn't *my* fault."

"No, it wasn't." Ivey wondered if seeing the way Corbin had handled the situation with Justin had brought up memories for Hope. It must mean something that she'd talk about it now.

"You know—" Hope gave a tremulous smile "—I think I forgive her."

Ivey got them walking again but at a very slow pace. "Why now?"

"Because I'm so happy, I guess." Hope looked up at the deck where Lang carried food to the table. "He hasn't made any promises, and I haven't asked for any. I don't know if this will last another week or…forever. But regardless of what happens between us, I know I'm better now. I know that tomorrow, I can face the day with less anxiety. The past seems less relevant now, so Charity's part in it is less, too." Shaking her head, she gave a crooked smile. "Does that make sense?"

"It makes perfect sense, and I'm so glad." New perspectives, that's what Hope had. Ivey knew her friend would prefer that her romance with Lang continued, but now she knew she could *have* romance, and that was the most important part. "The brothers have certainly taken Sunset by storm."

With a conspiratorial smile, Hope said, "At least for us." They were almost to the deck stairs when she paused. "You're totally, madly in love with Corbin, aren't you?"

Ivey didn't hesitate, but she did lower her a voice to a barely there whisper. It wouldn't do for Corbin to find out before she was ready to tell him. "Am I that transparent?"

"To me, yes." Since they each had their arms full, Hope merely leaned into her, shoulder to shoulder, friend to friend.

Sister to sister.

"You never looked like this with Geoff." Hope glanced around, then down at the dogs. "Here, with Corbin, in this setting and with his son, you're in your element, Ivey. It's as if you were put in the place you were always meant to be."

Oh, be still my heart. "That's such a beautiful way to put it, and pretty darned accurate. Everything about this feels so *right*. So much so, it's almost scary."

"Scary how?"

"Well, unlike some amazingly awesome woman I know, if things ended tomorrow, I don't know what I'd do. Ending things with Geoff felt liberating. With Corbin? It'd be like losing a vital piece of myself."

Lang leaned over the railing. "I can hear you both whispering, and it's making me think it must be something juicy. Either of you care to share?"

"Ah, no," Ivey said with a grin. "Are the ribs burned?"

"A little singed around the edges maybe." He left the railing, and a second later he came down the steps. "Here, let me help." He took the puppy from Ivey, put an arm around Hope, and together they moved up the stairs.

Yes, life here was idyllic.

Now if only she could make it last a lifetime.

That night, in bed, Corbin stared at the ceiling as shadows from the moon shifted and flowed. Arms folded behind his head and Ivey close beside him, he should have been falling asleep.

Instead, he thought about his son, about the things he hadn't known, the things that Justin kept bottled up inside. Life would be so much easier if Corbin could learn all the ugly details at once, rather than be blindsided again and again.

Remembering how Justin had flinched, as if he thought Corbin would hit him—

"Hey." Ivey's small, soft hand moved over his chest. "You okay?"

Uncanny how she always sensed when something was bothering him, more so than anyone else ever had. "I thought you were asleep."

"Something woke me." Sitting up, she balanced on one arm and looked him over. The filtered moonlight played over her cheek, her throat, the thrust of her breasts beneath a large T-shirt. She twisted around to see the clock, then stifled a yawn. "It's after midnight. Why aren't you asleep?"

He didn't want to get Ivey wide-awake, too, so he lowered his arms to hold her and tumbled her onto his chest. "I'm so glad you're here, Ivey." *With me.*

She made a soft sound of exasperation. "I'm glad, but that doesn't answer my question. You can talk to me, you know."

"Tomorrow I will."

"You're awake now, Corbin. Heck, I'm awake, too."

"I'm sorry." He pressed a kiss to the top of her head. "Sleep."

For nearly a minute, she was silent. "Justin is okay."

"Yes." Now. But for ten years…

"Shh," Ivey whispered. "Don't think about the past. Think about the future and how awesome it's going to be for both of you."

How could he not smile? "You think so?"

"With you as his father? Of course. You'll sometimes spoil him, sometimes have to discipline him." She stacked her hands on his chest and smiled up at him. "But most of all, you'll support him and love him and just be there for him. Always."

Corbin touched a soft curl that hung over her eyes. "Always." More and more every day, he wanted Ivey to share that future with him.

"Now," she said with great authority, "we can sleep."

Yeah, he probably could. Keeping her right where she was, Corbin adjusted the covers over her. "Good night, Ivey." He heard her breathing going deeper, and he whispered, "Thank you."

Chapter Twelve

Holding her phone in her left hand, ignoring the pain in her right, Ivey thumbed in a text to Corbin.

Be late tonight. Eat without me.

He immediately replied with: What's wrong?

So astute. Ivey smiled and returned, Explan latr. Blast. She didn't see the typos until she'd already hit Send. Texting left-handed wasn't easy. Be a few hrs yet.

OK but if you need me let me know.

Will do. Ivey sighed happily. It was so nice having someone worry about her. Not that Corbin needed more worries, and not that she needed that from him. He cared, and that's what she hugged to her heart.

The doctor stitching her arm glanced at her. "I take it everything is okay?"

From a chair in the small exam room, her friend, Ember Somerset, laughed. "She has a hot new boyfriend. Trust me, everything is fine."

"Ah," the doctor said. "Do tell."

"He moved here back in May," Ivey explained. Dr. Moore had stitched her up more than once, but this was the first time Ivey'd had an interesting story to share while she did. "He's gorgeous. Funny and sweet. And he has the most adorable little son."

Dr. Moore lifted one finely arched eyebrow. "Gorgeous, huh?"

"She's smitten," Ember pointed out. "But he really is easy on the eyes. Don't tell Mike I said that, though."

"Mike knows you aren't blind," Dr. Moore said. She tied off the last stitch, then sat back. "Done. That was quite the bite this time."

"It was quite the dog." Ivey exchanged a look with Ember. She and her sister, Autumn, ran an animal rescue farm. They had every type of animal from dogs and cats to cows and sheep and even a turkey and chickens. It was heartbreaking, sometimes backbreaking work, and yes, occasionally, in the course of assisting them with the medical needs of the animals, Ivey got bit. As much as the sisters did to help animals, donating her time as a vet was the least Ivey could do.

"He'd been mistreated," Ivey explained, "so he didn't trust us. He needed his own stitches, along with shots and a flea treatment." And a lot of love. "He'll be okay, though." The sisters would see to that.

"He bit Ivey before we could get him subdued. I think he was in pain, but by the time we left, he was already calming down."

"Autumn will coddle him, and soon he'll feel all the love."

"Yes." Ember tried and failed to remove her scowl. "If I ever find the bastard who hurt him, I'll…" She let the threat hang out there, maybe because she couldn't think of anything dire enough.

Ivey said again, more gently and with assurance, "He'll be okay."

Ember nodded. "We'll make sure of it."

"I don't know how you do it," Dr. Moore said. "I admire you both so much, and of course, Autumn, too."

"And Mike and Tash," Ember added. "They do a lot to help."

Mike, who'd already been a handyman at the rescue, was now married to Ember, and Tash was married to Autumn. Together, they made the running of the farm nearly seamless.

Glancing down at her blood-splattered clothes, Ivey wrinkled her nose. She'd need to shower and change before going to Corbin, otherwise she might scare Justin. And thinking of the boy...

"Tash's little girl has a real gift with animals, too." Ivey made the decision that she should introduce Justin and Sadie. The two kids had a lot in common.

"You're all amazing," the doctor said. "But I hope you start being a little more careful." She wrapped the wound, gave Ivey instructions for care and told her to return in seven days to have the stitches removed.

On their way out of the hospital, Ivey called Hope to make certain she'd gotten the clinic closed up for the day. Since Hope had handled everything without issue, Ivey put her phone away and glanced at Ember. "You really didn't have to drive me. I could have managed just fine."

"Ha!" Ember got into her truck and kicked on the air-conditioning. When Ivey slid into her seat, Ember reached past her for the seat belt and buckled her in.

Giving her a wry look, Ivey muttered, "Thanks, Mom."

Ignoring that, Ember got them on their way. "You were bleeding a lot, Ivey. And you got bit helping us. Of course I drove you." She frowned. "Does it hurt?"

At first, Ivey had been too worried about the dog to really feel the bite. Once she'd gotten control of the situation, yes, it had hurt. Luckily, the doctor had numbed her arm before the scrubbing began. "Superficial stuff, that's all. A few stitches fixed it. Besides, it's my forearm, not my hand, which means I'd have had no problem driving."

"Still," Ember insisted. "Are you sure you don't want me to drop you off at Corbin's house? Mike and Tash could bring your car to you." She waggled her eyebrows. "I'm betting your new guy would give you all kinds of delicious pampering."

"Nope, I'm fine." Ivey held up her arm. "Good as new. Besides, I want to go home to wash up and change clothes. Corbin's son, Justin, is super into horror flicks and monsters. If he sees me covered in blood, his creative little mind might think the worst."

"All right. If you need anything, though, please let me know. Autumn and I appreciate you so very much. We trust you, Ivey, not only with the health care of the animals, but with their sometimes wounded personalities. You're so good to them, and that's a huge thing to us. So thank you."

Such a kind compliment coming after a truly tumultuous day caused Ivey to well up. "Enough of that now," she groused playfully. "You'll get me bawling, and puffy eyes and a stuffy nose will only make me miserable."

Ember gave her a grin. "Okay, so here's a subject change. Tell me more about your hunk." She bobbed her eyebrows. "I've been so curious."

Oh good. That was a topic guaranteed to brighten her mood.

It was past suppertime when Ivey finally got to Corbin's house. All seemed quiet, but as she got out of the car, she heard a very distinct, "Psst."

Glancing around, she saw no one. With a frown, she started forward again, and...

"Psst." There it was again!

Hands on her hips, she surveyed the yard and the woods beyond. A chuckle mixed with a giggle brought her gaze to the
tree house. Aha! Walking over to the massive tree, she looked
up. "I've found you."

A quick shuffling of feet, then a hushing sound, got her grinning. Yes, her arm hurt. Already the bruising had spread up to
her elbow and down the back of her hand. Didn't matter.

Putting her purse strap around her neck and shoulder, she
carefully went up the unevenly spaced rungs.

Corbin and Justin had done an awesome job on the tree house.
It wasn't at all professional, not with the different colored boards
and a roof that sloped to fit the shape of the tree. Luckily, it had
been constructed on a lower, sturdy branch so she didn't have
to go too high.

When she reached the top, she peeked in the open window
and found Corbin attempting to quiet Justin's giggles. Very
loudly, she said, *"Psst,"* and they both jumped.

Justin charged toward her. "You're home!"

Oh, how wonderful that sounded. "Yes, I am." Teasing him,
she asked, "Did you miss me?"

"Sure." He stepped back. "Come on in."

Sitting against the wall, one leg bent and the other stretched
out, Corbin smiled at her—until he saw the bandage on her
arm. He was on his feet in a nanosecond. "What happened?"

She stepped in around him. "It's nothing. A small dog bite."

"That's what kept you?" He took her wrist and carefully
lifted her arm, his brows knitting as he traced a fingertip over
the bruises visible around the bandage.

Touched by his concern, she smiled and gently explained, "I
bruise easily."

"Stitches?"

"A few."

Justin moved closer to see. "A dog really bit you?"

She smoothed away a smudge of dirt on his cheek. "Yes, he

really did. He was horribly afraid because someone had been mean to him. He didn't yet know that I wanted to help, so he reacted out of fear."

Taking her hand, Justin moved closer. "He's okay now?"

"Yes. He's with my friends who run an animal rescue. They're wonderful people. You'd love them, and you'd probably really love their farm, too. There are so many cute animals."

"Many that you've helped?" Corbin asked.

She hedged her answer by saying, "Autumn and Ember carry the burden of the rescue, so I donate my veterinarian services."

He brushed a kiss over her lips. "I keep saying it, but Sunset is a wonderful place to be, and you are a wonderful person."

She was about to explain more when they all heard tires on the drive.

Justin raced to the window and looked out. "It's a guy." Turning back, he added, "I think it's the guy we saw at your office."

"Geoff?" It was Ivey's turn to hurry forward to take a peek. Sure enough, Geoff had just stepped out of his car and was headed for the front door. "What in the world?"

"Maybe if we hunker down and stay real quiet, he'll go away."

She laughed at Corbin's hopeful expression. "Don't be silly." She called out through the window, "We're up here, Geoff. Be down in a second."

With an eye roll, Corbin went to the door. "I'll go first."

Nudging Justin, she said, "He means in case one of us falls. Guess he thinks he's more sure-footed than us."

Justin grinned. "That's okay. I'm faster."

"You are, but we're not going to race down the ladder, okay?" Ivey ruffled his hair, let him go second, then she came down... with an audience of an ex, a current and a ten-year-old cutie.

Everyone looked at her. She pasted on a smile and said, "Hey, Geoff. What's up?"

His gaze dropped to her arm, which prompted him to come forward. "You got bit again?"

Brows up, Corbin asked, "Again?"

Sending him an impatient frown, Geoff explained, "She's been bitten a few times over the past two years. Usually on the arm, but once on the leg, too." Giving his attention back to Ivey, he touched her hair—then dropped his hand. "Are you okay?"

Wow, talk about awkward. Her gaze skittered over to Corbin, but with his arms crossed and his expression enigmatic, she couldn't gauge his mood. Justin just stared owlishly, as if he could sense the adult tension.

Shaking herself, Ivey said, "I'm fine." With a tip of her head, she asked, "What are you doing here, Geoff?"

His mouth compressed, but not with irritation for her. Leaning closer, he asked, "Can you send the kid inside?"

She stared at him. "Why ever would I do that?"

"Because I need to talk to you and his father, and it'd probably be better if he wasn't listening in."

"Um…" She chewed over the dilemma, trying to anticipate what Geoff might say, but not a single idea came to mind. "Give me a second." Striding over to Corbin, she whispered Geoff's request in his ear.

His eyes narrowed, but he didn't deny her. Voice calm and controlled, he said, "Justin? Could you go ask your Uncle Lang to heat up some dinner for Ivey? And check on the dogs while you're in there."

"Okay." He grinned at Ivey. "We had fried chicken with mac and cheese." With that announcement, he took off in a jog.

Corbin put his arm over Ivey's shoulders. "All right, let's hear it."

Running a hand over the back of his neck, Geoff shifted. "Look, I didn't particularly want to come here, okay? But Ivey's involved, and then there's the kid…"

Sensing something really was wrong, Ivey reached out to him. "What is it?"

"There was a woman in town asking about him." He nodded at Corbin. "She said you had her son and wanted to know where to find you."

"Jesus." Corbin's eyes, his face, the set of his mouth all went hard. "You told her where I live?"

"No. I wouldn't do that." Shoving his hands in his pockets, Geoff scowled. "I mean, I knew Ivey was staying here with you and the other woman looked…" He searched for a word, then shook his head. "She was loud and angry. I didn't think it'd be a good idea to send her here."

"So you came to forewarn him?" Ivey asked gently.

"Seemed the right thing to do. She was pretty unhinged." He shot another wary look at Corbin. "Pretty sure she was high or drunk or something. I didn't talk to her, but I can't guarantee no one else did."

Corbin drew a deep breath. "When was this?"

"A few hours ago. I was just leaving the bar and she was there, in the parking lot. Basically causing a scene, if you want the truth. Someone might have called the cops."

Holding out his hand, Corbin said, "Thank you for letting me know."

Geoff hesitated, then accepted the offering. "No problem. You, ah, might want to keep a closer eye on the kid. From the things she was saying, she might make a grab for him."

"I won't let him out of my sight," Corbin promised, without explaining that he already closely supervised Justin.

"Geoff." Ivey stepped forward and gave him a platonic hug. "Thank you."

For a second, he returned her embrace, his jaw to the top of her head, then he stepped away. "Take care of yourself, okay? And if you need anything, let me know."

She and Corbin stood together, watching him go. Ivey waited until his car disappeared along the drive, hidden by the trees, before she turned to Corbin. "What will you do?"

"Get hold of my lawyer first." He steered her toward the house.

"And then?"

"I have an idea." He stopped without opening the front door. "I don't think she really wants him. There has to be another reason she's here."

Ivey felt a little sick. "Money?"

"Even though she hasn't asked for it, I owe her for back child support."

Resting a hand on his chest, she felt the steady thumping of his heartbeat. "Because you didn't know."

"Regardless, there had to be sacrifices."

"I'm not sure you can buy her off." She wasn't even sure if that was the right thing to do. "It could be like paying a ransom—and you don't know yet if Justin wants to see her."

"I'll work it out. Sooner than I meant to." He paused at the entry to the kitchen where Lang and Justin were getting her food together. "Guess Geoff isn't so bad after all."

"Guess not." She put her arms around Corbin and rested her face to his solid chest. "But he's not you, and he was never right for me."

While Ivey ate, Justin kept her company, answering the many questions she managed to think up so that Corbin had time to tell his brother about the newest development.

Justin talked fast, his stories running together in his excitement. One of the puppies had pooed on the floor, and apparently Lang had stepped in it.

They both laughed over that. Overall, the pups were trained to go outside, but they were still young and accidents happened.

He showed her a scratch where a sharp puppy tooth had snagged his knuckle, and another on his knee from a puppy's claws. Added to his bruised elbow, he was pretty banged up.

It made Ivey realize yet again that she'd burdened Corbin with a few too many dogs.

Maurice, apparently, had smacked a pup that got too frisky, and Justin thought that was hilarious, too.

They discussed ways to keep other accidents from happening. It seemed that earlier Corbin had decided that Justin could take them out front—away from the lure of the lake—several times a day.

Ivey assumed that plan would now change. She didn't want Justin out front alone in case his mother showed up, so she knew Corbin would be even more adamant about it.

She wondered when, and if, life would finally settle down for him. Corbin deserved peace and calm and an opportunity to be a father without all the chaos.

Corbin spent much of the morning on the phone, always watching for Justin so that he didn't overhear anything troubling before they could have their own talk.

It was a godsend, having Ivey there to help with the animals and to keep Justin occupied, though she'd need to head to work in the next few minutes. It took some doing, and his lawyer wasn't entirely satisfied with his strategy, but he finally had some plans in motion.

He disconnected just as Ivey was preparing to go. He and Justin each gave her a goodbye hug. It did his heart good to see Justin accept her kiss on his cheek, and the way she squeezed him just a little longer than usual. Ivey wasn't his mother, but she fit the maternal role to a tee.

After they watched her back out of the drive, Corbin put a hand on Justin's shoulder. He'd waited until this morning to discuss things so that Justin wouldn't have to go to bed with heavy concerns on his mind. "I'd like to talk to you for a minute, okay?"

Going very still, Justin asked, "Did I do something wrong?"

"No." Corbin hugged him into his side. "I'm a talker, re-

member? This won't be the first time or the last where I want
to have a man-to-man chat with you. I don't want you to worry
every time I do."

Looking very unconvinced, Justin nodded. "Okay."

Corbin led him to the kitchen table. It seemed a good place to
have important conversations, probably because it was a practice
familiar to him. His own parents had always congregated at the
table for big discussions. "Where's your Uncle Lang?"

"Said he was taking a shower but would be up soon." Justin
fidgeted. "He took the dogs out first, though, cuz he wanted
me to stay inside."

"That's why you thought you were in trouble?"

One narrow shoulder lifted. "Usually I do it."

After pouring another cup of coffee, Corbin took the chair
nearest to his son. "Do you like having your Uncle Lang here?"

"Sure." His face scrunched up with worry. "He's not leaving, is he?"

So often, Justin worried about losing the people he'd grown
close to. "Nope. Even if someday he doesn't live in this house,
he said he plans to be close by. He's your uncle, he loves you, so
you'd still see him a lot."

With that now familiar skepticism, Justin said, "Kay."

Inside, Corbin cringed. For every inch of progress he made
with his son, there seemed to be some force pushing back against
him. "I wanted to talk to you about something else."

Justin appeared to hold his breath.

God, how to say it? His son looked so distraught, Corbin figured it'd be better just to plow through it. "Apparently, your
mother is in town."

Horror froze him with his eyes open wide and his mouth
clamped tight.

Corbin reached for his hand. "I don't know how you feel
about seeing her—"

Before he could finish, Justin launched himself at him, grabbing him around the neck and clinging tightly. The jarring movement knocked over his coffee cup, but luckily the hot liquid only spilled over the table, not on his son.

"You said I could stay here!"

The anguish he heard was unbearable. Corbin gathered Justin into his lap and held him to his heart. "I keep telling you, you aren't going anywhere. You're mine, and I won't ever let you go."

"But you said Mom was here," Justin accused.

"She probably wants to see you."

"No."

Christ, what had Darcie put him through? "If you don't want to see her, you don't have to. I promise." He only hoped he could keep that vow. "I mean it, Justin. I won't let anyone hurt you." Thank God he had resources. His mother and father hadn't believed in using money as power, but now? Corbin would use whatever means necessary to ensure Justin was protected. "Believe me?"

Without raising his head, Justin nodded.

"Good. So knowing that you aren't going anywhere and knowing that I'll always be your dad, would you want to see her if I was with you?" Quickly, he added, "I'd be right by your side. You wouldn't be alone with her."

He felt Justin wipe his face on his shirt and knew that he was crying. There'd been a few occasions when he'd come close, but this was the first time that he'd actually broken down. Corbin thought that having his heart cut out without anesthesia would have been easier than this.

With a wet sniffle, Justin sat back, but he kept his head bowed. "Do you... Do you want me to?"

"I want what is best for you." Honesty was the only way to go now. "Your mother might want to see you, but you don't have to if you don't want to. It's up to you, okay? Whatever you decide, I'll keep you safe."

Justin knuckled his eyes and drew a ragged breath. "What if she takes me away?"

"I would never let her do that." Corbin sensed when Lang came to the doorway. He looked over Justin's shoulder and saw the same emotion on his brother's face that he felt. "That's why your uncle didn't want you outside alone. Until I can get things worked out, I want you to always have an adult with you, even when you're in the yard. Okay?"

Justin nodded fast in agreement.

"If your mother shows up here, I want you to stay away from her, and I especially want you to trust me to protect you. Do you think you can do that?"

Justin dragged a forearm under his nose, sniffled again and gave another nod.

Lang disappeared for a second, then returned with a tissue box. Hunching his shoulders, Justin refused to look at him. For a little guy, he had so much pride.

Corbin handed him a tissue. "Blow your nose, son."

He made a half-hearted effort, then handed the tissue back to Corbin. It was a moment that made him smile, yet another novel experience, and he hugged Justin again. "We're going to get it all worked out."

No reply.

Lang pulled out a chair. "So, you know what I want to do tonight?"

Suspicious, Justin asked, "What?"

"I want to camp out in the living room. Just you and me, bud. What do you think?"

"Camp out?"

"Yup. We'll get in some practice with our sleeping bags before we try sleeping in the tree house. We'll use a flashlight to read one of the comic books Ivey gave you. It's extra creepy that way."

Justin gave it a little thought, then said, "I have a good Creature from the Black Lagoon one I've been saving. We could read it."

"That sounds perfect. I even have a tent we can put up. Won't that be cool?"

Amazing how Justin could go from tearful with worry to anticipating a new experience. And bless Lang for thinking of it.

When Justin left his lap, Corbin stopped him with a hand on his shoulder. "I wanted you to know what is happening so you'll be extra cautious, but I don't want you to worry."

"Kay." Justin swallowed heavily. "I don't want to see her. Not yet."

With a smile of encouragement, Corbin nodded. "Okay. If you ever change your mind, just let me know and we'll try to work it out." He smoothed down his son's hair. "I love you, Justin."

After a loud sniffle, Justin returned his smile. "Love you, too." Then he raced off, calling for Daisy.

Corbin shared a look with Lang. "That kid packs such a punch."

"No shit," Lang said, and he heaved out a breath. "I'll watch him for a bit. We'll make plans for tonight."

"Whenever you can without being too heavy-handed, reinforce the importance of being aware of his surroundings, okay?" Corbin didn't think Darcie would show up to steal him away, but when it came to his son, he wasn't taking any chances.

"Sure thing." Lang squeezed his shoulder. "Someday, somehow, it's going to be okay."

And until then, Corbin had his brother and Ivey, and he had his son. Someday, somehow. He had to believe that.

But first, he needed to find Darcie and make an offer.

He tried calling the number she'd originally given him, but it didn't connect. Leaving Justin with Lang, he went into town to try to find her. Sunset was small enough that it shouldn't be too difficult. In the meantime, his lawyer was drawing up new legal papers.

With any luck, he'd have it all settled in no time.

Chapter Thirteen

On a dreary evening one week later, Ivey was outside with the dogs. She'd gotten her stitches out that morning and her arm felt much better, the bruises already fading. For much of the day it had rained, and dark clouds still crowded the sky, making it seem later than it was. With the ground damp, she couldn't sit in the grass, so instead, she sat on the front step and kept a very close eye on the dogs.

If she was honest with herself, they were more than ready for homes of their own. She also wanted to spay Daisy so the sweet little dog wouldn't have to go through another difficult birth.

There'd been too many distractions lately, though. Corbin hadn't yet been able to locate Justin's mother. He'd checked all over Sunset, and although many people recalled her because of the scene she'd caused, no one knew where she might be. It was possible she was staying outside Sunset.

Until Darcie was found, Ivey feared that Corbin would be

tense and Justin would remain wary. She loved them both so much that it made her tense and wary, too.

So many times she considered telling Corbin how she felt, that she wanted more than another day, another month, or even another year. She wanted *forever*. At a time when she'd thought to expand her horizons, he'd come along and shown her that she didn't need that.

She needed him.

"Hey." Stepping out of the house, Corbin closed the door quietly behind him. "They haven't finished yet?"

"Maybe. But I was enjoying the night air." And thinking deep thoughts about love and the future. "Is Justin down for the night?"

Nodding, Corbin sat on the step behind her, his runner's thighs open around her. He kissed the top of her head. "He's clingier than he was before, and I think he's afraid to hope that things are settled, but he's dealing with it all in that silent way of his."

"You need to find Darcie so he can move beyond this."

For an answer, Corbin pulled her back to rest against him. "I'm working on it. Without a number to reach her, it's pretty damned impossible."

Humid air blew against her face, and she knew it would storm again. "It's so unfair of her to do this, to disrupt his life even more."

"I agree. In the beginning, I was angry about it. But now? I realize how much help you and Lang are, how you both made the transition easier, and it makes me...not sympathetic, but maybe more understanding? Little by little, Justin talks about her. He never knew her parents, so it was always just the two of them. I'm not sure she had anyone as backup, and I'm afraid she might have a drug problem, based off what he's said, what Geoff said and what I saw when she gave Justin to me. All combined, that's a hard life."

"I guess." Loving Corbin and Justin as she did, Ivey really didn't want to cut the other woman any slack. She had to admit, though, it sounded as if Darcie had some serious personal problems. And because of those difficulties, she'd made many horrid decisions and basically destroyed her own life. One mistake had led to another, until she probably couldn't see a way out.

It made Ivey admire Hope even more, because her life, too, had been incredibly hard—obviously, in very different ways— and yet her friend had remained motivated, optimistic and caring.

One thought led to another, and Ivey asked, "Do you think you'll ever want more children?"

His startled gaze shot to hers.

D'oh. She did seem to blurt out the most outrageous things. But she couldn't help wondering. He was such a great dad.

Looking out at the darkened yard, watching the antics of the puppies, Corbin considered it. "Actually, I've wondered about that, too, about all the things I missed. Diapers and formula, first laugh and first steps... I wonder sometimes if Darcie has any photos, and if she'd let me make copies."

"If you find her, you should ask. The worst that can happen is she might say no."

"If she's gone again, I'm not sure if I should contact her or not. Then again, for medical reasons, it'd be nice to have her family history." A small smile curved his mouth before he slanted her another look. "If I do ever have another child, I can guarantee I'll be with him or her from the start."

"I already know that." Beyond a shadow of a doubt, Corbin had proven that he took his responsibilities seriously.

She'd been thinking about kids recently. Her own.

That was a first. Before Corbin, the idea of kids hadn't occurred to her. Even when she'd been with Geoff, she'd never pictured them together as parents.

Now, with Corbin? The image was all too clear.

Watching her, Corbin asked softly, "What about you?" As he so often did, he toyed with her hair, teasing it with his fingertips, tucking it back. "Can you see yourself as a mother?"

"Don't let it freak you out, but I already do." To keep it light, she tipped her head back to look at him upside down. "I know Justin isn't mine, but I wish he was. I want to mother him. I want to show him how it should be when decisions are all guided by love, when he can feel that he's cared for and safe."

"He adores you," Corbin said with significance. "It's a big plus for me. At this point, I'm not sure I'd bring someone into his life who he didn't like."

"Then yay for me." She smiled. "He's pretty easy to adore right back."

Behind them, the door opened, and Lang stepped out. He'd walked Hope home a little while ago, and it looked as if he'd just gotten out of the shower. An ominous shadow filled his eyes. "Sorry to interrupt, but your cell phone rang, so I answered it."

Corbin turned, took in Lang's expression and went rigid with alarm. "Who is it?"

Jaw tightening, Lang said, "It's Darcie. She's waiting to talk to you."

A sort of suspended dread held them all immobile, then Corbin got to his feet with a rush of determined resolve. "At least she waited until Justin was asleep." He held out a hand to Ivey, but said to Lang, "You'll help her gather up the dogs?"

"Sure." Lang searched Corbin's face. "I'll also listen for Justin, just in case he wakes up."

"Thanks." Corbin gave Ivey a quick, soft kiss. "Go ahead and get ready for bed. I'll fill you in when I'm done."

Her heart beat too quickly, but Ivey hoped she projected an air of calm. "All right." She stopped him with a touch to his shoulder. "Good luck."

His brief smile held no humor, then he went inside.

"It'll be fine," Lang assured her, but he looked worried, too.

They got the pets inside and settled. Maurice stuck close to her while she showered and changed into a sleep shirt and shorts. She'd left Lang sitting in the great room looking morose while Corbin had carried the phone downstairs, to ensure Justin wouldn't wake and overhear.

She joined Lang on the couch. The TV was on, but neither of them were watching. They didn't engage in idle chitchat or try to pretend nothing was wrong. Ivey stroked Maurice, taking comfort in his nearness as always, and Lang occasionally patted her knee.

It was every bit of an hour later when Corbin finally finished his call. Cell phone in hand, he came into the great room and stood facing them both.

After a quick glance toward the stairs, he said, "She's in the hospital. Apparently she collapsed outside her hotel room."

"Here in Sunset?" Ivey asked, alarmed by all the complications winging through her brain.

"Next town over." He took a seat on the ottoman. "I'm going to see her tomorrow morning." He turned to Lang. "That is, if you can keep an eye on Justin."

Sitting forward, Lang set aside his beer and nodded. "Absolutely. No problem." And then, "She didn't ask to see him?"

"She did, but I said no. There are things we need to discuss first." Corbin rubbed his mouth. "She didn't confirm it, but I think she OD'd."

"Dear God," Ivey whispered. It was a selfish thought, but she was grateful the woman hadn't been in Sunset when it happened, otherwise gossip would have run amok through the small town. Corbin and Justin lived here now. This was their home, and Ivey would rather they have some space between problems as serious as that.

"I might be there all day." Staring into Ivey's eyes, Corbin said quietly, "She's getting discharged soon, but she doesn't have any money, and she doesn't have anywhere to go."

Shock stole through her, making her jaw loosen.

Lang gave a muttered curse, then got up to pace.

"You…" Her mouth was too dry. Without giving it a thought, she snatched up Lang's beer and took a long drink. Licking her lips and drawing a steadying breath, she asked, "You're bringing her *here*?"

"Christ, no." Corbin's mouth firmed. "I'm going to make her an offer of assistance and hope like hell that she takes it."

"An offer of assistance?" Ivey repeated.

He lowered his voice. "I don't think she really wants him. I'm hoping if she gets on her feet, if she has other options, she won't focus on him. But even if she does, it'd be better if she was stable."

Ivey stared at him in wonder. "Good God, you are wonderful."

"A freaking saint," Lang complained, sounding very unhappy about it.

"No," Ivey whispered, and she got up to hug Corbin tight. "He's a man who loves his son and wants the best for him."

Corbin closed his arms around her, and even after Lang headed off to bed, they stood there like that.

Yes, Corbin would do everything in his power to take care of his son.

And while he did, Ivey would take care of him.

It was late morning by the time Corbin arrived at the hospital. He'd told Justin that he had some business to take care of and might be gone for a while, but repeatedly affirmed for him that he would be back before bedtime. He assuaged his guilt with the reasoning that it was only a small lie to protect his son from anxiety.

Right now, his visit with Darcie *was* business—the business of protecting Justin's future.

Making himself smile for Justin, Corbin had done his utmost

to treat the morning like any other. Overall he'd been successful, but there had been a few moments where Justin had seemed to see right through his bullshit, as if he knew a lot was on the line.

Someday, with enough love and security, Justin would stop waiting for the worst to happen. What Corbin was about to try was a risk, but Ivey understood that it was necessary. For his son. For himself.

For their future.

He wanted her in his life, now and always. He wanted peace in his household, too. To that end, he would try anything, no matter how difficult it might be.

Walking into the hospital, Corbin thought about Ivey and Lang, about their help during a time of his life that was both jubilant—because he had his son—and the scariest thing he'd ever faced—because his son's mother was so unpredictable. They were forced to worry right along with him, and even while he regretted that, he was grateful that he had them.

His brother loved him, so his support was a given; he'd had it all his life.

But how did Ivey feel? It couldn't be easy for her to get involved in his mess. There were so many things he'd like to do with her, and none of it was possible. Yet. Would she still be around when he got things in order? Christ, he hoped so. He couldn't really imagine life without her.

It was as if he'd met the perfect woman for him, right when he needed her the most.

Dressed in casual tan khakis and a dark polo shirt, Corbin stopped outside Darcie's hospital room. A heavy weight settled on his shoulders, keeping him from knocking on the door. So much rode on the success of this visit. He knew Darcie's issues wouldn't be easily resolved, but at least he had a plan. From there, he could only do his best.

Stiffening his resolve, he knocked on the door and waited.

"Come in," came the weak reply.

He pushed the door open and came to an abrupt halt. Across the room, lying limp in a white hospital bed, Darcie looked like hell. Seeing her brought on a wave of sympathy that totally took him by surprise. Shaking himself, he continued in and tried for a moderate tone. "Hey."

Through bloodshot, bleary eyes, she stared at him. "You better not gloat." Her lips trembled, much as Justin's did when he was afraid. "I don't want to hear any lectures."

The hospital room was as cheery as possible, but it didn't affect the depressed atmosphere. "I don't have any to give."

"Good."

Darcie was emaciated, her pasty skin lacking any real color, and with the dark smudges under her eyes, she looked as if she'd gone through hell and back. Real concern brought him closer. "You're doing okay now?"

"Yes, so don't hold your breath waiting for me to croak."

"Darcie." He pulled a chair up near the bed and slowly sat down, giving himself time to formulate the right words. "You're my son's mother. I don't relish interference in his life, but I don't wish you any ill will, either."

"Ha!" At the outburst, she groaned, a hand to her stomach, her eyes closing.

Corbin waited, seeing the way she struggled.

"I almost died." With a caustic glance around at the room, she said, "You think this place is bad, you should see the ICU."

Bad? He thought the room looked comfortable and convenient, set up for someone who needed a lot of care. "I'm glad you were able to be moved."

She swallowed heavily. "I looked everywhere for you." She breathed a little harder. "But you were hiding."

"Actually, I looked for you as well."

Her gaze shot to his. "Why?"

"I knew you were in town. Others had…remarked on it. But I couldn't find you."

"Because I got dumped here." Her hand curled into a fist. "Cops brought me in after I crashed."

"The police were involved?"

Her mouth firmed. "People accused me of harassing them. Cops got there before the EMTs."

Dear God. "Where was this?"

"Local bar," she said without any further clarification.

"I see."

She shook her head as if it didn't matter. "Guess I had too much to drink."

If by too much, she meant she'd damned near drunk herself to death, then he'd agree. She still looked two breaths away from death. "It wasn't only alcohol, was it, Darcie?"

"So? Don't act like you have all the answers."

No, he wouldn't. He couldn't. There were too many occasions when he second-guessed his every decision. This was one of them.

He reached for patience. "How much longer will they keep you?"

Rolling a shoulder, she said, "They'll let me out soon, but I don't know what to do." Very deliberately, she smoothed the sheet over her chest. "You might not believe this, but I never wanted to hurt Justin. He's a good boy, just more than I could handle on my own."

Corbin noticed that she hadn't yet asked how Justin was doing. Seeing her so thin, more so than when she'd given him Justin, he couldn't take offense. "I can understand that."

"I thought Carl was going to marry me, but that fell apart." Defensively, she said, "That's the only reason I got so messed up. The damn pills didn't mix well, I guess." Tears welled in her eyes. "Now I have nothing and no one. I'm all alone."

The piteous tone grated. "That's not actually true." He hesitated, feeling both compassionate and repelled. To think that his son had spent ten years with this woman, that he'd had no one else around to protect him, made Corbin's blood burn. "You have your life, Darcie. And if you think you'd like to get things back on track, I'd be willing to help."

Her eyes, the same shade of blue as Justin's, took his measure. Miraculously, the tears disappeared. Letting her voice drop, she tried a coy smile that was ludicrous under the circumstances. "Our son could use two parents. It'd be easier together. I bet Justin would like that."

It took all his concentration not to jolt away from that repugnant suggestion. Him, with Darcie? The things he felt for her, resentment, anger, remorse and pity, were not conducive to a romantic relationship. She was the opposite of Ivey, lacking her vitality, her spirit and her huge capacity for love.

Insulting Darcie in any way wouldn't help his cause though. "I'm involved with someone else."

"You're not married," she shot back with sharp annoyance.

Her mercurial moods likely explained a lot of Justin's wariness. It wouldn't be easy for a kid to never know how a parent might react. "Not yet, no." He definitely wanted a lifetime commitment, though. *With Ivey.* "But our relationship is serious."

Alarm flashed over her ravaged features. "Since when?"

"Darcie," he chided. "I came here to see if there's a way I can help you, not to talk about me."

She eyed him. "So you'll do what? Give me money?"

Money was what she'd asked for, and initially, even before her call, it was what he'd planned to give. But he sensed that would only make things better for the very short-term. There was also the worry that she'd use cash for drugs.

For Justin's sake, Corbin wanted to see real, substantial change. "What do you hope to see for your future?"

Her expression made it clear she saw that as a trick question. "I love my son."

In her own way, she likely did. "I assume that's why you gave him to me. You knew you needed help, didn't you? You wanted what's best for him."

She jumped on that with desperate haste. "Yes! I knew you could take care of him. It was past time for you to have a turn."

He'd have been there from the start if she had seen fit to tell him…but he resisted saying so. "I agree. I'll see to him from now on."

With belligerence, she argued, "He's still my son. I have a right to see him."

She'd signed away her rights, but again, he tried to keep things civil. "I agree."

That stunned her silent.

"I think you know that it'd be best if you were…in better shape first?" Corbin rushed on before she could take offense. "You spent ten years caring for him on your own."

"And it wasn't easy!"

He acknowledged that with a nod. "Now that you know he's safe with me, you should concentrate on yourself for a while. This could be your turn at a better life. A life that could start right now, don't you think?" He couldn't say she looked interested, but at least she was listening. "There are programs, Darcie. I understand they can help. I'd like you to complete one." He knew it would only work if she wanted it, too, so he needed her cooperation. "What do you say?"

She took plenty of time to think about it. "I'm not admitting I have a problem, because I don't. Besides, even if I finished rehab, then what? I'm back out on the streets?"

"Not if I repaid you for those ten years of single parenting."

Stark suspicion narrowed her eyes. "Repay me?"

"Consider it back child support." After long talks with his lawyer, he was able to drop a number that made her eyes bulge.

Calculating, she licked her lips as she watched him. "I guess that would be a start."

A start—and a finish. He wouldn't allow her to manipulate

him more than she already had. "After you've completed rehab, I'd not only give you that money in monthly payments, but I'd also help you get back on your feet."

She sat up a little higher in the bed. "Help me, how?"

"I'll get you set up in an apartment, with several months paid in advance. I'll also make sure you have reliable transportation so you can hold down a job. But, Darcie? It'll all be dependent on you staying clean."

Skipping past his stipulation, she asked, "Why would you do any of that?"

Here was where it got tricky. He couldn't say she was a problem he wanted to resolve. That attitude would infuriate anyone, but especially someone in her stage of recovery. He'd planned his response in advance, and he hoped it was good enough to convince her. "Despite everything, I think Justin would be happier if he knows you're okay."

"Of course he would. I'm his mother. I bet he misses me, doesn't he?"

Corbin studied her. Already he could see the wheels turning and knew she was making plans of her own. Plans that weren't about their son. Plans that would do nothing to make Justin's life easier.

"I'm only doing this for him." Sitting forward, his elbows on his knees and his fingers laced together, Corbin stared into her still hazy eyes. He needed to make sure that she understood every word. "I'll only assist you as long as it's in his best interests. If you can't be sober, then I'd have to rethink everything."

Angry color rushed into her pale face. "You bastard. You think you can call all the shots, don't you?"

"No." Life was never that simple. He stood to pace around the room. "For now, if you want to see Justin, it would only be through supervised visits."

"He's my son!"

Her raised voice didn't faze him. In contrast, his own was soft with conviction. "You gave him to me. You signed away your rights, remember? I'm willing to work with you, but every decision I make will be centered on whatever is best for Justin."

"I'll sue you," she threatened with heat.

"If you want to take your chances in court, then we will. But if you go that route, I won't give you a dime." He looked around the room. "When you leave here, you'll be on your own. Think about that." Before he lost his temper, he headed for the door.

"Wait."

The desperation in her tone tore at him, again causing sympathy to war with resolve. He turned back to face her.

With her gaze downcast, she muttered, "I want to get better."

Closing his eyes in relief, Corbin nodded. "Then I'll do what I can." In that moment, Darcie looked small and afraid. His heart ached, not only for his son, but for her, too. No one wanted a life of dependency. No one made a conscious decision to be weak, to be arrested—or to court death through drugs. It was one of those awful things that happened, and he quickly counted his blessings that his parents had given him such a solid foundation.

Darcie rubbed one eye, making her look very young and frail. "Cops will be in to talk to me today. I… I don't want to face them alone."

He stepped closer again. "You want me to stay?" The idea had merit, because it would give him a clear view of what he was up against.

Her chin angled up. "Unless you have something better to do."

Parenting his son was definitely better, but he shook his head. "I can stay for a few more hours."

Relief stole some of the strain from her features. "I figure they'll lock me up this time."

This time?

She turned to look out the window. "It's not fair. None of it is my fault and now I have nothing."

If it wasn't her fault, then whose? Did she blame Justin for being born? Corbin for not somehow knowing he had a son, even though she hadn't told him? "Let's figure out what to expect first, okay? We'll take it one step at a time."

Her frowning gaze returned to his face. "You promise you won't leave me hanging?"

"I'll keep my word, you'll keep yours and we'll both get it worked out."

Ivey ended the call with Corbin just before she pulled into the drive at his house. God, it had been good to finally hear from him. She'd been so worried, anticipating the worst, wanting to be there with him but knowing that wasn't a good idea.

He'd be a while yet getting home, but he sounded cautiously optimistic about his visit with Darcie.

The officer who'd talked with her at the hospital had explained there would, in fact, be some jail time, followed by a mandatory program and counseling. Darcie would also have to submit to random drug testing.

Corbin had surmised that she was a multiple offender.

Ivey knew that had to be tormenting him. She, too, was thinking about the things Justin might have gone through.

The rest of Corbin's trip had been spent learning what he could about his son. Darcie had managed to unearth a few photos off her phone, but the younger ones of him were gone forever when she'd lost an earlier phone.

She'd claimed that everything she owned was stored in her car, now abandoned at the bar. To keep it from getting towed, Corbin had offered to move it for her. She'd readily given him the keys and told him to take anything of Justin's that he wanted—as long as he planned to help her once she was free again.

Corbin now had a box of items he was anxious to go through, but he wanted to get home first.

To his son.

And to *her.*

Ivey couldn't wait to see him. The future looked a little brighter with one problem addressed.

She was smiling as she drove up to the house—until she saw the RV taking up a considerable amount of space in the drive-way. She assumed whoever it was had just arrived, since the motor was still running. When she pulled up alongside it, a woman gave her an assessing stare from the passenger seat, then grinned. Ivey watched her disappear into the back of the motor home with someone else.

Unsure who they were or why they were there, Ivey hurried to the front door and poked her head inside. "Lang?"

He came out of the kitchen, drying his hands. "What's up? Is Hope home, too?"

She almost grinned. His constant distraction with Hope seemed like a very good sign to her. "Probably." She glanced back outside and saw the two people step down from the ve-hicle. "You have company."

His brows came down. "Not..." He looked to where Justin laid on the floor coloring.

"No." Before Ivey could expound on that, the woman was right behind her.

"Where is my grandson?" she boomed.

Lang dropped his head back and groaned.

The man with the woman laughed. "We just got here, Vesta, and you're already shouting questions."

Grandson? Ivey thought. She saw the expression on Lang's face, which was comically pained, and noticed that Justin was now paying attention, too. He had that alert, guarded posture about him.

Blocking the doorway to give Justin a moment to under-stand the visit, Ivey turned to face the couple. "You're Corbin's mother?"

"And his stepdaddy," the man said, extending a hand. "Hagan Phillips."

Ivey accepted his hand. "Ivey Anders. It's nice to meet you."

"He's not their stepdaddy yet," Vesta said with good humor.

"Not for lack of trying," the man shot back.

Ignoring him, Vesta opened her arms with a huge smile and grabbed Ivey in for a crushing hug.

Given the woman was nearly as tall as Corbin, Ivey got squashed in her impressive boobs. Laughing, she patted Vesta's back. "Hello to you, too." She remembered what Corbin had said about his mother's propensity for hugging. She supposed she'd passed muster—at least so far.

Thrusting her back to arm's length, Vesta asked, "Are you here with Lang or Corbin?"

"Let her breathe, Mom," Lang said, coming to her rescue. He caught Ivey's arm and pulled her to his side.

It gave Ivey a second to really look at Corbin's mother. She was...remarkable. Tall, with a stocky, commanding figure under casual but obviously high-end clothes. Bright silver hair in a pixie cut framed her face and contrasted with her light brown eyes.

"Lang!" Vesta cried with obvious glee. "You finally found a good one." She pulled Lang away from Ivey and gave him the same demonstrative affection.

The difference was that Lang squeezed her right back. "She's not mine, Mom. Corbin claimed her first."

Vesta eyed her again while speaking to Lang. "Your brother always did have a lot of sense."

Lang glanced at Ivey. "What she means is that Corbin had more sense than me."

"Where women were concerned," Vesta confirmed. "Now where is he?"

"Corbin?" Ivey asked. "He should be home soon."

Vesta pressed her way into the house, spotted Justin and squealed.

Justin looked frozen in indecision. All around him, the animals sat in fascinated silence. They all stared at Vesta.

Lang caught his mother before she could move. "Take a breath and let me introduce you properly."

Coming in behind them, Hagan said, "That's like asking the wind not to blow." He smiled at Justin. "Look at that. Such a cute kid."

Clasping her hands to her chest, Vesta moved in. "So incredibly cute. Oh, sweetheart. I'm your loving grandmother. Now give me a hug."

Chapter Fourteen

Ivey quickly took in the situation.

Justin appeared ready to make a run for it. The instinct to shield him got her feet moving. She quickly stepped into Vesta's path, stationing herself in front of Justin and trying to placate Vesta with a smile. "He's still a little shy."

"No, I'm not," Justin said. "Babies are shy."

Figured he'd take that moment to disagree. Plastering on her smile, Ivey said, "He's also opposed to being compared to a baby in any way."

"I completely understand." Vesta slowed her approach and made a visible reach for patience.

Ivey knew it was difficult for her. This was a grandmother meeting a grandson for the very first time. An emotional occurrence for both parties. If only she'd called first, Corbin could have prepared Justin...or at least been present. Then again, she supposed Vesta wanted to surprise everyone, much as Lang had.

Turning, Ivey tried to nudge Justin forward. "Would you like to say hello to your dad's mother?"

"Maybe." Resisting her efforts, Justin peeked around Ivey. "I don't think I want to be squished, though."

"Being squished is nice," Lang said. "My mother is a world-class hugger. Give it a try."

Vesta was far too quiet, and Ivey realized she had tears in her eyes. Gently, she asked Justin, "How about a nice adult hand-shake?"

"I guess that would be okay." Reaching out past Ivey, Justin offered his small hand.

Taking it in both of her own, Vesta smiled. "You have the look of him, you know." Slowly, she tugged him closer. "Dif-ferent colored eyes, but the shape is the same."

"As my dad?"

"Yes." Her smile wobbled. "Seems like only yesterday your dad and uncle were young like you. Time goes by much too quickly."

Coming up beside her, Lang said, "He has our height, too, Mom. Did you notice?"

"Yes, a very big, strong, handsome boy." Vesta breathed a little faster. "Sorry, but the hug is busting out of me. You'll just have to suffer through it." She tugged Justin forward, but em-braced him more carefully than she had Ivey or Lang, giving him plenty of room to push away if he chose. He didn't.

Rocking him side to side, she whispered, "I am so very pleased to be your grandma, Justin. Very, very pleased."

With a grimace on his face, Justin held his arms stiff at his sides, but he didn't look afraid. He merely looked uncomfort-able, as any ten-year-old boy might under the circumstances.

Vesta didn't take it too far. Releasing him, she asked, "Now who are all these delightful critters watching us? Goodness, there are a lot of them."

Oh, score one for grandma, Ivey thought, feeling impressed

with Vesta's tactic. Few topics would get Justin going like a discussion on animals.

Wiggling free, Justin said with pride, "They're my pets."

"All of them?" Vesta asked, giving Lang a curious blink.

"Long story," Lang said. "Or maybe a short story, once you learn that Ivey is a veterinarian."

"Ah, I see."

Justin lifted Daisy into his arms. "She's mine, and the puppies are hers. Maurice—the cat—is Ivey's, but he likes me, too."

"Well, of course he does. Why wouldn't he?" Kicking off her sandals, Vesta lowered herself to the floor, then patted a spot beside her. "Come sit with me, young man, and introduce me to all these wonderful animals."

More at ease now, Justin plopped down beside her and was immediately mobbed by the puppies.

Hagan sighed. "Told her I was hungry, and what does she do? Pets and kids are guaranteed to sidetrack her for a good long while."

"Oh." Ivey quickly shut the door. "I can get something together for you."

"Lang can do it," Vesta said. "Isn't that right, son?"

Looking suspicious as to her motives, Lang cautiously agreed. "I have dinner almost done anyway. Should be enough to go around as long as no one is a glutton."

Insistent, Vesta patted the floor at her other side. "I want Ivey to sit right with us so she and I can get acquainted."

"Oh, um…" Why did Ivey have such a bad feeling about this?

With precision leverage, Vesta suggested, "Justin will probably be more comfortable with you near."

Well, that cinched it.

Ivey shrugged her purse off her shoulder and set it on the entry table. She put her shoes by the front door and joined Corbin's mother.

Lang and Hagan looked at each other with male-inspired

smiles. "Come on, Hagan. You can snack on something while I mash the potatoes." Together, they headed into the kitchen.

Vesta allowed Justin to guide the conversation, but in between kid-appropriate questions, she asked Ivey about her relationship with Corbin. Ivey answered where she could, being judicious with little ears nearby.

"I take it you live here?"

"Sort of? I mean, I stay here often since it's more convenient—"

"She lives here," Justin confirmed. "That's why all the animals are here. Isn't that great?"

Pleased with Justin's attitude, Ivey met Vesta's curious gaze and shrugged. "I still have my own house, but yes, I stay here most nights."

"Wonderful," she murmured, and Ivey could see the wheels turning.

Lang chose that auspicious moment to poke his head around the corner. He eyed both women, then said to Justin, "Time to wash up for dinner, bud. Make sure you do a good job, okay?"

"Okay." Like a shot, Justin was off, the animals chasing after him.

"He's a bottomless pit," Ivey explained. "I think he could eat sunup to sundown and still be ready for more. Of course, he's always active, too. Probably burns it off quickly."

Vesta smiled at her. It was a cunning smile that made Ivey uneasy.

She tried to excuse herself on the pretense of supervising Justin.

Vesta didn't give her a chance. "You're good with him."

Funny how such a simple compliment could immediately put Ivey at ease. "Thank you. I don't have any children of my own, but he's so sweet, how could I not love him?"

"Exactly." Vesta leaned closer. "You love my son, too, don't you?" When Ivey hesitated, Vesta gave her a nudge that almost toppled her. "You can tell me, honey. He's wonderful, isn't he? I know because I raised him to be that way."

That made Ivey laugh. "Not that you're biased or anything."

"Of course I am, but it doesn't change the facts. Both of my boys are incredible men. I couldn't be more proud of them."

"They really are," Ivey agreed. "Corbin bowled me over as soon as I met him. He's so warm and caring about Justin, but also *hot* in the extreme." She fanned her face. "Scorching hot."

"Takes after his father that way," Vesta whispered. "Lord, how I miss that man. But I don't want Hagan to hear me say that. It would hurt his feelings, you know."

By the second, Ivey liked Vesta more. "Hagan seems nice."

"He dotes on me," she confided. "When I was at my loneliest, Hagan brightened my spirits. I adore his company—but I can't see me ever marrying him."

Fascinated, Ivey turned to fully face her. "No?"

"Shhh… He can't hear that, either." She peeked toward the kitchen, must have decided they had privacy and admitted, "My finances would all have to be redone if I married again. Besides, I rather like the no-pressure aspect of just being together." Turning up her nose, she added, "I'm the independent sort."

"I can understand that."

"Can you?" Vesta's piercing gaze dissected Ivey until she blushed. "If my Corbin asked, would you marry him?"

"In a nanosecond. I'm not a fool." Until the words left her mouth, it hadn't occurred to Ivey that she should censor her reply. After all, this was Corbin's mother. What she said to the woman might very well go directly into Corbin's ear.

Well, shoot.

Unfortunately, Ivey had never been very good at censoring. "The thing is, Corbin has plenty going on right now. He definitely doesn't need any other complications."

With mock sympathy, Vesta asked, "Are you a complication, honey?"

The woman was damn tricky with her questions. "No, at least I hope not." Was she a complication? What a repugnant thought. She'd have to ask Corbin. "What I'm trying to say is that I'm happy just to be with him." For now.

Vesta snorted. "You're not me, so don't let him get too comfortable with that arrangement. Tell him how you feel and what your ultimate expectations are. You have to be firm with men, you know."

"Mom," Lang warned, interrupting.

Ivey looked up and found him leaning in the doorway, arms folded over his chest, his expression chiding.

Hagan sidled past. "I left my heartburn medicine in the RV. Be right back."

Vesta watched him go, then turned back to Lang with a frown. "You're interrupting some serious woman talk."

Not in the least intimidated, Lang moved farther into the room. "Are you meddling already?"

"Get over here and help me up," Vesta said by way of a reply. She held out her arms and Lang obligingly hauled her upright.

Next he caught Ivey's elbow and brought her to her feet, too. "Word of advice, Ivey. Don't listen to my mother."

"Nonsense," Vesta said. "Have I ever steered you wrong?"

"No," Lang said. "But I'm your son. Besides, Corbin knows what he's doing. There's no one more levelheaded than him. Let him do his own thing in his own time."

Appearing far too wily, Vesta asked, "Why, Lang, are you saying you don't approve of Ivey as a sister-in-law?"

He didn't take the bait. "Ivey knows better."

"Then you think Corbin doesn't really want her?"

"Of course he does," Lang growled.

Ivey tried to run interference. "This isn't necessary. Corbin and I are happy as we are."

"You'd prefer to marry him," Vesta said. "You already told me so."

Face hot, Ivey muttered, "I thought that was a private conversation between us."

Vesta turned on Lang. "There, you see? Now you've made
her uncomfortable."

"Yeah, right." Deadpan, he said, "That was me who did that."

Again, Ivey tried to intervene. "Really, this isn't—"

Vesta spoke over her. "Don't you want your brother to be
happy?"

With an eye roll, Lang said, "Of course I do."

Ivey saw the open front door move, but it wasn't Hagan's
shadow looming. Uh-oh. She had a bad feeling. "Um…"

"So you don't think Ivey can make him happy?"

"Corbin can make himself happy," Lang stressed. He glanced
at Ivey. "No offense."

"None taken." She watched as Corbin appeared around the
door that Hagan had left open. "So, guys—"

"If he marries Ivey, and I'm not saying he shouldn't," Lang
tacked on, "it won't be to make her responsible for his happiness. That's not how Corbin operates and you should know it."

"The right woman makes everything better." Vesta folded her
arms in the same stubborn way as her son. "Shame you don't
know *that* yet."

"Who says I don't?"

"Oh? So who's making you happy?" Vesta paused. "Dear
God, you and Corbin don't want the same woman, do you?"
She turned to Ivey. "Are they both after you, honey?"

"Ha!" Ivey couldn't help but grin. "There's a fantasy, right?"

They both stared at her, Vesta amused, Lang a little appalled.

"Kidding," she quickly assured them. Giving Lang back some
of his own, she added, "Sorry, but there's no competition. I'm
on Team Corbin." And speaking of that…she glanced at Corbin,
rooted to the spot, appearing both horrified and amused. She
winked at him.

Lang and Vesta started in again.

Deciding it was time to end the comedy before Corbin got offended, Ivey called out, "Justin, your dad is home," which effectively quieted mother and son. Darting between them, Ivey made a beeline for Corbin.

He watched her approach with an incredibly intent expression that made her stomach tumble.

When she got close, she whispered, "Sorry," and went on tiptoes to brush her mouth over his.

Evidently with other ideas in mind, Corbin drew her closer for a longer, more thorough kiss.

Yeah, well, she could just imagine how his mother would interpret that!

Just then, Justin bolted around the corner. "Dad!" Full of excitement, he came to a skidding halt in front of Corbin and Ivey. The dogs and even Maurice bounded around him. "Guess what?" Justin said. "Your mom is here."

The silence lasted a good three seconds.

Ivey cracked first with a sort of snorting chuckle. When Justin eyed her curiously, she hugged him close and lost it, laughing out loud.

Laughter being contagious, Justin started to giggle.

Soon Lang and his mother joined in.

Corbin watched them all with a funny, crooked smile on his face. He didn't look offended. Nope, he just looked like Corbin. Gorgeous, calm, rock-steady. Yes, she wanted to marry him. Who wouldn't?

Even his family was wonderful.

And best of all, with Vesta around, Ivey knew she didn't have to worry about talking too much or saying the wrong thing.

She'd be lucky to get a word in edgewise.

Corbin glanced at the clock. For over an hour, Ivey had been soaking in the jet tub in the master suite. At his house, she tended to take quick showers. He assumed so they could spend more time together.

Tonight, as soon as dinner had ended, she'd excused herself to let him catch up with his mother—or so she said—and then she'd disappeared into the master bedroom.

A few minutes later when she didn't return, he knew she was indulging in a bath.

It was incredibly distracting. He kept picturing Ivey in the tub, her flyaway hair pinned up haphazardly, her smooth skin wet and warm, her body relaxed.

At the same time he enjoyed that visual, he tried to rein in his mother's gusto, while also fending off her matchmaking efforts. Now that Lang wasn't in the hot seat, he appeared to enjoy seeing Corbin put there.

Hope hadn't joined them for dinner tonight, and Corbin wondered if his brother had warned her away. It had become the norm for them all to eat together. Given that Hope was still so reserved, sometimes more so than Justin, Lang probably thought it would be better to introduce them once their mom had wound down a little. Corbin would ask his brother about it in the morning.

The unexpected visit had really thrown off his plans. He'd wanted to go through the box of stuff he'd amassed from Darcie's car: photos of Justin, a few things he'd drawn, an old toy. The idea of sitting with Ivey and looking at everything together had appealed to him.

Instead he'd walked into a circus. Nothing new with his overly exuberant mom. She brought a whirlwind with her wherever she went.

To his relief, she and Hagan had declined the offer to stay in the house, and instead planned to sleep in the RV parked in the driveway. Hagan claimed they already had everything set up. Corbin had the feeling they wanted their privacy—but yeah, he didn't want to dwell on that too much. He liked Hagan, the two of them got along well together, but he didn't want details of his mother's romantic adventures.

Tomorrow they'd need to recharge the RV, so their plan, according to his mother, was to find the nearest RV park for a nice long stay, then they'd rent a car so they could drive back and forth in frequent visits.

It hadn't taken long for Justin to warm to his mother, a fact that surprised Corbin since she could be overwhelming. Or maybe Justin hadn't been able to catch a breath to object.

He grinned at that idea.

Either way, his mother doted on Justin and he seemed to like it.

As far as Corbin was concerned, his son couldn't get too much love from family. His mother came with a lot of chaos, but she also brought a lot of love.

Finally, the house was quiet again. His mother and Hagan were settled in the RV, and after seeing Justin ready for bed and giving him a good-night hug, he'd left Lang reading to him.

Corbin went into the master bedroom and tapped at the bathroom door. At Ivey's lazily murmured "yes?" he stepped in.

With damp curls all around her face, she smiled. "Oh good, you survived."

No matter how much time they spent together, it never failed to strike him just how perfect she was for him. "By the skin of my teeth." Coming to stand by the bath, Corbin looked down at her utterly relaxed posture. "You've been in there over an hour."

"So? It was a hectic day." She heaved a long sigh. "You should try it next. You still look tense."

Walking in to hear his mother trying to marry him off could make anyone tense. "I already took a quick shower."

"Too bad." Ivey closed her eyes as if she planned to be in there longer still.

Bubbles circulated around her, constantly stirring the water but not doing a damn thing to obscure her body. "Enjoying yourself?"

"It's very relaxing."

Letting his gaze roam over her, Corbin felt her never-ending effect sink in. That, more than a jet tub, worked to unkink the stress knots in his shoulders and neck. "Ivey?"

"Mmm?"

"Did my mother embarrass you?"

"Of course." Her mouth curved in a small, secret smile. "I like her, though. She's funny, boisterous and well-intentioned."

Yup, that summed up his mother. "She likes you as well." To resist reaching down to touch her bare body, Corbin flattened a hand to the wall. Ivey wasn't yet ready to leave her bath, and he didn't want to cut her time short. "About what she said—"

Green eyes that looked amazingly bright opened to stare up at him. Very softly, she said, "I do love you, you know."

His breath stalled. She loved him.

As if that weren't enough to level him, she added, "Someday, when you're ready...*if* you're ever ready, I would love nothing more than to marry you. With you, Corbin, I feel more like me, if that makes any sense."

"It does." He pulled off his T-shirt and, wearing only sleep pants, knelt down at the side of the tub. "Because with you, I feel like myself, like I have a grasp on things." It was a wonderful illusion, one he wanted to hold on to.

Ivey drifted her fingers along the surface of the water. "You have a better understanding of life and the people you love than anyone I know." Her gaze trapped his, and her voice lowered. "When I think about Justin and all the things he might have gone through, I'm so grateful that *you're* his dad."

Corbin swallowed heavily. "Me, too."

"Justin needed someone strong, someone who would accept him, appreciate him and love him unconditionally."

What did Ivey need? Was he enough for her? Could she overlook all the challenges that lay ahead? Despite her assurances, he didn't want to put it to the test. Not yet.

Dipping a hand beneath the water, he stroked her thigh. "So you love me."

Her smile twitched. "Yes."

"I like hearing it."

Her gaze warmed. "I love you, Corbin."

There were a million things he needed to say to her. A lot of things they had to work out. But in that moment, he wanted her. No, actually, he *needed* her.

So damned much.

Without explaining, he turned off the jets and pulled the drain on the tub.

Ivey laughed. "I take it my bath is over?"

"Sorry." Very seriously, he said, "If I don't have you soon, I'm going to explode."

Satisfaction replaced her humor. "All right."

Coming to his feet, Corbin shook out the towel and held it open for her, then wrapped her up when she stepped into it. He didn't bother drying her, not yet. Not now.

He couldn't.

Instead he backed her to the wall, heard her quick inhalation as her warmed skin met the cool tiles, and he kissed her.

God, he loved kissing her.

Her lips were open, her tongue inviting. Ivey always gave so much. All that she had. Everything he needed.

After indulging her mouth for several minutes, he shifted to trail his teeth along her throat, then her collarbone.

Reaching out, Ivey pushed the lock on the door.

Yeah, good idea. He didn't want any interruptions—and he didn't want to take the time to find a bed. Having her right here, against the wall, seemed like a fantastic idea.

To ensure she was onboard with that idea, he kissed a path to her breasts. The towel dropped.

Neither of them cared.

Ivey tunneled her fingers into his hair and guided him to right where she wanted him to kiss her. Honestly, it was where he wanted to kiss her, too, so he closed his teeth gently around one ripe nipple, tugged, licked and finally sucked her in.

Going to her tiptoes, and arching forward, her body tightened. That reaction only spurred him on. Switching to the other nipple, he let his hands roam all over her. Every inch of her satiny skin fascinated him.

Driven to make her as heated as he was, he slowly moved down her body, lower and lower until he dropped to his knees. With his hands on her backside, he pressed hot, open-mouth kisses to her stomach and each hip bone.

He glanced up and found her with her head tipped back, lips parted and eyes closed.

She was the most compelling, interesting, sexy woman he'd ever known.

Nuzzling against her in the most intimate of kisses, he listened to her escalated breathing. She was warm and silky wet, ready for him. Maybe anxious for him.

He murmured, "Widen your legs."

Without hesitation, she stepped one foot out from the other. Corbin used his fingers to part her, then kissed her again, licked...and sucked.

He couldn't get enough of her, fast enough.

One hand released his hair so she could put it over her own mouth, muffling her small cries and groans. After a few minutes he felt her trembling, and knew she was close.

He stayed with her, attuned to her every response, until she came undone. Ivey never held back.

He loved that about her.

Once she started to ease, he came back to his feet, kissed her mouth and said, "I don't have a condom here."

"In the bedroom down here?"

"No. I meant to store more in the closet, but…the day went off the rails."

She gave in to a heartfelt groan, rallied a second later and with a sated smile she stepped around him to snatch up her clothes. He helped her get on her nightshirt and panties and then, ignoring the shorts he held out to her, she grabbed his hand. "Come on."

Together, they rushed from the bathroom, through the quiet house and up the stairs. Ivey's shirt barely skimmed beneath her bottom cheeks. Her breasts bounced beneath the soft fabric of her shirt.

Carrying her shorts for her, Corbin couldn't help but grin. He felt like a kid again, sneaking around for a quickie.

It was a wonderful way to end a tumultuous day.

They'd almost reached his bedroom door when Lang stepped out of Justin's room. Surprised to see each other, especially since it was obvious what Corbin and Ivey were about, they stared at one another.

Lang gave a quick glance at Ivey, then to her shorts in Corbin's hand. Fighting a grin, he said in a barely there whisper, "He's asleep, and the lights went out in the RV a few minutes ago."

"Good to know."

Saluting them, Lang said, "See you both in the morning." He whistled softly as he headed downstairs.

His brother knew he loved Ivey.

His mother had taken one look at her and known she was a keeper.

Justin adored her.

And Corbin couldn't get enough of her, not just physically, but in every way he could imagine.

Ivey was the type of woman you never wanted to take for granted. Soon, very soon, he'd ask her to marry him.

He needed her in his life—now and always.

An hour later, Ivey lifted her head from Corbin's chest. Drowsily, she asked, "Can't sleep?"

His eyes gleamed as he looked at her. "Did I wake you?"

She shook her head and hugged him. "I wasn't asleep yet, either." She could feel his turbulence, but she wasn't sure how to make it better. "Things were rough with Darcie?"

The bed shifted as he rolled one shoulder. "Like I said on the phone, it went better than I had expected."

She knew there was more to it. "And?"

After a brief pause, he scooted up to sit with his back against the headboard, then pulled her into his lap. "This will sound nuts, okay? But I felt sorry for her."

"Not nuts at all. She's in a terrible predicament, one that will be difficult for a long time." She cupped a hand to his face. "And you, Corbin, are a very good man."

"It's a strange feeling," he confessed. "In some ways, I despise her for what she did to my son and for what she did to *me*. I lost so much time with him. Time that I'll never get back."

Ivey tucked her face into his throat. "But you'll have him for the rest of his life. That's such a gift."

His hand idly trailed up and down her spine. "Yes, it is. And she's so...vulnerable. So many times today, she looked like a kid herself, lost and afraid."

Ivey quickly blinked back tears. Corbin didn't need that from her. Right now, he needed her to be strong. "There's only so much you can do."

"I know." He kissed her temple. "I hope she gets it together, but mostly I want to protect Justin." He was quiet for a few moments, then asked, "Are you sleepy?"

Without him saying it, she understood. "No, why? Did you want to talk more?"

"Actually..." He reached over and turned on the bedside lamp. They both flinched at the intrusion of bright light.

Ivey slipped away from him and pulled up the sheet. She admired his body as he left the bed and went to the closet, returning with a cardboard box.

Intrigued, she came up to her knees. "What is it?"

Sitting beside her, he pulled out the top photo of a chubby-cheeked toddler. "Justin."

"Oh my God," she whispered, taking the photo and smiling at it. "He's precious."

"She didn't have any photos of him as an infant, but she told me he was over eight pounds and bald until he was two and a half." He smiled.

Together, with the box between them, they went through everything.

"I want to show Justin this stuff, but he's smart. He'll ask me where I got it, and he'll know I saw Darcie." Corbin rubbed his neck in frustration. "I don't want to add to his worries."

"One thing at a time, okay?" Leaning over the box, Ivey kissed him. "Why don't you wait and see how Darcie does, and then you can figure it out?"

He nodded at that plan. "Until then, I'm going to keep the box in the top of the closet. I don't want him to accidentally run into it."

"Agreed." With a stretch and a yawn, Ivey slipped from the bed to pull on her shirt, panties and even her shorts. It hadn't happened yet, but if Justin ever woke and came into the room, she wanted to make sure she was decent. "Will you show your mom?"

"Eventually." He grinned. "For the next few days, she's going to be inseparable from Justin. I know her and she's going to want to spend as much time with him as possible."

Ivey laughed. "She can be very compelling."

"Tell me about it." He put the box back in the very top of the closet. "Once she's gotten her fill enough to relax, then I can get her alone to show her."

His mother was a special woman who had raised special sons. Ivey had no doubt she'd be a phenomenal grandmother, too. "She's something else."

"Too much?"

"No." Ivey snuggled back under the covers, close to Corbin. "I'd say she's exactly right."

"It's been a week," Hope complained, even though she'd tried not to. "Lang comes over for a while once I get home, but I'm not seeing him nearly as much. He said he's running interference for you and Corbin."

"And Justin," Ivey agreed. "Wait until you meet their mom. She comes on strong, but it's with love, you know? Not judgment or anything like that."

Sinking into a chair, Hope stared at the sandwich she'd brought for lunch and knew she didn't want it. "I don't think I'll ever meet her. In a lot of ways, it feels like whatever Lang and I had is over." The sinking feeling in the pit of her stomach made the thought of food impossible.

"Definitely not true," Ivey said, biting into a leftover piece of chicken. "I think he's protecting you."

Because she was damaged goods. Hope sighed. "He doesn't need to do that."

"I don't know. Vesta is a lot to take in. For one thing, you can't be hands-off with her. She's going to *crush* you in one of her massive hugs, believe me. The woman is like a lumberjack and doesn't know her own strength. And you should be prepared for personal comments galore. She pries without remorse and has zero filter. Remember, within a few minutes of meeting her, she wanted to know if I was in love with Corbin and if I'd marry him."

That earned a small smile. "She sounds perceptive. You *do* love Corbin. She just saw through your no-pressure efforts." For that reason alone, Hope liked the woman. Not many people could put Ivey on the spot, because usually it was Ivey doing that to others.

Hope wanted to meet Vesta—even her name was incredible.

But how did she bring that up with Lang? If, as she suspected, he wanted some distance between her and his family, she had no right to press the issue.

Ivey patted her mouth with a napkin. "The thing is, I'm not shy. I was telling Corbin exactly how much I wanted to share, then Vesta came in and boom! She threw it all out there. I have to say, though, it feels good to admit out loud how I feel. To Corbin, I mean."

"What does he do when you tell him?"

"Usually we have phenomenal sex." Ivey gave a satisfied smile. "Now I tell him every opportunity I get."

Hope laughed, but deep inside...she wanted to try that phenomenal sex for herself. Setting her sandwich aside, she glanced at the door to ensure it remained closed, then leaned toward Ivey. "Suppose I want to advance things—" she flagged a hand "—physically, I mean. How would I go about it?"

Freezing with her can of cola almost to her mouth, Ivey blinked at her. She quickly set the can aside. "You want to have sex with Lang?"

Hope felt her cheeks getting hot, but this was Ivey. Her best friend ever. All the family she had now. Someone she trusted without exception. "Pretty sure I do."

A huge grin broke over Ivey's face. "Is that because he's been enticing you for a while now?"

"For sure." Lang did a remarkable job of teasing her. A kiss here, a kiss there, the slight grazing of his fingertips over a spot that shouldn't have been sensitive, but with him, most definitely was. Like the side of her neck, her wrist.

Over her lips.

He did take pleasure in touching her, yet he never crossed the invisible boundaries she'd drawn. That had to mean something, right? Maybe she'd been overanalyzing things, worrying for no reason.

"Wonderful!" Ivey exclaimed. "That makes me like him even

more." She, too, sat forward. "So you think you're ready for the next step?"

"I think so. I hope so." In the back of Hope's mind, the fear remained that she might react badly. "What do I do?"

Ivey gave it a quick thought. "You know I'm not big on faking things, right? I'm all about tossing it out there and seeing how it lands."

"Right." Hope snorted. "You weren't that way with Geoff."

"No, because Geoff wasn't the right one. I couldn't be myself with him. Corbin is different, and I'm positive Lang is, too."

"Agreed. I'm just not sure how to proceed."

"Next time he's kissing you, if he starts to pull away, don't let him."

"I hardly think I'm strong enough to manhandle him."

Laughing, Ivey said, "Definitely not. The brothers are both fine specimens, right? But what I meant is that when he starts to end things, keep them going. I promise, he'll catch on real quick, and I'd be willing to bet he'll let you set the pace. If you start to get tense, ease up. If, though, you like what's happening, let him know."

Wide-eyed with fascination, Hope whispered, "You mean by moaning or something?"

"Ha! That's not generally something you can control anyway, not if the guy knows what he's doing. So feel free to tell him, if not with words, then with enthusiasm. Or just tell him not to stop. As long as you're enjoying things, keep telling him that."

Hope considered the advice, which to her sounded pretty daring, but then, she knew she was totally out of her depth when it came to sexual matters. "What if…" Her voice sounded scratchy with misgivings. She cleared her throat and tried again. "What if things get too far along and then I want to stop, and he can't?"

"Pfft. That's a huge myth. There is *no* point where a man can't stop. They're not animals." Ivey paused, her expression going grave. "At least most of them aren't."

Hope knew they were both thinking of the animal who had mistreated her. Lang had nothing in common with him, though, and she knew it.

Taking her hands, Ivey lowered her voice in understanding, but the smile remained on her face. "Lang is a really good guy, hon. If you're not into it, he won't be, either. I promise."

Biting her lip, Hope considered that and finally agreed. "Pretty sure I'll see him tonight."

"You've seen him every night, haven't you?"

"Yes." He still visited her, he just didn't bring her home. "You really don't think it's over?"

"If it was, Lang would say so. He's not a jerk."

"Definitely not." Since it was Saturday, she hoped they'd get to visit more over the rest of the weekend, but given how he'd switched up their routine, she just wasn't sure. "This might be my best chance."

That made Ivey laugh. "Pretty sure you could call him in the middle of night and he'd rush over, but by all means, let's make tonight the night." She sat back in her chair. "I've got it. Why not invite him up to your place? That ought to be a big indicator for him, and that way, it'll be easy to keep things going." She wrinkled her nose. "If you were at the main house with the rest of us, privacy would be hard to come by."

"Speaking as someone who knows?"

"I shouldn't complain. I get that Vesta is excited now that she's a grandmother." Ivey took another drink of her cola. "She and Hagan finally found an RV park they like, and it's forty-five minutes away. That means I won't run into them when I leave for work, and they won't still be there when I'm falling asleep. I had actually considered moving back to my own house, just to cut back on the commotion, but Justin is so used to me being there now, I'd hate to do that."

"Besides," Hope said, finally finding some interest in her sandwich, "it's not like you to give up."

"Who said anything about giving up?"

"You didn't have to." Hope imagined it was extremely difficult for Ivey. She'd admitted to loving Corbin, and yet she knew he hadn't returned the sentiment. If he had, Ivey would have already told her about it.

"Well, I might be a bit discouraged, but I'm not throwing in the towel. Honestly, Hope, I love him enough that I can't see ever giving up on him. If two years from now we're in the same place, I wouldn't end things like I did with Geoff."

Hope smiled. "At least with Corbin, you're having a really good time." She couldn't recall ever seeing Ivey so content. Even when she had concerns, optimism ruled her day.

"Life is very full, you know?" Ivey gathered up the trash from her lunch and deposited it in the can. "Justin is a constant source of amusement—and a few tears here and there. Lang keeps me in stitches. And now Vesta, too. I have to be on my toes around her."

Karen ducked into the room. "Your noon appointment just arrived early. She'll be the last of the day."

"Thank you, Karen. Go ahead and take your lunch break now. And, Hope, don't rush. I can handle Mrs. Roberts. She and her sweet dog are always a pleasure to see."

"Thanks," Hope said. Now that she and Ivey had talked it out, she wasn't as worried about her relationship with Lang. In fact, it made sense that he was only trying to shield her from his mother's assumptions. With that possibility, she was actually hungry, so she finished her lunch with Karen for company—and all the while, she anticipated the coming night.

Chapter Fifteen

Instead of going to the house and hanging out with Corbin and Ivey, Lang kept Hope out on the boat. Not that she minded, since she enjoyed being on the water. She now had a tan and badly tangled hair.

She was curious about his mother, about why he wouldn't introduce her, but she never asked. He had his reasons, and they might be that he didn't want her involved with more of his family. That didn't really make a lot of sense, because she already knew Corbin and Justin.

But meeting a guy's mom… That was a whole different deal. Maybe a little too familiar, especially if Lang wanted to keep things casual between them.

After all, they had kissed, but they'd never done anything more. Now, walking with him along the path from the dock to her home, Hope considered everything she and Ivey had discussed. She contemplated how to get things started. Something subtle, like a stroke over his hip. Or maybe she could put her hand under his shirt...

"You're awfully quiet," Lang said. "Tired?"

"No." She kept pace beside him, aware of the heated scent of his sun-warmed skin and the sizzling awareness of being near him. "I was just thinking."

"About?"

Getting you into bed. Of course she didn't say that.

It was nice that Lang always seemed so interested in her, in what she thought and felt. Seeing it as a slight opportunity, she lifted a shoulder. "Us?"

Pausing, he looked down at her. "Us?"

What she wouldn't give to be able to read his inscrutable expression. She saw interest, yes. Maybe a little caution, too. It almost appeared that he held his breath.

"I've been thinking about...things. With you, I mean."

He stepped closer. "What about me?"

God, this was harder than she'd imagined. How dumb. They were both adults, and she was sick and tired of being so hamstrung by her past. She loved kissing him, and not once had he pushed for more. He didn't even seem frustrated by her limitations, though they frustrated her.

It sometimes boggled her mind how or why she'd ever gained his attention. He was...everything. Strong, attractive, cocky and confident, even financially set. And yet he'd dedicated so much of his free time to her.

Lang was incredibly casual about her difficulties, which helped her to deal with them as well. With him, she didn't feel damaged.

With him, she wouldn't be.

She licked her lips, trying to find the right words—and they both heard a sound from the vicinity of her driveway. Almost like a car door.

Lang's gaze went past her and he frowned.

Hope turned and saw a sleek red car in the driveway.

Company? She *never* had company. Why in the world would she now, when she was just about to make a proposition?

Lang's arm went around her in what felt like a protective gesture. "Do you want me to see who it is?"

She considered it, but… "No." She was different now, she reminded herself. She could handle something as simple as an unexpected caller. "Will you stay with me, though?"

His hand held hers. "It's where I want to be."

Oh good. That sounded promising, especially after the difference in their routine all week. She'd gotten so used to spending dinner with Ivey, Corbin, Lang and Justin that she'd been feeling a little left out.

But that wasn't why she wanted to take things to the next step. Nope. She just flat out wanted Lang.

And with that decision, she got her feet moving through the lush grass. The sooner she got rid of her visitor, the sooner she could get things rolling with Lang.

They got closer…and she stalled.

A woman stood staring up at the deck over her garage, as if trying to figure out how to get up there. Her hair was shorter, and she was hugely pregnant, but of course Hope recognized her right away.

It had been four long years since she'd last seen her sister. Seeing Charity now sucked all the oxygen out of her lungs.

Like a zombie, Hope continued on until her flip-flops crunched on the gravel.

Charity turned, and her gaze locked on Hope's. They stared at each other, each sister silently appraising the other.

Lang released her hand and instead put his arm around her shoulders. Very quietly, he asked, "You okay?"

She blew out a tight breath and nodded. "Lang, this is my sister, Charity."

"Hi," Charity said in a dazed voice, her gaze bouncing back and forth between them.

Lang studied Charity. "I'm Hope's neighbor, Lang Meyer."

Charity's mouth lifted into a tentative smile. "A little more than just a neighbor, I think."

"A lot more, actually."

Hope felt herself blushing but wasn't sure why. Maybe it was the way Lang said that, as if they were committed to each other.

Oh, how she wished.

Taking her by surprise, Charity grinned. "Good for you, sis. I had worried... But here you are, looking so happy and with such a hunk." Charity laid a hand over her stomach. "Oh, Hope. I'm so glad to see you."

"No." The word emerged as a hoarse whisper. Anger stirred, and by God, it felt good. Refreshing. *Healing.* "How did you find me?"

"Facebook. You have the town listed and the animal clinic where you work." She glanced back at the house. "You even shared a pic of your new place—which is beautiful, by the way."

The casual way Charity acted only fueled her resentment. "You can't just show up here and act like nothing has happened."

"I didn't mean to do that." Charity glanced nervously at Lang. "I was hoping we could talk."

"It's been four years." She started to shake and couldn't seem to calm herself. "*Four years*, Charity. I haven't heard from you once in all that time." *You never even asked how I was doing.* "I assumed I'd never hear from you again."

"I know, and I can't tell you how sorry I am." Charity shifted. "For everything."

Hope cut a hand through the air, dismissing her sister's apology, surprising herself with the curt gesture. "Why are you here?"

"I guess I need to get right to it, huh?" Charity lifted her chin. "I'm pregnant, as you can see. I'm going to be a mother. You're going to be an aunt."

Good God. Hope fell back a step and felt Lang's arm tighten

around her. She hadn't considered her own connection to the baby her sister carried. *I'm going to be an aunt.*

Seeing her retreat, Charity rubbed her forehead. "I know, it's complicated, isn't it? I hope eventually we'll be able to talk it out, but the punch line is that I know my daughter will be better off with you in her life."

"What?" She couldn't have heard that correctly.

Big tears welled in Charity's eyes. "I know that I was unfair. I know I was selfish and misguided." She swallowed heavily. "Christ, Hope. When I think of my daughter going through what you did… I am so damned ashamed. I know down deep in my soul that I would never, ever turn on her the way we all turned on you."

The words stabbed into Hope, piercing her newfound peace of mind. "Stop," she whispered.

Instead, Charity took a step closer. "I would die for my daughter, Hope. I knew it from the moment I found out I was pregnant. She isn't even here yet and I love her more than anything. She's changed me."

Hope shook her head. It couldn't be that simple. Never, not in a million years, had she ever expected to hear an apology, much less an admission of guilt. At most, she'd thought she might hear from her family in passing, but as the years went by, she'd even given up on that.

This visit leveled her. Tears tracked down her cheeks.

"Mom and Dad should have done the same for you. They didn't. *I* didn't—and I'm sick with regret." Charity drew a shuddering breath. "When I realized I couldn't be like them, not with my own daughter, I knew I had to find you."

Lang turned with Hope so that she faced him and his back was to Charity. It broke the frozen connection between their gazes, allowing Hope to gulp in needed air.

Cupping her face in his hands, he stroked away her tears. "What do you want to do, honey? I can tell her to go." He waited a heartbeat, then added, "Or you can go inside and talk. It's up to you. Whatever you want."

Her mouth felt insanely dry, prompting her to lick her lips. She felt silly, but this was Lang, and she knew he'd understand. "You'll stay with me?"

His smile held reassurance, and a promise. "I'll be right by your side."

That helped so much. She nodded. "I guess I should invite her in, then?"

"Might be a good idea to hear what she has to say." His gaze searched hers. "You deserve an explanation."

"Yes, I do."

With a nod, Lang stepped to her side again.

Charity stood there, one hand still resting on her rounded middle, anxiety tightening her face. It was such an uncommon expression for her. Usually her sister was full-steam-ahead without a single doubt.

Not this time.

Hope cleared her throat. "Would you like to come up?"

Relief loosened Charity's entire posture. "God, yes." She looked around again. "I didn't see a way to get there, though."

"The stairs are inside the garage." Knowing nothing about pregnant women, Hope asked, "Will stairs be a problem for you?"

"Not at all, but I can't promise I won't huff, and I'd dearly love to put up my feet." She made a face. "My ankles swell."

Something warm and familiar unfurled inside Hope. It was recognition of things she'd lost. An easy camaraderie with her one and only sister.

It was…love. Sibling love.

A new wash of emotion sent more tears trailing down her cheeks. God, how she'd missed her sis.

She hadn't dwelled on it, not for a while now. What would have been the point? Bitterness was still there, but now it was more of a shadow than a sharp pain.

Trying to sort out the stew of conflicting emotions, Hope led the way into the garage and up to her small apartment.

Lang hadn't been in here since the day he, Corbin and Ivey had helped her move. Tonight, she'd planned to invite him inside, but these were very different circumstances than she'd initially anticipated.

Though the sun hadn't yet set, Hope flipped on a light to chase away the shadows and gazed around with pride.

It was a small space, but she'd made it her own in numerous ways. The furniture was for *her* comfort. The colors were to *her* liking. There were no personal photos, but she'd hung eclectic, affordable, textured art pieces that pleased her each time she gazed on them.

"How nice," Charity said as she looked around. "This looks like you, Hope. I like it."

The praise shouldn't have mattered...and yet it did. "Make yourself at home. I'll get us drinks." Always in the past, she and her sister shared icy colas. She paused at the kitchen counter as a thought occurred to her. "Can you have cola?"

"No caffeine." Sinking onto the sofa, Charity put her feet up on the poof footstool and sighed. "It isn't good for the baby."

"I have water or orange juice?"

"Water would be great. Thanks."

Lang sat on the edge of a chair, elbows on his knees, his fingers forming a steeple. "You and Hope share a similar look."

"More so before I got so big," Charity said easily. She touched her hair. "I've always worn my hair shorter, and I don't think I've ever seen Hope in makeup."

"She doesn't need it."

Charity smiled. "No, she doesn't. She's always been naturally pretty."

Before that could go on, Hope returned, handing a can of Coke to Lang and a bottle of water to Charity. "When are you due?"

"Three weeks, and I'm beyond ready. There are days when

I feel like I might pop." She took several long drinks of the water, then grimaced. "Mind if I use your bathroom? It was a long drive here."

This was all so strange. She, Hope Mage, was entertaining her own sister as a *visitor*. "It's there by the stairs," Hope said, then watched as Charity hauled herself inelegantly from the seat.

Once she'd disappeared behind the door, Hope turned to Lang.

He slowly grinned. "Threw you for a loop, didn't she?"

"Completely. I haven't heard even a squeak from her since I left home so long ago. No calls, no cards. I assumed they'd all written me off."

"Or maybe they're just too proud to come after you. People do really shortsighted things, honey."

"But for her to just show up here? Pregnant? I don't know what to think."

"Want my impression?"

Because her own thoughts were so muddled, she nodded.

"Coming to you face-to-face was a lot harder than a call, and a thousand times more sincere than a card. She made the trip because it mattered." He brushed his knuckles along her jaw. "*You* matter. I think your sister realized it and she genuinely wants to make amends."

Hope didn't dare jump to conclusions. Not after so long. She glanced toward the bathroom door, ensuring it was still closed. "I suppose getting pregnant, knowing she'd soon be a mother, might have had some influence."

"I know it did for Corbin." He tugged Hope onto his lap, one arm around her back, the other draped over her thighs. "My brother was off doing his own thing, as far from settling down as a man could be. Now he's changed literally everything in his life, all for Justin, and he did it without any qualms."

Hope considered that. "I'm going to be an aunt."

THE SUMMER OF NO ATTACHMENTS   259

"A wonderful aunt," he agreed warmly. "Your niece will be so lucky to have you in her life."

From behind them, Charity said, "I agree." Keeping a hand to the small of her back, she made her way to the couch again and settled gratefully onto the cushions. With no animus at all, she said, "I'm a selfish bitch, Hope, and I know it. But as soon as I found out I was pregnant, I desperately wanted to talk to you. I wanted to share everything with you. From the confirmation to the doctor to the ultrasound to my first stretch mark. God, it was so hard, not being able to call, to complain to you when I was sick, to tell you when I first heard the heartbeat." Her eyes welled up again. "When she first moved..." Her bottom lip trembled. "I wanted my little sister so badly. Not being able to share everything with you really drove home how much I've missed you."

Unsure what to say, Hope asked, "You've been well overall?"

"I puked my guts up for a month." Charity made a face. "It was miserable, and you know Mom. She's not exactly the nurturing type. But yes, the baby and I are fine. I was so excited when I found out I was having a girl. I kept thinking of all the things we did together." She added to Lang, "Sisters are special."

Lang lifted a brow at the irony of that statement, but he didn't reply.

Hope felt obligated to fill in the silence. "You were far more adventurous than me."

Charity laughed. "True." Again including Lang, she explained, "I was all about boys, and Hope was happiest in a cozy chair with a book in her hands."

"I can see that," Lang said, and gave Hope a squeeze.

The humor slipped away under poignant memories. Eyes solemn, Charity smiled. "I always envied you that. How self-possessed you were. How you didn't really need anyone."

A rush of hurt got Hope back on her feet. "That's not true." She stared at the sister she'd once considered her best friend. "I needed my family." The crack in her voice shamed her. Self-possessed? She, who had only just learned to enjoy a kiss? What a laugh.

"I know." Subdued, Charity stood, too. "I don't expect you to forgive me, sis, because I can't forgive myself." She swiped at her eyes impatiently. "Damn it, I've been so emotional since getting pregnant." After a deep breath that she let out slowly, she faced Hope. "I'm not married. The second I got pregnant, Will took off. He wanted no part of it, so I'll be raising the baby alone, and I'm okay with that. But you know, that's two major strikes against me. First, my fiancé turned into the worst sort of—"

"Don't say it," Hope whispered with feeling. *Don't say molester.*

Nodding, Charity went silent. Finally, with feeling, she said, "That was clearly a huge mistake on my part. He's a bastard and I hope he comes to a very bad end."

"That's two of us."

"So, loser number one. Then I hook up with Will, and he bails on me because we're having a baby. It's not like I planned it. He's the one who didn't…" She broke off again. "Sorry. It's all so dumb, but honestly, I'm as responsible as Will. You'd think I was old enough to know better."

Reeling, Hope asked, "He's out of the picture for good?"

"God, yes. Mom and Dad are annoyed that, the way they put it, they have to tolerate another wayward daughter." She swallowed heavily. "It really drove home the fact that you weren't wayward at all. You had the guts that the rest of us didn't. You stood up for yourself, and we were all… We were awful. You're the best of us, Hope. I want you in my daughter's life. Hate me if you want, but please." More tears spilled over. A damn river of them. "*Please.* Love my little girl."

There wasn't enough oxygen in the room. With a sob, Hope reached out and grabbed her sister in a tight hug that was so long overdue. "I will," she promised. "I already do." In that moment, she knew that no matter what her sister had done, how she'd turned her back on her, how badly she'd crushed her spirit, Charity was still her sister.

Now and always.

"I don't deserve you," Charity whispered.

"Maybe not, but you're stuck with me anyway." Getting her arms around Charity wasn't easy. Her sister had doubled in size. With a small laugh, Hope held her back. "Are you sure you aren't carrying twins?"

Wiping her eyes yet again and totally ruining her carefully applied makeup, Charity sniffled. "Don't even joke. I'm going to have my hands full with one." She smiled. "Oh, Hope. I'm sorry. I'm so damned sorry."

All Hope could manage was a nod.

Charity stroked a hand over her stomach, staring down at where the baby grew. "I laid awake one night, feeling her move and thinking about you, about what you'd been through. And... and I made myself think about my daughter. If something that awful happened to her."

"Shh. Don't."

"But it *could*, because it happened to you." Charity grabbed Hope in for another choking hug. "That means it could happen to anyone. I swear to you, I'll take better care of her, though. I'll protect her the way we didn't protect you. I'll do better. For you and the baby."

So much emotion had worn Hope out. She realized Lang was quiet and when she glanced around, she found him standing at the window, his back to them as he looked out at the woods. He'd given them as much privacy as he could—without leaving her.

God love the man.

She certainly did. The realization made her laugh. She loved him so very much. Not because he was the first guy she'd been involved with since her assault, but because he was special, to his brother, his nephew...and especially to her heart.

"Lang?" She held out a hand.

Troubled, he looked at her, his gaze probing as if to be certain she was all right. "It kills me to hear you cry."

That made her smile. "I'm okay," she promised.

And she was. A year ago, she wouldn't have been. Even a few months ago. But now, after having him in her life? She felt like she could do anything. And even if their relationship ended tomorrow, she knew she wouldn't retreat back to that protective shell where she feared everyone and everything except her closest friend, Ivey. She would never again be that person.

Immediately Lang came back to her, folding her hand gently in his, tugging her close to his side. "Where are you staying?" he asked Charity.

"I have a motel room. It's not far from here and if Hope is willing, I'd like to visit with her over the next few days."

"I'd like that," Hope assured her. "You're on vacation or something?"

"Actually, I've relocated. It was time to get away from Mom and Dad. Not for good." She gave a wry twist of her mouth. "For better or worse, they're our parents, and they'll soon be Marley's grandparents."

"Marley? That's what you plan to name her?"

"Marley Mage. It has a ring to it, don't you think? I'm still stuck on middle names, though." She shot Hope a look. "Mom hates it."

The grin took her by surprise. "I think it's beautiful." Marley Mage, her niece. She couldn't get used to that—but she wanted to.

"I needed some distance from Mom and Dad, you know? When I see them, and I will, it needs to be a planned visit, not a day-to-day thing." She chewed her lower lip. "I'll actually be closer to you, now."

"You moved here?" One surprise after another.

In a rush, Charity explained, "Don't be mad, Hope, please.

I'm not going to impose or anything like that, but I figured even if you hated me, you wouldn't feel that way about Marley."

"Of course not."

"I meant what I said. You'll be such a good influence on her, and no child can have too much love."

Hope smiled at Lang, since he and Corbin had often said the same about Justin. "I agree."

"I want you in our lives, but at least in *her* life." She didn't give Hope a chance to reply to all that. "I'm looking at a place only fifteen minutes outside of Sunset. I've started my own business. I'm a social media consultant for big firms. I help them get organized, show them where to put their advertising dollars and all that. I won't be rich, but I'll get by and I'll have time with Marley."

Hope looked from Charity to Lang and back again. For some reason, her sister's uncertainty struck her as hilarious. It was such a comical look for her confident sister. "I know you, Charity. You'll do great, I'm sure."

"That means so much." With a sappy smile, Charity picked up her purse. "Well. I should get going. I'm completely exhausted after my trip, but I had to see you or I knew I wouldn't sleep at all tonight."

"You have to go so soon?"

Expression softening, Charity said, "Tonight, I really am tired, and I didn't mean to interrupt your plans with Mr. Hotness here."

Lang laughed, taking the compliment in stride.

Full of uncertainty, Charity asked, "I hope you have time to visit more soon?"

Hope gave her a nod. "We'll figure it out."

"You are so amazing." Digging in her purse, Charity located a card. "I have a new number, but give me a call, and I can be over in no time." She hesitated, then asked, "Is your number different?"

"Oh, yeah, it is. I'll text you so you have it, okay?"

Charity nodded. Her watery gaze shifted to Lang. "Take very good care of this one. She's special."

Lang drew Charity in for a hug, and Hope heard him say, "Believe me, I'm aware."

Once Charity drove away, an uncomfortable silence settled around them. Lang kept his arm over Hope's shoulders, so he felt how rigidly she still held herself.

He didn't want to leave her, damn it. Not tonight. Maybe not ever. "Hope." After turning her toward him, he lifted her chin. Her dark blue eyes were still liquid with emotion. He saw the faint tracks left on her cheeks from her tears and felt his heart wrenching. Leaning down, he kissed each cheek very gently. "Are you sure you're okay?"

"Will you stay the night with me?"

Her blurted question hung out there, stealing his breath, making his brain scramble. Surely he'd misunderstood, right?

Yet she didn't blink. In fact, she seemed incapable of blinking. "Stay the night?" he repeated.

Three quick breaths later, she nodded—then promptly bit her lip. "Unless you don't want to."

"You mean…" It occurred to him that they were likely talking about two different things. His body had already leaped to lust-inspired conclusions. Knowing her as he did, he readjusted his thinking real fast. "You don't want to be alone?"

Of course that was it. He drew her in against his chest, rested his jaw on the top of her head.

"Sure, honey, I can stay. I can camp out on the couch, okay?" He'd be close, but she wouldn't feel uneasy about his nearness. He hoped. "It's not a problem."

"You want to sleep on the couch?"

Ah, hell. There his body went again. "I want to do whatever will make you feel better. Always."

"You're almost too nice."

Was she laughing at him? Something in her tone made him think so. Lang set her back so he could see her face. "I care about you, Hope. You have to know that."

"Yes, I do. I care about you, too…and I want you."

Yeah, okay, no mistaking that one. "You mean…?"

She tucked back her hair and gave him a slight smile. "I can't guarantee I won't falter, but I *really* want you, Lang. Enough that I want to try." She touched his jaw. "Would that be okay?"

His instinct was to crush her close, kiss her with all the hunger and need he'd kept under tight rein for so long. But they were standing in her driveway and she'd just had an emotional shock with an estranged sister.

The very last thing he would ever do was take advantage of her.

Her hand fell away and she took a step back. "You're, um, thinking about it for so long, I'm starting to get nervous. Ivey swore to me that you'd be on board. If she was wrong, I think I'll—"

Screw it. He hauled her in and kissed her—not the way he wanted to, but in the ways they'd indulged already. Hope enjoyed kissing, and God knew he loved everything about her.

"I'm on board," he swore, once he came up for air. "I just don't want to misstep and upset you." Cupping her face, he said, "Promise me right now that you won't hesitate to tell me if I do or say anything that makes you uncomfortable."

Nodding, she breathed, "I promise."

He rubbed his mouth, his thoughts bandying about as he tried to settle on a plan. He'd need to let Corbin know—which meant Ivey would know as well. Not much was private when those closest to them lived a short walk away and were family.

Another problem was that he only had one condom on him.

Given Hope's past and everything she'd just gone through, who knew if he'd even need it? But if he did…

At least he had that covered. One wouldn't be enough for him, but for her? Damn it, he was already getting half hard.

Insane. He was thirty years old, not eighteen. Hope deserved more than raging gonads. She deserved a lot of consideration and finesse and—

Hope grinned. "Will you promise me something, too?"

"Yes." He'd promise her anything. Hell, he'd *do* anything, as long as she was happy.

"Will you try not to worry?" She stepped into him, her arms tight around his waist. "I don't want to be treated differently."

"Sorry, honey, but you are different." How could she not know that? "It's not only what you've been through, but the way you and I click. I've known plenty of women through my life, but none that I wanted more than you. And I don't just mean sex, okay? If you find you can't after all, that's okay. I still want to be with you."

With her face tucked against his chest, she asked, "For how long, though?"

Was that her worry? That if they didn't go to the next step soon, he'd lose interest? Determined to get things rolling, he turned her back toward the garage and started in. "For as long as it takes." After pressing the button to close the garage door, he urged her to the stairs.

Breathless, Hope rushed to keep up. "I don't want you to have to wait."

He didn't want *her* to have to wait. He wanted her to experience everything, to get all the joy out of life that was rightfully hers. "I'm a big boy. I can handle it." At the top of the stairs, he kissed her again. "I just prefer to handle it with you."

"Lang." She hugged him again. "You make my head spin, and you make me feel things I didn't know I could."

"I hope you always feel that way."

Her eyes rounded at the word *always*. Yeah, he'd thrown that out there just to see her reaction.

Not promising.

Maybe she only wanted him to kick-start her sex life in gear again? What if she wasn't as crazy about him as he was her?

No, he wouldn't think that. Hope wasn't the type to use anyone.

But he couldn't let her delude herself, either. Plenty of people turned to sex when they needed an outlet. Him included. If that's all Hope needed, he'd be there for her, but one way or another, he'd earn her love, too.

"You look drained," he said. "Why don't you take a quick shower? I'll give Corbin a call."

"You're calling your brother now?"

The grin surprised him. "Not to gossip about you or what we do together. Corbin and I outgrew that a long time ago. But I live there, remember? He might wonder if I don't come in. He has enough on his mind right now without thinking something has happened to me."

"Oh yeah." She shook her head. "I hadn't thought of that."

"I usually read to Justin before he goes to bed."

"Darn. I'm keeping you from that, aren't I? You could run home and just come back later—"

Pressing a finger to her soft lips, Lang quieted her. "I guarantee Corbin will be happy to fill in. He's grumbled multiple times over me getting to do it."

She heaved a heavy sigh. "You're sure I'm not interrupting your routine?"

Silly Hope. The woman offered him sex, something he'd wanted within minutes of meeting her, and then she worried that it might inconvenience him.

"I'm sure." He gave her a quick kiss. "Go on. I'll be here when you come out."

More than a little reluctant, she went into the bedroom and opened the closet. Lang dug out his phone and dialed Corbin while striding to the far end of the living area to look out over the deck. Her apartment was small enough that there was really no place to go for privacy, but at least this way they weren't tripping over each other.

Corbin answered on the second ring. "Hey, what's up?"

"That's what I was going to ask you." He glanced back as Hope left the bedroom and ducked into the bathroom.

"Get this," Corbin said. "Mom took Justin with her to the RV park."

Wow. That was a big step for Corbin to let the boy out of his sight. "No kidding. How did Justin feel about it?"

"He's excited to sleep in the RV, and he wants to see the setup of the park. Mom described it to him, with a pool, a playground and a lot of other kids around. She made it sound exciting."

"So you're letting him go?"

"She swore she'd keep an eagle eye on him. You know how she is. She's a good watchdog."

Lang laughed. "That she is. I'm glad you agreed."

"She'll have him tonight and all of tomorrow, but they'll be home in time for dinner."

"Sounds good." Then, with more gravity, Lang added, "He's doing great, Corbin. Every day he's more and more like any other kid."

"Not so afraid of screwing up? Not as stunned every time something good happens?"

"Yeah." That about covered it.

"Monday, Mom's taking him clothes shopping."

"Huh." Lang heard the shower start and stared hard at the bathroom door, imagining Hope in there and what she might be doing. With effort, he drew himself back to the conversation with his brother. "I was there when you asked him about shopping for new clothes. He acted like you'd asked him to eat a whole jar of olives or something."

"I know. That's why I haven't gotten him new stuff yet. I was biding my time until he got more comfortable, but all his clothes are either too small or too big. The thing is, Mom asked, and he agreed."

"She convinced him?" Their mother could be *very* convincing.

Corbin laughed. "Actually, Justin whispered to me that it might hurt her feelings if he said no. Plus, Mom is going to let him pick out a few new books, too. He was totally on board with that."

Nice. He could see their mom using whatever leverage was needed. The woman was a master at getting her way. "So this means you and Ivey have the rest of the weekend to yourselves?"

"We're not running you off."

Ha! No, Corbin would never tell him to get lost, but he'd probably be glad to hear he'd have some privacy. "Just as an FYI, I'll probably be staying here for the night."

Surprise hung in the air. "Here?"

"With Hope."

After a slight, suspended silence, Corbin said, "Move with caution, okay?"

"Gee, thanks. What would I do without your advice?"

"Probably screw up."

Lang chuckled. "Possibly—but I doubt it. Not with something this important." *Someone* this important.

"I know," Corbin said more seriously. "I'm just giving you a hard time. I'm glad to hear things are moving along. She deserves to be happy."

"Agreed." Could she be happy with him? God, he hoped so.

"Not that you need it, but good luck."

The hell he didn't. Right now he needed luck and control in equal measure. "Thanks. I'll see you tomorrow sometime."

Just as Lang put the phone back in his pocket, Hope stepped out of the bathroom. She wore a white, wraparound terry cloth robe, tied at the waist with a matching belt, had her towel-dried hair combed back, and she looked at him with great expectation.

Yup, he was definitely getting hard, and there wasn't a damn thing he could do about it.

Except love her and hope it was enough.

Chapter Sixteen

Despite the urge to rush, Lang took his time in the shower. While he went over plans in his head, he realized he had nothing to change into.

Would Hope mind him wearing only a towel? She was a sensible woman, so odds were she'd already considered the complications of her spontaneous invite. Still, he didn't want to alarm her.

Losing a towel would be so easy.

Losing her robe, too.

Yeah, and thoughts like that would not help him keep it together.

After fifteen minutes, the water started to run cold and Lang knew he was pushing his luck. After drying off and finger-combing his damp hair, he folded his clothes—with his wallet on top of the stack—and wrapped the towel around his hips. He stepped out of the bathroom.

He wasn't sure what he expected, but finding Hope standing right there, her shoulders against the wall, her fingers playing with the terry cloth belt to her wrap, was a total shocker.

Her gaze shot up to meet his, and they stood there like that, no more than two feet separating them, while the tension expanded, throbbing in the air.

With her place so small, the bathroom and her bedroom were right next to each other. She'd left the bedroom door open.

She'd even turned down the bed.

Those realizations all closed in on him at once. While trying to sort it out, he stepped into the bedroom and set down his clothes, then moved the wallet to the nightstand.

Hope stood in the doorway, her gaze tracking over him, across his shoulders and chest, down to his abs, lower—as if she could see through the towel.

When she stepped toward him, the groan came of its own volition. "You're killing me, honey."

Crossing the last few steps in a rush, Hope came up against him, her arms sliding around his neck and her mouth seeking his.

Definitely not what he'd expected.

Probably more than he deserved, too. But yeah, he loved her eagerness.

He gently cradled her close while devouring her mouth. It wasn't easy, but he kept his hands still on her back.

Hope didn't. Her hands were everywhere, over his chest, up to his shoulders, along his arms. She freed her mouth, but only so she could brush her nose over his chest, breathing him in and all in all acting like a woman well primed, without a single nervous qualm.

He tangled a hand in her hair and tipped her face up. God, she looked beautiful to him, petite and pretty with her dark, baby-fine hair and her deep blue eyes now dazed with need.

Lang considered things, then asked low, "Want to try the bed?"

"Yes." Snagging his hand, she attempted to drag him toward the mattress.

He laughed, but damn. "Slow down, babe."

Rounding on him, she said, "Over four years I've gone without wanting anyone, and now I want *you*. I want *this*." She pulled the belt of her robe open and let the material part. "And I want it now."

It struck Lang that he'd been completely wrong in his thinking. Hope was a smart woman who knew her own mind. She'd lived through the awfulness of her past and had learned to deal with it. In all the time that had passed, no one had managed to pressure her in any way—because she hadn't let them.

Why would he think he'd be any different? Obviously, she wasn't shy with him, so he'd been worrying about nothing, instead of proceeding naturally.

The smile came slowly. "You're really sure, aren't you?"

"About you? Yes, definitely." As if to prove it, she shrugged off the robe and it landed in a fluffy white heap at her feet.

Lord help him.

As if in challenge, she stood with her hands at her sides, her shoulders back and her chin angled with determination.

So many nights he'd thought about her body, but he still hadn't been prepared. Lust clamored against protectiveness and then melded with love. It was all okay, because it was with Hope.

Watching her, he loosened the towel and let it drop.

She swallowed heavily, her gaze darting all over him, her breathing deepening.

Using care, Lang stepped closer and eased her bare body against his. "Okay?"

She tucked her face into his neck. "I want you so much."

That honest admission was all the encouragement he needed.

After that, everything happened as it should, without unnecessary caution. He stopped worrying about offending her and instead loved her as he wanted.

As *she* wanted.

Stretching out on the bed together, they both grew bolder.

Lang discovered that she was keenly curious about his body and not at all timid in exploring. When she curled her small hand around his erection, he closed his eyes and concentrated on not coming.

Once he had himself in control again, he showed her how to tighten her grip, how far to stroke, how fast.

Such exquisite torture.

"My turn," he said, moving her hand and bending to kiss her breasts while pressing a hand between her thighs.

Thrilled to find her already hot and wet, he utilized every ounce of experience he had, and every drop of patience he could muster, until she gave a throaty, vibrating moan. As soon as her climax started to ease, he shifted to grab the condom, quickly rolled it on and then came down over her.

Using care, he parted her thighs and settled against her. "Open your eyes, honey. I need to see you."

She chuckled and lazily did as he requested. "I think you can see plenty of me."

"Yes, and I enjoy looking at you. But I want to see what you're thinking, too."

Her gaze warmed. "I'm thinking that you've changed my life, and I will never, ever regret that."

It wasn't quite a declaration of love, but he didn't care. He took her mouth and slowly eased into her. She was so tight, it made him a little insane, but her enthusiasm sparked to life again.

Half an hour later, he really wished he had another condom— or ten. He could have made love to Hope all night long.

He could definitely love her…for the rest of his life.

"Lang?" Cuddled together, Hope relished the closeness and comfort of being like this with him. For an instant, she thought of all the time she'd wasted being afraid, and then she shook her head.

It hadn't been only fear that held her back. No man had offered even a slight temptation.

Not until she'd met this man.

"Hmm?" His fingertips trailed up and down her spine in a never-ending caress.

"Will it ruin the moment if I ask you something?"

He shifted slightly, scooting her up so he could see her face. "You can ask me anything, at any time. Okay?"

Shoot. She hadn't meant to imply it was something monumental, but now he looked so grave, she smiled. "How come you don't want me to meet your mom?"

His brows shot up, the seriousness vanished, and he laughed. "God, I'm not sure I want to talk about my mother while we're naked in bed together."

Oh. She hadn't thought about that. No, she wouldn't want to talk about her mother, either. "Sorry."

"Kidding." He rolled her to her back and turned on his side to face her. Now his big hand, fingers opened, rested on her stomach. "I don't mind if you meet my mom. Actually, I think you'll like her. For sure she'll like you."

"Then why have you excluded me all week?"

His brows leveled. "I'm sorry if you thought I was."

Hope shrugged. "You've spent time with me, and I've enjoyed the boat rides. I'm not complaining about that. Everything changed, though, and I wasn't sure...what to think."

"I should have explained." Pressing a firm kiss to her mouth, he said, "I wanted to protect you. Not only does Mom come on strong, she's a master at making assumptions. I'd worked so hard not to pressure you, I didn't want her to, either."

That sounded like a convenient excuse, yet as soon as Hope thought about it, she discarded the notion. Lang wasn't that way. Far as she could tell, he was always honest with her. "Ivey told me that about her."

As if they'd been in this very position numerous times, he

put a leg over hers. "If Mom has her way, Ivey and Corbin will be married before they know what hit them."

She knew Ivey would be thrilled—if Corbin was willing. "How does Corbin feel about it?"

He slowly grinned. "This is the strangest after-sex convo I've ever had. First questions about my mother and now my brother."

Hope pushed at his chest. "Well, I'm not exactly up to speed on these things."

Laughing, he kissed her. "You could try complimenting me. Tell me I'm the best—"

"You're the only," she pointed out, then balked as ugly memories tried to intrude. "The only one that matters."

He smoothed her hair. "You amaze me, Hope. I had all these dumb misconceptions about how you would handle things. I underestimated you, I'm sorry for that. The truth is, I'd love for you to meet Mom. She'll be there at dinner on Monday if you want to join us."

Cue the guilt. Knowing she'd just coerced him, Hope frowned. "I didn't mean to twist your arm."

"That could be kinky if you want to give it a try."

The grin threatened; he was always so funny, even now. She loved that about him. "Be serious."

Turning to his back on the bed, Lang pulled her half over him. After a yawn, he said, "When you meet her, you'll understand. Going forward, though, know that I want you in every part of my life. If I screw up and don't make that clear, call me on it, okay?"

She froze even as her heartbeat picked up speed. "Every part?"

Warm brown eyes smiled at her, and he said gently, "I love you, Hope, so yeah. Every part."

"Lang!" When she tried to sit up, he tightened his hold, keeping her right there against his heart.

"I'm not pressuring you, okay?" His hands gentled, fondling her in delicious ways. "But it's the truth, I've never known anyone like you. I think I fell in love with you that first day I met you in your driveway."

"You did?" All she remembered of that first meeting was how she'd cowered in her car.

"I swear, I don't plan to live with Corbin forever. In fact, I've been checking into property around here to open a sports complex, so I won't be a man of leisure forever, either."

That he wanted to share his plans with her filled her with warmth. "You don't have to explain yourself to me." Had she given that impression? "I know you're here for your brother."

"And my nephew, yes. And now you." He squeezed her again. "I love the area, I love my family and I want us to have a life together. Here, in Sunset."

So much excitement made it difficult for her to organize her thoughts. "Are you...?" Did she dare say it?

She didn't have to, because Lang did. "Asking you to marry me? Yeah. What do you think of that?"

This time he couldn't restrain her. She bounced up with a loud squeal that had him laughing again.

"Can I take that as a yes?"

Throwing her arms around his neck and kissing him multiple times, Hope said, "Yes, absolutely yes." She could barely catch her breath. "I love you so much, and I think you're incredible, but I wasn't sure how you felt so I didn't want to make assumptions."

"I admire you, Hope. Especially your strength."

That slowed her down enough to ask, "My strength?" Overall, she was pretty darned scrawny.

"Strength here." Smiling, he touched her forehead with a fingertip. "And here." He rested a hand under her breast. "The way you handled your sister today proved you have a great well of strength, enough to forgive, and that's more than many people have."

Her heart felt full enough to burst. "I admire you, too, you know. You're so loyal to your family, and you're funny and smart."

"And handsome," he teased.

"Definitely that." Another thought occurred to her. "One thing, though."

His dark eyes drifted over her face with so much heat, she felt singed. "Anything you want."

She liked that idea a lot. "Let's take our time. Not because I don't love the idea of being married to you, but Justin is still adjusting and Corbin is already slammed. Plus I know Ivey feels a little bit in limbo right now. I want to share with all of them, but I don't want to add to the chaos."

"Understandable. As long as you don't mind if I stay with you often. I like holding you like this, Hope."

"I like it, too."

"Then we're in agreement." Tugging her back into his arms, he said, "Now that we've got that settled, let's get some sleep—and tomorrow I'll store a box of condoms in your nightstand."

Loving that idea, and especially loving him, Hope fell asleep with a smile on her face.

On Monday, silence reigned at the dinner table. Corbin glanced around, taking it in. Everyone seemed cautious, except for Justin, who chatted about everything, and his mother, who smiled conspicuously as if she knew a secret.

On her drive over from the RV park, she'd picked up barbecue for dinner with coleslaw, pasta salad and a cake for dessert. It was a simple meal, but the company was a little complex—or so it seemed to Corbin.

His mother had, of course, enveloped Hope with her boundless affection. And why not? Hope was a doll, plus she made Lang happy. Her quiet demeanor didn't put off his mother, it just gave her additional opportunity for hugs because Hope didn't protest.

A few times there, it actually looked as if Hope relished the embrace. Maybe because her own mother hadn't been very demonstrative. Just the opposite, from what he understood.

Thank God she'd had Ivey.

Again and again, Corbin's gaze was drawn to Ivey. Today she had her riotous curls somewhat contained atop her head, which produced a sort of poof that he thought looked adorable. He didn't know how it happened, but every time he saw her, she somehow got prettier, and sexier.

Or maybe it was just his growing feelings for her.

Having her all to himself for the weekend had given him a taste of how it would be if they made things permanent. He wanted that. So damn much.

His gaze went to his son, currently with barbecue sauce smeared over the corner of his mouth and, somehow, across one cheek. His mother had apparently let him swim right up until it was time to head home; a touch of color brightened his cheeks and nose, and his hair had that dried-in-the-sun look.

Picking up a napkin, he handed it to Justin. "Right here," he said, touching his own cheek.

Without much thought, too intent on his food, Justin swiped at the mess.

It made Corbin smile to see his son like this now. Surrounded by people who loved him. Happy. Carefree.

But he knew it was a fragile time for Justin. It was still too soon for him to accept all the changes. He'd keep at it, of course, keep showing him how a child should be loved and sheltered. Eventually Justin's trust would grow.

Beneath the table, Ivey touched Corbin's thigh. That silent support proved yet again the depth of her ability to care. She had an acute awareness of others and never hesitated to give comfort when she sensed it was needed. With him, she was always cued in, as if she shared his every thought.

Smiling at Justin, she asked, "How did you like the RV park?"

"It was awesome. I had a TV near my bunk and Grandma let

me watch a movie last night. Today we swam and swam, then she took me for a ride on her golf cart and we found some other kids to play with."

Corbin noticed the beaming smile on *Grandma's* face.

"They shot hoops," Vesta said. "Did you know Justin is really good?"

Blushing, Justin said, "I missed a lot of times."

"But you also made a lot of baskets." Briefly, Vesta touched his shoulder. "And you played well with the others, even when one or two of them were rude."

Justin hitched a shoulder. "Kids are like that sometimes," he said with world-weary cynicism. "There was a kid where I used to live who was always mean. I didn't like him, but I felt sorry for him. He never had anyone to play with."

Vesta put a hand to her chest in a show of emotion. "Were you nice to him?"

"I guess." He looked up. "His dad would smack him in the street sometimes."

Corbin slowly lowered his sandwich.

"It's okay," Justin said quickly. "Some cops came and arrested him for it and they told the boy they'd figure things out for him." Scrunching his nose, he added, "I didn't see him after that."

Ivey swallowed heavily. "I'm glad you weren't mean to him. It shows what a wonderful person you are."

"I wasn't mean to anyone. Well, 'cept this one kid who was throwing rocks at a dog." His eyes narrowed. "I threw rocks at *him* until he quit."

Before Corbin could figure out how to reply to that, Ivey said, "Bravo! I'd have done the same."

"A few of the rocks hit him," Justin said.

"Good. He probably deserved it."

Lang snickered, and Vesta quickly covered her mouth with her napkin.

Belatedly, Ivey realized her faux pas and cleared her throat to add, "Though we probably shouldn't do things like that. Some people just need to be taught kindness."

Justin missed the impromptu correction. "I really like the RV. It has a refrigerator and table and beds and everything. It's cool. The shower isn't very big and Hagan says he barely fits, but there's a hose on the back that Grandma let me use for showering. *Outside*," he added with emphasis. "I left on my trunks, though."

Corbin grinned. Clearly the idea of bathing outside was a treat.

"So," Lang asked with interest. "You really liked the RV, huh?"

Corbin immediately pointed his fork at him. "No more extravagant gifts."

Surprised, Ivey said, "You wouldn't." When she saw Lang's face, she laughed. "You would! Oh my gosh, Lang, you're outrageous."

"I try to be, but Corbin ruins all my fun."

"Is that so?" Ivey glanced at Hope and Lang both with suggestive meaning. "I heard differently."

Hope went bright pink but smiled.

Lang just grinned.

"What's this?" Vesta, never one to miss a thing, pounced. "Something happened recently?"

Lang gave her a long look. "I always have fun with Hope. That's nothing new."

Hope got redder.

Vesta bounced her gaze back and forth between them. "So. When are you getting a job?" she asked Lang.

"Mom," Corbin said. "You know he just sold his business."

Ignoring that, Vesta asked Hope, "Do you approve of my son being a deadbeat?"

"He's not!" Hope went straight to his defense. "He's already thinking of another business, but for now he's just enjoying the family time."

"Hmm," Vesta said.

Hagan put down his napkin. "Justin, if you're all done eating, would you want to show me the boat? I admit I'm curious." He smiled at Vesta. "Been thinking of getting my own, you know."

"Can I, Dad?" Already out of his seat, Justin jammed the last bite of potato salad into his mouth.

"You can," Corbin said, "but remember to get a life preserver first."

"I'll make sure he does," Hagan promised. With his hand on Justin's shoulder, they started out.

Vesta turned to grin at them all. "Hagan knows me so well. He understood I had questions—oh, so many questions—but with Justin here, I was hampered."

Lang snorted. "Nothing hampers you."

She threw her napkin at him. "Behave yourself."

Half hiding his smile, Lang folded the napkin and handed it back to her. "Yes, ma'am."

Corbin jumped in before his mother could get going. "Justin's birthday is in two months. I've been thinking about this, and we should all cut back on the presents until then. That way, his birthday, and then later Christmas, will mean a little more."

"Oh my gosh," Ivey gushed, "I hadn't even thought about his birthday. We could do an entire monster party! I have so many things we can use…" She jumped up from the table to rummage in a drawer until she found a pen and paper. Hurrying back to her seat, she started a list. "This is going to be so fun."

As Corbin watched her, contentment settled into his heart. Ivey not only loved his son, she loved caring for him, loved surprising him and making him happy. She would be an amazing stepmother.

Suddenly Ivey stopped her feverish writing. She glanced up at Corbin with an expression of uncertainty. "Am I assuming too much?" She sat straighter. "Damn it, I didn't mean to suddenly take over."

"You're fine," Corbin promised her, but she didn't appear to be listening.

"It's just that he enjoys monster stuff so much and he's always so happy whenever I give him something from my collection. There are so many more things for him to enjoy, and I'd already decided to hand the whole lot over to him…"

Corbin touched a finger to her mouth to stop her rambling. He was aware of his mother smiling in satisfaction, and of Lang and Hope watching with affection. Of course everyone loved Ivey. How could they not?

If they didn't have an audience right now, he'd kiss her silly. "I love your idea, and I know Justin will, too."

Unconvinced, she chewed her bottom lip. "You said it's two months away." She glanced around the table, then lowered her voice as if everyone couldn't hear. "I assume I'll still be here?"

If he had his way, she'd be with them always. He'd thought about it a lot and as much as he wanted to marry her, he'd kept thinking that it would be best to wait a year, maybe even two…

But now? Now he faced reality. *He* couldn't wait that long, even if she was willing.

Ivey sat back. "Well, you're taking an awfully long time to think about it."

"Because," Lang said, giving Corbin a provoking look, "my brother is sometimes a little slow on the uptake."

"I'm not, actually," Corbin promised Ivey with a smile. "Yes, I want you here. Always." He brushed his knuckles over her cheek. "Now that you've been staying here, I can't imagine this house without you in it."

"Awww." Ivey put a hand to her throat. To Vesta, she said, "Isn't he just the sweetest?"

"I raised him right," Vesta replied. "So will there be a wedding?"

Damn it. He really wished his mother didn't bulldoze through every situation. He needed to talk to Ivey alone, without everyone listening in.

After a beat, Lang filled in the silence. "In fact, there will be, because Hope and I are going to get married." He lifted his glass in a toast. "I'm *not* slow."

Screeching, Ivey was out of her seat and racing around the table to Hope, while Hope hurriedly pushed back her chair.

They embraced tightly.

Grinning, Corbin watched them. Ivey wanted to marry him. He knew that because, as usual, she hadn't been shy about telling him. But clearly she didn't resent Hope's good news. She glowed with happiness for her friend, and just as she had with Justin's birthday party, she immediately started making plans.

Corbin looked at his brother. "Congratulations."

"Thanks." Lang nodded at their mother. "The news struck her silent. Who knew that was even possible?"

Wow. Their stalwart mother looked positively leveled. She even had tears in her eyes. When she turned her dazed expression to Lang, the emotion overflowed. "I'm finally going to be a mother-in-law!" she wailed, making both brothers jump.

Surging to her feet, she snatched Hope away from Ivey and crushed her. Hope only laughed and hugged her back.

While they were all otherwise engaged, Corbin pushed back his chair, took Ivey's hand and led her through the dining room and out to the deck. He closed the slider firmly behind him.

Flushed with excitement, Ivey sighed. "Isn't it wonderful? Oh, Corbin, I was so afraid Hope would never find the right guy for her, but your brother did the trick. She is *so* happy. And that makes me happy, too." She wiped at her eyes.

Corbin gently pulled her into his arms. "What about you, Ivey? Have you found the right guy?"

"Pfft," she said, resting her head on his shoulder. "I found you. It doesn't get more right than that."

No, it didn't. "I love you, Ivey."

It was as if time and space stopped, she went so still—then she exploded from his arms. "You *love* me?"

"Shhh. Sweetheart, you'll tell everyone on the lake."

Laughing, she surged back against him. "Who cares? I have a right to shout it."

Corbin tugged her to a chair, sat down and situated her in his lap. "At first I was thinking that we should take it slow—"

"Slow is fine by me." She pressed her palm to his jaw. "I don't mind waiting."

"—but every chance I got, I included you more in our lives."

"That was for convenience."

Laughing, Corbin shook his head. "Just shush and listen to me, okay?"

Her brows shot up. "You're telling me to *shush*?"

"Please." He kissed the disgruntled set of her mouth. "It'll be easier for me to propose."

Her jaw loosened, then her lips parted. She didn't say a word.

"I love you, Ivey. Life is so much better with you, for so many different reasons. You see the best in me, you're the most understanding person I know. The kindest and sweetest." He lightly tugged on a bouncy curl near her temple. "Definitely the sexiest."

She bit her lips as if to keep from talking, but he saw the happiness glowing in her mesmerizing green eyes.

"I had worried that it might be too much for Justin. I wanted his adjustment to be as smooth and easy as possible."

Nodding fast, Ivey again showed the depth of her care for his son.

"But that was just dumb. How can it hurt him to bring more people into his life who love him and who make him a priority?"

Ivey whispered, "I do love him, Corbin. So much."

He knew it. He'd seen it, felt it. And so had Justin.

"Now I realize that the more he sees of good relationships, the better it is for him."

"We do have a good relationship."

"The best," he confirmed. Her relationship with Justin was also amazing. And she got along great with his brother and now his mother. All in all, Justin had something he never had before—a big, loving family. No matter how old he got, he'd have their support. "We can't pretend that things are settled with Darcie. We both know better. And I can't promise my mother won't overstep at times."

"With the best of intentions," Ivey added.

"Yes." His mother could smother a person, but she smothered them with love, not ill will. "It won't always be easy."

"Corbin," she whispered. "I'm a veterinarian. I deal with wonderful people and awful people. Beautiful animals who have love and animals that have been horribly mistreated. I heal some and lose others. I still love my job and wouldn't trade it for anything. Nothing in life is always easy. But together, I believe it'll be easier."

"Agreed." He was kissing her, loving her, wishing he had time to get her alone, when voices carried up from below.

Justin and Hagan were returning from their tour of the boat. In his growing, carefree way, Justin talked about life on a lake, and Hagan—who really was a good guy—gave his agreement.

Ivey kissed Corbin's throat. "Justin is flourishing with all the attention."

He really was, and it gave Corbin hope. "So will you marry me, Ivey?"

"Yes. But for right now, let's keep it to ourselves, okay? This is such a momentous thing for Hope, I don't want to steal any of her limelight."

Grinning, Corbin said, "I'm not sure my mother could suffer the shock anyway. We'll let her get used to one wedding at a time."

"As to the wedding…are you wanting something big?" Ivey rushed on before he could answer. "Because I'd rather something small and simple. I could invite my folks and your family and Hope, of course."

God, he loved her. "Whatever you want is fine with me." Thinking it through, he added, "We'll let Mom get it out of her system with Hope and Lang."

Ivey laughed. "There you go."

Just then the patio doors opened and Justin came out. "Hagan wants to try tubing. Uncle Lang is going to take us out. Do you want go, too, Dad?" He turned to Ivey. "It's super fun."

"I would love to go," she said. Leaving Corbin's lap, she caught Justin in a hug.

He didn't resist, just hugged her briefly and then wiggled free. "I gotta put on my trunks. Go get ready!" And he took off.

Having Ivey as his wife was going to be amazing.

Corbin couldn't imagine a better life.

Chapter Seventeen

"All week," Hope complained, "you've been keeping a secret. Don't deny it, because I can tell. Give, already."

Ivey laughed. She and Hope were so close, it was impossible to distract her. God knew Ivey had tried, talking about Hope's upcoming wedding. And then there was news of her expanding relationship with Charity.

Ivey had met Hope's sister when she came to the clinic to share lunch. It was obvious the woman was truly remorseful. Not only because of what she said, but how she confided in Hope and how Hope reciprocated.

They'd fallen into an easy rapport that belonged exclusively to sisters, whether they were blood sisters, like Charity and Hope— or sisters found through friendship, as was the case with Ivey.

These days, her heart felt so full it was almost scary.

Because Lang slept over with Hope each night, Ivey and Corbin had switched up reading to Justin. Neither of them was as dramatic a reader as Uncle Lang, but Justin preferred snuggling close to her.

With his dad, he had long talks before each book. With Lang, he laughed a lot. And with Ivey, he indulged all the cuddles.

"I'm just happy," Ivey finally said to Hope as she finished stitching up a bite mark in a cat's side. Apparently the cat had slipped out the door, then gotten a little too close to a neighboring Rottweiler who wasn't a fan. Luckily the cat wasn't seriously hurt. The bite would heal, but Ivey knew it could have been a lot worse. And elderly Mrs. Tassie would have been devastated.

This was one of those very rewarding circumstances where she could heal an animal and reassure a truly wonderful pet owner.

"It's more than that," Hope insisted while keeping all her attention on the cat. "Yesterday when we were floating in the lake, you had this faraway look in your eyes, and you kept smiling for no apparent reason."

Ivey had all kinds of reasons, actually. "The water was warm, Daisy enjoyed her swimming lesson, I love my flamingo float you gave me and it was so pretty how the blue skies reflected on the surface of the lake. It was all just so relaxing and serene."

"Daisy did like swimming, didn't she?"

"She gets more confident and outgoing every day." Much like Hope. "Justin has been good for her. I was afraid she'd miss him when he was off playing with his grandmother, but so far, she's adapted well even to that."

"Yes, she has, and I agree that's all wonderful," Hope said. "But I know you too well to think that's all it is. So *tell* me, already, because I'm dying to know."

"All right." Ivey smiled as she put in the last stitch. "Corbin said he loves me."

After a suspended second of silence, Hope snorted. "That's not news. Everyone knew he did."

"Well, now he's admitted it. And that *is* news."

As if she couldn't credit such a thing, Hope asked, "Were you really uncertain?"

"No. He made me feel loved in a hundred different ways. I did worry that he might be too overwhelmed with worries to realize it, though. But, Hope, he said the sweetest things about me."

Teasing, she replied, "I say sweet things about you all the time."

"And I love you for it." With the surgery complete, the conversation paused as they moved the cat to recovery.

With that done, Ivey removed her gloves and washed her hands. "I'm going to stay here a while to monitor him until he's fully awake." She didn't want to let Mrs. Tassie take him home until she knew he'd be okay.

"I can stay with you," Hope offered.

"No way. You and Lang are still celebrating."

"We have our whole lives to do that." She hesitated, then added, "But Charity was coming by."

"Wonderful." Ivey was so happy that Hope had her sister back, she would never get in the way of that. Shooing her, she said, "Go on. I'll be fine."

It took some convincing, but Hope finally gave in. She opened the door to step out and nearly collided with Karen.

Looking back over her shoulder, Karen slipped in and closed the door. "Your last appointment of the day is here, but it's your ex. He has a kitten with him, and he wants to see you specifically. I told him that you were in surgery, so—"

Ivey laughed. "Thank you, Karen, but it's fine. You can send him to one of the rooms. I'll be there shortly."

She got Hope on her way, texted Corbin that she'd be late, checked the cat one more time and then hurried to the exam room.

Geoff was there, waiting, a small kitten in his lap.

"Ivey, hello." He got hurriedly back to his feet. "I'm sorry about this. I know it's the end of your day and—"

"It's okay. I planned to stick around a little while anyway to monitor my patient, at least until his anesthesia wears off."

"I know you have techs, and Hope could have dealt with it, but I wanted to talk to you anyway."

She gave a polite smile. "So. You got a kitten?" She took the adorable little fur ball out of his hands. It was an all-black male with blue eyes, looked to be three or four months old and had a very sweet meow.

Geoff cleared his throat. "It's actually my girlfriend's cat. She got called into work."

Whoa, what was this? "Girlfriend?"

"That's why I wanted to see you. To let you know I won't be a pest anymore."

She frowned. "I don't understand."

"Because I'm blundering." He ran a hand over his hair. "I didn't want you to think I was still being an ass. Like you suggested, I moved on. Now I'm with Amy, and…" He shrugged. "I just thought I should tell you."

She saw the sincerity in his eyes and knew he needed her to really see him, to know he wasn't still hung up on her. "What wonderful news. Geoff, I'm so happy for you."

His gaze searched hers, then his smile came slowly. "I believe you really mean that."

"Well, of course I mean it. You're a terrific guy and you deserve the best. Tell me about her."

"Her name is Amy. She's pretty and smart, and she has a lot of style. You'd like her, Ivey. Everyone does. She's a buyer for the department store. We're, ah…living together."

"Already?" Truly, Geoff looked madly in love. "Good for you."

"I won't screw up again," he stated. "I'm sorry that I had to learn with you, Ivey. You deserved better. But I *have* learned, and I think Amy and I have the real deal."

"I'm glad." She really was. Now that she was so happily involved, she wanted the same for everyone.

Still with a smile, he said, "You never loved me, did you? Not really."

Since he appeared so well-grounded, Ivey didn't mind giving him the full truth. "No, I don't think I did. At least, not the way I love Corbin."

"He's a good guy, isn't he?"

"He's…incredible." She gave a soft laugh. "Don't get me started or I'll spend this whole appointment singing his praises."

"I wouldn't mind." He smiled again. "His kid is cute."

"I love him like he was my own." She couldn't wait to get home to see Corbin and Justin both.

Geoff tipped his head, studying her, then nodded. "I'm sorry I wasted two years of your life. I mean that, Ivey."

"Nonsense." She began to look over the cat. "It wasn't a waste at all, because it helped me understand what I really wanted."

"You didn't already know?"

"Until I found it, I had no idea."

Slowly, he grinned. "Same for me."

This new, easy camaraderie with Geoff felt far more special than what they'd had as a couple. "If anyone should apologize, it's me. In many ways, I used you. I wanted something specific in life, and even though our relationship wasn't it, I was afraid to let you go."

"I understand that. After you ended things…" He rubbed a hand over his face. "I felt like I'd been kicked in the teeth." He gave a crooked grin. "I *did* love you, Ivey, but Amy is… She's everything."

Ivey touched his arm. "With her, you feel like the best version of you?"

Surprised, he lifted his brows, considered it and then nodded. "Yeah, that's it exactly."

"It's a wonderful feeling, isn't it? And who knows, Geoff?

Maybe we needed that time together to figure it all out. I don't regret it, I promise."

"Whew. I'm so glad. And seriously, Ivey, I'm happy for you, too. Friends?"

This time she gave a firm "yes," because she knew it wouldn't be misconstrued. "Very good friends. Always." She lifted up the cat to look at it. "Now, what's the problem with this handsome fellow?"

"He keeps scratching at his ears and then crying."

"Likely just ear mites. A little medicine will fix that."

"Thanks. I told Amy I'd get him to the vet today if possible, so I appreciate you making time for me."

"No problem." Ivey hadn't realized that the discontent of her breakup with Geoff had lingered, until they put it all to rest. She'd begun to feel bad about how she'd handled things, especially in light of how Geoff had taken it. Seeing him not only fully recovered but happily involved in this new phase of his life truly set her heart free.

All the stars had aligned—she loved Corbin and Justin, and the future loomed bright.

By the time she left the clinic, she felt like dancing. It was late, but Mrs. Tassie had rushed right over to collect her kitty once he'd recovered from his anesthesia. Ivey gave her instructions on how to care for the cat, then took another few minutes to close up the clinic.

It was nearing nine o'clock and the sun hung low on the horizon for her drive home. She should make it in time to visit with Justin before he had to go to bed.

Her new sense of peace shattered when she pulled into the driveway and saw the police car. Heart hammering, she gathered her belongings and jogged in.

The house felt unnaturally quiet, no animals running to greet her, no chatter from Justin—in the kitchen, expression grim,

Corbin spoke quietly with two officers. His gaze briefly met hers, and she saw his torment.

Going through her routine by habit, she put her cell phone in her pocket and her purse on the foyer table. She left her shoes to the side of the door and slowly went into the kitchen.

The officers gave her polite nods, but they, too, looked solemn.

"Justin?"

"He's upstairs with Lang." Corbin pulled her close. "Darcie overdosed again."

Her stomach bottomed out. "How bad?"

"She's…gone."

Oh, dear God. Tears burned her eyes. "Does Justin know?"

"We didn't talk in front of him, but the look on his face…" His mouth flattened. "I think he's guessed."

"Do you need anything?"

"No. I'll be done here in just a minute." He touched her cheek. "I'm worried. Would you check on Justin?"

Nodding, she said, "I'll go to him right now." On impulse, she went on tiptoe and hugged Corbin. To the two officers, she nodded her thanks that they had given the news in person.

Not knowing what she might find, she took the steps upstairs two at a time. At the moment, seeing Justin, ensuring that he was okay, seemed the most immediate concern.

Justin's bedroom door was closed, likely so he couldn't overhear. Ivey lightly tapped her knuckles to the wood, then turned the knob and stepped in.

Lang stood with Justin at the window, looking out at the lake.

"Hey, guys," she said softly, aware of how Justin hunched his shoulders.

Lang turned with a forced smile. "You really ran late today. Everything okay at the clinic?"

With a questioning look, she said, "Yes, just had a few last-minute things to do." She came farther into the room. "Justin?"

Lang shook his head, indicating that Justin didn't want to talk. Unsure how to proceed, Ivey came closer.

In a raw whisper, Justin said, "Police are here."

She stopped in her tracks. "Yes, I saw them." Emotion tried to choke her, but Justin didn't need her to be weepy. "You okay, honey?"

"I'm not a baby," he snapped, and then he sniffled, wrapping his arms tightly around himself.

She reached out to him, but Lang took her arm and urged her to follow him to the room she shared with Corbin across the hall. Very near her ear, he said, "I think he's guessed, but I haven't confirmed anything. Corbin needs to be the one to talk to him."

"I agree, but we can't leave him alone."

"Why don't you stay with him? I'll go downstairs with Corbin." He frowned. "Or vice versa. Whichever you want."

"I'll stay with Justin." At the moment, wild horses couldn't have dragged her away. The urge to comfort him, to shelter his feelings, to help him believe that a bright future was ahead whether he could see it right now or not, flared inside her.

Going back into his room, she pasted on a smile. "Guess what? I had to do some quick surgery on a cat today."

Grudgingly, Justin glanced at her. His eyes looked red but dry. "Is the cat okay?"

God love him, could there be a more compassionate little boy? As she'd hoped, the cat's welfare drew him out of his own misery. "Yes, honey. He's fine. He'll probably be groggy for the rest of the day, though. Odds are, he'll throw up a time or two." She sat on the side of his bed and began talking about the cat, ad-libbing his adventure sneaking out and trying to tangle with a Rottweiler.

Almost against his will, Justin moved closer. "Why did the dog bite him?"

"I'm pretty sure he was surprised to find a hissing cat in his bushes." Taking his hand, she guided him to sit beside her, then stroked his hair—and he let her. "It would have been really easy for a dog that size to kill a cat, but I know Rory. He's a good dog, friendly, and usually he's great with other animals." She leaned closer and said in a conspiratorial way, "That is, when they don't jump out at him from the bushes."

A ghost of a smile, there and gone, teased over his mouth. "I'm glad the cat is okay."

"Me, too. Mrs. Tassie loves him as much as I love Maurice. And speaking of Maurice, where is he?"

Justin looked down at his hands. "He went to bed with the dogs."

Ivey felt him struggling, and because of that, she resisted the urge to baby him. Instinctively she knew it might cause him to lose his fragile hold on control.

"I was getting ready for bed, so they all went into the laundry room." He fell silent again. "I'd just finished brushing my teeth when the cops got here."

"I see." They both heard the front door open and close.

Justin stiffened, his bottom lip quivering. "I gotta go to the bathroom." He stood again, looking as if he wanted to escape the reality of what would come.

Corbin stepped into the room.

Ivey took one look at him and her heart crumbled. No man should have to tackle so much in such a short period of time. She wished for a way to help but didn't know what to do.

Corbin's hands flexed, he watched his son, then came closer. "Justin, I—"

"I gotta use the bathroom," Justin blurted again and darted past his dad into the hall. They heard the bathroom door close a little too hard.

Ivey was horribly afraid that Justin had just sought privacy for a good cry, and she wasn't sure if she could stand it.

"I'm so sorry," she whispered to Corbin.

He came over to sit beside her, his elbows on his knees, his head bowed. "The fact is, I knew this could happen. But I couldn't help hoping…" He shook his head. "She had my information on her. That's why the police came here. I don't know anything about her parents, and neither did the cops."

Their shoulders touched, and their voices were low. Corbin heaved a long sigh and straightened, glancing back at the door. "He's struggling."

"He doesn't want to cry in front of anyone." She touched his jaw. "But you're his dad, Corbin. He loves you, and I know he trusts you." Her own eyes burned with the truth of that. Yes, Justin had a very difficult background, but that wasn't his future—and he knew it. "Don't let him be by himself. Go to him, show him that it's okay to cry and hold him while he grieves."

As if that settled the indecision for him, Corbin stood and crossed the room in a few long strides.

Ivey watched him go, praying that father and son could console each other…and wondering how much right she had to take part in it all.

Corbin returned in mere seconds. "He's not in the bathroom."

"Oh no." Already on her feet, Ivey followed Corbin as he jogged down the steps.

"Justin?" he called but didn't get an answer. He went through each room, then started to go downstairs and practically ran into Lang. "Is he down there?"

"No." Lang looked around. "You check the animals?"

"He's not with them." Corbin suddenly straightened. "The lake." His stride long and full of fear, he headed straight for the patio doors, Lang right behind him.

Ivey called, "I'll look out front!" She didn't pause for her shoes, just darted out, her gaze searching. Except for the chirping of crickets and the occasional long croak of a frog, the yard was quiet. Dusk had settled with all the bleak gloom of bad news.

Damn it, she should have known Justin would try something

like this. He was so stubborn in his pride—but then, for years, pride might have been all he had.

She started to turn around, praying he wasn't anywhere near the lake, when a low sound reached her ears, a sound that didn't belong to the quiet night.

Heart pounding hard, she listened…and realized it came from the tree house. It was a low, muffled, heart-wrenching sound that got her feet moving.

Never before had she scaled the ladder so quickly, but this time she practically flew up the thing. When she peeked in, she found Justin sitting with his knees to his chest, his head in his folded arms, crying out his little heart.

As quietly as she could, she texted Corbin: In the tree house. Then she crawled on in.

It didn't matter that she hadn't given birth to Justin. It didn't matter that she'd met him only months ago, or that she and Corbin weren't yet married. In every way that mattered, Justin was hers now. She'd be side by side with Corbin to love him for the rest of her life, and by God, she intended to start right now.

"I'm sorry. I know you wanted privacy," Ivey whispered as she sat behind him and wrapped her arms tight around him. "I need to be with you right now."

"I'm not a baby," he cried.

"No. You are an absolutely amazing little boy and I love you so much."

He twisted suddenly, hugging her neck, his face to her throat as he tried to stem the tears soaking her skin.

She hugged him more fiercely, rocking him a little. "I'm so sorry. Sometimes life is incredibly hard, but you don't have to go through it alone. I'm here for you, and so is your dad. Your uncle and grandma. Daisy and Maurice and the pups. You are loved by so many. We'll get through this, all of us together. Okay?"

He choked on a breath. "*She* didn't love me."

What an awful thing for a ten-year-old boy to believe. "I think she did. It's just that your mother wasn't well."

He settled against her more comfortably, his cheek to her shoulder, his face still hidden. "What do you mean?" he finally asked, anxious, maybe, to find a reasonable explanation for something no child could possibly understand.

Corbin came through the doorway, saw them huddled together and briefly closed his eyes.

It amazed Ivey how he filled up the space, how his calm presence already made things better. Unlike her, he was able to quickly hide his upset. She'd never minded her emotional nature, and she figured Justin would get used to it soon enough. In that way, she thought, she and Corbin complemented each other.

When Corbin sat close beside Ivey, Justin wiped his eyes and looked up at him with his little face ravaged, his nose running and his breath uneven. "I didn't mean to cry."

"You have every right to your feelings." Corbin lifted him into his lap, and together the three of them leaned against the rough wooden wall. Justin held on to Ivey's hand—but no more tightly than she held his. "You have a right to anger, son. To happiness. To worry and fear. To laughter and yes, to tears."

Justin sniffled. "Is mom…gone?"

With only a single beat of hesitation, Corbin said, "Yes." He kissed the top of Justin's head. "But she did love you, son. I know she didn't always show it. As Ivey said, Darcie was ill. She'd been ill for a long time, I think."

His solemn gaze met Corbin's. "You mean she was sick?"

"It was a sort of sickness." Corbin rubbed up and down his back. "I should have explained this sooner, and I'm sorry that I didn't. I wanted to protect you, but now I realize that the better way to protect you would have been to give you the information."

Justin stared at him, his blue eyes swimming with more tears. "It's okay, Dad."

For a single second, Ivey saw Corbin's composure crack. He swallowed heavily, nodded his gratitude and managed to say, "Thank you." He enfolded Justin in his warm embrace while he struggled. "That means a lot to me."

Ivey brushed at her falling tears.

When Corbin loosened his hold, he had himself in check again. "Your mother was an addict. That means she took drugs, too many of them."

"Why?"

"She was unhappy with herself. But those type of drugs aren't good for you, and they ended up making her even more miserable."

"Do you ever...?"

"No," Corbin promised. "Not ever."

Justin's questioning gaze switched to Ivey's.

"I don't, either, sweetie." She brushed her thumb over his small knuckles. "I was fortunate that I was always close with my parents, and when things bothered me or when I needed something, I could go to them. I don't think your mother had that."

Releasing her hand, Justin sat up on Corbin's thighs and knuckled his eyes. "Mom used to drink a lot."

"I know. That's part of it," Corbin said. "When people can't deal with their problems, they sometimes turn to crutches— like drugs and alcohol."

"I tried to make her happy."

At this rate, Ivey knew there was no chance of stemming the tears. "Oh, honey. You weren't responsible for her happiness."

"No, you weren't," Corbin said. "The way it's supposed to work, and definitely how it will work for us, is that a parent is supposed to care for their child. In your mother's case, and in other cases, too, the parent has issues that aren't easily solved." He lifted Justin's chin. "I saw your mother not too long ago."

He startled, his eyes flaring. "You did?"

"I was going to talk to you about it soon." Corbin cupped

Justin's cheek and used his thumb to wipe away the tears. "I put it off because I didn't want to worry you, but like I said, that was the wrong thing to do. You and I made a deal to talk things out, right?"

Justin nodded.

"So that's what I should have done, and I promise, I'm going to do better."

Justin nodded. "Me, too."

"And me," Ivey offered, and got a slight smile from both of them.

"Your mom was in the hospital because of all the pills she'd taken. It made her really sick. She wanted to get well, and I tried to help her, but it's not easy for an addict to stop doing what is making them sick."

Justin's expression was tight, wary. "That's why she died?"

"Yes. But when I saw her, she told me how much she loved you. She said she wanted to get well, and she wanted to see you again."

Mouth pinched, his voice very small, Justin whispered, "I didn't want to see her."

Ivey thought there was a big difference in Justin not wanting to see his mother as she'd been, and wanting to see her as someone who loved him. Unfortunately, the latter had never happened…and now it never would.

"It would have been your decision," Corbin said. "But if you'd changed your mind, I wanted to help your mother to get well. Understand me, son. Only so you could visit her if you'd wanted to. I wasn't going to let her see you without me, and I was never going to let her take you away. This is your home, and this is where we'll be together."

He seemed to be weighing the words, maybe trying to understand them since the concept was difficult for a child to grasp. His gaze slanted over to Ivey. "Will you be here, too?"

Overwhelmed, Ivey nodded. "I know I'm not your mother,

Justin, but I love you. You're important to me. In my heart, where it matters most, you are always going to be my son."

He reached out to her, and she gladly embraced him. "So," he said, sniffling again, thinking it through. He kept his face tucked close to her throat. "You'll be like my mom now?"

She flicked a glance at Corbin, he smiled at her, and she positively melted. "Nothing in the whole world would make me happier than being your mom."

"Okay," he said, with a child's simplicity.

Lang poked his head over the top of the ladder. "Hey," he said, glancing warily at everyone.

"Come on up," Corbin invited. "We were just working out a few things."

Hastily, moving off of Ivey's lap, Justin wiped his eyes and his nose.

Good old Uncle Lang produced a few tissues that he passed around to everyone, then he made a big show of dabbing at his own eyes. "Emotional night, huh?" He plopped down next to Justin, pretended to blow his nose, then let out a long sigh. "Is this where we go to cry? Because I need a place, you know."

Justin laughed. "You don't cry."

"Who says?" It was Lang's turn to snag Justin to his lap. "Anyone who is upset is allowed to cry."

"Only if it's something really, really bad," Justin decreed. Then he whispered, "Or if you're Ivey."

Ivey choked on her laugh. "Just so you know, not all girls cry as much as I do. I just happen to be a very emotive person."

"I guess sometimes I'm 'motive, too," Justin decided. He narrowed his eyes. "But I'm not gonna cry much."

Smiling, Ivey said, "I'll probably cry enough for both of us."

They all sat in companionable silence until Justin whispered, "I might miss Mom some."

Corbin clasped his shoulder. "You know what we could do? Your mom gave me a box of your stuff. Pics of you when you were a little squirt, a few things you'd drawn over the years. You want to go inside and we can go through everything together?"

Boggled by the idea that his mother had anything of his, Justin asked, "For real?"

"Let's do it," Lang said. "Anyone else in the mood for a little popcorn?"

"You could invite Hope over," Justin suggested. "She'd like to see my pictures, I bet."

Corbin smiled. "I'm sure she would." So would his mother, when she found out what had happened. He wouldn't call her tonight, but he'd take care of it first thing tomorrow. That would give Justin another chance to talk it out even more, to show the things Darcie had saved...and to feel loved.

"Consider it done." Lang moved Justin to his side and headed out. "I'll go get her, then I'll start on the popcorn. And maybe I'll make some milkshakes, too."

Justin followed him to the doorway, saying, "I want chocolate."

The resilience of children, Ivey thought. "I love you, Justin."

"Love you, too," he replied, still looking out the door, no doubt watching Lang cross the yard. "Can we let the dogs and Maurice back out since I'm not going to bed yet?"

"Sure," Corbin said, and Ivey heard the relief in his voice. He leaned close to her ear. "I'm so glad you're here with me." He nodded at Justin. "With us."

"Me, too."

It would be all right. The worst had happened, and they'd get through it. Together.

Epilogue

Justin looked amazingly handsome in his suit—and he knew it. He strutted around, sometimes with his hands in his pockets, sometimes with his thumbs in his belt loops, continually with a smile on his face. He especially liked his boutonniere.

Every few minutes, Vesta caught him for a hug.

The wedding ceremony had been put off by more than two months, first so that they could hold a service for Justin's mother. Darcie had a nice headstone in the local cemetery, because that's how Corbin wanted it. If, or maybe when, Justin wanted to visit her there, he could.

Corbin had discovered that Darcie's mother passed away long ago, and her father had relocated, never to be heard from again. His own family had attended the service, and Ivey knew they were there for Justin.

Justin seemed to know it, too.

After that, they'd celebrated his birthday with a small party at the beach. He'd met new friends that he'd get to know even better with school starting up soon. The collection of monster paraphernalia had been enormously popular with all the children, especially Justin. He'd decided to start his own collection, so part of the basement was set up with display shelves.

He still had occasional worries, but they didn't seem quite as dark.

The wedding vows had been short and sweet, as per Ivey's insistence. Together, she and Hope had compromised on a double wedding. Neither had wanted to go before the other. They loved each other enough that sharing seemed like the perfect idea.

Though they had very different styles, they had coordinated. Hope wore a long, flowing white dress with a full skirt overlaid in lace that made her look like a fairy princess and kept Vesta wiping her eyes.

Ivey wore a tea-length dress with quarter-length sleeves of the same material. Instead of a sweetheart neckline, hers had a rounded neck. The same lace on Hope's gown was used as a sash on her own.

Fragrant white roses, accented with tiny blue forget-me-nots, filled the outdoor tables and served as bouquets for Hope and Ivey.

Corbin and Lang had mixed it up as well. Instead of tuxes, they wore suits—Corbin's jacket was black with a pale blue shirt and black tie, same as Justin's. Lang, always flashier, wore a blue jacket with a black shirt and blue tie.

Both men looked incredibly handsome.

Set up in the yard, they'd kept the wedding small with only family, which included Hope's sister, Charity, and Hope's precious new niece, Marley. Marley had kicked up a fuss during the short ceremony, and Justin, serving as best man for his dad and his uncle, had grinned through the whole thing.

Now Hagan sat with Ivey's parents, holding Marley to give Charity a break, and together they all laughed at something that was said.

Justin bowed gallantly in front of Vesta. "You want to dance, Grandma?"

"Oh my, I would love to." She took his hand and together they went out to the wooden dance floor set up by the lake.

A small local band played, and Justin danced as if he couldn't be happier. All in all, Ivey decreed it an absolutely perfect day.

"I can't wait to get you alone," Corbin whispered in her ear.

Leaning back against his solid shoulder, Ivey said, "A few more hours." Then Justin would go with Vesta and Hagan to spend a few days at the RV park, the guests would head home, and she and Corbin could indulge in a short "honeymoon" where they'd probably spend the entire time in bed.

Joining them with his arm around Hope's waist, his jacket off and his shirtsleeves rolled up, Lang said, "I just thought of the perfect wedding gift you can give us."

"Yeah?" Corbin smiled and sipped at his glass of wine. "What's that?"

"The guesthouse. What do you say? I'll expand on it, but it'd be nice to be close and still separate."

Looking struck by the suggestion, Corbin said, "Great idea. Consider it done."

Ivey gawked. Hope looked equally stunned.

"What?" Corbin shrugged. "He gave me a boat. And you know Justin will like having *Uncle Lang* near."

Slowly, Ivey grinned. She couldn't deny that she would love having her best friend close by. "On one condition."

"Anything," Corbin said, sounding as if he really meant it.

"They have to take two of the puppies as a wedding gift to us. Five pets are just a few too many, but I couldn't give them to just anyone."

"Done and done," Lang said, then he thought to ask Hope, "That is, if it's okay by you?"

"It will make me very happy," Hope promised. "Justin will still be able to visit them, so he won't miss them too much."

"The same applies to Ivey," Corbin teased with a grin.

"About the house," Lang said, "the garage could be made into living space, right? I was thinking of a great room and another bathroom, of course. Maybe a kitchen."

"That's what I was thinking," Corbin agreed. "The upstairs could just be a master suite and sitting area."

"I could build another garage off to the side." The two brothers stepped away to discuss floor plans.

"On their weddings," Ivey noted, shaking her head.

"You're the one who didn't want it to be too formal." Smiling, Hope hooked her arm through Ivey's. "Though I have to say, it was absolutely perfect as is. I'm not sure I could have handled a huge crowd."

"This was just right," Ivey agreed, pleased with how it had all turned out.

With her gaze on the guests, Hope said, "I love you, Ivey."

Oh, now see...the tears started again. "Not as much as I love you."

"Debatable. But the point is, I always thought we were lucky to have each other, and now we have so much more."

"We're the luckiest." For a woman who had planned a summer without attachments, Ivey had ended up with something else entirely. A husband, a son, his family...and an incredible love she knew would last forever.

"Come on." Ivey took her hand. "Let's dance."

To her surprise, Hope laughed—and took over the lead to the dance floor.

★ ★ ★ ★ ★

Here is a sneak peek at New York Times *bestselling author* Lori Foster's Stronger Than You Know, *the next exciting novel in the McKenzies of Ridge Trail series.*

Even before Kennedy Brooks's Uber driver turned the corner to where she lived, her skin prickled with alarm. It was well past midnight, a fact that couldn't be helped.

She should have been home at dinnertime.

One delay after another had obliterated her schedule, to the point she had to rebook her flight. After she'd spent hours sitting in the airport, exhaustion pulled at her. She wanted nothing more than to collapse in her bed, with her own sturdy locks in place.

When the scent of smoke infiltrated the closed windows of the car, her heart beat harder. She had a terrible feeling that there'd be no rest for her tonight. Maybe not even in the foreseeable future.

"What do you suppose happened?" her driver asked, pointing to the strobe of red lights that pierced the dark night.

"Fire," she breathed. And not just any fire, but from the apartment building where she lived.

Fire trucks, police and EMTs were everywhere. Neighbors she recognized clung together, many wrapped in blankets to ward off the cool Colorado evening air. Crowds of curious onlookers also lined the street, had poured out from other buildings to gawk.

Lifting a shaking hand to cover her mouth, Kennedy took in the enormous blaze that engulfed the entire building—including the floor where she would have been sleeping.

The driver couldn't get close, but then, she didn't want him to. "Stop here."

He glanced at her in the rearview mirror. "Hey, you okay? Is that your building?"

"Yes." She swallowed heavily. *What to do, what to do?*

Because she'd learned caution the hard way, Kennedy pulled additional money from her wallet. "Wait here, please."

The young man eyed the cash, glanced back at the fire and finally took the bills. "For how long?"

"I just need to make a call." She hesitated again. "I'm going to stand directly in front of your car, in the beam of the headlights." She needed privacy for the call, but she didn't want to be alone in the dark. "Leave them on, okay?"

"Sure."

Knowing she couldn't delay any longer, Kennedy hooked her purse strap over her shoulder and neck to keep it secure, dug out her phone and stepped out. It was an uncommonly cool September night, yet she felt flushed with heat, as if she could feel those flames touching her skin.

There was only one person she knew who might be able to deal with the present situation.

It was fortunate she had his number programmed in her phone, because her trembling hands refused to cooperate.

As the phone rang, she kept constant vigilance on her surroundings. She could almost swear someone watched her, yet when she glanced back at the driver, she couldn't see him for the glare of the lights in her eyes.

"Hello?"

Reyes McKenzie's sleep-deep voice caused her to jump, and not for the first time. He was six feet four inches of hewn strength, thick bones and confident attitude. A man with a big, sculpted body thanks to the gym he owned.

Pretty sure he had other interests as well, which would explain the edge of danger that always emanated from him.

Just what she needed right now.

Clutching the phone, hoping he'd be receptive, she whispered, "Hey. It's Kennedy."

Sharpened awareness obliterated his groggy tone. "What's wrong?"

Yes, Reyes was definitely the right person for her to call. Never mind that he had a wealth of secrets, for some reason, she trusted him. Mostly anyway.

Tonight she had little choice in the matter. "Reyes, I need you."

She could hear him moving as he said, "I can be out the door in two minutes. Fill me in."

God bless the man, he didn't hesitate to come to her rescue. Before anything more happened, Kennedy gave him her address—something she hadn't wanted to share before now. Life had a way of upending plans, and hers had just been sucked into a treacherous whirlwind. "I'm not actually in the apartment building, though. I'm at the corner, behind a line of emergency vehicles, with an Uber driver. I don't know how long he'll let me hang out, though."

"Are you hurt?"

That no-nonsense question held a note of urgency.

"No." *Not yet.* "Could I explain everything once you're here? I'm afraid it's not safe." She felt horribly exposed.

"Forget the Uber driver, okay?" The sound of a door closing, then jogging steps, came through the line. "Get close to a firefighter. Or an EMT. *Stay there.* It'll only take me fifteen minutes if I really push it."

Nodding, Kennedy looked up the street, but the officials all seemed so far away and there was a lot of dark space between here and there. "I... I don't think I can."

"Shit." A truck door slammed. "I'm on my way, babe, okay? Get back in the car with the Uber guy and drive around in congested areas. Don't go anyplace deserted, and don't sit in one spot. Tell me you understand, Kennedy."

"I understand."

"Circle back in fifteen. I'll be waiting."

Yes, that sounded like a more viable plan. "Thank you, Reyes."

"Keep your eyes open." He disconnected, likely to concentrate on driving, and suddenly she felt very alone again. Reaching into her purse, Kennedy found the stun gun and palmed it. She'd practiced with the damn thing but had never actually used it on anyone.

She didn't want to use it tonight either, but she felt better for having it.

All around her, smoke choked the air and tension seemed to escalate. She opened the car's back door and slid in, saying to the driver, "Could you drive, please?"

Exasperated, he twisted back to see her. "Listen, I have to pick up another guy from the airport. I can't just—"

"I'll make it worth your while, I promise."

He eyed her anew, his gaze dipping over her body. "What's that supposed to mean?"

Oh, for the love of... Kennedy knew she was a mess. She'd pulled her hair into a haphazard ponytail, her makeup was smudged and her clothes were sloppy-comfortable, suitable for a long flight. There was absolutely nothing appealing about her at the moment. "It's not an invitation, so forget that. Just lock the doors and drive for fifteen minutes. Stay in busy areas—no dark, empty streets—and then you can bring me back here. I'll give you another forty bucks."

Considering it, he continued to study her.

A movement beyond him drew her startled attention. There, from the long shadows, two men crept toward them. "Lock the doors and freaking drive!" she shouted.

Disconcerted, he, too, looked around, and the second he noticed the men, they broke into a jog.

Coming straight for them.

"Jesus!" Jerking the car into Reverse, he backed away with haste, almost hitting a telephone pole. Spinning around, he punched the gas and the small economy car lurched forward down the empty street. Again his gaze went to the rearview mirror. "Who the fuck was that?"

Looking over her shoulder, seeing the men fade away, Kennedy sucked in a much-needed breath. "I don't know," she whispered. *But I know they haven't given up.*

Reyes drove with abandon. His Harley would have been quicker, but he couldn't quite picture Kennedy strapped around him with the wind in her hair. Plus, he had no way of knowing if she'd be dressed for the cool night. Grim, he pulled up to the cross street in front of her apartment building. The road was closed off to through traffic, and the firefighters were still hard at work. Crowds had been pushed far back, held at bay by police officers.

Glancing around, he didn't see Kennedy.

But he did spot two shifty-looking creeps keeping watch on everything. Dressed all in black, with black knit hats pulled low, they watched the streets instead of the fire.

Narrowing his eyes, Reyes did a quick survey of the area and didn't see anyone else. Most people appeared to be enrapt with the fire—but not these two.

Getting out his phone, he pulled up his recent call list and touched Kennedy's name. She answered before the first ring had finished.

"Reyes?" she asked with breathless urgency.

"Where are you, hon?"

"I couldn't come back. Two men are watching for me."

"Yeah, I see them. Did they bother you?"

"They charged the Uber car, but my driver got us away. I... I don't know what they want."

"I'll find out. Give me two minutes then circle by. I should be ready by then." Belatedly, he added, "I'm in my truck." Because Kennedy came to the gym he owned, and because they'd partnered in the rescue of a big alley cat, she was familiar with his ride.

"What?" She screeched with panic, "What do you mean you'll find out? You can't possibly—"

"Sure I can." For a while now, he and Kennedy had been dancing around the fact that they both had secrets. When faced with danger, she'd called him, so obviously she understood his ability.

Tonight seemed like a good night for her to learn a little more about him. "Did you hear me, Kennedy? What did I say?"

"Two minutes," she repeated blankly. "Reyes, don't you dare—"

Seeing that the jerks had noticed him, Reyes smiled and disconnected. Leaving the truck, he started toward them, his attitude amicable. "What happened, do you know?"

The men looked at each other. The tallest of the two said, "Looks like an apartment fire."

"Yeah, I can see that." He was only ten feet away now. "Who started it?"

They shared another glance, and Stretch spoke again. "Who says anyone did? Might've been faulty wiring."

"Nah." He continued to close the distance, his stride long and cocky—with good reason. "Pretty sure you yahoos had some-thing to do with it." He grinned. "Amiright?"

Stretch reached inside his jacket, and Reyes kicked out, send-ing him sprawling backward. He landed hard, the wind knocked out of him.

His shorter friend took an aggressive stance.

Bad move. With a short, swift kick from his booted foot, Reyes took out the guy's braced knee. He screamed in pain as his leg buckled the wrong way.

Quickly, Reyes patted him down and removed both a knife and a Glock. Still squatting, he shifted his attention to Stretch just as the guy got back to his feet.

Maybe hoping to mimic Reyes's moves, Stretch tried to plant his foot in his face.

Reyes ducked to the side, grabbed his ankle and yanked him off balance again.

Down he went, for the second time. Unfortunately, he cracked his head and, without so much as a moan, passed out.

"Well, hell." Turning back to the shorter dude, Reyes prod-ded him. "Who are you and what did you want with the girl?"

Dazed with pain, his face contorted, the guy gasped, "What girl?"

"Dude, you are seriously whack. Want me to bust the other knee? I can, you know." Using the Glock, Reyes tapped his crotch. "Or maybe you want me to smash these instead?"

Rolling to his side, he cried, *"No."*

Heaving a sigh, Reyes stood. "What a wuss. C'mon, man. Give me something. It's not like I really *want* to hurt you, you know." *Not much, anyway.* But when he thought of these two planning to harm Kennedy…yeah. Red-hot rage. "I'll give you to the count of three. One. Two."

"All right! We were hired to grab her. That's all I know."

"Bullshit. There's always more. Like where were you to take her? Who wants her? And why?"

"I don't know, man! We were paid half, told to take her to an address and then we'd get the other half."

"Yeah? What address?" Reyes heard Stretch groan and knew he was coming around. Probably a good thing.

"Bolen has it in his pocket."

"He does, huh?" Going over to Bolen, Reyes quickly searched him, removing another gun and also taking his wallet. Inside he found a stack of hundreds and an address scrawled on a torn-off corner of a pizza box. When Bolen tried to sit up, Reyes pistol-whipped him. He collapsed again.

Glancing back at the other guy, who made a failed attempt to get up, he asked, "What's your name?"

"Herman."

"Ah, dude, you said that so fast I'm not sure I believe you." When Reyes reached for him, the guy flinched away. "Man, you are seriously not cut out for this line of work." He shoved him to his side and pulled his wallet from his back pocket. It, too, was padded with bills. "You guys got a nice paycheck for kidnapping, didn't you?"

"I need an ambulance."

"Yeah, probably. Pretty sure I fucked up your kneecap. You might never walk the same." He searched through the wallet, curling his lip at a condom, a few interesting business cards for local joints, a coupon and a receipt. "Tell you what. Once I'm gone, you can try to crawl down there by the fire you set. EMTs are still caring for the people you hurt. Course, that might raise questions you don't want to answer, right? One thing could lead to another, then you and your busted leg might end up rotting in prison." Reyes pulled out the man's driver's license. "Huh. Herman Coop. Well, Herman, now I know how to find you. And trust me, if you ever bother the girl again, I will. You won't like the outcome of that."

"God," Herman groaned, sweat soaking his face from pain.

"When good old Bolen comes around, you tell him I'm watching him, too, yeah?"

"Who the fuck are you?"

Headlights bounced over them, and he sensed it was Kennedy returning. With an edge of menace, he intoned, "Your worst nightmare." Seeing Herman's face, Reyes barely bit back his laugh.

He did enjoy spooking the knuckleheads.

Coming to his feet, he considered alerting the nearby cops, but he didn't know how that might implicate Kennedy. Hell, he didn't know her secrets or how serious they might be.

Should have listened to his family and researched her. In fact, he'd be willing to bet that his computer-tech sister hadn't listened when he'd told her to step down.

Research was what she did, after all.

Then he and his brother followed up in whatever way was necessary.

For now, though, all he knew for sure was that there was more to Kennedy Brooks than she let on.

He nudged the thug with the edge of his boot. "On your stomach, lace your fingers behind your head and don't move or I'll send your balls into your throat."

It took a lot of effort for Herman to painfully maneuver around, but the ball threat often worked wonders. Choking on his every agonized breath, Herman got into position.

"Stay like that," Reyes warned again as he began moving away, one of the guns held at the ready in his hand, the remaining weapon and wallets balanced in his other hand. He glanced behind him and saw Kennedy stepping out of the car, her eyes huge in the shadows. The driver lurched to the trunk, practically tossed out a rolling suitcase and allowed her to snatch out of his hands a laptop case. While she tried to get her luggage upright, the driver sped away.

Leaving her standing there alone.

Giving up on the goons, Reyes jogged to her. "Come on."

Staring at the load he carried, she whispered, "What did you do?"

"Gathered intel, that's all. Move it." He got her to his truck, dumped the confiscated items onto the floor and nearly tossed her inside. "Buckle up, babe." He took her laptop case from her and jammed it under her seat as well.

After putting her enormous suitcase into the back of his truck, he gave one last look at the fallen men and a quick glance at the still-raging fire. The night had turned into a clusterfuck of the first order. But hey, Kennedy had called him, not anyone else.

Overall, he'd call it a win.

Don't miss Stronger Than You Know *by*
New York Times *bestselling author Lori Foster!*